ROSS RAISIN

Ross Raisin is the author of three previous novels:
A Natural, *Waterline* and *God's Own Country*,
which was shortlisted for nine literary awards.
Ross has won the Sunday Times Young Writer of
the Year Award and was named on *Granta*'s Best
of Young British Novelists list in 2013. In 2018
he was awarded a fellowship by the Royal Society
of Literature.

Ross teaches at the University of Leeds, for the
Guardian Masterclass programme and for the
education charity First Story. He lives in York.

Find more on Ross, his books and teaching here:
www.rossraisin.com

ROSS RAISIN

A Hunger

VINTAGE

1 3 5 7 9 10 8 6 4 2

Vintage is part of the Penguin Random House group of companies whose addresses can be found at global.penguinrandomhouse.com

Penguin
Random House
UK

First published in Vintage in 2023
First published in hardback by Jonathan Cape in 2022

Copyright © Ross Raisin 2022

Ross Raisin has asserted their right to be identified as the author of this Work in accordance with the Copyright, Designs and Patents Act 1988

penguin.co.uk/vintage

A CIP catalogue record for this book is available from the British Library

ISBN 9781784702779

Printed and bound in Great Britain by Clays Ltd, Elcograf S.p.A.

The authorised representative in the EEA is Penguin Random House Ireland, Morrison Chambers, 32 Nassau Street, Dublin D02 YH68

Penguin Random House is committed to a sustainable future for our business, our readers and our planet. This book is made from Forest Stewardship Council® certified paper.

For Pebbles and Stripes

Their bodies hang around my head, strung from the ceiling hooks, everyday as washing. Six quartered torsos, sliced apart on the slaughterhouse floor. Mothers, sisters, children, all scrambled parts now; push them closer and you might see how to start putting them back together again. Today's is marked up. A smeared docket pinned to her flank. She's too heavy for me to lift on my own. The boys probably still muck about in here competing to see who can hold up a carcass for the longest. Not in front of me, though, not any more.

Turtle should be back by now. It's almost five minutes since he went for a pee. No doubt sneaking a fag. On the other side of the walk-in door the din of the kitchen is a world away. My body is already working to stabilise itself. Hands and earlobes losing sensation, the blood vessels narrowing under my skin — pushing warm, thick blood deeper into my core — the nerve endings at the back of my throat tingling with the shock of refrigerated air. My arm, reaching towards the heifer, has gone numb. It feels good just to rest it there, the dead tissue against my palm as firm and smooth as a punchbag. Let him take as long as he wants. It's better alone in here. Time moves differently. There's the same stillness that draws me in at the end of service after the boys have left, willing the click of the final kitchen porter closing up, not wanting to go home and deal with whatever state Patrick is in.

The walk-in door is opening, Turtle coming back in. He is looking at his phone and he doesn't see me behind the joint. He comes through the gloom staring at the phone and nearly walks into one of the sides of beef. Now he looks up – jumps when he spots me.

'Fuck, Chef, I almost shat myself.'

His warm cigarette breath twirls in the dim blue light.

'Put your phone away.'

'Right. Sorry.' He goes over to the wall for the little stepladder. He carries it back and places it next to today's forequarter, mounts the few steps and wraps an arm around the shin. With grunty effort he heaves the joint up, his skinny legs trembling inside his trousers. He grimaces down at me. 'Fuck me, it's heavy.'

'Yes, Turtle. It's a cow.'

The stepladder rattles as he unlatches the hook from the ceiling ring. My knuckles are whitening on the side rails, supporting the ladder. 'Steady, Turtle. You're doing fine.' But he doesn't have control of it and the joint is teetering, his hands scrabbling up the flesh for purchase as it begins to fall.

The wallop on my shoulder nearly knocks me over.

'Shit, sorry, Chef. Are you okay?'

'Yes.'

Together we pick up the joint from the floor, holding an

end each, both of us wheezing. It weighs more, this carcass, than Patrick does now.

'Carefully, Turtle. Let's get it into the kitchen.'

Even steering out of the room he is clumsy, manhandling the joint, bumping into a shadowy pair of hindquarters. Someone is opening the door. Kitchen brightness floods the walk-in, lighting up the full crate of staff beers on the floor next to two cans of deodorant and a box of fresh cut flowers from the market. Anton's daily pineapple. Behind us, before the door closes, the remaining bodies are still lit, twisting and swaying on their hooks like the last stoned dancers at a party.

'Backs, everybody. Give us space.'

The boys move to let us past, Freddy pushing forward to help hoist the animal up onto the metal. It lies gleaming under the pass lights. Everybody is watching in silence, crowding round, floor staff appearing at the pass, as if they've never seen a joint broken down into primals before. One of the waiters turns away, squeamish, at the first cut into the elbow joint – slicing, pushing with my other hand, slicing, pushing – until the whole shin pulls free and the elbow socket is shining in the light, smooth and white as the inside of an oyster shell.

Turtle is at the front of the boys, showing Sandy where the marbling through the flesh builds up, telling her that it's when the cow started getting fed more. He keeps looking up at her and the rest of the floor-staff audience, wanting them to know that he's been part of this. He doesn't pay any attention to the large muscle exposed by the division of the

ribs – the eye – through which the real history of this creature is being told. It is darker, stickier than it should be, signs
of stress; but he is not thinking, none of them are, about the
electric goad, or the trainee inseminator. They only see the
meat in front of them. They don't see the rest of her: her
stomachs, her womb, the four chambers of her udder, the
tongue long enough it could wrap around Turtle's neck.

One of the waiters leans over the pass. He is recording a
video with his phone.

'Get that away from here.'

He pulls his hand back, mumbling an apology.

'The bread's up. Go and cut it.' And off he goes. Tail
between his legs.

My whites are smudged. Probably from the carry, not my
work. My work has been meticulous. Just as it will be during
the rest of this forequarter's processing, then lunch service,
and clean-down, dinner prep and service, and on – on into
the night and the second job, Patrick, lying in wait for me at
home.

Her eyes are shut on the cushion but her mouth is moving a bit. She's saying something that's too quiet to hear. She probably wants me to leave her sleeping so there's nothing to do now except the telly. My lunch is still on the table and there's bits of food on the floor and my toys. She's not hungry, is what she always says, that's why she's not had lunch too, she's just tired. Not all of her is asleep though because she's still saying things in her dreams and her feet are stroking each other on the end of the sofa.

'Mummy.'

She can't hear me. The telly is too loud but the presser isn't here because she might be lying on it. She's too sleepy to wake her up. It's cold now even though it's a sunny day outside and she's got goose pimples on her arms. She'd be warm with her bed things on her but they're too heavy to pull through so it's no point trying. My cat jumper is hiding in a big mess of clothes on the floor and it won't pull out, it's too heavy as well under all the wet clothes. There's some of the man's clothes in the pile. A shirt, and a sock that must be his because it's as long as my arm.

It's warm in by her tummy and it feels nice. The droopy flowers on the table are trying to find the sun but it's went behind the curtain so they can't find it. There's just a little bit of it on the table and it's going more away from the flowers since lunch. Mummy should wake up now. She's going to be sleeping still when the man gets back and he won't like it. She is starting moving a bit with my fingers tapping on her head. She opens her eyes just a little and she can see me.

'Come here, my love.' She strokes my hair. 'Come here.' She is speaking very quietly, stroking my hair more and she's starting to sing a song, but not out loud, just inside her. It's 'Oranges and Lemons', and we've both got our eyes closed now, because it's a very sleepy song.

His armpit is hot against my neck. His mouth pressed to my skull breathing determined little whimpers into my hair.

'Do you want to have a rest for a moment, Patrick?'

He snorts. No, he doesn't. He is weak today, still stiff from yesterday's fall, but stubborn as ever.

'Nearly there now.'

It's only about a dozen steps, bedroom to bathroom. Right now it feels like a pilgrimage. His refusal to give up is steeling me, though, dragging me on. The thought of failing, even at this small task, getting to the bathroom – it's not going to happen.

He lets go of me and leans against the wall to let me open the bathroom door.

'Are you sure you don't want a bath instead? I can run you a shallow one.'

'No.'

The water comes cold through the showerhead for a while, then suddenly too hot. He is standing at the side of the bathtub, waiting for me as water falls loudly onto the porcelain.

'You can go out now.'

'You're not strong enough to do it on your own today.' The wrong choice of words. His face hardens against me. 'At least let me help you in.'

Grudgingly, he lets me lift his feet one by one over the white wall of the bath. He stands inside it, next to the waterfall, still in his dressing gown. He's waiting for me to leave. He doesn't want me to see him take it off. With one hand against the wall tiles, he grabs at the shower curtain and with a surprisingly nimble flick pulls it across. His silhouette, through the thin mouldy curtain, doesn't move.

'Go out.'

'I can just wait here, in case you need me.'

'Please, go out. And close the door.'

Out on the landing the sound of the England match is coming through the wall from next door. This, really, waiting for him to finish in there, should be my opportunity to change his dirty bedsheets, but already tonight's service is running through my mind: planning when to take Jonas aside for a quiet word about the sloppiness of garnish last night; the timing of the three big tables and the push that will hit just before nine. The hiss of water has not changed pitch, so it doesn't sound like he's washing himself. He is probably still standing next to the shower in his dressing gown. Maybe he just wanted a few minutes on his own, without the threat of being intruded on. Without me staring at the blue ruin of his body. Or – who knows? – maybe he's having a wank.

At some unmarked point we have become something

different to each other. We are not a partnership any more –
or, instead, we're a different kind of partnership, no longer
simply husband and wife. When did that change begin? Was
it on the deck of the cruise ship? In the first doctor's office?
The first night-time screaming fit? Or was it with the slow
withdrawal of touch – and what touch is turning into now:
gloves, sprays, wet-wipes. That is why Emily and Matthew
don't want to be here. From a distance they can pretend that
he still exists. They don't want to stop caring, don't want the
word to change its meaning. At least, that is why Emily
doesn't want to be here. Matthew, of course, has his own reasons. A loud squeak. It sounds like his foot slipping on the
bathtub.

'Are you okay in there, Patrick?'

He growls at the door being opened. 'Don't you come in.
Do not come in.'

His leg's doing a mad spasm, splashing, kicking at
something – a glimpse of it beneath the shower curtain –
there is a mouse in the bath.

'Get out, get out, get out!' He is shouting at me, or the
mouse, kicking frantically at it, trying to stop me wrenching
the curtain from his grasp.

'Patrick, stop.'

The curtain comes free – and it isn't a mouse, it's a poo.
The streak where it landed is painted against the white of the
bath side. He is still booting it about.

'You're going to fall over. Stop. Please stop. It's okay. It
doesn't matter.'

He won't stop. He's trying to kick it towards the plug. With every strike it is breaking up. Bits of it are floating in the pool of water, each of them circled with a delicate brown bloom, like jellyfish. Parachutes in the sea. At once he goes still.

'It's okay, Patrick. I'm going to put my arms around your tummy and help you out.'

It is difficult to guide him over the side, his legs, feet squirming over the rim, losing balance, his arm swinging and we are tumbling together to the floor, the whole lump of him landing on top of me. A sharp pain shoots through my shoulder where the back of his head wallops against the same spot the cow fell on me a week ago. Water is seeping into my clothes as my front presses into his back, his bottom. He is getting worse all the time. There is no point pretending otherwise.

It is strangely peaceful, lying here like this with my arms still wrapped around his stomach, like lovers.

'I thought it was a mouse.'

He is making a thin wheezing noise. Laughter. 'Squeak!' His tummy and his bony bottom twitching with amusement.

'You see, Patrick. It's okay.' My lips are touching his ear. 'It doesn't matter.' Our four feet sticking up together. One of his toes has poo on it. 'It doesn't matter. Everything is going to be okay.'

The assurance repeats in my head, those familiar, failed words rebounding from the past, making me hold him tighter, squeezing him hard and remembering her in the bathroom with her dressing gown open, gazing into the mirror – *Everything is going to be okay, Mum. I promise* – until Patrick wriggles in my grip, piping a little noise of discomfort.

'I'm crushing you. Sorry.'

There is a faint cheer through the wall from next door.

'No, no, fine, not *you* sorry. I crapped in the bath.'

1971

She's looking through the dresses now. She's going through all of them with her fingers and stopping when she finds one she likes. She's forgot what she said about going to the toys after she'd finished looking at the shoes.

'Mummy, can we go now? I want to see the Clothkittys.'

She's bending down putting her hand on my arm. 'Course we can, my love. I just want to try this on first.' She's taking a dress off the rail. 'Come on.'

The woman working at the counter is looking over at Mummy walking to the changing rooms with the dress. Mummy knows the woman's watching because she does a check over her shoulder at her but she doesn't put the dress back and she starts going a bit quicker to the changing rooms.

Inside the stall Mummy is humming to the music they've got playing in the store. She's not like she was earlier when she was crying with Eddie or after that when she was all quiet on the bus. She puts the dress over the mirror stand and she starts undoing the buttons on her blouse.

'You coming inside, then?'

She moves forward and leans over me with her boobs in my face to close the curtain.

'I want to see the Clothkittys, Mummy.'

'In a minute, Anita. Just let me try this on, then we'll go down the basement and look at the toys, I promise.'

Her body is bright white and soft without her clothes on. If someone opened the curtains now they'd be able to see her right there just in her Alan Whickers. She's giggling at me looking at her and she blows me a kiss. The store woman's feet are outside the curtain but my hand is keeping it closed so that she can't come in while Mummy is putting the dress on. It's got orange flowers and a big collar and the sleeves come all down her arms. She looks nice, like she's in a magazine.

'What do you think, sweetie? Will Eddie like it?'

'It looks nice. Are you going to buy it, Mummy?'

She laughs, whispering, 'No, course I'm not going to buy it—Oh! Listen. I love this song.' She grabs my hands and starts to dance. 'Come on, Anita!'

Mummy is spinning us round the stall. My bum knocks the mirror and it wobbles a bit but it stays stood up. She is singing out loud – 'Oh, sugar, sugar' – and she doesn't care who else can hear her or that the woman's feet are still there behind the curtain, she just keeps on singing – then she stops spinning around, because she wants me to copy her dancing: lifting up her knee, then her other knee, until we're both doing it together and laughing and if the woman outside the stall opened the curtain right now she'd think we was both off our heads.

Freddy is chuntering to himself at the fish section.

'Freddy, talk to me. How are you looking?'

'I'm hit, Chef. Spanked. I'm good on these four monkfish and the sole but the salmon needs me for the whole cook and I don't want to burn it.'

'That's okay. I can take the salmon.'

Right away he is shuffling his pans on the stove, making room for the bullseye. All around there are arms and hands moving, faces down. At the pass, the mechanical stutter of the Ramenco starting up again, another order coming in.

'Give me some space, Freddy.'

The salmon fillet is ready on a board, roomed-up, seasoned – its skin freckled with tiny beads of moisture drawn out by the salt. Some lucky diner is about to eat a beautiful piece of fish, even if they have only chosen it because it's the most expensive dish on the menu.

The flesh is firm in my fingers. This wild, summer creature that has returned from the ocean, swum thousands of miles across the Atlantic then, against the river current, jumped up weirs and waterfalls to lay its eggs in the same headwater it was born in and now lies in my hands, a gorgeous thing, as closely related to all the pellet-gulpers headbutting each other in their sea cages, bound for Tesco, as Turtle is to Escoffier.

The pan is raging, smoking with oil. At the first touch of heat the fillet buckles, its skin contracting. Freddy is glancing across from his monkfish. He might be slammed, but he'll still be wishing that he was cooking this. He has come on, this last year in the kitchen before Frank made him fish CDP. He would have this same discipline as me to resist moving the fillet now, to let it relax, applying just the correct fingertip pressure to feel for the minute vibration of skin bubbles nubbling against the pan. For these hushed seconds, the kitchen is a world apart. With me away from the pass and nobody expediting, bridging them to the outside, each chef is completely focused on his own element, a chain working together to the background hum of the extractor, the squeak of clogs on the non-slips. The dark beyond the hot lamps a foreign land – of floor staff and conversation and clueless diners not giving a second's thought to what they are eating. All of life is controllable in here, inside the den of the kitchen, safe, away from that other world: the restaurant, the city – and further out, later, the night bus; the tired, apprehensive journey home to Patrick.

The pan is ready to move to a quieter place on the stove. Further down the kitchen there is a loud whoosh, like surf, as Jack lowers a full chauffant basket into a pot of boiling water to bring up the garnish for the monkfish. Jack's left cheek and the left side of his neck are blazing red. His come-face, as Turtle has started calling it. For the first time today both of them are fully focused, undistracted by their novelty St George's Cross clogs or the World Cup wallchart Frank finally let them put up this morning. The skin is beginning to brown at the edges, the salmon already three-quarters, ready for finishing. Butter, Maurice, flip – and it comes away without a shred missing, skin crisp as a biscuit.

'Spoon, Freddy.'

He passes one across, looking at the salmon, nodding. The first hot, yellow spoonful coats the skin with a thick gloss. To the tap, tap, tap of the spoon against the pan, lapping butter over the fillet, the kitchen is gradually lulled, the metallic rhythm passing into each of us, a pulse, a joining of our blood.

'Coming up on table nine!'

Lemon juice strains through the cloth and over my fingers. It emulsifies with the butter in the pan, the final spoonful glazing the fish. A sprinkle of salt flakes and it is ready for the pass, where waiters are hovering, waiting for the shout.

1972

'Do you need anything, Mum?'

She's shaking her head.

'Cup of tea or something? I know how to do the kettle.'

'No, I'm all right now.'

She looks like she is, too. She's gone still and quiet in the chair, staring out the window at the tops of the other towers. One of her feet's a bit twitchy but that's all, and if somebody was to see her now and ignore the rug all snarled up and her handbag spilled out over it, they probably wouldn't even guess that she's just fell out of her chair. She is smiling up at me putting the blanket down over her legs – but all of a sudden she's going stiff because there's someone bang-and-rattling at the door.

'One of you open it, will you?' It's Eddie. Forgot his own key soon as Mum's agreed to give him one, or he's been at the pub.

'I'm coming. Wait a minute.'

He's still yanking at the lock not waiting for me to get there, and he manages to do it himself. The door swings open and he's stood there in the doorway looking at me with a great smile on him and a big fish wrapped in newspaper in his armpit.

'I caught a fish, Anita! Look – I caught a bloody fish!'

The fish smells. Eddie's holding it out in front of me like he wants me to take it off him but there's no chance that's happening. He comes inside and he puts the fish down next to the kettle. He's seen Mum by the window. She's watching over at what's going on, confused as anything, as if a horse has just walked in the flat.

'I caught one, Jane. Me and Bobby, we got one each. Down where the creek goes in the Thames, we were there with his rods all afternoon and we caught two the same, hell knows what they are. Flounders, Bobby thinks.'

Mum is looking at him with a smile that's not changing shape.

'Come on, get up. You can cook it for us.' He looks down for a second at the rug. 'Up you get, come on. Do something, Jane, will you, for a change. I'm going to get myself washed up.'

He is off to the bathroom and Mum's staring into space again, still with a bit of the smile left on her mouth.

'It's all right, Mum. I'll give you a hand.'

It's easy enough to help her get stood up, there's that little of her. She walks slow, leaning in to me, like an old person, over to the fish on the counter. Its head is poking out the top of the newspaper. She starts peeling off the paper, all wet with fish slime. Then she just looks at it.

'What do I do?' she says, really quiet.

Her hands are shaking a bit and she puts them onto the counter, around the fish. Through in the bathroom Eddie's got the shower running and me and Mum are just looking at this fish that he wants to eat.

'I'll do it, Mum.'

She lifts her face up to me. She doesn't think that's a silly thing to say. She's just pleased.

The dead fish is in front of me, brown and slimy with dark spots all over it. It's got about as much clue as me what needs doing with it. Mum is still stood next to me, not watching but not looking at anything else either, and she doesn't say no to me taking the sharp knife out the drawer. The fish is wide and flat, so it feels like the right thing is to cut it down the middle. When the knife goes in, it's crunchy, not soft. It doesn't cut smooth – and it's difficult because the knife keeps getting stuck and needs taking out and digging in again. Little twigs of bone are sticking out all the way down the middle until where its weird googly eyes are, one of them in the middle on top of its head, the other next to it a bit lop-sided. It's disgusting thinking about keeping cutting down the middle, through its brain, if it has a brain. Better just to chop its head off.

After the head is done, and the tail, it's all looking a bit of a mess. There is bones and pink mush coming out of all the cut bits. It's in two parts, though, and now that it is, it doesn't look like there's going to be enough for the three of us. Still, Mum hardly eats nothing, and thinking about putting any of this fish into my mouth is making me want to be sick in the sink. It's Eddie's fish. He can eat it. He's getting changed in Mum's room now. He'll be back through soon enough and he will see it's me not Mum has been doing the fish so it's time to get going quicker – putting the oven on and getting the bag of chips from off the freezer shelf and a great pile of them onto the oven tray. When that's done, the two pieces of fish balance easy enough on top of the chips. Mum is smiling. It's hard to know if it's because it's a mess or because she's not had to do it herself, but she's happy, and it feels good knowing that this has made things easier for her. On one of the pieces of fish, next to where its head was, there is a small, hard bit. Turning the fish around, there's another on the other side, the same stiff feathery stump – its fin, where it's been snipped off. And it's only noticing the fins makes me notice as well that there is a hole cut into what's probably its tummy, too neat and wide that it was my knife did it by mistake. All at once it makes sense. It's from the market, this fish. It's probably yesterday's and he's been given it by the fishmonger. Or he's nicked it. He is coming back through now, his hair wet, and he looks pleased as anything, watching Mum move forward from the counter with the tray in both her hands to put it in the oven. A couple of the chips fall off the pile onto the floor and she waits, holding the tray steady where Eddie can't see us because we're bent down together by the oven, for me to pick them up and put them back on. Her face has already gone a bit pink from the hot air and even with her eyes swollen and her hair a dog's breakfast, she looks beautiful, up close like this.

Eddie's voice comes from the sofa: 'It's going to be delicious, that is, Jane.'

We look into the oven at the fish, which looks like a bus has just gone over it, and both of us start to giggle quietly. But it's in there. It's food and he's going to eat it and be pleased and Mum is going to be happy, maybe, for the rest of the day.

'See, Mum. I can look after us now.'

She is moving her hand towards me and she touches me on the cheek.

'I know, my love.'

She smiles at me and closes her eyes, shutting the oven door.

A stale skin of onion and grease is radiating from my trousers, my undershirt, my hair. Dried service sweat. The bedroom is so hot that it is starting to come on again, but Patrick is calmly asleep, the bedcovers gently rising and falling, his eyelids quivering. There is a piece of paper underneath his hand on the other pillow. He's written something on it. He didn't say what he wanted the pen for this morning but it looks like he's made some kind of list. The lines are numbered. The word *Lock* stands out on the first one.

He wakes up at me trying to take the paper from under his hand.

'What? Oh. You.'

'I'm just back from the restaurant. Do you need anything?'

'No.' He is picking up the piece of paper, looking at me with suspicion. 'Rules.'

'Rules?'

'Yes.' He hands me the paper.

'What is this?'

'Read them.'

There are six bullet points in different-sized writing, fairly neat at first then getting more erratic and finishing in a huge scribble, like a child's Christmas list.

1. *Lock for bathroom door*
2. *Cup of tea only when asked for*
3. *Digital clock for bedroom*
4. *NO VISITORS*
5. *No carrots*
6. *I can feed myself*

He is waiting for my response.

'What do you want me to do with this?'

The question confuses him.

'What should I do with it? Put it on the fridge?'

'Yes, good.'

His rulebook has energised him. His house, his rules. The impulse to crumple it up and throw it across the room squeezes my fingers against the paper. 'And if Emily or Matthew want to visit, will they be allowed?'

He puffs out his cheeks. 'Don't need to worry about that.'

It is the most coherent, and true, thing he has said all week. In the anxious aftermath of his first stroke, almost four and a half years ago now, hard as that is to believe, it felt like Emily was home most weekends; this time, she has still not managed to find a date to come down since Easter. And in a couple of weeks it will be a whole year since the bitter, explosive afternoon when Matthew finally left.

'What happens if you fall in the bathroom and the door's locked?'

'I won't fall.'

'What if you do?'

'I have a right to privacy.'

'Do you think I want to be in there with you?'

As soon as the words leave my mouth and he turns his face away, pity, then guilt – the fleeting thought of Peter; wanting to be with him, away from here – seize me, making me get up and move off to open the window. Neither of us speaks. The undigital clock is ticking away on his bedside shelf. Through the window the houses across the street all have their front doors open for the draught. Everybody is in their living rooms, the England match playing on every television. The road unusually calm, trafficless.

'Tell you what. Instead of crunchy ones, later I'll cook you the softest, tastiest carrots you've ever eaten.'

'No. No carrots.'

'No carrots at all? Not even soft ones?'

'No. I don't like carrots.'

'You don't like *carrots*?'

'No. I never have.'

There it is, then. He doesn't like carrots. Thirty-two years of marriage and we're still discovering these titbits about each other. Would he find that funny? He might.

'Who'd have thought, Patrick? Thirty-two years of marriage and we're still discovering these titbits about each other.'

But he has closed his eyes. He's going back to sleep.

24

1973

It's all gone quiet. Really it's worse waiting for if the shouting is going to start up again, and it's not knowing what is
going to come next that's making me squash my ear up on
my wall, listening in. It's dangerous quiet in their room.
Eddie is talking, though, his voice soft and sorry. It's not his
fault, he keeps saying, it's not his fault. Their door is opening. One of them coming out – Mum – because Eddie's still
in there talking. Feet outside my room. A calm feeling filling
me up inside as their door closes shut again, because it's over,
and nothing more's going to happen now that the door is
between them.

The flat is dead still. Eddie has stopped talking and wherever Mum is, she's not moving. An idea comes in my head
that she might have gone out, even though that's not possible
because the flat door hasn't been opened, but the thought of
it is too big for me to stay put in my room.

She is looking at herself in the bathroom mirror. She
doesn't see me coming towards her. Even if she does, she's
not turning round. Her dressing gown isn't tied up. The front

of it is all open in the mirror and there's bright red bits on her skin either side of her belly button. She's still not moving and she's let me get close enough now to be able to count them, four splodges on both sides above her hip bones, red as anything, like a finger painting. If she was crying it would probably feel better than this, more easy to figure her out. She's completely still. She must know it's me behind her, though, pulling her dressing gown around her, tying the belt back up for her.

'Are you all right, Mum?'

She just keeps staring into the mirror.

'Can I get you anything?'

Eddie's voice comes sudden through the wall: 'It's not my fault, Jane.' He's not shouting but his voice is that clear it's like he's here in the bathroom with us. 'You don't *do* anything. What's wrong with you, woman? It's not my fault. You're a bloody nutcase.'

She's still standing there in front of the mirror.

'Everything is going to be okay, Mum. I promise.'

Mum is opening her mouth, like she's going to say something, but nothing comes out and now she's lifting my hands gentle off her tummy and pulling away from me, going back.

Peter is there, waiting for me. Chatting to the fish man. His stall is closed up, the vegetables bagged and boxed out back. My feet sound against the stone floor, the market hall cool and echoey as a church after coming in from the sweltering city outside. The fish man has spotted me. He gives Peter a little nudge. After half a dozen years of monitoring me in here, they all have their presumptions about me and him, the other traders. Peter is smiling.

'It's the lady chef, look. Hello there.' He is coming over, saving me the awkwardness of an exchange with the fish man. 'How are you?'

'Knackered. A hundred and five for lunch.'

'Bloody hell.'

We are falling into step as we walk through the market, passing through the ghosts of cured meats, cheese, shellfish, flowers. He nods at another stall owner still shutting up shop.

'How long've I got you for?'

Already the feeling of wrongdoing is making me want to be away, to get home. 'Just the walk to the station.'

'Quick cuppa, then, on the way?'

'Okay. A quick one.'

People are crowding the pavement, on the walk to the station or standing with plastic pint glasses outside the bars, most of which still have England flags and scarves up in their windows even after yesterday. People with normal jobs who finish at the same normal time every day. They're too focused on themselves to see anyone else but the possibility that they could notice us is unsettling – that they might understand the trespass; that they, like the market traders, will presume what is going on here. When we reach the café, Peter holds the door open for me – pointing to where in the distance the yellow quiff of the Trump blimp that the boys were talking about earlier is momentarily visible, floating above the buildings.

Inside, the heat is stifling. There is the babble of conversation. Milk being steamed behind the counter. What *is* going on here? Nothing – and in all the time that we've known each other there never has been anything – but all the same something has started, in these few months since Patrick's last stroke, as he worsens, to feel increasingly untoward. The nothing of it is growing. Peter is going to the counter. Outside the window, an ambulance siren is moving down the road in the direction of the protest and my legs cramp up against the table as it comes past. It is too easy to imagine what other people would think. What Emily and Matthew, if they were ever to meet him, would think.

He has bought me a piece of cake.

'Thank you, but you have it.'

He shakes his head at it being pushed back to him. 'It's for you.'

'I don't want it.'

The cake is poised, between our mugs, on the table.

'Come on, Anita. You don't have to feel bad for having a slice of cake.'

'I don't. I just don't want it. It's too hot for cake.'

'Fair enough.'

He starts to eat the cake. The light through the window, as he puts it into his mouth, is shining on the left half of his head. 'You should think about yourself more,' he says, finishing his mouthful. 'Your own needs.'

'You thought I needed a lemon drizzle cake?'

'You daft? I'm not talking about the cake. You can't just give yourself up to work and caring. You'll expire.'

'What choice have I got?'

'You need some help.'

'You're offering, are you? He'd love that, a man he's never met coming by to spoon him his dinner and sponge his armpits.'

It is over the top, unfair. Peter is clearly hurt – but he is the one apologising, telling me gently that he was being thoughtless, that it's not what he meant.

'That wasn't fair, Peter, I'm sorry.'

'There are other people could give you a hand.'

'My children, you mean?'

'Well, have you asked them? Directly, like?'

'They have their own lives. Anyway, he wouldn't allow it. Sacrificing themselves to look after him.'

'What about your sacrifice, Anita? He not mind that?'

'Well, we've been married over thirty years and it's not come up so far.'

'Funny girl.'

A full English breakfast is coming towards the man at the table next to us. The growing smell of it makes my stomach wither with hunger. 'There's other kinds of help you could get,' Peter is saying. 'Professional help. You don't have to do it all on your own.'

It is too much: this idea, his kindness, the thought of Patrick still on his own in the house.

'I should go. I'm sorry.'

My chair shrieks against the floor and the man looks up from his afternoon breakfast. It is not right being here now, while Patrick is alone, going hungry without another meal in him since me leaving for work. Peter is coming around the table. 'It's all right,' he says, reaching for me, his arms around me, pulling me in. 'You go, pet. You go.' The earthy smell of his clothes, his face next to mine and a void opening up inside me, yearning to give in and let go, needing him to hold me tight to him, safe.

1974

The park's chock-a-block because the sun's out, people all up the paths and around the deer park and the Observatory. No one's on our bench at the pond, mind, so Mum's straight off to it. She sits down and lets me get her settled in with her bag next to her with all her things, and her sunhat on her properly.

'You comfy enough, Mum?'

'Yes. Thank you, sweetie.'

Down the edge of the water there's a little pile of ciggies where people have been stood here looking at the pond, smoking. The nest is gone. And the birds, too. There's other birds about, ducks and geese and some pigeons where people have dropped bits of bread, but the two little black ones who should be here have gone. Something tight is straight away happening in my tummy, wanting the black birds to be here like they normally are. Babyish to cry about it – and there's other people about too, some teenagers over the other side the water, a boy and a girl kissing each other. Behind me on the bench Mum's settled and peaceful, humming to herself,

31

away with the fairies, so there's nothing to do about it except stand here and look for the birds, listening to the drizzle of the fountain on the pond, trying to stop myself crying, wanting the birds to be okay and everything to be normal again.

But now one of the black birds is coming out the bushes, right the way over the other side near the teenagers. And the other one's there too, following straight behind. They both of them do their funny little run up the mud and splash into the pond. They swim over to where the nest should be and stop.

'What's happened to the nest, Mum? Why's it gone?'

The sun is on her face and she's got her eyes closed.

'Council probably demolished it, Anita. Slum clearance. They'll have the towers up by the time we're next here, you'll see.' She is laughing away, shaking her head. She's sparky today, all right, but in a good way that doesn't feel like it's a worry, not the scary way.

One of the birds is standing up, like it's standing on the water, while the other goes off to the bank again – and it's obvious now from the little shadow under the water that the nest is really still there, just fallen down a bit. The bird on the nest sits down. She's the mum. The water is up over her bum and almost to her neck but she's just sat there like everything's normal. The dad walking round the bank, patting across the mud with his big clown feet. He sticks his head in a big tuft of reeds and rips out a great mouthful, then he's off back to the nest with it. There's something about watching them that makes all my body stop still. The way they just get on with it, same as they have these last few Saturdays, like there's nothing else matters in the whole world. Nothing's going to put them off, not even the nest getting sunk, which couldn't've been a big surprise, really, because it's a right mess the way they build it.

Mum's got her arms folded over her chest and her legs stretched out. She opens her eyes, sees me go into the bushes.

The dad bird takes no notice of me coming out with a bunch of twigs and putting them on the ground for him. He's pretending he doesn't need any help. He's got more reeds in his mouth but soon as he's gave them to her he starts swimming straight back for my pile of twigs. Mum's watching too now. She's grinning, watching the bird take some of the twigs and go back to the nest. He lifts up his beakful, putting on that he's found them himself.

It's not long before some of the nest is showing again on top of the water, they're that quick about it. All the twigs are almost used up, and there's not much else on the bank near here. There is another patch of trees and bushes over by the teenagers, though, who don't take any notice of me coming round because they've still got their tongues in each other's brains.

Through the bushes, back by the pond, there is voices. Turning round, the sight of three boys makes my heart near come out of its sockets – how they're just suddenly there, out of nowhere. They're only nine or ten same as me but they're big, especially one of them, who looks a bit older. They're stood down at the side of the water below Mum, where my twigs were, and the dad bird thinks there's more twigs for him so he's swimming right towards them. One of the boys has got a stone in his hand. He holds it up and throws it at the bird. There's a great splash right next to him and he's all ends up, he's that surprised, wings flapping, rushing back for the nest. The boys think it's the funniest thing ever. The biggest one is going off in the other direction around the pond.

My skin is all goose pimples, listening to the water drizzling on the pond, and my brain and my bones are thumping inside me, an out-of-control feeling growing and growing – of wanting Mum, just to be my mum, needing her to keep me and the birds safe and everything to be all right.

The birds think it's me doing this to them. These boys are going to hurt them and smash up their nest but my legs won't move. The boys have taken over this place. They don't know about me here in the bushes and even if they did it wouldn't matter to them, they'd ignore me or they'd make me go away, because the pond is theirs now.

The big one is back, carrying a great load of stones. He hands them out. All three of them start taking turns throwing them at the nest. Both the birds are on it now. A stone hits a bit of the nest away and they're in a panic, bouncing up and down and flapping about. They're still not moving off though. The boys are going for more stones but the birds are staying put. *Over my dead body*, they're both saying, like Dead Grandma in that photo of her stood on the broken bricks behind her house after the council knocked the rest of her street down, digging her heels in right until they came and demolished her house anyway – before they came for Mum's street too and then my dad left and Mum got housed in the towers and went off her head.

The boys are coming back with an armful of stones each. The big boy's got one that looks as big as the birds. He thinks he's strong enough to throw it as far as the nest and if he can then that will be it destroyed in one go.

Mum is coming down off the bench. They haven't seen her. They're lobbing off another round and she's running towards them and the big one has his arm back ready to throw when Mum surprises him and gets hold of him by his ear. He does a loud squeal. She's twisting it and his back is curling over. The other two are frightened now, their hands going down by their legs with the stones still in them. Mum shouting, 'Go on and clear off then!'

The teenage kissers are staring across the water. And now they're scarpering too, like the boys, because they're scared she's going to come after them next.

The birds are sat on the nest nudgying up together. They're probably wondering what the heck's just went on. Mum is walking towards me, telling me to come out of the bushes. She looks happy. She takes hold of my hand. Hers is a bit warm and sweaty but she's gripping tight around mine.

'Come on, my love. Let's go say hello to the deers, shall we?'

We start walking away from the pond, the drizzle of the fountain behind us getting quieter, Mum not letting go of my hand and the pair of us smiling away because she's seen those boys off and we've both got the same feeling: that no one can lay a finger on us. More people are about, walking past in all directions and none of them are looking at us because we just seem normal to them – Mum talking now about her and Eddie getting married, the chapel she's thinking of having it in and the dress she wants me to wear – and everything feels so simple, holding her hand tight like this, like we're the right way round for once and there's nothing else to have to think about except going to the deers and whether we might buy an ice cream before we get to them.

Maybe it's the physical sensation of it, or my clumsiness, or maybe just the novelty of being touched, but he is chortling.

'Hey you, keep still. I'll chop your face off if you're not careful.'

The blade slides down over his jaw. It is surprisingly firm. He's jutting it out, wanting me to know this, that not all of him has gone to the dogs yet. The hair on his top lip thick and strong, vitality pushing up from under the skin as if to say, *Here is a man, still.* He used to let Emily shave him sometimes. Not Matthew. Did he ever ask Matthew if he would have liked to do it, or was that a job only for a daughter? Not that Matthew would have wanted to, either way. He would have found the prospect of stroking the razor across his father's face too intimate. Or, more likely still, a test. A dollop of cream drops onto his lap. It sits there obscenely on the lap of his dressing gown, beneath a slit below the belt where his tummy is poking out doughy and white around the red pit of his belly button.

There are longer tufts of hair underneath his bottom lip. Around his ears, too. Slowly, precisely, the blade takes them. The intimacy of this moment is making me gradually forget myself, his carer. That other work for now at bay: changing and cleaning him, fighting with him until he allows me to help him with his food, sliding the spoon between his lips while soft wet slop dribbles down this same chin that is now almost perfect: bright, strong, alive. He is looking at me in the mirror. For an instant the eyes, meeting mine, are Mum's. They are pleading with me, asking for my help. The blade comes to rest in my hand as we regard each other, the eyes in the mirror moving, alert, watching my hands come down onto the bony shoulders, my lips lowering towards to kiss the scalp through the thin hair. Which stinks. But one thing at a time.

1975

She's in my room again. Not in my bed today, though, not asleep. She's in my drawers by the bed, rooting through them.

'Mum?'

She turns round, her face frozen.

'I'm sorry, Anita.'

She is lying down on the bed. Her eyes fixed on my flaky ceiling. She keeps mumbling she's sorry, over and over. The middle drawer of the chest is open and the lid's off my Milquick pot.

'Mum? What were you doing?'

She twists her neck to look me straight in the eyes. She's not crying but her face isn't good. Her hair's dirty and will need washing if she'll let me and her lips are cracked from me never managing to get her to drink enough water.

'Will you do something for me?'

'Course, Mum.'

'Will you lend me some money? Just whatever you can?'

'I've not got any, Mum.' She is looking at me like it's a lie but it's not, it's three weeks since he last gave me any money – cassette and a magazine and that was it spent. 'Have you asked Eddie for some?'

'He won't give me any. Says it's for my own good because I can't be trusted with it.'

'What is it you need?'

She's turning her face away from me, all the energy gone out of her again. 'I want something that will help me. I can't live like this any more.'

A dizzy, sick feeling is at once going through me.

'I don't understand.'

'Please, Anita. *You* could just ask him for some – tell him you need to go up the market and get some things we need for the flat. I can't ask him because he'll want to know what it's for and—'

'What *is* it for, Mum?'

But she's tired out, shaking her head slowly like she expected me to help her but she's been let down and now there's no point in anything except going back to sleep.

'I don't know what to say to you, Mum.'

'Oh, you don't need to say anything, my love.' She is squeezing my hand, using my weight to pull herself back up again. 'You just need to promise me you'll turn into someone else.' Her eyes are yellow, looking right at me. 'You have to fight for something better than all this.'

Something has broken the hush of the kitchen, the stirring of activity up on the floor filtering down. Turtle looks up from his mise. 'Why-aye! It's Potato Man!'

Peter is up there, in the restaurant, the top of his bald head bobbing above the service gangway, floor staff flocking towards him as he hands something out, like a favourite uncle. My knife flashes with the pulse of my wrist, roll-slicing a length of salsify without pause while everyone else moves to the pass where Peter is coming down the gangway steps.

'Get stuck in, lads. Some British beauties here.'

There is a carton of strawberries on the pass, already crawling with white hands. Peter standing on the other side with his arms folded, chuckling. He is sweating slightly from the heat outside on the street. He gives a quick look at me as Frank walks over to him. They shake hands. Peter's other hand opens to reveal a strawberry, reserved for Frank. He holds it out on his palm, as if he expects Frank to snaffle it off him like a horse. Frank ignores it at first, then picks it up, pops it into his mouth.

'Your autograph please, Chef.' Peter places a docket onto the steel while Frank searches the pass top shelf with his hand.

'No pen. Hang on.' He turns his attention to the chefs still hanging around the empty carton – 'You lot, back to work' – and goes out to the office.

Peter is alone at the entrance to the kitchen, looking at me. My eyes go back to my task, peeling a new length of salsify, concentrating on the rhythmic scrape of the action, exposing the white flesh. He comes beside me, putting something onto my board. A baby leek. Frank is returning from back-of-house, stepping into pastry to say something to Xav then looking into the plonge, instructing Isaac and Musa to go and collect the crates of veg. Peter moves off towards him. They speak a few quiet words while Frank signs the docket. Then Peter is leaving, calling out his cheerios as he moves from section to section – Freddy at fish, Jonas juggling new potatoes at garnish, Anton at meat slicing up his daily pine-apple ready for morning break – and slaps Jack and Turtle on the shoulders. He gets more laughter and conversation out of them in his ten minutes here with the morning delivery than they give me during five doubles.

The leek is hiding amongst the salsify. Something is pro-truding out of it: the central cylinder of leaves has been taken out and a tightly rolled pipe of paper is wedged in its place. A peek up – nobody seeing the leek go into my pocket, or the little smile on my mouth. What a ninny.

Inside the walk-in, in the seclusion of its dingy light, the paper slides smoothly out of the leek. It unfurls to show a couple of lines of writing. Scribbled notes, it seems, is how the men of my life have decided they want to communicate with me. There are no rules on this paper, though:

I've found your restaurant. It's perfect. Insolvent Vietnamese place in Lambeth. Call me x

1976

'Do you want to go sit on the chair, Mum, eat it through there?'

Her body's all fidgety, like she's about to take off from the bed.

'No, no. I'm happy here, thank you.'

As soon as the plate's on her lap she gets tucking into the mash, hungry, saying how nice it is – and at once she's talking while she eats, words rushing out of her: '. . . the one says Eddie needs his head seeing to even more than I do, staying with me and still planning on us getting married, but Eddie knows that's just her talking rubbish—' She stops. Her first mouthful of sausage going in, coming straight out again, too hot. She is staring at it hovering on the fork in front of her face, damp and grey, steaming, as if she's just pulled out a piece of her brain. And now she's off again, ten to the dozen, the heatwave and how hot it is for Eddie working down the underground and she can't stop thinking about him trapped in down there after the bombings. '. . . and I can't stop thinking, Anita, it's just that sometimes I can't stop thinking.' She's nodding, but not at me; she's nodding like there's someone else in the room talking to her. 'He's right, you know. My head's gone. God knows why he still says he wants to marry me. Marbles and conkers, I am.'

We sit there, her hand on top of mine on the bed and there's nothing to say. It's not like she's wrong.

'He wants to send me over the doctor's again but how am I supposed to go if I'm not even allowed to leave the flat? And he's not going to take me himself, is he? *Here she is, Doc, here's my wife-to-be the nutcase.*' She's looking at me like she's expecting me to say something. 'Am I raving, sweetie?'

'A bit, Mum.' She laughs, which starts me laughing too. 'It's all right, though, I don't mind. I'm here. I'll go make us a cup of tea.'

She's smiling away, eating her food, shifting her legs to let me get off the bed and go put the kettle on.

It's cooler through here, all the windows open, a few flies buzzing about. Even if she's like this for the next few days, it's good that her dark spell of the last couple of weeks looks like it has passed, as long as Eddie can help me keep her inside the flat now. Good that she's eaten too. And if Eddie buys in some Chinese after work like he said, that could be two meals in her today – and the hopeful thought comes of the pair of them sitting in front of the telly with their trays on their skinny legs and the salt shaker sliding about over Mum's jumpy knees. Outside, the river is blazing in the sun. Boats going up and down, a flock of birds, smoke puffing up into perfect clouds above the Dogs. The thick tide of the market and people going in and out of the pubs all down the High Street. Children, across the water, playing on the Muddy. Everywhere busy with life.

She is not in the bed. She must have gone to the toilet – so there is a chance now to change her sheets while she's not here, because they're stinking to all hell with her being in them all through the heatwave. Soon as the teas are down on the floor, though, there's the sound of her coughing, loud, like she's choking, through the bathroom wall.

'Mum, you all right in there?'

She doesn't hear, or she's ignoring me. Getting closer, there is the noise through the door of the tap on full.

'Mum? Is everything all right?'

The tap is turning off. For a bit there is no sound at all. Then her feet coming to the door. She slides the latch and opens the door – and is standing there with an odd look on her like she's been caught in the act.

'Mum?'

There is water splashed onto the floor and the mirror on the medicine box is slid open.

'I'm sorry, my love. I'm so sorry.'

'What is it, Mum?'

There is a little pile of capsules on the sink next to the toothbrushes. They're the blue bullet ones, her Barbaras.

'I need you to help me, Anita.'

It's almost a whisper, how she says it. A panicky feeling is going through me, because normally it's when she's in the dark spells that she's started asking me this but now that she's up on her feet and ten-to-the-dozen there's no telling what she might do.

'I don't have enough. The doctor won't give me any more and this isn't enough.' She's looking me in the eyes, trying to convince me, like it's something normal she's asking for. 'I just need a bit of money so I can get something else as well that can – that will help me – but I don't know where he keeps it so I need you to—'

'No. Stop talking like this, Mum. You've had a bad spell for a while and now you're not yourself at the minute but that'll pass over too soon enough and then everything's going to be okay. You'll see. Everything is going to be okay.'

She looks at the capsules on the sink, then she moves towards me and puts her cheek down on my shoulder. 'Yes,' she says. 'What would I do without you?'

The sucking of our shoes on the greasy lino tears through the empty, hot space. There is a bad smell. Something dead. Peter goes ahead to what was the bar. He peels a takeaway menu from the counter. The agent's voice from the kitchen doorway: 'It's actually quite big.' An imprint of the menu is left on the bar counter, the only legible thing the numbers down one side. 'Great condition, really, this kitchen,' the agent is calling through. 'Stainless-steel extraction system, new prep benches . . .'

A terrace of battered rodent bait boxes lines the floor behind the bar. Peter is staring at them. He looks up at me, winks. 'Christ, it's mafting in here.' He wipes a hand across his forehead. 'Come on. Let's see in this kitchen, then.'

He goes first through the beaded curtain across the doorway, which has patches of missing strands, like balding dreadlocks.

The kitchen, in reality, is a shithole. A tidemark of yellow scum is climbing the walls. The paired fryers still filled with fat. In one of them, something large and dark has sunk to the bottom.

'I know why they went out of business,' Peter says,

pointing to a chalk board on the floor that is leant up against a wall: *starter and main free* is scrawled amidst the rubbings out. It all feels surreal. Examining the wreckage of someone else's failure like this, in secret.

'Here, come look at this.' Peter leads me back out of the kitchen. On the wall by the beaded curtain is a calendar with a picture of a fisherman casting a net from a little, wooden boat. Things are written in another language inside the date boxes, all abruptly empty from halfway through the month. Peter has started walking through the restaurant. He goes around a corner into an alcove naturally lit from above through a mottled glass panel. With the electricity cut off and everywhere else in the half-dark, the sun beams down here like a stage light.

'You could get a big table in here,' he says. 'Group bookings.'

'Yes, we could.'

'Put a booth in. Banquette seating, curved into a horse-shoe. Big oval table.'

He's right – in everything he has said about this place since his message-in-a-leek: it does have potential. It is not difficult to imagine how it could look. The arrangement of the tables along the large front window. Stools along the bar. Waiter and bread stations, flowers, around the central pillar.

'I don't know why I'm here, Peter.'

He is looking at me severely. 'Because this is what you want, Anita.'

'It's a fantasy.'

'No, that's you talking yourself out of it. This place has got something. It's a damn sight better than that old boozer we saw last.' He steps towards me, takes my hand and keeps hold of it. 'It's not a fantasy.'

A thrill of excitement is passing through me – the sudden unobstructed vision of this restaurant full of noise and heat and movement – until the agent appears again from around the alcove corner. Peter lets go of my hand. The agent, seeing how close together we are standing, moves back around the corner.

'Shall we go and see the rest of it?' Peter asks.

'Yes.'

In the main floor area of the restaurant, as we come back through to it, the agent is gazing into the fish tank by the toilet corridor. It is full of green, murky water. Best not to think about what happened to the fish. The agent gestures down the corridor: 'Well-specified toilets.' There are peeling, white-lettered stickers on each of the two doors: *Ladies. Gents.* He doesn't look like he's joking. 'Twelve hundred square feet, prominent trading position, good footfall, passing vehicle trade . . .' He is directing all of these details, automatically, to Peter – who is listening intently, his finger tapping on his bottom lip as he takes it all in. Peter hasn't asked, this time, whether Patrick knows about the viewing. Already, the deceit of it has become normal. Implicit. The agent is calling Peter's attention to the EPOS booking system by the fish tank. Its screen, in the light from the road window, is stippled with fingerprints, people, life. Everywhere the evidence of this past lies abandoned: the tower of yellowing polystyrene take-away boxes on the bar counter and the worn patch of floor below them; the sad outpost of dipping sauces by the till. Even the tables and chairs are all still in place, as if mid-service one evening the whole place had to be evacuated.

'Why didn't they take any of this?'

The agent shrugs. 'I think the end came quite quickly,' he says, deadpan.

It was somebody's dream once, this place. A family, by the looks of it. There are photographs stuck to the open storage-cupboard door on the way to the well-specified toilets. Happy faces in another world, a turquoise sea in the background. Hopefully they have gone back there, made a life again.

'You've got a customer already, look.' Peter points at one of the tables. A long, pale rat is sitting on top of it. The agent claps his hands, walking towards the rat. The rat doesn't move. It is watching the agent, who is slowing down, losing his nerve. He stamps the heel of his pointy, black shoe. The rat stays put.

'You'd need to fumigate, obviously, get the exterminators in.' He turns around and comes back to us. 'Clean it all up, make the place your own.'

In the reflection of the front window, Peter is looking at me. His eyes, unaware that he too is being observed, seem to be holding me keenly, longingly, even – and for a few liber-ated seconds it feels as though this half-real man in the glass is going to step forward out of his trance, and touch me again.

Eddie's smoking out the window, spying down on it all, his face a picture, getting all worked up and muttering at the glass every time he sees something new happening.

'Half the bloody Met's out, look.'

From up here the police are two dark lines stretching out of sight behind the houses up the New Cross Road.

'Go get your mum.' He's annoyed – shouting through to the bedroom: 'Jane! Come out here and look at this. It's all about to kick off.' There's no sound from the bedroom but he's too distracted to care for long. 'Look at all these clowns. Rubbing shoulders with the blacks.' He's shaking his head. 'Wait till they get home and can't find their wallets.'

The crowd of demonstrators has got bigger. It's down every road and pavement. Deptford High Street, all the way down to the river, is jam-packed.

'They'll be here soon. Just wait till they come marching through. Now that'll be a sight. Just you wait.' He chucks his fag out the window and goes off to try and get Mum out of bed, shaking his head again as he walks away. If he keeps his promise and they do get married next year, then it'll be made official: this clot will be my dad.

There's horses down there. People who've climbed up on top of roofs and traffic lights. Parts of the crowd look like they're rippling. Lines of people are moving forward together inside it like veins, all these people together like a living thing, a body, calling to me, drawing me towards it, away from here.

Eddie will play hell later, course he will, but sod him.

Strange how quiet and normal it is at the bottom of the tower. It's only by the High Street that it gets clear something's different. People smiling, excited, all of them moving slowly forward up the market with the thick of the crowd. It's easy enough darting through them, though. A great low noise up ahead that sounds like a chant without the words, like the march up the Den, except everyone's cheerful. Some of the demonstrators have got flags. Great whopping banners. *They Shall Not Pass. Defend the Lewisham 21.* It's only now that it hits me there is no children about, not even that many my age, their own mums keeping them inside in case there's a battle when the fascists arrive. There's a bottleneck at the turn into the New Cross Road and everyone's come to a standstill. Straight above my head a man's sat on top of a street sign. He's looking right down at me. Blows me a kiss. Bursts out laughing when he sees me stick my tongue out and give him the Vs. It's possible just about to squeeze on through, getting further in, the chant starting up again, the words of it clear now, loud: *Workers, united, will never be defeated* . . . as if this is a strike or something, which doesn't make much sense but everyone's singing it anyway, the noise building, the marchers slowing down, a group of three black men just ahead with a couple of white women not much younger than Mum, all just chatting away, happy and together. The crowd's getting slower and thicker but it's not frightening. A kind of magic is happening: everything bad up in the tower is disappearing and it is possible, here in the crowd, to lose myself.

A sharp stink is up my nose. Above the heads there's a cloud of orange smoke, people running now, one man being chased by a bunch of coppers all holding on to their helmets with one hand, like a party game. The lot in front are trying to step back but people are still coming up behind, squashing me in between, ramming the breath out of me. My legs are going funny but it's too cramped to fall. A woman has her hand in my armpit keeping me up, a great booing getting up all around because the coppers on the other side the road are making a line to stop people getting past. Hiding behind big rectangular shields. Their faces through the clear plastic look like all the same face. The same moustache. 'Disgrace!' The woman is letting go of me, jabbing her arm out to point at them. 'You're a disgrace. What you protecting *them* for?' The police creeping forward now behind their line of shields, like Ireland on the television, things being thrown at them, bits of rubbish, an apple. The crowd behind are pushing at our backs but the woman's got hold of my hand and we're moving down the street together. What would Mum think of me here holding this woman's hand? Nothing, probably. She'd just keep staring at the walls. Whispering she's sorry for everything and her head's gone and I need you to help me, Anita, please listen to me, Anita, I can't live like this any more.

There are coppers everywhere, behind the shields and on horses clopping down the road, big black batons bouncing on the horses' bums. The coppers are dividing the crowd up into portions. Back in the distance the lad up the signpost is gone and in front a girl is screaming – some coppers around someone on the floor, kicking him. Closer to us a man is getting carried off. He's coming past, people shouting, more coppers coming to pen us in, their helmet straps pushed right forward to the front of their chins away from their sideburns. The man's throat is covered with gloves. One of his shoes has come off. He's got stripy red and yellow socks underneath. 'Here they come! Here they come!' Through the line of shields an army of British flags is on the approach up the road. Someone up the front of the crowd starts chanting, '*Sieg Heil!*' at them and now everyone's joining in or booing. There's electrics going through the crowd, watching the fascists march past. The chant is getting louder and louder when everyone sees that the NF's outnumbered by us. Even if there wasn't all the coppers they couldn't come it with us because there's not enough of them, never mind it's them has travelled here from all round the country; it's us who's the real army. They are being led off down a side street by the police. One of them, holding a flag taller than two men, is turning his head to look at the crowd – it feels as if he's looking right at me, hearing me yell out louder and louder, my throat burning with new words – and it's like being carried inside a wave, the outside of my body disappearing until there's no beginning and ending of me, there's just the crowd, carrying us all away together somewhere pure and happy.

Next door's cat is watching me wash up. She's stretched herself out full length on top of the fence and is following the movement of my hands in and out of the soapy water.

A bang upstairs. Then footsteps, moving slowly across the ceiling.

He arrives at the top of the staircase. One arm reaching for the banister, the other for the handrail.

'Do you need something, Patrick?'

'No, no. Coming down.'

'Hang on. Let me just dry my hands. I'll help you.'

He is lifting an arm. He wags a finger. 'No, on my own.'

It takes him just over two minutes to get halfway down. He stops, blowing hard, and starts off again with the same repeated motion: working his left hand down the banister, right foot down a step, left foot slowly joining it. He looks up. Grinning. 'Keeping you?' He stumbles – he's over-reached, attempting the stairs and a joke at the same time – but he's gripping on to the banister with a remembered strength, bracing himself.

Two steps from the bottom a huge silly smile comes over his face. It stays there as he completes his mission. To my applause, he breaks into a sprightly little jig – jerking his shoulders up and down, hands on his hips, waggling them from side to side – like a quirky wind-up toy.

There are knickers in this drawer that haven't seen the light of day in decades. A whim almost takes me, now he's asleep again, to put a pair on. This lacy number here, that he bought for the anniversary weekend in Paris. What would he do if he woke up and saw me in them now? It would probably finish him off. My fingers glide beneath all the extinct pants, to feel the familiar smoothness of the drawer lining, finding its edge, lifting it up – a quick look to check he's still asleep – sliding my hand under for the two pieces of paper beneath.

It's a bit cockeyed, the new bathroom lock. Not my best handiwork, but at least it's appeased him, even if it has taken me more than a month to carry out his request. The bolt slides stiffly into the barrel and already the usual sick excitement is churning in me, before even sitting down on the toilet seat and laying the letters out on top of my lap. The words ingrained enough in my mind now that my eyes don't even need to take them in, not properly. It is enough just to know that they are there.

Everyone's stood about waiting to be let inside the chapel. They're all smoking, not saying a lot to each other, an hour or two yet before they can go and get sozzled. Eddie's stopped gabbing on at them all. He's done the rounds, shaking hands and exchanging friendly words, so now he's just stood smoking and complaining about his shoes. It's funny seeing him in a suit. He looks good in it. Strange too, this feeling of needing to stay close to him before we go in, not wanting to go near any of these people. Most of them have never met Eddie before, and probably haven't even seen Mum since her wedding with my real dad. There is a woman, one of Mum's relations, her cousin or maybe in fact just the daughter of one of Dead Grandma's friends, who keeps looking over at me. Even with Eddie in the way her eyes are on me, past Eddie's blotchy neck, while she talks to her husband, probably saying how the last time they saw me it was as a baby at that wedding and isn't it a shame how that all turned out, him up and leaving Mum and me like that before we got put up in the towers and Eddie came along.

A new couple has arrived and Eddie's going off to greet them – the woman taking her chance to get an eyeful of me in my dress, comparing me to Mum, looking to see if there's anything of her in me. She gives me a smile, then she turns back to her husband. For a moment it feels good to think of Mum being happy on that wedding day, in a nice dress, laughing and chatting to people, introducing them to her baby. None of these here still waiting outside the chapel – that woman, or her husband, or the couple who Eddie's gabbing on to now – know that it's me who's looked after *her* since before it's possible to remember, that she is the one needed feeding and putting clothes on her and making her take her pills to stop the dark thing living inside her from climbing out of her and coming for us all. My legs are itching like hell inside these nasty tights but there's nowhere to go and nothing to do except stand here waiting until Eddie is finished talking and comes back. All of a sudden, though, the doors are opening and everyone's turning to look, and there's a man in robes coming out, beckoning us in with his friendly giant hands.

It's too bright inside. As soon as they start walking in it feels like everyone's looking at me. Nobody's told me where to sit so for a few seconds they're all coming past me, nodding, smiling with pity.

She is there, up the front on a stage. Eddie didn't tell me that. That we'd have to see her. There's strange quiet music playing and brown curtains on both sides of the coffin, maybe so that you can't tell which side they're going to burn it. A big bunch of flowers on top of her. Two candles on tall metal stands at the back. Eddie is here by my side again, his arm going around my shoulder. He's crying already. He sits me and him down in the back pew, people still coming past looking and it's impossible to stop thinking that she only had me and it was supposed to be my job looking after her, but it wasn't enough. And that she asked me and asked me to help her do it an easier, gentler way, and all those times of telling her no is what made her do what she did. The policeman's face at the door is coming for me again. My head burrowing up now inside Eddie's jacket, into his stale armpit, and there's no stopping me, sobbing and shaking, it's all come rushing out, him too, the both of us going full steam, filling the chapel with the sound of our wailing.

Emily isn't picking up. She's still at work. Soon she'll see the missed call and it will alarm her; she'll wonder if something is wrong. Her voicemail message – assured, professional – turns into beeps.

'Hi Em, just calling to see how you are, fill you in on Dad. He's fine. Everything's normal here. Speak soon.'

Everything's normal. An interesting choice of words. Since her Easter visit Patrick has started waking in the night not knowing where he is, shouting about dentists.

It is blissfully cool out here in the courtyard, now that the heatwave has broken. Through the fire exit, Jack is in the kitchen hauling the cauldron of risotto over to the pass, where the floor are lining up for staff food. It is a surprise how hard it has hit me, Peter's news this morning that the Vietnamese place has gone – even if the truth is that the unsettled, knotty feeling in my stomach is not so much for the place itself, as the anxiousness of how long Peter will tolerate me stalling for. Although his mood, for now, is as upbeat as ever: *It's all good. I've found somewhere even better.*

The phone against my ear again. A shard of longing pressing at my temple.

It is a foreign dialling tone. He's still abroad, then. Morocco? Spain? Who knows? Emily probably knows.

'Mum?'

'Hi, Matthew.'

'I can't really talk. Is Dad okay?'

'He's fine. I'm about to start service, but I just wanted to give you an update.'

'Has something happened?'

'Nothing's happened.'

A pause. 'Right.'

He has been updated. In his silence now, waiting for the purpose of this call, he is letting me know all that he needs to: he only wants to be contacted when something changes, which, seeing as the chances of his dad getting better are long gone, means that he wants to be updated when the next bad thing happens, or the worst thing happens. No change for a couple of months is not news. Never mind that a month and a bit ago Patrick could still sleep through the night and put his own socks on. That person is already becoming forgotten. How quickly each decline beds down into a new kind of normal. What *was* the purpose of this call, though, except to hear him? What else is there to say?

'Emily and Morgan have made a date for the wedding. September next year.'

'Yes, I know.'

So they are in touch. They speak to each other.

'Do you think you'll come over for a while around it?'

'I don't know, really. It's a year away. Look, Mum, can I call you at the weekend if it's important?'

'I'm at the restaurant all weekend.'

'Right, of course.'

Barman Danny is at the fire exit, waiting for me to move out of his way. He mouths thank you and comes out into the courtyard, dragging the bottle empties tub loudly behind him. There is a small sigh of irritation down the phone line.

'Just wait a second, Matthew.'

The tub judders over the broken concrete. Then the continuous violent din of shattering glass as Danny throws the bottles into the glass bin. A part of me wants it to take longer, to keep Matthew here by my ear. As if he might want at last to talk, to tell me where he is, or if he's working, or with somebody; if he is okay – healed, a little, by the gap of time since his desperate words of that tearful afternoon last summer. If his anger towards his dad has calmed, or if it is still raging as fiercely as it did when Patrick finally told him the truth, before Matthew fled.

'Sorry, but I have to go, Mum. Call me at the weekend if you need to.'

'Okay. Bye, Matthew.'

'Bye, Mum.'

It will be weeks now until we speak again. The same brief conversation, nothing to say. He doesn't want to talk about Patrick, less still to be here with him. Does he know that by punishing Patrick like this, cutting himself off, he is punishing me too, punishing himself? A waiter has appeared from the kitchen. The new one. Jared? Jonjo? He is topless, his shirt in one hand, an iron in the other, ludicrously muscular.

You wouldn't know it with his shirt on. Barman Danny, trundling the empty tub back, is smiling at him.

'Jimbo, you fucker!'

The two young men hug beside me. Tubers of muscle swell in the waiter's arm. Their bodies are momentarily locked together; the easy communication of young men. Other young men, not Matthew. Matthew, it's fair to say, is not a hugger. They come apart and slap each other's triceps. They don't seem to have noticed me staring at them. Their sous chef boss, the old kitchen lady, ogling their showroom physiques. Bodies they have never imagined will eventually fail them. Enjoy them while you can, boys. You'll be pooing yourself in the shower one day. An observation which, if it had been out loud, probably wouldn't have made them think much differently about me.

The music has changed, louder now, something punk. It's coming up through the floor, rebounding around the walls and the ceiling, the whole room shaking with it. A clothes rail at the bottom of the bed. Skirts on it, belts hanging down and a line of Daisy Dukes all queued up. My mouth is dribbling on her sheets but my head is clearer now. She won't be happy. My tummy cramping again, remembering the stream of sick on the wall downstairs and the bloke dancing with me, moving closer, smiling and holding me up, all the other bodies dancing around us. There's a crack in the doorway – the flash of somebody coming past – their feet on the stairs, winding round and round, people sat drinking on the steps, damp clothes all up the banister. Where is this place? Bits of it are trying to come back through the foggy mess. Running. The woman calling after me down the street. The open door and the boys outside on the pavement smoking. There's a suede coat on the back of the door. Nice things, she's got. Her shoes and boots lined up neat along the carpet. It's not right, being here in her room. She's going to come in and see me in her bed, the sick on her pillow, and she'll be raging.

'Hello, there.'

It's a boy. A man. He might be the one danced with me, or he might not, it's hard to tell.

'Aren't you in a pickle?' He's grinning. 'Few too many?'

He is sitting down on the bed. His bum pushing up against my leg.

'What's your name?'

He's twisted round looking at me and the air behind his head is wobbling with the music like a heatwave. What would Eddie think, me in a stranger's bed in a house somewhere and this man leaning over me touching my face, his hand moving onto the bedsheets, onto my hip? Eddie! He wouldn't think nothing at all – he's likely pissed somewhere too, or in the flat gawking at the telly and drinking his cans.

'John?'

He sits up straight, looking at a girl in the door.

'Who's this?'

'I don't know. I found her in here just now.'

'Jesus, she's a state. Look at her.'

She is coming towards the bed and she can see the mess on the pillow. Him standing up to let her get closer. She's kneeling down by the bed, her face near me.

'What are you doing here, sweetheart?' Her hair is soft and spirally down her cheeks. A white flower in it above her ear matching the flowers on her dress, and just like that my brain is right back to Mum in a clothes store asking me how she looks and the two of us are dancing in the cubicle with the store woman outside the curtain on the watch for Mum stealing the dress.

'How old are you?'

My throat is closing in on itself.

Another girl coming in the door.

'What's going on? Who's she?'

The boy saying, 'I don't know. I found her in here about a minute ago. I just came in now.'

'She's a bloody kid.'

'I don't think she knows anyone here. She's bunked in the party.'

The two girls are kneeling by the bed. Him standing behind.

'Where do you live?'

'Oh, fucking hell, she's been sick, look.'

'It's okay, sweetheart.' The first girl moving sticky hair off my face. 'We're going to get you home.'

All their hands are taking the sheets off and lifting under my knees and my armpits, him too, picking me up. A new bolt of sick racing up me and into my mouth – spewing onto the carpet and their legs and feet, the boy swearing, pissed off, sick on his shoes. They are carrying me out the room. People are sitting on the stairs, turning round to look. There's a bathroom up here. They're taking me in, putting my legs down, the nice girl holding me up under the armpits.

'That okay?'

'Yes.'

'Here, hold on to the sink. Put both hands on it. You can be sick in here if you need to.' She is smiling at me in the mirror. 'You're going to be fine now.' My knuckles are bright pink. She's rubbing my back and it's too much looking at her face in the mirror thinking about the sick in her bed and knowing it's my fault.

'It's all right, have a good cry, let it all out.'

My head is clear now, empty, but the tears are keeping coming, bucketfuls, down my face and dripping off my nose into the sink. There's blood too. A cut on my forehead from somewhere.

'How old are you?'

'Fifteen.'

She's nodding. The other two have gone and it's just me and her. She is washing my face. Dabbing a towel at the ends of my hair, staining it red.

'Come on, let's get you home.'

There's people everywhere, all of them looking up at me at the top of the stairs, some of them getting to their feet at the sight of me with blood on my face and hair, moving sharpish out the way: Hell's teeth, they're thinking – everybody run! – it's Carrie! The girl is helping me down the steps, her arm around me, saying, 'It's all right, keep going' in my ear. A thick smog at the bottom where there's a crowd of people talking and smoking, some of them screwing up their noses or laughing when they see me but the girl's moving them out the way, 'Coming through, coming through,' and we're at the front door – someone opening it for us – and out into the cold, clean air outside.

'So,' she is saying, 'which way?'

'The river.'

One foot, two foot, down the pavement. It's dark now. She doesn't have to be doing this.

'You've got to be careful, you know. Girl your age. You shouldn't be going sneaking into parties like that. Most boys are a good lot but there's always one or two. You've got to learn that.'

We're coming down the High Street. The black shapes of the towers up ahead. Little lights scattered about all through them. My legs feel so tired. There's market spills and smells in the gutter, a fish stink, but she's got her arm tight around me and it's too much effort to lift my hand to cover my nose, the queasiness coming again.

'Can you tell me where you live?'

'There. That one.'

'That tower block?'

'Yes.'

She's puffing some but she's on a mission and we're not far off now. Soon she will be gone again, away back to the party, and knowing it makes me grip on to her even tighter, not wanting her to leave me yet. It's too tiring, even to talk to her, tell her sorry for the sick on her bed and offer to come and help her clean it up in the morning. Which is a stupid idea, anyway, because she'll have to do it tonight, unless she can sleep somewhere else. She could stay at ours! Here we are – you can stop on the sofa if you like, don't mind him there with his face in his chips, he'll clear off to bed if you give him a kick.

'This it?'

'Yes. Thank you.'

'You promise me you won't do something silly like that again, will you?'

'No, I won't.'

She's seeing me in the entrance before she steps back. The doors close behind me but she's waiting, she wants to make sure. She starts waving goodbye when the lift doors start to slide shut, then she's gone. It smells of sick in here, too. Unless it's me. Or maybe it's Eddie. The lift starting to move up is making my tummy lurch again. The metal walls spinning, graffiti whirling round me – *R.I.P. Gary Wilson Fuck the GLC tits! EAT THE RICH* – the doors opening but my body not able to move. The stairwell in front narrowing. Gone. The lift starting back down and tiredness is taking over me, making me sit down here in the corner, wanting to just go to sleep. The doors opening. Nobody there outside the entrance. A new energy is coming into me, making me stand up and go out the lift, out the entrance, into the night.

The need to be close to her is carrying me forward, under the concrete webs of walkways, into the park. Dead quiet in here. Dark. Only the sound of my own feet and breath all the way down the path, speeding up through the last stretch of trees, imagining what it would have been like for her on that final walk from the flat, listening to her feet and the stones clacking in her pockets in the stillness of the night – until, out the other side, there it is, the sudden black hole of the river.

He's right. This one was the best so far. Small. Old wooden floorboards. High windows. The L-shaped interior and the pavement space for a few tables at the front, opposite the green. Footfall, too. Even on a Tuesday morning the stretch was busy: locals, shoppers, moneyed retirees with dogs. Peter's enthusiasm walking to the bus stop afterwards: 'I swear down, Anita, we'll not find anywhere more perfect than this place. And it's far enough from a tube that even the rent's not that mad. Obvious it's some rich kid whose parents have gave him the money to open his own coffee shop and he's went and buggered it up. We could make this work. If you really are serious about it. We could find backers for this one.'

We, he has started saying. Maybe he doesn't realise he's doing it, doesn't notice how it makes me go quiet, keeping from him the anxious tingle of it being made real: him coming in with me and everything that would mean – the house in front of me now, only a twenty-five-minute bus ride from the place – the real cost of going ahead with it.

It's hot as all hell inside. On the hallway wall, the thermostat light is glowing. Somehow, Patrick has managed to get downstairs and switch the heating on. My arms and legs, slogging up the stairs into an even stuffier atmosphere, are being tricked into thinking they are at work already. From the bedroom there is talking, singing – the television. Patrick sitting up in bed wearing a scarf and a red, woolly hat.

'Hello. Are you really that cold?'

'Yes.'

His hands, to the touch, are icy. Even though the heatwave has passed it is a lovely late-summer morning outside, probably twenty degrees, and five degrees hotter still in the house, but he's sitting in bed freezing. It is snowing on the television screen. A black-and-white film. He seems to be watching it, engaged. Could that be why he is cold? Is that possible? The botched wirings of his brain connecting him to an altered reality, one that has nothing to do with the sunny day out of the window.

'Would you like a hot-water bottle?'

He looks up at me, confused and distressed, his mouth open.

'A . . . A . . .'

'A hot-water bottle, to keep you warm.'

He keeps looking at me with his mouth open, still distressed, then lets his chin fall to his throat, defeated.

'I'll go and make you one.'

Turning, my eye catches the drawers. All of them are open. Panic climbs inside my chest – needing to know, not even disguising my urgency to get across the room and see which he has been in. My hands feel in the underwear drawer, pretending to neaten it, searching for the tiny rise of the lining paper and finding it still there, understanding with relief that the drawer is exactly as it was, the inside of it untouched.

He is looking at me. He has sensed my agitation.

'The hats,' he says, pointing, with some effort, to the bottom drawer – which is opened slightly wider than the others – and the rummaged jumble of winter woollies inside.

1980

'You going to take that job, then?'

Deb's finished her burger, looking at me for my answer.

'Not sure. Maybe. Probably be better than making sure Eddie's got something to eat every night when he staggers home from the pub, even if the pay's not up to much.'

'You should take it. You're lucky she asked you. Not many other jobs going, you know. And it'll be nice and all, cooking for little kids. I'd like that. She looks out the window at the street and all the people already going inside the Rex. 'Come on,' she says. 'You ready?'

She's all chat as we come out from the warmth and noise of the Wimpy, saying how her mum thinks eating in the cinema is disgusting and she agrees with her but lots of people do it anyway.

'Well, tell your mum that last time I went to the Rex there was people doing things she'd think are more disgusting than eating.'

Deb's laughing but the thought of Mum is trying to steal into my head and everything in me is straining to shut it out.

Deb is leading us up the steps to the entrance. It's heaving inside, a long line at the ticket window, Deb saying, 'Bloody hell, we should have got here earlier.' There's one or two boys from school up the front of the line, who neither of us have probably spoke to since we left but Deb's clocked them too and she's off to announce herself.

'You stay here in the queue, will you? I'll just go say hello.'

She goes away down the front and a pair of little lads scoot out the line in front of her, pretend laser-fighting. She skips round them, patting on top of their heads, the queue moving forward now and suddenly a hand is on my bum, pressing, squeezing, then gone. Stupid to turn round, even for a second, but – two men's faces are staring straight ahead like nothing's happened. They were in the Wimpy, the booth next to us. The air is being sucked from my chest, a scream forming, dying in my throat. My eyes searching for Deb up ahead but she's not there through all the heads. The men are keeping quiet behind me, probably trying not to laugh. Nobody else has seen what happened, or is doing anything. The left side of my bum is throbbing like it has been kicked. The queue's moving forward again and it's probably my imagination but it feels like their breath is on the back of my neck. Every inch of me is burning up, ashamed, expecting it to happen again. Just leave. Deb would be annoyed but so what? Just leave. The urge to do it is almost too much – to escape from here, down the river, or down some street where there'll be a door and music and voices and another night to get lost and forget myself into. Deb is coming back, though. She's smiling, coming in next to me and talking, but her words are disappearing, all my senses still turned around the other way, on guard. One of the men is saying, not quiet, 'May the arse be with you, Luke,' and it doesn't even make sense but they're both pissing themselves. A group up ahead is kicking a fag packet about between them, and instantly it's obvious that the queue is all men and boys. Deb's looking at me funny for taking hold of her hand and gripping tight around it. She doesn't know that my heart's going like the clappers at the thought of going into the dark of the auditorium, the boom and flash of it, in their space, surrounded.

My eyeballs are hammering. Heat and steam and fat blurring my vision as we all follow Frank out of the kitchen into the gloom of the service gangway. Frank goes ahead up the steps for a recce of the floor.

'Still punters. Let's go onto the terrace.'

We file up the steps and to the far end of the floor, the last table of customers in the middle of the restaurant turning round to observe us – nine tired, pasty figures in white jackets emerging from our enclosure, a mental asylum outing.

The terrace heaters have been turned on ready for evening service and we huddle clammily around the circular ten-seater. The tablecloth has been cleared and crumbed but not changed yet. It is stained here and there with the yellows and greens of lunch, the red round kiss of a badly poured wine bottle. In front of me, a small dark spot of my sauce Périgueux.

'Sous is running dinner, so she'll brief you on service in a minute, and we've got the three new mains on from tomorrow, so I'm going to take you through those.'

Sandy is sliding open the terrace door. Frank makes a deliberate show of having to break off what he's saying.

'Coffees?' Sandy asks.

She comes round taking our orders, keeping them all in her head. In the distance behind us, the City skyscrapers sparkle in the lowering sun. Sandy leaves the door open so she can return with the coffee tray and Frank resumes his briefing. Through in the restaurant, there is a loud bark from one of the last diners. Even from here, his face looks pissed red. It doesn't take a genius to guess that his order was the fiddly idiotic one, with the lobster mash from the turbot dish requested under his blue steak. His table doesn't look as though it's leaving any time soon. There is a magnum on the table. Three men, suit jackets on the backs of their chairs; a woman with them. Her body upright, contained, sitting in conversation with the red man whose chair is pushed back, one leg stretched out and his wine arm dangling towards the floor holding the glass by the rim with his fingers.

'So keep an eye out for consistency,' Frank is saying to Jonas. 'I've spoken to him about it, and he knows it's not good enough, especially the quality of the aromatics. We can get them from a different supplier easily enough, I've told him. It's not like his produce is cheap.'

Heat is rushing to my face. He's talking about Peter. My gaze fixes on the sauce spot, willing Frank to keep talking so that nobody will notice me. Sandy is back with the coffees, though, diverting their attention as she comes through the door with the tray of mugs on the arch of her fingers. Murmurs of thanks as she glides around the table putting them down. Freddy looking up and smiling at her. The boys pick up their mugs and start blowing at the hot coffee. Their faces are puffy with weariness. Everybody, since Marco went back to Australia and Christian was fired, is on their fourth straight double. Someone's knees jitter under the table. Jack is fidgeting with the edge of the tablecloth. In another world, Patrick will be sitting in bed in a woolly hat.

'All right, you lot,' Frank says, 'when you've finished creaming yourselves over the waitress.'

Sandy is sliding the terrace door shut. The waitress. She has been at the Longwool for at least two years. She walks away towards the bar and is called over by one of the diners. There is a long exchange, the men all leering at her, Sandy saying something that makes them double over laughing and the red man seize a chair from the next table, whirl it round and pat on its leather bottom. The woman is watching, saying nothing, smiling. Sandy shaking her head, the red man getting to his feet. Sandy takes a step back, him one forward, a tango, then his hands shoot to her elbows, keeping her in place. He puts his palm flat onto the top of her head. Slowly, he draws it back until it meets his chin. A lowing sound comes through the glass. A few of the boys, hearing it, look over at the diners, who will have been paid more during their pissed-up lunch than our table will be paid all put together for today's fifteen-hour shift. Sandy is facing away from us. The man is touching her again, his hands moving quickly down her arms, to her hips, clasping, turning her around so that her face, stony, comes into view as she breaks free. Another of the men glances, uncertain, at the female colleague. Xav is tutting. 'Cock tease.' Nervous sniggers from Turtle and Jack; Anton looking at him coldly. The instinct to speak out and defend her forms, but dies inside my throat. The man is waving goodbye to her as she walks off to the bar, then the man says something to the rest of his table and the other men break into new laughter, one of them clapping his hands together in delight while Sandy pauses briefly to speak to Barman Danny – polishing glasses next to Jimbo with an earphone in his unseen ear – unknots her apron and hurries away, flinging her apron to the floor before she disappears into the service gangway.

'Chips or faces?'

'Faces.'

'Beans?'

'No, thanks. Beans is disgusting. Can I have an extra pizza bread?'

'No, you can't, cheeky thing.'

'More faces, then?'

Chrissie's giggling next to me, listening to this. The girl is still stood there, tray in her hands, looking up at me.

'Go on, then. You can have a couple of extra faces.' The girl is staring up in wonder at me winking and whispering to her: 'I'll hide them under your pizza bread.'

'Thanks, miss.'

She is away to Chrissie on puddings, pleased as punch at her extra potatoes. Her hairband has slipped down and half her hair's fell out of it. She's talking to Chrissie now, nattering away and waiting for Chrissie to pass over her jam sponge.

The next boy is looking at me. 'You gave her two extra faces. I saw.'

83

'You saw, did you?'

'Yes, you gave her two extra ones. Can I have that too, please?'

Chrissie is peeing herself now. She taps her nose and turns around, scouting the kitchen for Donna. There isn't much choice now except giving the boy more potatoes too – and he's made up, he even rubs his hands together like an old man, eyeing up the extra faces being slid underneath his pizza bread. His expression going all serious when he sees me put my finger to my lips.

They've all cottoned on now, course. The next one doesn't even ask, just copies what he's just seen and puts his finger to his lips and waits. Behind us, Donna is back in the kitchen putting her nose about, so it'll have to stop soon enough. Look how happy they are, though! Two bonus smiley potatoes and it's made their day.

'You are good with them.'

It's hard to tell with Miss Gates whether she's pulling your leg or not.

'It's just a couple more potatoes. You can have more as well if you like.'

'All right, then,' she says in a quieter voice. 'I will. Thank you very much.'

The way she's looking at me it's uncomfortable holding her eyes and she can probably see that my face has gone red. The little girl after her in the line is right up close behind. Obvious how pleased she is to have got this spot next to Miss Gates. It's hardly surprising, how much they all like her, the gentle way she has with them, with her kind face and her smiles and her proper clothes-shop dresses.

She's laughing at the little pile of potatoes on her plate, saying, 'I mean it, you know. You are good with them.' Her plate's done but she's not moved on, she's staying there with this playful smile on her. 'You'd be great in a classroom, I bet.'

It's only when she's moved off it sinks in that she means as a teacher. Chrissie is raising her eyebrows at me. She's heard what Miss Gates just said and now that she's served her the rice pudding she is watching with me as Miss Gates walks out into the dinner hall, a little mob of followers gathering behind her, going to a table where she's at once chatting to them all, putting her tray down and going over to a boy at the far end of the table. She starts helping him with his knife and fork, guiding him to cut up his food, the only child in the school who's chosen the liver.

At the next table along, the girl who first charmed the potatoes out of me is already on to her jam sponge, chattering with her friend next to her. All down the dinner hall there is the happy racket of children's voices and underneath it the clinking music of their knives and forks on plates – setting off the usual rush of satisfaction that it is me who has filled their bellies, looked after them. Miss Gates is getting sat to eat now. She must sense me watching because she looks over and meets my eye, just for a second or two, wanting to remind me what she said. And for a moment the picture of it – a classroom of children looking up at me, safe and fed and happy – is in my head, before Chrissie gives me the nod that Donna's on her way down the line and we're both right away all spoons and spatulas, giving what's left of the food in our maries the comb-over.

The bed is empty. The tray teeters in my hands, the tea he requested almost dropping to the floor.

He is not in the bathroom.

'Patrick?'

Or Emily's room; Matthew's. Consternation quickly taking hold of me.

'Patrick!'

He can't have come downstairs, it would have been obvious. The windows in the bedroom are all closed. The television still on, the sound barely perceptible. A dry cackle comes from behind the bed. His head is appearing above the mattress. He has been playing hide-and-seek.

My body is shaking with a sudden fit of laughter.

'You silly old git. How did you get down there?'

'Oh. Yes. I fell.'

My phone is downstairs in the kitchen and there's nothing to do but sit here by the bed while he sleeps. A moment of calm before the intensity of service. It is quieter now in this room, he's not wrong, without the 'bloody tick-tockery' of the old clock. The new one lets the time pass silently into the afternoon. His mouth is opening. A long, queer note comes out of him – and he is awake. Coughing. Eyes on the ceiling, frightened. He ignores me, my palm on his forehead, shushing him, *shh, shh, shh*, like a baby.

'Toilet,' he says decisively.

'Okay. Do you know which it is?'

His eyes dart to me, angry and lucid.

'No, not the toilet – I mean, is it, you know, a one or a two?'

He is looking at me with disgust. His brain has woken up a year ago, alert.

'Just, after last—'

'I need a piss.'

He is struggling to get out of the bed on his own. He needs my help, puts his arm around my neck and lets me support him across the carpet. It was a thoughtless question. He's not that far gone yet. An image comes to me, as we move out of the room together, of Matthew – a toddler on the toilet, bending over to look between his legs: *Oh, it's a poo.*

He tells me to wait outside the bathroom door as he goes in. A few seconds later the lock slides very slowly into place. It feels merciless, an intrusion, listening to him go to the toilet. Imagining him as he struggles to undo his trousers, master his bladder. At the rate he is deteriorating, it will not be very long before even this is beyond him, before his dignity is gone for good, and it is too cruel, the inevitability of this fate; it is not fair on him, this so proud man, that he has to suffer it.

Faint sounds of discomfort are coming from inside the bathroom. Wheezing. Then the sound of the toilet-roll holder spinning. A loud explosion.

'Patrick? What's happened? Are you hurt?'

Nothing.

Then: 'Fine. It's fine. The plant.'

The lock is sliding open. The door handle trembling. He comes out and grips my arm. Behind him, there is soil all over the floor. Shards of pot. The succulent is all the way over by the sink.

'Yes, yes,' he says. 'I've been gardening.'

He smiles all the way back to the bedroom.

'I'll be going to work soon, Patrick. Would you like the television on?'

'No,' he says, inching himself back into bed. Rain is slanting heavily at the window; the kitchen boys will be skittish tonight, like little children.

'Shall I put the blanket back over you?'

'Yes, please.'

His eyes stay open as he lies there. His big lips quaking slightly. He is cold, maybe, or thinking. He turns onto his side, to look at me.

'I don't want this life.'

He keeps his eyes on me, then closes them.

'I know.'

He is asleep as my feet pad quietly across the room to the chest of drawers.

There is enough time before setting off for the restaurant to read the letters once more, sitting on the toilet with the plant pot lying shattered at my feet and a cold, scandalous anticipation growing, examining every word, testing for their meanings — *I do not want to become a burden* — trying to imagine what they will sound like to other ears.

1982

The police patrol boat is cruising past. The usual copper up the front, giving me a wave, going inside the cabin to tell the others: 'The dinner-lady girl's there again, boys!'

The sandwich bread has gone a bit damp from the tomato. Not like my tummy will care, it's been that long since breakfast. It's peaceful down here in the sunshine. The great mucky river sliding on and the little sound of the waves the police boat made pattering on the pebbles of the beach.

It would have been a boat like that. Maybe the same one. Maybe even one of those same coppers; it's only a few years gone and they're old enough most of them have probably been doing this job a while – travelling up and down the river, searching for wherever the city has emptied its sins and secrets.

The bloke from the newsprint warehouse has come down the slipway and is sat smoking a fag. He's minding his own business as always, but still – best not stopping here too long, the way some of them get with the uniform, the magnet it is for them. This one's not trouble, mind. Just smokes his fag, chucking bits of gravel into the river. He only bunks down here for a bit of quiet, same as me. The swan that came out the creek with her babies a few minutes ago is gliding by him now. He stops throwing his gravel, waits for her to come past.

She's a clot, Donna. All that rubbish before lunchtime about the children being ungrateful. She hasn't got a clue. Ungrateful! Their only proper meal of the day, a lot of them, but she just wants to get them in and out quick and easy as possible so she can flapmouth on about her bad ankles and her brave boy Joseph all the way over the other side the world, risking his life to defend two birdshit-coated rocks in the ocean no one had never heard about before last month. Too away with her own voice to even notice me and Chrissie slipping out second sausages until that git Year Four teacher put the squeak in. The sandwich is over too quick. It wasn't big enough, after making Eddie's. At least there's the stolen Battenberg left, foiled up, waiting for its little ceremony. Thank you for that at least, Donna, you dozy mare.

It still feels odd Eddie didn't say anything this morning. Surely he's remembered. He's not that tunnelled into himself he could have forgot. Another boat coming past. A tug. Brown peaks riding to the shore. A mirror set of them going the other way toward the Dogs to knock against the north wall. The Dogs looks strange without the flour mill, like a wasteland. Pretty much what it is now. Eddie's wrong. They'll never get it back like what it was. It's moneyland now and money will do what it does, build it over, clear the people out. They should fight for something better, all those people, not stay and fight for the past. What's the point roping yourself to something that's already sailed off? They need to make themselves up new. And straight away the jitters are coming on, agitating the sandwich in my tummy, remembering that my teaching course starts three weeks Monday; Miss Gates's words on the last day of term: 'Don't worry, you'll be a natural, and you're as clever as any of them.'

A hoot from the tug. Time for cake.

The Battenberg sits steady enough on a flat stone. She'd like this. The silliness of it. Her favourite cake, here, on this same bit of shoreline she said she used to drag my real dad to back in the days she was happy and she still had all her marbles and everyone used to come down here in the summer, before they closed off the steps.

The bridge she did it from isn't visible from here. The shape of the river cutting off the sight of it. The wharf is, though, in the distance across the other side. Its wooden posts going down deep into the water where the current and everything it's carrying meets the bend of the river.

The sponge is dense enough the candle stays in no problem, right in the middle of the squares. The first match won't light, probably from Eddie leaving the packet by the sink. But the next one starts sparking up, and the candle lights first time. It wobbles in the river breeze. The blue spiral of wax starting to soften.

'Happy birthday, Mum.'

The wick is smoking. A thin plume of it carried off in the air. The first bite of the cake is horrible, all sugary and unnatural. Her old joke: it's that chemically it turns your poo pink.

An acute pain — my own cry waking me. His toenail has dug in, ripping into my calf. An impulse to hurt him back flares, briefly, before there is another spasm of his leg, then a loud moaning noise. His head is shaking slightly, the moan getting louder, becoming a different kind of noise, a howl.

'Patrick. Patrick. Shh. It's okay, Patrick.'

But the sound is getting louder, a scream now. He is screaming as if he's terrified but his eyes, through the dark, are open, locked on the ceiling. The scream is one continuous noise and it is getting louder and louder. The neighbours on both sides will have been woken by it.

'Patrick, please.'

The scream is broken by a coughing fit — and then it is over. His eyes closing and only a quiet, exhausted whine coming from him, his body still once more.

He is asleep. The heave of his outbreath into the dark. My limbs are stiff, on guard for another spasm — and his leg is moving again, but slowly, stretching out, our feet coming together under the sheets.

The number changes on the new clock: 03.41. Somewhere, in the distance, our children are asleep. Dreaming in their own worlds.

What would happen if he woke to find me gone? Would he realise? His eyes, beneath the lids, are twitching, the motor of his brain alive. It seems for an instant that my fingers, stroking his forehead, can feel it at work under the surface. An old expression, a tiny electrical movement of his skin, passes over his face, and is gone. His nose is cold. My fingertips press gently at either side, feeling the firmness of the septum between his nostrils. For two seconds, my fingers hold his nose shut. His face does nothing; his mouth still closed – on the release of my fingers, a wet sound as his nostrils open. Once again, this time longer – four seconds, five, six – and his mouth opens, swallowing in a deep breath. As he exhales, he sighs a long, spoken, 'Aaaah', like a person sinking into a nice warm bath.

Is there some part of my brain that makes me choose Emily's room and not Matthew's? Both sets of bedding are untouched, although for long enough now that they probably should be changed anyway. Both beds would be just as comfortable, too, being exactly the same size, bought together – that same week that Duncan the lamb man was sentenced for killing the burglar boy – despite Patrick's insistence that it was senseless spending money on a new bed for Emily when she obviously wouldn't be at home for much longer.

It is invitingly cool and dark inside her room. This is the right thing to be doing. He needs the space of his own bed, for his own comfort. At the touch of the cold undersheet, a weight of tiredness slugs through me with the force of something unblocked – stuck waiting for weeks, months, anticipating this moment, sleep, almost at once, coming for me.

My phone alarm is going. Confusion, getting my bearings – the dreadful thought rushing through my mind that this is Peter's room, his bed – until an awareness of the night that has just ended slowly returns.

The light comes in differently in this room. The knowledge that this is the light, the ceiling, that Emily used to wake to every day keeps me in the bed, inside the momentary shared experience, all these years later. Imagining her burying herself deeper into the covers, not wanting to get out of the warm bed, then stretching out and turning over towards the window to say good morning, one by one, to her Polly dolls lined up on the sill. There is no sound on the other side of the door. If he is awake, he will know that he is alone. Will he be distressed, or just presume me gone to work? Or will he think nothing at all? He is so different from day to day, hour to hour, that it is impossible to predict. It is time to go back to the doctor to ask, again, about a diagnosis. He has been getting worse markedly enough, for long enough – the hidden chambers of his brain host to untold silent events – that they might, now, be ready to put the word to it. The lamp by Emily's bed is fixed to the wall. There is no bedside table in here. No desk, nowhere even to sit. She always did everything on her bed.

He is asleep. But at the sound of me opening the curtains, he wakes up. He comes to, groaning, shifting under the covers.

'I'm making myself a cup of tea, Patrick.'

'Yes,' he says bluntly. The tactic of not asking him directly is still working.

In the private space of the kitchen, the kettle begins to rumble. It would be possible simply not to say anything about going into Emily's room. He might not even care, or know, and as the kettle finishes boiling it feels clear that this is the best way, not to make a fuss about it.

He watches me put the tea on his bedside shelf.

'You were gone.'

'I went to make us a tea.'

'No, the . . .' His speech trails off, his face contorting. '. . . the night.'

'Yes. I went to a party.'

He laughs. Frogspawn bubbles of saliva are blowing from his mouth. Sudden compassion, love, punches blindly inside me, sits me down next to him on the bed.

'You were sleeping badly, so I went through to Emily's room to give you more space.'

He screws his face up again, bemused.

'You kicked me. Look.'

He stares blankly at the red slit on my calf.

'It's fine, it's nothing. But I'm worried about hurting you, rolling over onto you or something.'

He takes a short, loud breath through his mouth, sucking in the remaining bubbles.

'I think it might be a good idea for me to sleep through there again, just for another night or two.' The lie of the last part, whether he understands it or not, hovers between us. 'Do you think that would be a good idea, Patrick? More comfortable for both of us?'

He is looking at the bedcovers. Can he hear the echo of his own words, years ago, when it was him decamping to Emily's room, unwilling to deal with the first of my night sweats?

'Yes.'

He doesn't see me come for my bedside table because he is asleep, and it feels worse this way, underhand, like stealing. There is an old box of Kleenex on the carpet underneath where the table stood. Used tissues are littered around and on top of it, crumpled stiff as dried flowers. We never were, even before, the cleanest of families. Collecting them up now to clear away into the box, each of the tissues is its own delicate sculpture in my hand, collapsing, disintegrating, as it is stuffed back in. Patrick is trying to turn over, his breath whistling with the effort of it, in this same bed where we used to hold each other, to have sex; where the children long ago climbed under the duvet to be read to before bedtime. The past is there, in touching distance, but it has been altered. It cannot be looked back on in the same way any more – as if all the memories we thought were real have been replaced, put back disfigured. The understanding of this, though, is not upsetting. My only feeling now, picking up the table to carry through to Emily's room, is relief.

1983

The staffroom is along a corridor the children aren't allowed onto. The school secretary stops outside the door and says she's off to get her lunch. 'Good luck,' she says, opening the door for me and walking off, leaving me in the doorway like an offering. All the eyes inside are on me. From their sofas and plastic chairs they watch me come through the smoke. The uptight woman who's had me kept mum in the corner of her classroom all morning is at the far end of the room at the only table. She doesn't look up to acknowledge me. She's done her stint. My heart is going some now, my skin probably shining. There is a space against the wall by the kitchenette. It's as safe a bet as any, a minute or two of busyness to be had from the kettle, making myself a cup of tea.

The kettle going, there's a chance to study the room. All the seats are taken. Everyone's in little groups. Men, women, old ones, younger ones. Even the younger ones, mind, are much older than me. The kettle's coming to a boil. In the cupboard above it is a tin of teabags and four mugs on a shelf. Behind me, it feels like they're all still watching, judging me. There's no way of knowing if any of these mugs belong to anybody, but there is one tiny cup behind the others, too small surely that anyone would ever use it. The teabag pretty much fills it.

With the tea made there's nothing else to do but stand by the wall. On the other side of it there is the noise of children in the canteen. A pining for my old job, that school and its canteen and all the lovely little children makes me want to sit down on the floor and disappear. All these teachers are looking at me drinking from the dinky dickhead cup, all of them thinking: *She's on the wrong side of the wall, that girl.* An old geezer in an elbow-patch jacket that even from here is clearly falling to bits gets up and opens a window. A draught of air flows in and the fag fog doubles over, a ghost punched in the stomach, and through the smoke there's a flash of green out the window, all the streets of trees and big, posh houses that feed this school with children who look at me in the corner of their classroom and know without me even speaking that they come from better. The school's not called a grammar any more but, all these children with the same voices, the same look about their faces, it's obvious that's what it is. Maybe it was for a joke that they've placed me here. Challenging me to stick it out. Or maybe – the image of her on the bed, looking at me with her yellowed eyes – she's the one pulling the strings from up high, directing all my actions, turning me into someone else. Another man, a younger one, is walking over to the kitchenette. He comes behind the counter and starts making himself a tea. It's obvious, from the way he's pausing between his actions, the little movements of his head, that he's going to speak to me. The room watching, waiting for him to do it.

'First day?' He turns to face me.

'Yes.'

Stirring a spoon of sugar into his tea. 'How's it going?'

'It's going all right. I'm in with Miss Swerner.'

'Ah. Miss Swerner.' He's smiling. 'Well. In good hands, then.' He's younger than some of them but he could still be my teacher. He's got a large head. Black hair swept back wet, receding a bit already at the front. 'So, you're an English teacher, then?'

'Will be, when I've finished my training.'

He takes a slurp of his tea. He has big lips. His mouth, when he smiles, is not unattractive. He puts his mug down on the counter and looks round at his colleagues. 'You always wanted to be a teacher, did you?'

'Not really. Until I started my course I thought maybe I wanted to be a cook.'

He doesn't laugh. He's listening, his eyes on mine.

'What about you? Did you always want to be a teacher?'

'More or less. I come from a family of teachers.'

'That right? I come from a family of nutcases.'

His eyes have lit up. He wasn't expecting that. Behind us everyone else is starting to get up, the bell going, Miss Swerner already heading for the door without me.

'Well, then, back to it. Good luck with Miss Swerner.'

There's something soft and teasing in the way he speaks, his smile. Easy enough to imagine him speaking to his older girls like this, and how they might like it.

Service adrenalin continues to beat in my veins. All the boys will still be up, no doubt, in a bar or a club somewhere, a toilet, inhaling their evening's wages. And why not? Is it any more normal to be sitting in your daughter's childhood bed, eating Shreddies at two in the morning? Who's to judge?

There are pronounced crease marks now, despite the months of careful handling, along the central fold of both letters. Soon, they will be unusable. Too obviously written when he was at a different stage. There is no logic to the inclination that draws me always first to Emily's. The words written to Matthew are identical, after all. But it is Emily that it somehow feels more real, more painful, to imagine reading it.

Dearest Emily,

This is not an easy letter to write to you. Or to your brother. If there was a better way to do it then I would. You should know that the law in this country is an ass. It does not allow a person to decide for themselves. But I have decided. I do not want to become a burden. A drooling fool in a home. If I could do this on my own I would. But I cannot. So I have asked your mother to help me despite her reluctance. She is assisting me already by typing this. I need you both to know that this was not an easy decision. There might be some fuss and nonsense. I might make the papers! I have thought at length, though. I ask you to please understand this. And that I love you, for all my failings. It is the only way.

Yours always,
Your Dad

The moment is getting closer. The distance widening, every day, between the person he is reducing into and the person in the letter — whose determined wish, in these words, is clear to read. Will either Emily or Matthew believe that it is the man who is now disappearing inside himself who has been able to dictate this? Will anybody? The doctors? The police? The courts? That he will be making a clear and informed decision, once the time comes? Soon he will not be able to write their names. Their addresses. If Matthew has one. He wrote his list of rules, though. He was capable of that. By hand, only three months ago. And in the blackness of Emily's room, with the letters folded away and the light off, his words of only a fortnight ago come back to me. *I don't want this life.* The person he is now and the person he was after the second stroke — *I do not want to become a burden* — agreeing with each other, asking for the same thing.

1984

The corridor is hushed. With no children about, the sunshine that's flowing through the big windows is shining like glass all the way down the polished wood floor. The silent toil of lessons presses against the walls. Above the corridor ceiling there is the muted rompadomp of instruments my school never had. She wouldn't hardly be able to believe it if she could see me walking through this place now, a proper person. Up ahead, there is a small noise of footsteps. Approaching down the steps from Fifth Year, getting louder, a girl's voice, a man saying something quiet back to her.

It is Patrick. He is coming down the corridor with the redhead girl in his form, Jane Dicky. He smiles without thinking, seeing me. A look of glee on Jane Dicky's face, too; she's even putting her hand to her mouth, the two of them walking up to me. Of course all the students know, however much he might say they don't. Not like he could keep it secret for ever.

'Off you go, then, Jane,' he says.

'Bye, sir. Bye, miss.'

She scampers off, already planning what she's going to tell her friends. She can say what she likes, though, it doesn't matter, because it's me who's got something on them: being with Patrick; having a job like this. And me who's got something what they'll never have because books and learning is all second nature to them; their parents probably read them the Brontës for bedtime stories. They don't know what it's like to learn that world fresh, to open your eyes to it.

Patrick is stood in front of me, a big smile on his face. Blatant flagpole in his trousers – which hopefully wasn't there when it was just him and Jane Dicky. Best not sharing that joke with him. Not one he'd appreciate.

'Fancy this,' he says.

'Fancy this.'

'I'm skiving lessons, what about you?'

'Something like that.'

He puts his hand on my back and escorts me away down the corridor. To one side of us there comes a muffled burst of laughter behind the wall.

'Are you going back to your form room?'

'Yes,' he says quietly.

'I'll walk with you, then.'

Our feet have fallen into step, echoing down the long, empty corridor. Our arms swing in time together. When the backs of our fingers brush against each other a spark of excitement runs through me. A mischievous thought: will he allow us to hold hands, here, in the open? Our fingers, for a couple of seconds, fasten together, before he pulls away.

'Spoilsport.'

He is shaking his head. A little smile.

At the door to his room he hesitates, but he's weakening, opening the classroom door – and there is a fire in me now, being wanted like this, wanting him back. He closes the door behind us.

'I think you might need to lock that, Patrick.'

He's not used to me behaving like this and he's not quite sure what to do. He lets me take his key from his pocket to lock the door, then lets me take him by the hand to lead him towards the store room at the back of his class.

It smells faintly, in the darkness, of children. The sweet chemical trace of deodorant, and hair spray, bubble gum. Maybe he shuts them away in here when they misbehave. With the door closed he's not hanging about, his fingers already at my knickers, his mouth warm against my neck, our breathing loud now in the pitch black. He is moving his hands to my hips, wanting to turn me around.

'No. Not in here, not in the dark.'

He stops, reaching for the door to let a crack of light into the storeroom. He gives a happy hoot of surprise as my hand closes around his penis, pulling him into me. In the cramped space we both grip on to the wooden sides of the cubbyholes past each other's shoulders. Our breathing coming faster now and if we're caught that'll be curtains for me here – but the door is locked and there's no holding me back, wanting him, wanting everything that's ahead of us. The column behind the dark shape of his head is partly lit up by the sliver of light from the door: a jiggling treasure trove of rulers, protractors and compasses all meticulously ordered into jars. A carton of brand-new pencils just beyond the tight clamps of my knuckles, the neat rows of little pink rubbers at the top of them watching us like a class of startled children.

Once upon a time, before the place became a coffee shop, this room would have been the kitchen. Madness that he just left all the equipment in here instead of selling it. The hot cupboard alone would have fetched five hundred quid. He didn't know. He was dead set on his coffee shop and he had no use for this room, so it obviously went the way of any space with no purpose and became a storage room, then ended up a dumping ground. Broken chairs and tables. A cracked toilet mirror. Gimmicky coffee paraphernalia, like this stack of vintage metal etchings propped against the wall — each of them an ornate cartoon of coffee pickers with toothy smiles, big hats and bosoms, which, maybe he needed somebody to point out to him after he'd paid a pretty penny for them on eBay, are plainly offensive. The whole room is a catalogue of bad decisions. Here, though, beneath the service hatch, caked in grime, the long, wooden prep board has survived. It is original, built into the worktop. Whatever kind of restaurant and history of restaurants before it these premises used to be, this board has lasted. My finger runs a slow line across it, feeling the years of use, the middle of it dipping slightly, like the small of a back, a centimetre lower than the sides. How many

hands have worked on this piece of wood? Chopping, kneading, sifting the hundreds of clouds of flour that have settled
here – my own hands out of instinct able to feel now under
my palms a chilled block of dough, centring it on the wood
with thumbs and heels before taking a roller by each handle to
gently smooth it out, turning, rolling, slowly and methodically
away from me until the sheet of dough almost meets the edges
of the board; placing a cool slab of butter-flour on top and
folding the sheet over, one point of the square at a time, tight
as hospital corners, folding and squeezing out the air so that
the melted fat will steam and puff into the dough's own tiny
warren-bubbles, folding, wrapping the slab up for it to be
rolled again, moistened with a fingertip in the middle, and
folded once more, from the bottom, from the top, until the
laminated package of pastry is tucked and swaddled for the
fridge, waiting to be rolled and folded again, then again,
smoothing, firming, hour by hour.

Peter, through the hatch, is making the most of these few
minutes before the agent returns. He's doing his chair thing.
It is obvious how serious he is about this place. The number
of times he's pushed me for this second viewing, and now the
chair thing. He hasn't spotted me watching him through the
hatch, my eyes following him – unafraid, here in this hideout,
of being found out. He walks a few steps across the floor,
stops, puts the chair down. Sits for a moment, stands up
again, turns the chair ninety degrees, sits. He keeps going,
rotating the chair like this, testing each angle for light and
view – until he is facing me.

'Oi, don't laugh. It's important, this.'

'Of course, Peter. It's very important.'

'What are you up to in there, anyway? You cooking something?'

'A pie.'

'Oh, don't do it to me. I'm that hungry.' He closes his eyes. 'What kind of pie?'

'Any pie you like.'

'Corned beef and potato.'

'Any pie apart from that.'

He stays there smiling with his eyes closed, probably still imagining his disgusting pie, even as he can hear me walking out of the kitchen towards him – only opening his eyes and lifting his face to look up at me when he senses me beside him, feeling the pressure of my hand on the back of his chair.

'We really could make this work, Anita.'

His face, this close in the urgent daylight, is intimately new. There are soft pouches under his eyes. Fine lines spreading from the corners of his mouth. A memory of Tristan shoots through me, his sleeping face on that final morning; the sharp clarity that he could not be my life.

An old couple are outside the window. They are both cupping their hands around their eyes to peer through the glass.

'Hell's teeth,' Peter says, 'who are this pair? Look – they're coming in.'

The woman is opening the door, looking about her, inquisitive, while the old man follows in behind her. It takes them a few seconds to notice us.

'Hello there,' Peter calls to them.

They are gawping at us across the empty floor, Peter in his chair and me standing behind him like a hairdresser.

'Can we help you?'

'We would like a cup of tea and a slice of cake,' the woman says.

Peter is getting up now. 'I'm sorry, but I'm afraid there's no kettle yet. Or cake.'

The old couple look at each other. 'Oh,' the woman says, 'that's a pity.'

The old man is courteously opening the door for her, and slowly they make their exit. We watch them proceeding along the outside of the large window, waiting for them to be out of sight before we both give in to laughter. From the other direction along the street, the agent is coming back. He sees us laughing as he enters with his takeaway coffee but he doesn't ask. He walks slightly away from us into the room.

'As you can see,' he says, picking up where he left off before he went for his coffee, 'this place speaks for itself. You're fortunate it's still on the market, to be honest. Is there anything else you want to know?'

Peter answering him: 'Not for the moment, thank you.'

The agent takes a sip of his coffee. 'Okay. Up to you now, then.'

He sees us out and locks the building up. 'Call me when you've made a decision,' he says, to Peter, then crosses the road, checking his watch, back towards his car.

'So. Fancy a stroll on the green while we're here?'

'All right. I've got a bit of time before I have to go in for prep.'

As we cross over the road, the agent, on his phone in his car, looks at us without acknowledgement. Peter takes in the green. 'Canny spot.'

It is kidney-shaped, with thick London planes all around the outside and a small fountain at its centre. The grass has been raked clear of leaves. At the other end of the green from the entrance that we have come into a fitness trainer is loudly counting the pad-punches of his bouncing client. We start walking in their direction, along the central path.

'So, what do you think?' He nods across the green at the vacant premises.

'I think it could be lovely.'

'If we took the plunge?'

'Yes.' The steady beat of punching travels over the grass. 'If only it was that simple.'

'You know,' he says, a little touchily, 'it's as much a leap into the unknown for me as it is for you, Anita.'

'No, Peter, it isn't.'

He is looking ahead down the path, where the old couple are sitting on a bench contemplating the grass. Is that really what he thinks: that it is the same for him, who has no one depending on him, judging him; who has only his veg stall to think about?

'Here,' he says after the long silence, gesturing to a bench just in front of us. 'Sit yourself down and I'll get us a coffee. I've spied where our man got his from.'

The bench is cold and still a little damp from last night's rain. At the end of the path, beyond the motionless heads of the old couple, the fitness trainer is holding his pad out to the side for his client to kick. My eyes are fixed on Peter, walking away across the grass. A need increasing for him to return and calm this feeling of being suddenly alone. He pauses to say hello to a dog retrieving a ball from close to his feet, then he heads for another exit under the trees, only to stop another time to say something to a young couple both holding European flags who are obviously on their way to the march. The three of them laugh together at something and the young woman unfurls the banner she is carrying – *Put it to the People* – and Peter gives them two thumbs-up as she rolls it back up and they go on their way.

A daydream is creeping in, catching me off guard in the mild autumn sunlight: the restaurant through the hatch full, diners flowing out of sight around the L-bend, chatter and laughter and Peter appearing at the hatch, at ease, near me. Does he even know how folded into this dream he has become? As soon as the thought comes, however, others are queuing up to push it out: Patrick, money and – as out of the blue as earlier – Tristan, looking at me from the hotel bed; my vow to never let that happen again. But something has changed. A hunger is growing in me. During these site visits with Peter a foreign understanding of happiness has started to reveal itself. It feels shocking, selfish, the idea of being happy. Has there ever been a time – except, perhaps, for those few early years with Patrick – when it has even entered my mind that it is possible to want that for myself? Happiness has only ever meant the people around me – Patrick, the children, Mum – being happy. The instinct to make sure that they are okay; that they are safe.

Peter is coming back across the grass, a coffee tray in his hands. The air around me is pulsating. The thud of the punch-pad merging with my heartbeat, with Peter's footsteps over the grass. He is veering away from me now and an impulsion to cry out, to shout to him that he is going the wrong way, grips me, then passes, as it becomes clear that he is walking towards the old couple. There are four cups on the tray. He is bending down to talk to them, explaining, their faces in a stupor as he hands them each a cup. Then, from one of the tray's hollows, a small, wrapped package. Their cooing carries to my bench. Peter holding up his free hand to refuse any offer of payment. He starts walking back to me, the old couple watching, looking at me in delighted appreciation at my presumed part, our jointness, in this.

He sits down on the bench and passes me a coffee. 'I do understand how difficult this is for you,' he says. 'I do. Just, it isn't simple for me either, that's all.' He looks at me. 'I was thinking. Seeing as I'm closing the stall Mondays now, how's about we make a regular thing of it, a walk out? Bit of exercise now the weather's turning colder. Greenwich Park, maybe. What do you think?'

The first sip of coffee is scorching, stripping off a layer of my palate.

'I'd like that, yes.'

1985

His hand is resting on my leg. His thumb stroking against my seatbelt clasp. In front of us, the two bald brothers lean in to hear each other over the growing thunder of the jet engines, the pink crests of their heads coming together, peeping above the seat tops. Patrick's fingers are pressing into my thigh.

'What do you think it will be like there?' he asks.

'Hot.'

He is grinning, maybe about to make a dirty joke, but then he says, 'Eric told me it was ninety degrees when they went. Even in the shade.'

His hand, closing around mine, is clammy. Strange really that it's him, who has flown before, a few times, who is nervous. The noise is building outside the little window. The plane beginning to move. A woman and her daughter a few rows in front of us are holding hands across the aisle. My stomach muscles tighten against the sloosh of my guts, the runway racing outside, hurtling, our seats starting to shake and the wheels of the plane, now, letting go of the ground – a man with a flag, the airport's dirty rooftop, a kaleidoscope of parked cars, trees, houses, the slow, red dribble of a bus moving down a street, slower and slower until everything below is frozen, a picture, millions of tiny lives enclosed by fields. She never saw the world like this. It didn't look like this from up in the tower. She never got the chance to see things different, for me to show her there's other ways to live. She wouldn't have been afraid, here in the plane; she'd have been happy, going loopy for it, dancing in the aisles. Patrick is staring out of the window. He looks in a spell, like everyone else, until the grey and green land below all at once disappears, whitened out. A murmur of exhilaration around us. We are above the clouds!

'You do know that we're on holiday?' He is looking at my book. 'You don't need to do your lesson planning now, you know.'

'I'm not.'

'So, you're reading *North and South* just for pleasure, are you?'

'Yes.'

He purses his big lips, amused, then turns his head to look out of the window.

A minute later, he is touching me on the knee.

'Do you want a drink?'

'What, now?'

'Yes, you can have whatever you like.'

'Here in the seat? Is there other people drinking?'

For a second he does his teacher smile at me.

'Right here in the seat. And there *are* other people drinking, yes.' He stretches over me to crane a look for the air hostesses. 'I'll get you something.' He kisses me on the cheek, unbuckling himself. 'I can't wait for this week,' he says, standing up, and squeezes out past my knees.

My eyes close for the memory of last Saturday, the rain beating on the roof of his car, him saying how he is so happy he's found me and both of us knowing we'll be alone together this whole holiday with no schoolchildren or colleagues or anybody else to nosy in on us. The pilot starts speaking on the Tannoy. The temperature is presently 85 degrees in Malaga, he is saying, so he hopes we've got our suncream on already, and everyone laughs like lemons because we're in a box over the sea and all our lives are in his hands.

'Abracadabra!'

From behind his back Patrick holds out two glasses of fizzy wine. He hands them to me so he can clamber past.

'There's a couple further down drinking this, and I thought, Why not? We're on holiday. So I asked one of the flight girls and she poured them right there from her trolley.'

'Do you know something?'

He takes his glass from me before he sits down and raises it, with a big goofy smile, to the smokers at the back of the plane. He settles in, putting his arm around me and clinking my glass with his. 'What?'

'I'm so lucky, being with someone so sophisticated.'

He doesn't seem to understand it is a joke.

'No, it's me,' he says, 'the lucky one. I'm the luckiest sod in the world, I am.'

Some of the men are in their shorts already. They must have changed in the airport toilets. The whole coach in party mood now, a song going up – 'I came home in the morning light, my mother says when you gonna live your life right . . . ' – Patrick joining in with some of the words, laughing at the guy across from us who is standing up in his red trunks leading the singing, twirling side to side, trying to get everyone to join in. The man's shirt is unbuttoned, his chest hair dark with sweat. Up the front, the tour directors are smiling back, on the alert. They probably see him every week, this man.

'You happy?'

He is coaxing my head gently into his neck. The question has taken me by surprise.

'Yes. I am.'

And in the heat and smell of his body, the song still going around us, it is true.

'Look,' he says, reaching down for his sports bag. 'I think of everything, me.' He is taking out a bottle of Lambrusco. Two plastic glasses.

'Go on, then.'

The heat and the booze have made me feel sick. Patrick is leading me by the hand off the coach through a concrete forecourt with dry flowers into a giddy queue that is turning into a conga, one of the tour directors talking to him – 'Is she all right?' – and Patrick saying, 'She's fine. It's just the heat.' He is still holding my hand as we go into the hotel past all the suitcases and up the outdoor stairwell where it is cool and my sandals are tapping on the stone steps until we come out higher up at a balcony into shocking bright light. In the distance, between two concrete towers further down the hillside, there is the blue flame of the sea. He is leading me to our room. Letting us in, closing the door behind, taking me through and lying me down on the bed. He goes to stand by the window. He's feeling let down, all this money it's cost coming here and all the plans we had for what we were going to do, but now here's me lying sick on the bed spoiling them all. He is walking back from the window. He sits on the bed next to me, strokes the hair off my face with his finger and leans down, kissing me on the head. 'It's so beautiful here,' he is saying. 'Why don't you have a little nap? We can go exploring later. We've got all the time in the world, we have.'

We've come a long way down the beach, past most of the people, past all the sunlounger areas with their stripy brown parasols that looked, from up on our balcony, like trays of chocolates. Patrick is taking us towards the giant, square stones lined up into a breakwater at the end of the sand. There were some boys jumping off it into the sea earlier, but it's deserted now. He takes hold of my hand, leading me round where there's a path going up onto the top of it.

The stones are too hot for our feet. We skitter across them towards the sea, where the spray from the waves hitting the last block has cooled the surface enough to sit down. Our legs dangle above the drop to the surf. There is nothing ahead of us. Just sea.

'Where are we?'

'How do you mean?' He puts a hot arm around me.

'I don't know where we're looking.'

We gaze out together at the thick blue nothing of sea.

'South. South-east, maybe. Africa's out that way, anyway.'

For a minute we scan the horizon, looking for Africa.

From above, from up in the quiet sky, we are two white dots on a rock. Nobody else anywhere about. Closer in, we look happy, his arm around me, as normal as any other couple on holiday. The regular beat of the waves on the rock is spritzing our faces with cool seawater and it all feels so simple, sitting here in the rhythm of the surf, so clear that it is not just me, on my own, any more; that we are joined.

He stands up.

'Come with me.'

Down the other side of the breakwater there is a small patch of beach. He jumps down to it from the low end of the breakwater where the stones are buried into the hillside.

'Wait up there a minute.'

He's getting out his new Kodak camera.

'Smile,' he says and snaps me against the big sky. 'Right, now jump.'

He is putting out his arms, and it's only a little jump but he catches me, takes me firmly by the waist.

It is cooler on this side. The stones as high as our heads, shading us from the sun. A white bird flies overhead, away out to sea. He is moving my hair aside to kiss the side of my neck, my shoulders, undoing the laces of my top. The chill of the sea air on my chest turns on my whole body's electrics as he kisses me and lifts me with his hands under my bum towards the stone wall. The faraway sounds of people and cars are hardly registering, a different world. The cold stone against my back makes me take a sharp breath and he's apologising, waiting, until he feels my palms against his chest, taking charge, my mouth at his ear, telling him to lie down on the sand.

The kitchen stops. The hum of the restaurant beyond the pass audible, everybody waiting as Frank looks down at the plate under the hot lamps that was about to go out, wondering which unfortunate is about to get roasted. From behind his back there is no way of knowing what he's scowling at, which element is at fault. Anton can see the plate from his section. He glances over at me, edgy. Next to him, Turtle does the same. It is the halibut. My dish. The whole kitchen is watching. On the other side of the pass, Richard is instructing the floor staff to hold back: Sandy, Karolina, Jimbo – each of them watching in fascination. The senior sous is not supposed to be the one fucking up. It is supposed to be me that Frank entrusts with giving out the bollockings, on this rare occasion that we are both on the line together, and they all want to see how this is going to play out. If he's going to bawl me out. He is carrying the plate over, which they all know is already special treatment, not making me come up to the pass. He puts the plate down in front of me. Overcooked. He is sizing up my section.

'Jesus,' he says under his breath. 'This is a hole. What's going on?'

Tears are filming my eyes. The first, ever, in this kitchen – and they won't stop coming. Exhaustion is swimming through my limbs, marooning me, alone in front of the dry, toughened halibut with everybody watching. My brain is meat. It is an effort just to keep standing. To not cling to Frank's whites, the solidity of his body, and go to sleep.

He tips the fish into the bin and turns around to the kitchen.

'Back to it. Five minutes on table eleven. Everybody good with that?'

Nods and mumbles.

'Yes? No? Bollocks? Tell me: everybody good with that?'

'Yes, Chef,' the cry comes back.

He is looking into my eyes now. Seeing the bloody obvious tears there.

'Do you need to go home?'

He says it quietly enough for nobody else to hear him. Home. Where Patrick screams in the night and it is starting to smell of piss and the front door has to be locked at all times.

'No. I'm fine.'

'Good. Get your section in order. And refire that halibut.'

He will call me to the office after service and he will want to know if something is wrong. My answer: nothing is wrong. Eye off the ball, Chef, it won't happen again. Isaac is beside me, briskly removing the charred halibut pan and the dirty plate for me. Frank cannot know how bad it is getting. How relentlessly Patrick's brain is breaking down. That he has an appointment at the memory clinic next week and the GP wouldn't say it out loud but there can only be one reason for this referral. Or that the two halves of my own brain – here; home – are swelling against each other, the load of them tighter and tighter to my skull with every week that he regresses. And that the only place of refuge – the only place my tired bones want to be right now – is with his veg man.

'Are you okay, Lady Boss?' Isaac says very quietly.

'Yes, Isaac, thank you.'

He pauses momentarily in front of the bin, looking down at the fish at the top of it. 'My cat would be angry with this.'

'Maybe your cat would get along with Frank, then.'

'No, I do not think so,' he says, moving away. 'But she would like you, Lady Boss.'

Time is accelerating. Another order comes in and my hands, fingers, move without me. New pan on the bullseye. Butter. The new pavé of halibut roomed-up and ready. Jack and Turtle have appeared, thumbing through the tickets on the rail – the commis chefs arriving to help me out of the shit.

'We're confused, Chef.' Jack is wiping down my grimy boards. 'We're the ones that make the fuck-ups, not you. What do you need doing?'

'Check the beurre blanc while I do the refire. Turtle, can you dab these two bream dry with a C-fold?'

'No problem, Chef.' Turtle gives me a cheeky wink. 'You can give me my blow-job later.'

'Hey!' Jack giggling next to him. 'After me, pal. After me.'

'Sorry, Chef. Jack wants to give me a blow-job first, so you'll have to wait for him to finish.'

Both of them, all three of us, laughing now. Silly boys. This is all it takes, then, after all these years, to be accepted. A bollocksed fish. With their help, my composure rebuilding, the section is already coming back into order. The returning rhythm of actions repeated thousands of times. Control flowing again through my veins, separating me from everything outside of this kitchen, from home, letting me lose myself once more in the waves of service. Jack is looking over at garnish, where Jonas clearly needs him back.

'You can go now, boys. All good here. Thank you.'

The halibut is done. How can my hands move so quickly, arranging pans, basting, thumb-testing cuts of fish, while the other part of my brain is somewhere else? As if there are two people standing here, one cooking and the other slipping back again into last night, his yowling from the other room bleeding into the screams of a cat somewhere in a garden outside, calling my name over and over, even with my hand on his forehead and his eyes open, his breath catching in his throat – soothing him with a lullaby, trying to subdue the terrible, strange surging excitement that he was dying.

In the fluorescent lighting above the pub's toilet mirror, the cream fabric of both armpits is as damp and puckered as oysters. Through in the pub there is the hubbub of people taking their seats, getting ready for the speeches, the procession of men who are going to stand up and talk about me.

They smile and move back to let me past. The roomful of eyes watching me walk up the patterned carpet back to the top table.

Eddie plonks a shoebox on the table.

'My notes,' he says, and there is a ripple of laughter as he stoops to take off the lid. His nose bonks the microphone, opening fire at the room. There really is paper inside. Handwriting on it, which must be his, though it's hard to remember him ever writing anything. The paper is up to the top of the box, but when he picks up the top sheet there is a pile of old newspapers revealed underneath that the audience can't see. He's thought this joke through.

'In case anybody's confused . . .' He gives a chummy wink over my head to Patrick. '. . . I'm the one giving her away.'

He combs his fingers through his own still-thick hair. 'That one there is the husband.' Another wink. They've met each other twice before today. 'He done the right thing, though. Come to ask me for her hand.' Three times, then. Why hasn't Patrick told me about this? Trying to protect my feelings, maybe, not wanting me to know whatever Eddie said – about Mum, probably, and where marriage, women, get you. 'Course, I said yes right away.' He takes a shaky drink of his pint. 'Before he could change his mind.'

Bloody hell, Eddie. They're not exactly rolling in the aisles. One or two of them are snickering, though: the table from school at the back of the room listening closely, loving every word of this. Even after three years, me and Patrick are still the gossip that keeps on giving: *Not only is there a decade between them but look now at this cockney clown she comes from!* Patrick's got a fixed grin on him. Lord knows what he's thinking. His parents on the other side of him, po-faced, looking daggers every time Eddie opens his mouth. No prizes for what they are thinking: that their son is tying himself to someone below him. Not like their other son who they married off last year to someone more their own type, in a hotel. Mary's expression that day – the first time she'd ever laughed in front of me – listening joyfully to the speeches that she'd not been invited to take part in. Today she looks like she's at a funeral.

'. . . first brought him home I thought he was the social!'

Eddie's leg, next to my face, is quivering. Every time he stops to look at his notes he takes a drink. He's already halfway down the first of the two pints he's got lined up. Through the window at the back of the room, outside, some of the waiting staff have taken their chance to go for a fag.

'All joking aside, I know how much her mother would have loved it today. She'd have been proud as punch to see how beautiful she looks in that dress.'

A general murmur of agreement from the roomful of people who never knew her. The sudden thought of Mum is escaping its cage – Eddie's voice muffling and the room starting to blur as the piercing memory comes back of the policeman's face in the doorway looking at me and not knowing how to start saying it, then the thought of her walking through the night, the stones clacking in her pockets.

'Are you okay?'

Patrick is smiling at me, touching me on the shoulder, bringing me back.

'Yes. I am.'

And, really, Eddie is right: she would have loved this. This is what she wanted. Seeing me up here making something better of myself with someone so solid who loves me and will look after me, to have and to hold, those words that don't mean nothing to most people but would have done to her, who had no one to hold her, hearing them being said to me.

Eddie glances down at me, then at his wife up the far end, who doesn't meet his eyes. It's her shoebox on the table. The shoes she's wearing today, by the looks of it, the unshowy heels he's led her about in all day, introducing her to the few family members and former friends here who neither of us have seen since the cremation. 'You look lovely, sweetheart,' is all she's said to me, though to be fair she's about the only one of them on this table it wouldn't be so bad talking to. He's on to something else already. An old school report he's dug out that he obviously never read first time round and is probably going to use for a joke about me becoming a teacher. She's got a nice face, his wife. A mystery how she's ended up with him, somewhere out in Kent. Everyone is raising their glasses. 'To the happy couple,' resounding about the room. Patrick clinking glasses with me and his hand finding mine under the table, squeezing it, letting me know that me and him don't need any of this lot, it'll just be us a few hours from now, on our own. Already the two of us are peeling away from the whirl and din of this scene. He is going to care for me, his hand is saying. He doesn't need anything else from me; he just wants me for me. Music has started up. People getting up from the tables, laughing and clapping and Patrick is leaning in towards me, whispering into my ear, 'I love you, Mrs Kelly.' Our hands clutching together under the table, safe as houses.

He is watching the television. Sunshine is pushing through the gap in the bedroom curtains, onto the wardrobe. He's made no sign of noticing me come in, yet somehow it feels odd, the thought of undressing, releasing my towel, in front of him. The wardrobe handle is warm in my hand, opening it, taking out my clothes. He is entranced by the adverts and doesn't at first see me pulling on my underwear, underneath the towel, as if we are at the beach.

'Why are you here?'

It sounds more like surprise than annoyance. My back is turned to him, my arms reaching behind to fasten my bra. Does he think that it is someone else?

'I'm off this morning, remember?'

He switches off the television himself. 'I want a walk.'

'I don't know if that's—'

'I want to go outside.'

He is shifting the covers, trying to manoeuvre himself to the edge of the bed.

'Hold on, hold on. Let me help you.'

The bed releases a cabbagy gust as the covers lift.

'I want.' He is frowning. 'I want.' He bats away my hand. 'I, I . . .' He cannot find the word.

'That's okay, Patrick. We can go for a walk.'

'Breakfast,' he says finally. 'I want sausages.'

It is a beautiful day. Bright and crisp, leaves blowing on the pavement in the draught of passing cars. The slight incline of our street is proving difficult for him. He is leaning into me, my arm through his. His other hand a small cold skull around the handle of his cane. When did we last go out for a walk? The occupational therapist would be delighted. Fresh air and exercise will help his mood, she is always telling us, and natural fatigue will reduce stress: he'll be less inclined to fight if he's tired. We'll see. Once upon a time, when he was a baby, that's what the health visitor said about Matthew.

Before the end of our street, he wants to stop for a moment. He takes his arm out of mine and rests instead against the postbox. The image of Matthew on the pavement beside it steals into my vision – but Patrick is smiling up at the sky, cock-a-hoop. He is out on a walk in the sunshine. He starts rabbiting on as we continue. Telling me things. The news on the television earlier. A boy walking out of his lesson with no trousers on. He is saying it as though this happened yesterday. Who knows when it did happen, if it happened at all? It could have been last year, or just as easily forty years ago, the boy now a man with a history of his own behind him. It is difficult to follow the thread of what he is saying. It makes sense only in patches. Something else has, silently, closed inside his brain in this last few weeks. The step down in his functioning showing itself in these broken trails of thought and the unpredictable spells of concentration, the lost words.

There are lots of people about in the village. Locals, bustling in and out of the busy shops. Mothers and babies, weekend dads. Nobody that knows us well enough to come and talk, thankfully. He stops to gain his breath and look at the giant spray-painted spider's web in the window of the florist. 'Come on,' he says, and points towards the café, a childish excitement in his eyes.

There is a line of pumpkins on the windowsill of the café, each carved into a different personality: happy, sad, aggressive, confused. A cruel joke pulls at me – *Look, Patrick, it's you: there's Monday, there's Tuesday, Wednesday . . .* – but fortunately he is already trying to get through the door, a woman coming to help him open it.

As soon as we are inside there are the familiar café sounds of conversation, cutlery clinking, and guilt closes around me at the involuntary thought of Peter, the easiness of his company, away from this life.

An unfamiliar young woman in an apron is clearing a path for Patrick through the busy tables. People moving aside, polite, kindly. What they see is an old man. An old man with a cane. She is seating us, pulling a chair out for him.

'Do you know what you'd like, or shall I give you a minute?'

'Sausage. Poached egg. A coffee.' He states it with extreme deliberation, like a final meal, and she writes it down then looks to me for my order as the door opens again and Paul and Julie walk in. There is a two-second pause between them seeing us and their faces resolving into a course of action. It's too late for them to step back out, so they start moving towards us.

'Hello, Patrick.'

Julie stands awkwardly by his chair. Even as recently as a year ago, she would have kissed him. She would have kissed me, too. No longer, it seems. Paul is stiffly next to her, waiting for her lead. Patrick simply stares at them both; all three of us probably wondering whether he knows who they are.

'I wanted sausages,' he says eventually.

'Sausages, ooh, lovely,' Paul says, with the detached animation of a man speaking to a child. If it was cancer, or his heart, that would be different, Paul could respect that, the mechanics of it. Tell Patrick he's a fighter. The sight of Patrick now embarrasses him. All he can see in front of him is a doddery old man.

Julie is looking at Patrick, her face pinching with pity.

'How *are* you?'

The accepted thing to do would be to step in at this point. Say something meaningless: *He's doing well. We're coping fine. It's so good to get out and have some fresh air*. It feels good, though, watching her flounder. Does she even know that it has been confirmed now, that it is dementia, that the real answer to her question – 'How are you?' – is that he is at least one, known, brain disintegration removed from the person she saw when she last came round to the house? She's still not even acknowledged me. Neither of them has. They don't see me as a full person any more either. They assume me to be fulfilling the role everyone expects of me: the wife, the stoic carer, there entirely for his needs, like the stick. My career, my body, my future all collapsed now into a single feature, a pumpkin on the windowsill.

'It's really good to see you, Patrick,' she says, this woman who lives five doors down the street from us. And now she looks at me. They both do. 'How are Emily and Matthew getting on?'

An urge rises in me to punch her in the face.

What has started coming out of my mouth, however, is exactly what they want to hear, easy nothings, an opening to talk about themselves. '. . . she might be coming down from Manchester for Christmas actually.'

'Oh, that would be so good. With her fiancé?'

'If Morgan doesn't go to his own parents, yes.'

'And what about Matthew?'

'He's still in Spain, working in a hotel.'

It might be true. She doesn't know any better. Or maybe she does – Emily, it's quite possible, might have told Rebecca something. Paul is looking at his watch. Julie saying, 'Do just let us know if we can be useful. We have Becca and the baby with us for Christmas, so I'm sure we'll see you then.' Paul asking her quietly what kind of coffee she wants. If they had intended to sit down when they came in, they're not doing that now.

They walk away through the tables. They'll get their coffees and wait until they are out on the street before they talk about how sad it all is. That poor man. The shadow he is of his old self. His dying brain, his reducing mobility, the sexless waste of his body. Not that they'll talk about that part. The young woman is bringing our drinks. She puts them down in front of us and goes off.

There is no sugar on the table.

'Do you want some sugar for your coffee, Patrick?'

He nods. He is tired out. This has been too much for him. Looking at him across the table, his head tipped forward and to the side because he hasn't the strength left to hold it erect, a tenderness for him moves me to put my hand onto his – the dreadful thought of the letters, out of nowhere, running headlong through me.

'I'll bring you some.'

Getting up again, the noise of people and cutlery and the milk steamer enveloping me, my limbs fire with a sensation that Peter is in the café, that my feet are taking me, unbidden, towards him.

At my return Patrick lifts his face to me. His eyes look up at mine from underneath the roadkill of his eyebrows. His lips are tremoring with the effort to form what he wants to say, the word he is trying to find.

'Wankers.'

1986

The donkeys are lined up ready for us, their saddles garlanded with flowers. People start to laugh as they scramble to mount them, but the donkeys aren't fussed, they just keep gazing ahead. Mine is a grey. Flies move in and out of her ears and her stiff filthy mane. She gets going without any command from me, setting off with the rest of the convoy up the hillside, behind Patrick's donkey.

Every now and then, Patrick looks to the side of him – at the parched valley, the cloudless sky. There's something peculiar about watching him from behind on a donkey. Not knowing what's going on in his head, under that silly hat he bought on the beach yesterday. Maybe nothing is going on; maybe he's just listening to the hidden birds in the scrub or the donkeys' hooves on the path. It's the not knowing, though, that is making me feel queer. A new yearning is filling me up, wanting us to be completely together. The reality of being home again after the honeymoon, back in the routine of lessons and bell and staffroom, is each day that we are here making me feel more greedy to be near to him.

His donkey lets off a big fart. A few chuckles from the riders nearest to us. Patrick turning around, giving me a little smile and making known, to me at least, that it might not have been the donkey.

The line keeps winding up and up the hill, over the dry crumbled path past yellow tangles of thorns and abandoned outbuildings, a couple of sleeping goats, the sun directly above us now and on the other side of the valley, between two large hills, a deep blue triangle of sea. We are coming towards a small clearing. Some of the group have already got off their donkeys and are walking them to where the guide is explaining how to tie them up. My donkey comes to a stop. Patrick has slid off his and is trying with some difficulty to bring it round alongside mine.

'Come on, girl,' he is saying quietly. 'Come on, girl.' Not surprising, really, by the looks of its penis, that the donkey is ignoring him.

The hot firm belly of his donkey presses against my leg, the creature's hard breathing pulsing at my skin. A longing spirals up through me, wanting to be alone with Patrick, just the two of us. The guide is walking up to us. He takes the reins of both our donkeys and leads them to a post near where all the others are tethered. There is a small stone building a bit higher up, painted white. Two long tables with lines of chairs in the shade of some olive trees and, coming into view, a buffet spread out all along the wall of the building.

The other honeymoon couple that Patrick got talking to yesterday in the hotel reception are in front of us in the food line. Patrick is saying something to the husband about the food, pointing at the bowl of elaborately concertinaed melon slices that's first up. The line moves forward and the four of us gather around the bowl. The wife, Linda, in her elegant white shirt, takes a slice and passes me the tongs.

'Don't they look lovely?' she says. 'Did you see the fruit at breakfast this morning?'

'Oh, yes. Patrick can't get enough of these buffets. I think we was the first down this morning.'

She laughs and moves on to the next dish, a massive oval plate of neatly folded ham. Patrick looks at me funny for a second, before he arranges his plate with ham.

There's no space for the four of us together, so Geoff and Linda go up the other end and Patrick sits down next to me. '*Were* the first down,' he says, with his teacher's face, his father's face, and starts eating his food. Quick shame prickles at my chest. It's the second time since we got here that he's pulled me up for getting my language wrong. A long while since the days he used to do it all the time, making me monitor everything that came out my mouth, but he's stepped it up again this holiday, maybe because it's more embarrassing for him now we're married.

'Aren't you hungry?' he asks.

'Not much.' The thought of eating all this warm, left-out food is making me feel a bit sick. Even the melon, as it touches my lips, is warm. 'Ate enough at breakfast.'

Music starts coming from the building. Two men with guitars are stepping out. Behind them a pair of beautiful, tanned girls carrying large, brown jugs. There is spontaneous applause down the table. In the shade of the trees, the sun dappling light onto the table, some of the group begin clapping to the music. At the other end of the table, Geoff and Linda are smiling at each other, their arms thrust out, giving it some welly.

It is crema Catalana again for pudding. The ceramic pots get put down in front of each of us by the Sangria girls, each with a tiny ornate spoon. Across the table a sweating, older man is shaking his head, muttering something – *Bloody woman* – it sounds like, his wife's back turned to him because she's got her attention on the man coming down the table with a wicker basket of souvenirs. The husband flinches when her back touches his arm for an instant, and he shuffles a bit away from her. He thinks he's the one who's hard done by, while she's here trying to have a nice time – laughing now with the souvenir man as he gets to her – and he's just sat there going grumpily at his pudding with the little teaspoon. Were these two happy, once? It's hard to imagine that they were, that they ever had what we've got. You need to know what it feels like to have no one, to be properly alone, to really be happy when you find someone.

Patrick is getting up, other people too, the table wobbling. Patrick saying, 'I think it's the walking tour now,' and in the kerfuffle of everyone moving off from the table the man stands there wiping the custard off his lips with his napkin while his wife shows him the purple velour bull she's just bought.

The group is quickly on the move down the hill following the guide, but Patrick is delaying, wanting them to go on ahead.

He puts his arm about my waist and steers me down a smaller path, into an orange grove, wasps droning all around us.

'Are you enjoying yourself?'

Fallen smashed fruit is everywhere on the ground, twitching with wasps.

'Yes. I am.'

In the stillness of the grove, without the chatter of everyone else, the air throbs with buzzing.

'I love you,' he says.

His cheek is cool against mine. It feels unreal, picturing us, our faces touching above the alive orange ground, that this is my life.

'I love you too.'

The guide, when we break from kissing, has turned around and is smiling, signalling for us to follow on. Some of the group around him notice and seconds later a jovial cheer reaches us through the dry air.

Out of the orchard, the sun is directly on top of us as we join the back of the group and come to a narrow, dusty road. There are a couple of small, white houses along it and, round a bend, a village. The tour comes through it: a dozen houses, a memorial, an empty café. Two old men, standing by a dried-up fountain, pause to inspect our group filling their village, then go back to their conversation.

'It's like going back in time,' Patrick says.

That doesn't make much sense, mind. It was never like this where my family came from. Or his, even, across the tracks. The guide is explaining something that we're too far behind

143

to hear. At the back of the group the sweating man is peering down, not looking at the guide like all the other heads. He's staring barefaced at Linda's bottom. Linda doesn't seem like she's noticed, or Geoff, or the man's wife, who's craning forward to listen to the guide. She knows, though. Course she knows. She has chosen to ignore it, dutifully looking the other way. A wish to run into the group and expose him crawls in my toes. Although, what would be the point? All it would do is humiliate the wife, Linda and me in one fell swoop. He'd just laugh it off: *Had a bit too much sangria, this one. You've got a lively one on your hands there!* The wife is adjusting her sunhat. Nudging the old perv to alert him that the tour is moving on.

We are trailing behind again, adrift of the group. 'Come on, lovebirds!' someone shouts back, Patrick giving me a pinch on the bum, and it feels good being separate like this, shielded – the pervy man looking at us too, miserable as anything, probably grinding his teeth at the sight of this younger, better-looking man with his arm round me. Even Geoff and Linda, smiling sweetly over from in the group, aren't nothing on us. Everything bad, everything she wanted me to fight away from, is left behind me now. Together like this, there's no one can touch us.

'Look.'

Patrick is pointing across the valley to where the sea has come fully into view. A gorgeous bright slab of it twinkling between the hills. The group are stood around a donkey that they've come to beside a tree. The guide finishes saying whatever he's saying and they all move off.

The donkey, when we reach it, is on its own, tied to a tree trunk by a long rope. It is walking slowly around the tree. On the flat stone circle all about the tree base there is a feathery heaped sun of corn sheaves, which the donkey is treading over, trampling down. Patrick has took his hat off, his hair flattened and damp.

'What on earth?'

'It's threshing it, look. It's making the corn come loose.'

'Ah.' He puts his hat back on. 'Clever. Backward, but clever.'

The rope is tied to a hook that's screwed into the trunk, not looped round it – so that the rope wraps about the trunk, getting shorter, as the donkey walks in circles. The group are away out of sight now but it's too hypnotic, watching this donkey go round and round, to move away. There's nobody here driving it, but the animal is relied on to just keep going, muzzled, trampling the corn. What happens when the rope's out and the donkey is right up to the trunk? Does it just turn around and go again in the other direction? A strange anger is building up in me. Resentment at whoever it is has left this animal here trudging slow circles around a tree. And it is suddenly plain that there is nothing, nobody, to stop me from untying the rope.

'Come on, we should catch up.'

It's not Patrick, or what the group, the tour director, would say that is stopping me from doing it. It is the donkey. The quiet horror of releasing it but the animal just keeping going, dutifully round and round, without the rope.

It is calming, here in the small snug space under the staircase. Even on the little wooden stool, it would be easy just to nod off here for a while. To hide from the task at hand – Emily's number lying in wait on my phone, a press away. Patrick had a plan once to do up this space: to take out the landline and cover the whole snug with photographs. The landline, however, has outlasted him, still there intact on the wall, barely used in the last couple of decades. Emily's phone is ringing. Funny, really, how we all kept coming in here to use our mobiles, out of habit.

'Hi, Mum.'

'Hello, my love. How are you?'

'I'm fine. What about you? Is everything okay?'

'Yes. I just wanted to speak to you.'

'What about?'

'I'm thinking of getting some help, Emily.'

The bright gash down the inside of my forearm has fattened since this morning's fight.

'Help?'

'Yes.'

'What do you mean? Counselling?'

'No, God, no. I mean help for your dad.'

'Oh, I see.'

'Someone to share a bit of the load. A care worker.'

She will already be thinking about practicalities. Can she take more time off work? Would Morgan come with her or will he have to stay in Manchester?

'How often would they come?'

'I don't know exactly.'

'I could maybe . . . How much have you looked into it already?'

'A little. I've started to.'

'Is this so that you'll be able to work?'

'I am working. If I wasn't, we wouldn't be able to keep paying our bills, but he needs more and more caring for and it's turning into two full-time jobs. I need some help.' It isn't meant to be an accusation, although it probably sounds like one. She will take it as one.

'What does Dad think?'

'I don't know.'

'You've not spoken to him about it?'

She doesn't know what he is like now, since her last visit, doesn't understand the speed at which his brain is failing.

'He's not really at a point where he can make his own decisions any more.'

In the pause while she turns this over, the right words – to comfort her, to explain how this is the best thing for him – will not come.

'It's an idea, that's all. I just wanted to talk to you about it.'

'You know I'd jump on a train to be there myself if I

could, don't you? And I'm sorry – I do want to – but I really can't at the moment.'

Why not? It almost slips out. Who decided that it's not a child's role to do just that? Is a few days every six months the required amount? Is there a ratio: for each year of child-care you get a week of parentcare at the other end? If there is, obviously no one has told Matthew. Not that Patrick ever did as much as a year of raising either of them, before he made his bid for me to return to teaching and hand Matthew over to his mother.

'Of course, I know you can't. No one's asking you to give up your life. And I know how drastic this must sound to you, and how difficult it is to hear, but it's got to the stage where I need some professional help. Now the specialist has con-firmed it.' She says nothing. She is not ready to talk about that. 'He's getting worse, Em. He's had another sharp decline recently. He couldn't find the bathroom this morning, then he got mad and fought with me when I tried to show him.'

'This person wouldn't know him. They wouldn't know how he likes things.'

'I'd explain everything to them.'

Cup of tea only when asked for. I can feed myself. No carrots.

'I'm not sure about it, Mum.'

As if the final say is hers, remotely. She is right, though. It shouldn't be my decision alone. It should be all of ours. It should be his. If she knew that it wasn't actually my idea in the first place, that it was Peter, a man she's still never been told about, who made this suggestion about her dad during one of our now weekly strolls in the park, what would she have to say about it then?

'You've not told Matthew this, obviously.'

'No.'

'He'll be upset.'

Now is the moment to ask her if she knows how he is, where he is, but stupid pride won't let me.

'Matthew hasn't spoken to your dad for a long time.'

She has an opinion about this, clearly, but she's not saying what it is. Matthew must have told her something about what he found out before he left – it is there in her sensitivity about his distance now – but he has not told her all of it. He can't have. She is not the type, unlike the rest of us, to keep things held in, unsaid.

'Let me speak to Morgan. He's on location during the week but we might be able to come down one weekend. Or just me. Spend some time with Dad and give you a hand, before we come down again for Christmas.'

'Thank you. I'd appreciate that, if you can.'

It is hard to leave the shelter of the snug. Thinking about how Emily will relay the conversation to Morgan. The things they must talk about in private: what they say about me, about Matthew. Whether they should bring forward their wedding plans, while her dad is still mostly with us. Whether they should offer us money. Does she know just how *much* money his increasing needs are going to cost? That even though our savings were eaten into after his first stroke – savings which my years of work made grow but are inscribed legally, by his demand to put them in his name, to perish with him – the amount is still, just, over the state threshold. And a nursing home anywhere nearby will cost at least a grand a week. Of course she knows. This is Emily. She knows her father well enough too, the man he was, not to need telling that he would never accept being put in a home. As he put it, while he still could: *You will not, ever, banish me to one of those places to rot with all the other dumpling*s.

The gash in my arm is a deep one. It will join the others there, the kitchen ones. Christmas is another awkward conversation waiting to happen. She knows, from long experience, what my rota will be like. How much time she can expect me to be at home with them.

A low whine is coming from upstairs.

Was he listening? Would he have understood any of it if he was – some of the conversation filtering through to him, gluing up in the thick tallow of his brain? There will come a time, before very long, an event or two away, when it will be possible to talk about him while he lies in the same room, there but not there. With Emily. With a care worker, a stranger. She is right – the noise upstairs getting louder now – that it is uncomfortable to think about, getting somebody else to look after him, although of the choices yet to be made this is the only one, still remaining, that can be spoken to her.

1987

It doesn't feel right, having the seatbelt over my tummy. Patrick keeps looking across at me loosening it, poised to reach over and strap me back in if he needs to. He puts his gearstick hand on my knee.

'Nearly there now.'

The world outside the windscreen is already different, a place beyond me. Commuters, children at the bus stop. They move past like an exhibition. A need to be separate from this world is curled deep inside me, has been increasing since the moment yesterday when my waters broke over David and Ruth's sofa – all four of us standing up to watch the spot spread across the fabric and Patrick automatically apologising, saying he'd pay for it. His sister-in-law immediately pulling him up for it: 'Don't be ridiculous, Patrick, it's not toxic – and I hardly think my sofa should be high on your list of priorities right now.' How wrong she was: he's already got a quote from a dry cleaner. The shame, maybe, of imagining his parents sitting on my stain every other Sunday.

'What the hell is this clown doing?'

A van has stopped in front of us. The traffic on the other side of the road too congested for Patrick to pull out. A man is getting out of the van, walking slowly around to open its back doors.

'Get out of the bloody road!'

His fist is tightened around the gearstick, the eyeballs of his knuckles glowering at this fat man now lifting an office chair onto the pavement.

'It doesn't matter, Patrick. We've got time. Let's just stay calm.'

The side of his neck is hot, his shoulders rigid, loosening a fraction at the touch of my hand. 'She's not coming yet, my love. It's all going to be fine.' The calmness that is in me slowly crossing into him, joining us in a state of quiet togetherness, of joy.

She can hear all this. She has been listening in for the last five months, the midwife said — my organs thumping and fizzing around her, this tiny, invisible witness to my days: footsteps to the shop, the television, laughing at Patrick's silly jokes, the knife on the chopping board. What does she think of us so far, her parents? Does she understand that his angry muttering, as he pulls out at last into the other lane, is just because he's scared? Will she know, when she exits my body into a bright room of bulbs and metal, that she is, suddenly, the whole of our world?

A 'devoted husband' who helped his wife of 45 years to die in her own bed as he sat beside her has today walked free from court.

Father of three John Henley from Whittlesey, Cambridge-shire, who was arrested on 9 January on suspicion of assisting Huntington's disease-suffering wife Josephine's suicide after she died from a lethal overdose of prescribed medication, acted 'wholly out of love', Peterborough Crown Court heard.

Judge Roland Palmer, handing down a 2-year sentence, suspended for the same length, described Mr Henley's actions as 'an act of mercy' brought about by 'the unbearable strain' of caring for Josephine during her tragic decline.

That phrase, *2-year sentence, suspended*, brings back the thought of Duncan the lamb man – the footage of him being escorted into court; the dead boy's family on the news – before my eyes are drawn back to the screen.

The court heard how Mr Henley, 73, a retired maintenance engineer, had taken on the burden of being the sole carer for his wife since her diagnosis six years previously.

As her condition deteriorated last year following a lung infection and Mrs Henley, 67, became increasingly depressed and bedbound, finding it difficult to breathe or even to sit up, 'her last scraps of dignity had eventually gone', the judge told the court.

Passing sentence, Judge Palmer said: 'This is an especially harrowing case, and nobody can have any doubt about your longstanding devotion to your wife, or that you were disrespecting her final wishes.'

Mrs Henley, the court heard, implored her husband over several months to assist her to end her life. Together they considered different methods to do so, including research into the Dignitas assisted dying clinic in Zurich, Switzerland, although they were put off by the prohibitive cost.

In a victim impact statement, Mrs Henley's sister, Angela Gibbs, described how the couple had been left with no choice: 'If you're rich you can determine your own death by going abroad. For everyone else you're not allowed to decide yourself, so either you've got to go on living in misery or you take it upon yourselves and risk the ordeal of the one who remains going to prison. The law has it backwards.'

The same words as in his own letter, more or less. *The law is an ass.* All the same, Mr Henley is free. He is out and about at this very moment, at the shops, the pub. The unbearable strain of caring for his wife unbearable enough that he passed the six tests: not in the public interest to imprison him. If it had been the other way around − if it had been the wife massaging the pills down *his* throat – would the judge have ruled the same way? Or would Mrs Henley have been expected to deal with the burden, with or without the three children, to bear it for longer? There are, it is becoming clear, more men than women in these reports. The pensioner who tried and failed to get his wife to swallow four packets of paracetamol, then suffocated her with a pillow. The ninety-five-year-old spared jail for going at his wife with a lump hammer.

The bigger it gets, this freakish collection, the more unreal it becomes. The harder to understand who they are, these devoted lovers with their drugs and hammers. When was the moment that they knew it was the only choice left, the easier, kinder way, their options narrowed down to a nightmare interpretation of their wedding vows? What to make of it all? What would Emily and Matthew make of it – their mother lying in one of their beds with her laptop, bewitched by this macabre, growing catalogue on the screen, unable to stop searching for more?

1988

There is no sound from the cot. Pointless this holding my breath to listen in better, the racket he's making next to me. She must be asleep. Or dead: the blanket yanked over her face, smothering her. The brainless thought, as soon as it is allowed to creep in, impossible to ignore.

She is fast asleep. The soft little sound of her breath slipping in and out of her nostrils.

There she is. When she's awake, exploring, feeding, giggling, screaming, there's never a single minute to take stock of her. To understand properly that she is real. It's only these once-in-a-blue-bloody-moon occasions that she's actually asleep for more than ten minutes when the fact of her enters me, like a syringe, numbing me. There in her cot, the miniature shapes of her feet pushing up against the tuck of the blanket, she looks unearthly. Perfect. Her face is warm on the back of my finger. She feels the right temperature for once. Or maybe if she was even warmer she would stay asleep longer. Really, who the hell knows? Out of nowhere she starts her head-shaking thing – jerking it two, three, four times from side to side. Is she thinking something? Has she sensed me? She goes still again. Maybe Patrick's snoring has made her dream about his joke: her rubbing herself a bigger bald patch than his. Maybe she's thinking about me. Although, even after all these months of stalking each other about the flat, she still doesn't seem to have figured out that she is not me – something that hasn't rightly come to me yet, either. There's a whole crowd of me and her mingling around the bright bunting of her cot. All the women that used to be me, staring in at her; all the women that Emily is going to be, getting ready to climb out – each of them at the same time claiming and rejecting me.

The night light, for no sane-person reason, now looks much too bright. Out of its many mystifying settings, though, which would surely even baffle the hell out of somebody who hasn't had to stay awake for twenty-one hours a day for the last ten months, none of them will make it go dimmer.

With a bit of careful arrangement on top of the chest of drawers, the pack of nappies sits square in front of the night light and the room darkens a little. Only an idiot wouldn't be getting some rest now, while she is so fast asleep. But something won't let me leave her alone. An urge to be with her, watching the air flow in and out of her body, is keeping me here by her side.

From behind the shadowy mountain on the chest of drawers, the night light glows like a distant city.

'What are we going to do with you, hey, missy?'

The fox and the owl, hanging from their cords, stir with

my voice. Emily's eyelids stay closed. She is smiling. It's the wrong question. She knows precisely what we're going to do with her: we are going to feed and clean and teach and love her. What are we going to do with me? That is the real question.

There he is. The usual spot, outside the Observatory. He has seen me and is walking over, smiling, a big green scarf around his neck, my weekly hour off about to begin the moment he hugs his hello and my bones unstitch into a sinful pile at the top of the hill.

'I've got you a coffee.'

'Thank you.'

His arms around me. He smells of soil, even on his day off. 'How's about an aimless meander, then?'

'Okay. Let's go and say hello to the deer first, though.'

Other people are all around, not giving a second thought to us walking down the hill sipping our coffees, and it is so easy, not to have to do anything, to be anyone. Even as Peter starts chatting away about market this-and-that – the leak in the market-hall roof, the celebrity chef who has started coming to the stall every Monday for his Vitelotte potatoes – he doesn't need me to say anything, to give him something in return. He knows, he must know by now, that this stolen hour has become the high point of my week.

There is a young dad sitting in the bandstand, looking at his phone while his toddler splashes in the pile of leaves they have collected. The toddler stops to watch us come past and Peter gives her a wave.

'So. How is the new woman getting on?'

'It's hard to know. She comes, I know that, because she writes it in the care book. She gets him dressed, gives him his medication, leaves a sandwich by the bed. I think she's probably in and out in less than twenty minutes.'

'It's something, though.'

'It is. With a care bill at the end of the month that I have to work for a lot longer than the care he gets to pay for.'

He takes a drink of his coffee. 'And is he okay with her, like?'

'It's difficult to tell. He doesn't say when I ask him. He has these flashes of being almost normal but most of the time now he's so confused. I put a photo of the toilet on the bathroom door at the weekend.'

It immediately feels underhand, telling him this, a betrayal.

'It's the right thing to have done, you know, the care woman. You couldn't have gone on like you were.'

'Maybe. It's been difficult for Emily, though. I think she's in denial about how much worse her dad is getting. It wasn't like this last time.'

'She's not here with him now, though, is she?' Some of the deer are visible up ahead in their enclosure as we move down the avenue of trees. 'She still coming with the fiancé for Christmas?'

'Yes.'

'That's good. She can help you out. It'll be an eye-opener for her.'

'It will.'

'What about Matthew? Any word from him if he's coming?'

'No. Not yet.'

One of the stags is raising himself off the ground, lifting his face to the sky so that his antlers almost touch his back.

'I've got my own girls down with me next week, by the way, so I won't be able to come for our walk.'

'Don't worry. That will be nice for you.'

'Oh, it'll be canny.' He is smiling. 'They think you're quite the woman in lights, you know. Senior sous in a fancy-pants restaurant. Wanting to open your own place.'

'What?'

He has said this as if it's normal, speaking to his daughters about me. An impulse to leave makes me stop still on the path. Peter stops too. He is moving to face me.

'You not think they'd know about you?'

'What is there to know?'

'That you're someone important to me. They've been hearing about you for years.'

From near to the deer enclosure there is the soft drizzle of the fountain sprinkling onto the pond, the sound of it making me need to start moving again as an old hurtling weirdness sweeps up through me: the image of her, clear as if it was yesterday, sitting on the bench, humming to herself, away with the fairies. Then it's gone and there's nothing. A hole.

'I've not told them I'm thinking of selling up, mind, coming in with you.'

'Good. Because it's a bloody stupid idea.'

He laughs quietly, coming to a halt and turning to me again. 'I know, I know. You're a woman who goes it alone. I've been doing some more digging about the place on the green, anyway. Rates, local competition and that. The signs are all good. There's other interest, mind. I got that out of them.'

'That's enough now, Peter.'

'Oh. Fine. Okay.'

It is too much. It isn't possible to talk about these things yet, this first week of Patrick being cared for by someone else. Peter's hand is gently on the back of my head as it comes against his chest, my arms closing around him, already trying to resist the sensual memory of Tristan; merging this, Peter, with that time. The care worker is with Patrick right now. Heaving him in and out of the bed. What would she think about this picture?

A man – one of Patrick's old colleagues – is jogging up the path. A music teacher. Luke. The lines on Peter's forehead thickening: puzzled, impatient, at my sudden stepping back from him. 'Christ, what have I done now, Anita?'

Luke is almost level with us. He's in running gear. Why is he here? It's not half-term. He must have noticed me peeping over at him. There is no choice but to say hello. It would look even worse ignoring him now, even though he seems to be pretending not to have seen me, striding on with his earplugs in.

'Hello.'

He takes the earplugs out, stopping, flustered. 'Oh, hello.'

'It's Luke, isn't it? We've met a few times before at school events.'

'Right, yeah.'

Peter is still conspicuously close, listening just at the side of the path. It is becoming apparent, however, that Luke doesn't have a clue who he's talking to. He has probably taken me for a parent, or grandparent, not the wife of his former colleague who less than a year ago had a stroke during a history lesson.

'I've been running. Free period.' He checks his watch. 'Should be getting back, actually. Good to see you.'

He jogs away. A man who once spoke to me for the length of a summer-fair hot-dog-stall queue about the mileage range of hybrid cars, but who now no longer remembers my face.

Peter is coming back over. 'Are you all right, pet? You've gone white as a sheet.' He gestures towards Luke, running away. 'That was mighty odd.'

'Not really. Even a woman in lights becomes invisible when she gets past a certain age. Don't tell your daughters.'

1989

Emily does a little squeak at every push, as though each one is a surprise. This should not feel so much like a chore. It should be reaching some essential part of me, should be reaching inside my chest to fill me with contentment – but instead every heave of her, coming back at me two seconds later like a cannonball, is draining me of energy.

'More. More.' She is giggling. At the next swing along, the little boy's mummy is responding to his delighted burbling with baby noises of her own: 'Wee! Wee! Wee!' Resentment peps me up, listening to this woman hog all the sound space. The thought of me and her standing beside each other making the same noise – *Wee! Wee! Wee!* – makes me want to throw up. Or punch her. She's got an air, this woman, older than me, of knowing perfectly what she is supposed to be doing, of connection. She will no doubt push her toddler for as long as he is enjoying himself, before she takes him home for his cooked lunch and puts him down for a scheduled nap while she gets the craft box ready. Who does she think the silent, exhausted girl pushing the swing next to her is? The

164

nanny? Hardly. In this posh park even the nannies are older, and definitely more fun, than me.

Before long, this time with her will be over. A murmuring of grief is already in my ears, telling me to savour it because soon her face, her beautiful, chubby body, will be apart from me; she will be shrunk to a daydream during the dragging hours of school – the same lessons, the same tired, bored teachers complaining in the staffroom. A glimmer of my old job cuts through the thought – the rush of lunch service and camaraderie and the satisfied faces of the children – as the swing comes back again to me, the confusion of the future lurching forwards, backwards, unrelenting, forwards, backwards.

All across the playground there are mothers clapping and cooing. They're so wrapped up in their special baby bond that they can't see they're all the same. In five years, twenty years, there will be mothers and children here doing exactly the same things, round and round, up and down, forwards and backwards.

It cannot be normal, having thoughts like this.

And it's not her, it's not Emily. Like usual it is thinking ugly like this that now brings me back to her, guilty and powerless against the huge, confused love that swells up in me for her, the meatiness of her back, reassuring me how real she is. That she is mine and she needs me and it doesn't matter that there is nobody to tell me that my efforts are good enough, because she is saying it, giggling it, herself. Did Mum ever do this with me: take me to the park, push me on the swings? It is too far back to remember; there are too many other memories in the way. But she will have. She was well enough, when it was me in this swing, to have done this. And she would have wanted to punch this smug, happy-clappy mummy too.

She has stopped pushing, though, the other mother. She is telling her boy that it's time to go and he is throwing a hissy fit – Emily turning to look at his wailing, then beeping with pleasure as she starts going higher than before.

An older girl has climbed to the top of the witch's hat. 'Look at me, Mummy!' The woman below her pacing and fretting, wanting her to come down. Tiredness sludges through my arms. Oh, to just lie down, right here on the ground. The craving to do it is overwhelming. The ground – and Mum, her face smiling – beckoning me, saying it's okay. The little boy and his mummy are on their way now, him still bawling. Emily happily chatting away with her nonsense speak. Apart from the woman appealing to her daughter to come down from the witch's hat, would anyone else even notice? Just for half a minute, that's all.

'Get ready for some big ones, Em!'

It is so easy; the ground comes to me. Just half a minute. The swing will keep going for a while yet. The laughter and prattle of the playground sounds louder from the floor. 'Get down *now*, Gemma.' The creak of Emily's swing. Her little shoes racing against the sky. She hasn't noticed yet that Mummy is lying on the ground. No one has, it seems. What will they think, if they do? Maybe even now somebody is running over. They won't understand. They're too absorbed in the pantomime of their own devotion to judge this as anything other than an emergency. An unforgivable failure. But come on down, mummies. Come and join me. See how good it feels.

The air is buzzing. Even walking through back-of-house there is an early-morning crackle coming in from the kitchen that tells me this is going to be the kind of service that pumps life into your veins.

In the kitchen there is movement everywhere. Heat. A bright mad clash of smells: truffle, lardons, sofrito, blood.

'How are we looking?'

They lift their heads. Jonas raises his knife in salute. 'All good, Chef!'

Little candied fruits are arranged in concentric circles on the pastry stainless. Xavier picks one up, gives it to me. Papillae light up around my tongue as the intense flavour of the tiny sweet flows into my nerve fibres.

'You clever boy, Xav.'

He continues with his work. 'I know.'

A row of Sports Direct tankard mugs is waiting on the pass, a pint of coffee in each. Further along, the crates of meat, ready to be checked. Peter has been and gone too – a twinge of disappointment to have missed him moves through me – today's veg order propped against the plate hot cup-boards. At the top of a bag of carrots there is a large ginger root, its rhizome naturally shaped into a figure uncannily like a human body with arms and legs and, growing down from its middle, an enormous penis. Peter has drawn a face at the top of the root with a marker pen. The silly sod. Turtle has spotted me shaking my head, laughing to myself, and he comes over, curious, then cracks up when he sees the ginger man. He takes it away to show the others. He's different with me since my service fuck-up. Jack, too. Both of them more at ease with me now. Jokey. There is a small eruption of laughter over at garnish. They all want to touch the penis.

If these were my chefs, it could be like this all the time. Relaxed. Happy. As long as they worked hard. There would be no brigade, no hierarchy. Too small a team: just cooks, making lovely, unshowy food, the KP involved and properly paid too; front-of-house, all of them taking part, proud of what they are doing. At once, a convulsion of fear puts its hands around my bones and pulls me from the dream. But it is creeping in, the vision. With each update from Peter about the place on the green, and each furtive night at the laptop studying the deaths of other people's loved ones, it is taking form.

Anton is coming up to me. He has butchered the pig cheeks. 'How are these, Chef?'

Each cheek is perfectly trimmed, smooth, cleanly pared from the jawbone.

'Perfect, Anton. Wrap, label, store them in the walk-in.'

There is a box of aromatics to go through: alliums, hard herbs, spices. A couple of sixteen-kilo flour sacks for the dry store. All big orders this morning. The first office party is in tonight, although today's lunch looks quiet – Richard has taped the bookings sheet to the pass shelf – still the lull before the arseholed rampage of Christmas begins.

'Hey.' Sandy is at the pass. 'Coffee?'

'I'd love one, thank you, Sandy.'

She darts off – pausing to pluck a sliver of Ibérico from a side plate that the floor have stashed inside one of the gangway cupboards, then offering the plate to Musa in the plonge hatch, who says something to her that makes her laugh as he takes a piece – before she is away to the bar, singing to herself. Would Sandy come with me? She'd get paid less, but she might. She could run front-of-house. She'd be a natural. Who else? Anton. Freddy. Jack and Turtle, maybe. Musa. Isaac. Poor Frank; he'd hardly have anybody left to shout at.

In this moment, with the hustle of activity all around, it is not so difficult to imagine putting in an offer and making it real: the busy kitchen joining with a noisy restaurant, compact and full, spilling outside onto the pavement tables, Sandy floating around the space and Peter, behind the bar, joking with the regulars. The vision lingers again for a spell, broken eventually by Sandy returning with my coffee. A new life, pushing in.

1990

'He's fine, leave him.'

'He's not fine. Listen to him.'

The howling is getting louder, filling our room.

'It'll just confuse him if you go through.'

'He's confused now. He doesn't know where we are.'

'He'll get used to it. Emily did.'

Emily, who was nearly a year old before Patrick evicted her to the other room. Matthew's still too small to know that we are close by, that he is not alone. He doesn't even know that Emily's in there with him, somehow sleeping through the noise. She was never left to cry for as long as this. Patrick won't remember. He's forgotten all of that. He is pressing up behind me, his whisky breath hot and wet on the back of my neck, Matthew still howling. He starts kissing the top of my spine. His hand moving around me and onto my boob. He leaves it there. 'Is that okay?' Can he actually be asking if it feels good, his hand pressing against my gum-sore nipple, or does he just want permission?

'I'm not ready, Patrick.'

His hand, and the erection pushing at my bottom, stay in position, making his point for him: that it's me who is abnormal. What could be more natural than an erection? My own genitals are still trifle. The idea of anything going into them makes my thighs clench.

'It wasn't this long after Emily.' He was recording something accurately, then. 'But we can wait, if you want to,' he says, lightly kissing my ear, my hair, then pulling at my pyjama bottoms, ignoring his own words and moving on top of me. Matthew, finally, has gone quiet. The memory of that other time, the delicate web of stitches stretching, is bearing down on me. Past Patrick's deepened breathing my ears stay alert for any sound from the other room, and in my mind the baby is still here inside me, a fragile part of my being that Patrick, manoeuvring himself into position, is getting ready to pummel, to keep in there.

'I don't want to.'

He rolls away, sighing, and the wailing starts up again in the other room.

'Don't worry,' Patrick is saying, 'I'll bloody go.'

She is late. Fifteen minutes now. My bones are locked, waiting, all set here on the landing for the dull tinny rattle of the new key safe outside. A slow snoring is coming from the bedroom. Not like he knows or cares if she's punctual, or whether she stays as long as we are paying for. He won't even be expecting her. However many visits she makes, this woman appearing from the desert of his sleep will be new to him every time.

Do other people do this? Spend their half-day off spying on the care worker to make sure that their husband is being cared for properly? Probably not. Normal people – there it is finally, the scrabble and clunk of the key safe – are supposed to care for their own husbands. The door is opening. Time to move – quickly down to the floor where she cannot see me, on hands and knees, crawling softly away over the carpet into Emily's room, closing the door carefully shut. Anticipating the sound of her coming up the stairs. But for almost a minute there is nothing. She is still down there. The need to know what she is doing is too strong, my heart thumping at the risk of exposing myself – creeping back out of the room, towards the landing, the view of downstairs getting gradually bigger. And in the crowded reflection of the school photograph by the coat stand, there she is. Inside the snug. Sitting on the stool with the landline handset in her lap. She dials a number and puts it to her ear, listening. It's as much a surprise that it still works as the fact that she is using it. She is putting in another number. Listening again, then hanging up. She is moving now towards the stairs. For a second, in the hallway, she seems to be looking at the photograph – to have seen me – before my head disappears behind the landing and she starts coming up the stairs, four or five steps up by the time Emily's door is gently closed and my eye is ready at the keyhole. For a moment she is so close that there is only darkness.

'Coo-coo.'

She is going into our bedroom. My fingers are trembling on my watch button, the little beep of the timer starting so loud it feels that surely she will turn around and discover me. But she is at his bedside, her face moving close to his. She places a hand on his shoulder and lightly jiggles him. It is perversely thrilling, watching this. Twice a day, because of me, a woman comes into our house, to our bed. There is a splutter of breath. A frightened honk. 'There, there. There, there. Let's get you seen to.' She peels away the duvet. Although the smell doesn't reach me, the awareness of it makes me wince, but she doesn't bat an eyelid, she just carries on. 'Will we be having a wash today, Mr Kelly?' He is shaking his head, mumbling something, still flummoxed. 'No? You do not want to?' He keeps shaking his head. 'Shall we just get you dressed, then?'

He is turning away from her. 'We need to get you dressed, Mr Kelly,' she is saying. *We* – as if there are others gathered round the bed with her: the care manager, the occupational therapist, the care company shareholders, all of them needing him to do as he is told. Her hands are under both of his armpits, heaving him up to a seated position. She is stronger than me. He's gone limp, giving in to it. 'Very good. Well done.' She is unbuttoning his pyjamas. Pulling off the bottoms. What does she think of this old white man sat crumpled before her? Of our home, or the children on the walls who are not here looking after him? What does she think of me – leaving him to a stranger who will in a moment see him into the bathroom, then medicate him, before she moves on to the next house, and the next house, a Parcelforce of care? It is not her, however, who is keeping watch, judging another woman's actions – no different in truth to that other woman, Patrick's mother, nailed now to the wall in the bosom of her grandchildren. A woman who, it never occurred to me through all the years of hating her, behaved like she did because that was the only role anybody had given her, the only thing anybody, including me, could see her as: the harridan. For all her domineering, she was actually always the one without control – at the bidding of a man who never allowed her to work, or learn; two sons who never let her untie her apron strings. How simple it always was to think that she was the cruel one – to blame her, the mother – when it was Patrick, as much as his father, who never thought of her as a real person, let alone permitted her to be one.

It takes me by surprise still, being able to see her now, differently. Even if it does not, and will never, excuse what she did. What Patrick did. The pact they made that day and kept secret for so long.

Patrick is no longer fully in my sightline but there is enough of a view to see that he won't sit on the edge of the bed to let her dress him. My breath quickens against Emily's door, not so much in satisfaction at his resistance as excitement at what she will do about it. She waits. Patient, stroking his arm. 'What will she think, your wife, hmm? She will think I have not done my job.'

Now would be the moment to reveal myself: '*Ta-da!*'

He is giving in again. Slowly, she puts on his shirt. 'We can get your trousers on when you've been to the toilet and we've washed you, shall we?' And he gets off the bed, lets her support him out of the room, past my hiding place, to the bathroom.

Patrick's muffled shout, 'No!' carries across the landing.

When they return moments later he is fully undressed, obviously unwashed. She props him up in the bed and goes downstairs. A couple of minutes later she returns with a glass of water and a crustless sandwich. 'Here now.' He lifts his face and she sends the pills down his baggy white throat.

She is away down the stairs. Eighteen minutes. Pretty impressive, really. It would have taken me twice as long. He is sitting up, staring at the sandwich. He doesn't notice me coming out of Emily's room, moving past his doorway, onto the staircase.

She is on the landline again.

'Who are you calling?'

She sits upright at the sight of me in the hallway. 'I am calling the system.' She doesn't put the receiver down. There is something defiant in the way she looks away from me. 'I need to log out.' Something the care manager said comes back: electronic call monitoring, rota management, terms lost in the fog of unending jargon.

'You were only with him for eighteen minutes. And you were late.'

She puts the phone back on the wall. 'You have been here?'

'Yes.'

She nods slowly, twice, and gives a rueful smile. 'Of course. Everybody must keep watch on me.'

'He isn't getting the care that we're paying for.'

She stands up and steps out of the snug, forcing me to move aside. Unflustered, she walks to the hallway table and opens the care-book folder. She takes up the pen and begins to write in it. 'He is getting the care that I am paid for, Mrs Kelly.'

'You're supposed to wash him. He's not clean. His nails need cutting.'

'Nails is not in his care package.'

'I don't give a toss about his care package. They need cutting. And he should be washed every morning.'

She closes up the folder and looks at me, unflappably tolerant. 'If he refuses personal care, I cannot force him. I do the best I can.' She opens the front door, turning around to face me again. 'If you are in the house, Mrs Kelly, maybe you can wash him.'

Everybody is out in the garden. Sunny chatter carries down the thin, gravel path at the side of the house. People who know each other. Patrick rings the bell again. Still no one is coming. He moves to the gate in front of the path. 'Hello!' Leaning over it. 'Paul!' Over the roar of a motorbike zooming down the street, he calls again more loudly: 'Paul!'

'Why is Daddy shouting, Mummy?'

'He's letting our new neighbours know that we're here. So we can go to their barbecue.'

Emily goes to look through the gate. 'I don't want to.'

Matthew is wriggling in my arms. There's no sun at this side of the house and he is cold, probably hungry, too. The door opening. A man, red forehead, can of lager in his hand, Paul. 'Hi, gang.'

It is disturbingly intimate, walking through the house. Their shoes in the hallway. A battered, dog-hairy beanbag under the staircase. Smiling faces along the walls who will probably become our friends. The layout of the house is the mirror image of our own – showing up, with how full of the stuff of life it is here, how empty ours is still. Paul brings us through into the kitchen. Every surface is covered with drinks and plates of food. 'Put the bits and pieces you've brought in here if you can find a space,' he is telling Patrick. 'Then come outside and meet everyone.' He leads us into the sun-filled garden. People turn to look and smile at us. Emily's head is against my bottom, Matthew pressing into my chest, shielding me. A woman coming towards us. 'Oh, look! Hello, sweet pea.' Matthew twists away, her hands on him. 'How old is he?'

'He's one.'

'Coming up for two,' Patrick cuts in. If the woman detects the needle in it – his wish for me to have returned to teaching by now – she doesn't let on.

'Well,' she says, putting her face closer but moving her hands away, 'I think you're gorgeous.' Through her bright red slip dress the outline of her body is just about visible. Patrick, at least, appears to have noticed it.

'I'm four,' Emily calls out from behind me.

'Are you?' The woman kneels down, the crown of her blonde head ablaze with sunshine. 'And have you just moved into a new house?' She is speaking through my legs.

'Yes, I've got my own bedroom and Matthew isn't allowed in it.'

'Lucky you. And what's your name?'

'Emily.' Slowly, she creeps out from behind me to speak to the woman.

'Hello, Emily. I'm Julie. I'm your neighbour.'

'Which is your house?'

Julie springs up, suddenly animated, thrusting both arms into the air – she's Debbie McGee! – 'It's this one!'

We all look with her at the happy scene. Little groups of people chatting, a carnival of Bermuda shorts around the barbecue, the sun-blushed rooftops of an identical street beyond the bamboo screen. Paul gives Patrick a nudge, taking him off towards the barbecue men.

'How are you settling in?' Julie says.

'Really well, thanks. Everyone's been so welcoming.'

'It's that kind of street.' She turns again to look at the people enjoying her garden. 'All your neighbours are here.' Julie smiles.

By the barbecue, Patrick is rooting around in a cool box. He pulls out a can, then a bottle of wine. He says something to a man near him, who takes a bottle opener out of his pocket. They start talking while Patrick opens the wine bottle, then they both look over. Patrick points at me.

'How's this one sleeping?' Julie is looking at Matthew, then intently at me. After a couple of weeks of living next door to us, she probably knows the answer to that already.

'Good nights and bad nights. He's still getting used to the move.'

Patrick is walking back with Paul. 'Catford,' Patrick is saying.

'Oh, right. So, not far,' Paul replies. 'This is a much better area, though.'

'God, yes. It's like being in a different country over there.'

'You'll like it here, then. They don't call it a village for nothing.' Paul comes close to Julie, puts his arm around her waist as Patrick hands me a glass of wine.

Julie is doing her inquisitive face at us again. 'Paul tells me you teach together at Perrydale.'

'We do.' Patrick takes Matthew out of my arms. 'Well, we both will again from September, anyway.' He turns his attention to me, giving me a hard look while Matthew wrestles to be free of him. 'When she comes back to us.'

'It's a good school,' Julie says. 'My brother's son goes there.'

'Oh, yes?' Patrick wraps his arm around Matthew. 'What's his name?'

'Tom Banner.'

'Ah! Tom Banner.'

Tom Banner's little, sallow face is at once leering across the classroom at me, through the jellied curtains of his hair. Whoever the *us* is that wants me back in September, it's not Tom Banner. Matthew is squealing now, kicking his legs, but Patrick has angled his body to stop me taking him back. A girl, about Emily's age, is hovering nearby.

'Rebecca, darling,' Julie puts her hands on the girl's shoulders, 'this is Emily.'

Emily retreats behind my legs again. Rebecca walks round after her. 'Do you want to see my Troll Dolls?' Emily is weighing it up. 'Come on.' Rebecca takes Emily's hand. 'I'll show you.'

She leads Emily away, still holding her hand. No prizes for

whose daughter she is. Paul, seeing a new arrival, wanders off – 'Hola!' – and Julie blows a kiss at Matthew and goes with him.

Set down on the grass, Matthew is happier. The sticky, hot smell of the first meat drifts past us, sitting down with Matthew as people carry plates of chicken and sausages to the kitchen for the salads.

'Here's a thought,' Patrick says. 'Let's go on a proper holiday next summer. Somewhere hot.' He picks Matthew up and lies down on the grass, holding Matthew's body above his face. He swings him from side to side, making aeroplane noises. Matthew starts to giggle. His forehead is already turning pink; he should have suncream on. 'We won't have to tighten our belts as much next year,' Patrick is saying. Further down the lawn, Julie and another woman are looking over adoringly at Patrick and Matthew. 'When things are back to normal.' He plonks Matthew back on the grass and sits up. 'Love you, mate.' The surprise of him saying this to one of the children makes something release in me. The noise of people around us blurring. 'Right. What can I get you from the barbie?'

'Surprise me.'

He hobbles off, stiff from lying on the ground. At an upstairs window, Emily and Rebecca are sitting on the sill with their backs to the garden. Rebecca cupping Emily's ear and whispering something to her. As easy as that. A friendship made in minutes that might last for years, a lifetime. These are the friends she will make, here: girls like Rebecca, from houses like this. She'll never know anything different. But they've all gone now, for me, the girls of my childhood. Deb. Where is she now? All likelihood she's right where she was, working on the High Street, kids of her own, not much more than a half-hour walk from this garden and these people neither of us could've even imagined back then. Probably it should make me sad, thinking about her, but it doesn't. If anything, it's the opposite. People move apart, they get jobs, husbands, kids, they take different paths. Just that mine has took me somewhere better than before. A ginger cat has come over the bamboo screen. It parades across the lawn and is greeted by everyone it passes. Underneath the empty blue sky, the upstairs of our new house five roofs down from here is glowing in the sun. It looks solid, permanent. Patrick and his mother and the doctor can give whatever name they want to this last few years since Emily was born, but whatever it was – this, now, is what normal is going to be. And just like that – Emily and Rebecca waving out of the window at Patrick walking over the grass – it's clear as day that teaching is not going to be part of it. After four years away, there is nothing in me that wants to go back to the gossipy monotony of the school. That decaying staffroom. The same children in new disguises of braces and attitude and acne. Tom Banner. All of that is past now.

'Breast and sausage.' Patrick is grinning down at me, on his way to the kitchen with our plates. 'What more could we want for, eh?'

As he goes away to the salads his question stays with

me. He has made clear what he wants: for me to go back to teaching and contribute towards this big, new house, while Mary takes charge of the children. But right now, watching him talk to another man in the kitchen, a thought is budding: the possibility of evading this plan – and finding something new; something, whatever he and his parents might have to say about it, for me.

'It's not my place to put pressure on you, Anita. If we are doing it, mind, we need to move on it now, because it'll go. He told me this morning that the other party have put an offer in.'

A young family is coming out of the yard of the Christmas tree market. Peter's eyes instinctually moving to the two little children, one at either end of the trussed tree, carrying it slowly away, their faces as serious as pallbearers.

'I'm sorry, Peter. It's not fair leaving you hanging all this time while I can't make a decision.'

He is taking hold of my forearm. We stop on the path. A couple of teenage girls come past, both automatically glancing across at us, probably intrigued by the sight of two people our age looking at each other so intensely.

'Listen. Nobody's going to hurry you into anything. Now that the bank are making positive noises, and with the money we've been quoted for selling up my end of things, we're in a decent position. There will be other places than this one, if you aren't ready yet.'

Will there? Maybe there will, although my end of the finances are only getting worse and the other obstacles are not going to change, not as long as Patrick is alive. But – the thought prowling in the corner of my mind – what right does Patrick have, the Patrick of old, the Patrick who controlled our money and our mortgage and who never told me the truth about that day, to deny me now? The parents have taken charge of the Christmas tree, leaving the park just ahead of us. The two children either side of the tree, supervising. He seemed hardly to register me this morning while he sat in the armchair gazing at me putting my shoes on and waving him goodbye. How quickly he is degenerating. With each week, each day, even, that passes, he is losing himself. As we walk out of the park, going past the family all pushing their tree together through the boot of their car, a cold sureness begins to energise me: that it is me who has to decide the future – mine, his – and deciding it is the right, the just thing to do. It is what he deserves.

Peter's eyes are still on the family.

'Walk with me to the bus stop, Peter?'

'No bother.'

'Will you have your girls down with you for Christmas, do you know?'

'No, no. They'll be up there, with their mam.'

An image of him alone in his flat, cooking himself a Christmas dinner, almost makes me blurt out an invitation to join us, but he is speaking again, asking me about Matthew, whether he has been in touch yet.

'Still no word, no – but Emily and Morgan have said they're going to stay on until New Year.'

'That's great.'

He goes quiet, thinking about something. Possibly, because of me reminding him, his own children. In the unusual silence between us, the sound of our feet on the pavement, a fear is accelerating: of him growing impatient with my stalling – and moving on, leaving me behind. His frustration is starting to show itself: at my changeable moods, at the presumption that it is only me who has a life at stake here. A want to give him something almost makes me break the silence; to give him a reassurance, a commitment. To tell him that we should put in an offer for the restaurant. Or, to give him something more: something still unspeakable between us.

'Right then,' he says as we arrive at the bus stop. He reaches out his hand and puts it on my arm. 'It's all going to work out, you know?'

And as he keeps his big, soily hand there, gently pressing at my flesh with his fingers, hope blooms in me, believing that he is right.

Patrick is still in the living room, in the armchair, awake.

'Hello. What are you watching?'

On the news they are talking about the vote in parliament. The government has lost it and they're in contempt for not coming clean about their legal advice on the deal, and now this lot of cherry-cheeks all waving their arms about and guffawing like end-of-night businessmen will get to have control if the deal is defeated. Does he understand any of it? He's hardly spoken about this whole sorry circus in almost a year now, since the second stroke, although he's probably sponged up more coverage, given that the TV is always on, than anybody else actually following it. He's smiling at the television, anyway, so something has tickled him.

'Is it funny?'

Stuck to the bottom of the screen, it only now catches my eye, is a photograph.

'What's this?'

It is a photo of the first television we bought for this house. There is a cartoon on its screen, the top of Emily's bunches in the foreground of the shot. It pulls away easily, leaving a knob of Blu Tack on the plastic. He is clucking behind me.

'What's going on, Patrick?'

He is trying to lift up his arm, shaking with rasping laughter. It's something to do with the photograph, clearly, so at least it's not a stroke. He is pointing a finger to the side of his chair. On the floor is another photo. Face down, Blu Tack on the back from where it must have been attached to the fabric. The photograph, on turning it around, is of him, still with most of his hair, asleep in this same armchair.

'Oh, I see. Aren't you clever?'

He is laughing louder now, wheezing rhythmically like a trampoline. It is a comeback to my photo of the toilet on the bathroom door. A nervousness briefly immobilises me – watching him there, so pleased with himself – that he has been capable of something so normal: a joke. His mind has been alive enough to plan it, to achieve it, and now to take pleasure in the result. He's not only recalled where all the photographs are kept, he's managed to get them out of the cabinet and gone through them, ransacked the years of memories, when yesterday he couldn't remember the word for curtain. How he has even managed to find the Blu Tack is a revelation.

'Are there more of these?'

He nods, looking at the television again.

'Where?'

He stares at me, confused.

'Where are the other ones, Patrick?'

He doesn't understand, doesn't seem to know what we were talking about.

'Don't worry. I'm going to get you a glass of water now.'

Could the care worker have helped him do this? She wouldn't have had the time, surely, and the joke is definitely his. Silly, but something critical in it too – having a go at me for the bathroom photo. The kind of joke the old him would have made. And it is this, the sudden appearance of his former self, that is unnerving. The truth, pursuing me down the hallway, that it is simpler – coming home from meeting Peter, letting breed the black plot that is germinating upstairs – to believe that person has gone.

There is one on the fridge of a cow in a field. Another on the toaster, of his old car. Maybe his brain had run out of steam by the time he got to the kitchen. On the kettle, though, is his mother, drinking a cup of tea. The unexpected sight of her stops me dead. The thought tempts me, fetching his glass of water, to put her into the toaster. What did *he* feel, pulling out this photo? Love? A stab of conscience? Guilt? Or maybe he simply wanted to give me the willies.

He turns around straight away at my return to the living room. He has remembered.

'Yes – I've seen them all. You are a clever sausage, aren't you?' He looks exhausted. 'Come on. Let's get you upstairs.'

On the other side of the room by the cabinet, the photograph box is on the carpet. The lid is off, revealing the disordered mass of our past, taken out and stuffed back inside the burst box, like a glimpse inside his brain.

He is leaning heavily on me as we leave the room.

'Bloody hell, Patrick. How many of these are there?' Here now is me, sitting on these stairs with Emily chummily up against my side and a toddler Matthew on my lap. The day we moved into the house, in awe of the staircase. Together, we step over the photograph. Who is she, this woman? It is easy enough, convenient, to imagine that it is him who is a different person, robbed of himself, but isn't this young woman on the stairs with her children just as unrecognisable now? Or is she still somewhere here inside me? Does anybody, with the slow press of time, remain always the same person that they were?

He seems content, lying down on the bed, being tucked in. By my feet, at the side of the bed, the new commode is still untouched.

'I'm going to leave the photo on the bathroom door, Patrick. Even though of course you know where the toilet is.'

Another version of me is on the chest of drawers. In a

bikini, standing on one of the giant stones of a breakwater, a perfect blue sky behind me. The photo has been taken from below, making my legs look surprisingly long, my whole body shining with seawater.

'I'm going to let you rest for a bit. I'll just be downstairs.'

But the girl in the photo has enchanted me. It is difficult to stop looking at her: her confidence, smiling down from the huge sky, how happy she looks – and fleetingly it is possible to remember that moment on the beach, to share it with her; to believe that we are in fact the same person, joined, time-lessly, to the man who took the picture, this same man who is here now in bed, whose life – the judgement of what he deserves to happen to him – is in my hands.

This house is rotten with her. Even now that she's out of the room, checking on the roast, she is still everywhere. She's there in the prissy flowers and the daily-hoovered carpet. The expensive photoshoots on the mantelpiece that she made both families pose for. She's doubtless after a quiet word with Patrick now; he can't still be giving her a hand with the food.

Gordon is spouting on about politics again, this new Labour man who's got him so hot and bothered. Ruth catches my eye. Raises her eyebrows. Gordon doesn't notice. He's not talking to us, he's talking to David – who's not even looking at him, bored as all hell, his wine glass full again. The wives just sat here mute, both of us with an ear on the children off playing in the garden.

'He's gunning to be their leader, you mark my words, and then watch out. It'll be socialism with a shiny, new face.'

'He's not a real socialist, Gordon. He's against nationalisation, for one thing.'

Ruth has stopped him in in mid flow. He looks bamboozled. But he has listened to her, and he is waiting for her to say something else. The ambitious daughter-in-law, who he doesn't look down his nose at, the one who has not announced that she's about to chuck her career down the drain and start again from scratch.

'I'm going to check on the children.'

Gordon turns his face to me. He looks irritated, probably that Ruth knows more than him. 'Good idea,' he says. Maybe it's his age, or more likely mine, but the old coot definitely doesn't stare at my boobs as much these days. Small mercies.

The kitchen is empty. Cut vegetables float in the cold, still water of a line of pans. The Yorkshire pudding tray is ready on the counter, neat little turds of margarine in the middle of each trough. Margarine – really? The wrongness of it making me bend down for a sniff. Yes. Margarine. Through the window the children are log-roll-racing over Gordon's perfect grass. Emily, it must be Emily, has unwound the hosepipe and laid it out as a finish line, two of the stone goblins at either end. *She's got brains, this girl*, Gordon will no doubt tell us again at lunch. With that look that says, *Unlike her mother*. Emily is directing Anna and Ashley to lie down. Matthew, though, is not in the garden.

'Emily!' Em!' She doesn't hear me knocking on the window. 'Em – where's Matthew?' She still can't hear, too busy telling her cousins the rules of her game. He has probably gone inside for the toilet.

The downstairs toilet door is locked. 'Matthew, are you in there? Have you closed the metal thing?'

'Go way, Mummy.'

'Are you doing a poo?'

'Go way.'

'Do you need me to wipe your bottom?'

'No.'

'Okay. Can you let us know if you can't get out?'

'Yes.'

There are quiet voices upstairs. So, that's where they have gone to talk about me. She is saying something at length, and the sound of her voice draws me up the stairs – past the shut door of the bedroom and the secretive conversation inside, into the bathroom.

My wee pelts against the perfumed lavatory water for a long time. Probably a good idea to slow down on the wine. In the silence afterwards, it's Patrick whose words come through the thin partition wall.

'. . . bide my time. Things will look different by autumn term.' It is disorienting, hearing the soft dream of his voice like this, as if coming in here was to walk into his thoughts. 'I could be made head of department this time next year if I play my cards right. And then I'd be earning enough it wouldn't matter what she's doing. I just need to show willing. Put the hours in.'

'Which makes the timing of this whole cooking thing even worse.'

Patrick doesn't seem to respond. Maybe he's nodding. Or crying.

'It's what she wants to do, Mum.'

'And has she thought about you? The children? There's

nearly three years until Matthew starts school. Does she think that *I'm* going to keep looking after him all that time while she indulges this fantasy? They'll never see her, those children, the ungodly hours chefs work.'

For a while there is nothing. Flushing would alert them to my presence, so there's no choice but to sit here and listen, burning with the injustice of this – Mary complaining about looking after Matthew, and Patrick just sitting there agreeing with her – as if it wasn't their own campaign to try and make me go back to teaching and surrender Matthew to her.

There's a watercolour of a pastoral scene on the wall with the bedroom. Cows, a blue sky, two farmworkers in dungarees walking across a hay field with pitchforks over their shoulders. On the slim white shelf just underneath the picture she has positioned twin yellow loofahs against the field to look like hay bales. She's a humorous old thing, his mother.

'She's washed her hands of teaching for good, then, has she?' Again he doesn't speak. 'Does she know how lucky she was, to have been put in a school like that in the first place?' A school that is better than me, she means. A job that someone like me shouldn't have the right to reject. 'And to announce that she's turning her back on it after all this extra time you've had to support her. Really, Patrick.'

'She just wanted to be at home a bit longer, Mum.'

'Well, you know what I think. I don't see why baby blues should keep you from doing anything useful ad infinitum.'

What would they do if my face appeared at the door – striding in now, into that room the daughters-in-law have never entered – to shame them both? Shame Patrick, anyway. He would be mortified. Mary wouldn't. She would more likely take pleasure in knowing that her nasty words have cut me – that they are making me question whether actually they are right, that it is ungrateful and selfish to want this, to want anything, for myself. She probably knows already, in fact, exactly who is sitting listening on her khazi.

'And you don't mind, either, all those men she's going to be surrounded by?'

'It's what she's decided. What can I do?'

Nothing. You can do nothing, Patrick. Because even if it wasn't set in stone before, it is now.

One loofah, both loofahs, go into the toilet. A pee-soaking, a shake off, and back onto the shelf they go. A final firm flush of the toilet. To hell with the pair of them.

'Three minutes on table twelve! Anton – duck happy?'

'Duck happy, Chef.'

'Jonas – endives happy?'

'Yes, Chef, endives happy.'

'Sauce happy, Jack?'

'Sauce happy, Chef.'

Beyond the swirling yellow mist of the pass there comes a rumble of laughter and table-thumping from the restaurant. The big Christmas party up this end of the floor, sectioned off from the normal punters. Faces we will never see. The kitchen is perfectly quiet, working as one, no beginning or end of each other, just the wave of each dish coming together. The boys are no doubt loaded with painkillers or powder, coffee, or still shitfaced from last night, but they're on top of service. Sandy is coming to the pass. A film of sweat over her forehead, shining under the hot lamps, but she still looks lovely. She sticks her tongue out at Turtle working at the flat-top. Turtle, sweating too in his Santa hat, doesn't look so lovely. He sticks his tongue out back at her, and is still smiling after she's gone.

'Coming up on twelve!'

There is another rumble from the floor. Some hilarious

frivolity going on. Drunken moneymen loosening their belts after dessert, coming out of their shells. The landing cloth has a stain on it. The tape around its edge rips from the metal with a sound that is, for an instant, the undoing of a nappy. The thought of that, of Patrick, has to be banished immediately; it does not belong here. Anton is bringing the duck plates over, waiting for me to tape down the fresh cloth. He places the duck plates down beside it. The meat is pink, soft under my thumb.

'Soigné, Chef, well done.'

Jack is behind him with the sauce, wiping the pan bottom, stepping forward to place it on the landing cloth. The sauce coats a spoon, viscosity just right, pouring and moving slowly around the duck breasts as Jonas comes up with the endives and the fondants.

'Service!'

There is no other feeling like this. Knowing that everything is exactly under control, each one of us working in tune together, carried inside the wave. Most of the boys have been here for eighty hours already this week. They know the stink and laughter of each other, the movement of each other's bodies, better than they do their loved ones, if they have loved ones. All of us bled by now into the same being.

A diner has blundered down from the restaurant. He's cleared the steps, the floor staff, and is in the service gangway leaning over the pass, his fat drunk face breathing above the duck plates.

'Hello!' he shouts. 'Hello!'

'Excuse me, sir. Could you move back, please?'

He holds his palm up to me. 'Woah – cheer up, love. Just give me a minute.' He is looking at Anton, trying to get his attention. 'Hello!'

Karolina cannot get past him to the plates. Anton, unsmiling, comes up to the pass and the man puts his hand out for Anton to shake.

'Outstanding food, my man. Outstanding.'

'Don't thank me.' Anton gestures towards me, letting go of the man's hand. 'She's the boss.'

The man turns his head, confounded. A few seconds later he puts the hand out again, this time for me. It is moist and hot. Karolina reaches in for the plates and Richard arrives finally to shepherd the man away – his belly floating along the pass as the whole kitchen, in unison, gives him the finger.

Chef Terry continues his lap around the workbench, hands clasped behind his back, waiting for someone to answer. Everyone is staring at their fish. They are all thinking that it'll be me again. Chef Terry is waiting it out, though, giving them the chance to show that they were paying attention in the class this morning. On the other side of the workbench, Laurel puts his hand up. 'Yes – we do scale.'

'No, Laurel.' Chef Terry shakes his head. 'We do not scale our flounders.'

Everyone looks down at the ugly brown thing in front of them, its cartoon googly eyes, pleased that they won't have to scale it at least.

'What about plaice? Do we scale a plaice?'

Laurel and Hard-On, beside him, confer for a few seconds, but neither of them are risking this one. A few others have their hands up, though. He picks Kerry.

'Yes.'

'Very good, Kerry. Yes, we do.'

Kerry bows her head so that only the blue top of her cap is

showing. She's blushing. Backing up Laurel and Hard-On's theory once more that she won't last two minutes in a real kitchen because she couldn't say boo to a goose. Even though she has said boo to both of them already, directly enough that they've not tried it on with her since.

'Righto, chefs, let's process these flatties. I want four tidy fillets, speedy as you can.'

Straight away there begins the quiet clickety sound of fin-snipping. The perfect mechanics of twelve primeval creatures getting taken apart.

All the others are still on the fins as my knife sinks smoothly into the underbelly, a single motion carving open a gut flap just big enough to slide in a finger and hook out the gunk. A rinse under the tap and the rest of the fish's innards float away down the trough.

'We will be cooking with two of these fillets shortly. The other two are yours to take home. Flounders, you will notice, are small fish, which makes them more of a technical challenge, as well as being cheap. Two good reasons why we are using them today.' He is chuckling to himself, doing his lap, peeking in through each shoulder-gap to nod or point for something to be done different. 'And what should our fillets smell like, if the fish is fresh?'

'A walk on the beach, Chef.'

'A walk on the beach.' Chef Terry closes his eyes in happiness.

Laurel and Hard-On are smirking. Every week they're getting more blatant about taking the mick – wanting Terry to know that they think he's a failure, a never-was who has washed up teaching in a catering college, a cook. Because they are both going to be stars, of course. Hard-On, who has started to fillet his fish the wrong way round; Laurel, who's forgot to cut the pectoral fins off.

The fish lies on the board, camouflage side up. That's something to tell Emily tonight – how the top of them is the same colour as the seabed they skate over, she'll be interested in that. No chance in hell she'll eat one, mind. The two idiots opposite have realised that they're doing it wrong and are sneaking glances over at me doing it properly – sliding the blade gently from head to tail along the backbone, slow against the seam, feeling for the flicker of the knife over the bones until the flesh detaches from the frill, a clean, firm fillet, its muscle bands tight, smelling like whatever a walk on the beach smells like. Chef Terry has seen me holding it up to my nose and is coming over, all the others still busy with filleting while my hand itches to hold the knife again, to feel the control of my wrist, my fingers over it, the excitement of discovering my ability at this.

'Very good work.' Chef Terry points at my fish. 'This, people, is what your fillets should look like.' He walks on. Stopping round the other side of the workbench. 'Stroke, Laurel, don't force it. Stroke, stroke, stroke.' He moves on. Laurel and Hard-On start doing sex faces at me. Laurel closing his eyes and jerking his hand back and forth just above the bench, whispering, 'Stroke it, Anita. Stroke, stroke,

stroke.' When he opens his eyes, he sees me pick one of the mackerel pin bones from the last practical out of the trough, to hold up before him and delicately masturbate with my tweezers – Laurel's smile starting to give way as he slowly understands and Hard-On pisses himself next to him.

'That was so good.'

'It really was, Mum. Thank you.'

'Seriously. You should think about taking this up professionally.'

He is a sweetheart, Morgan. It was just a bloody turkey. After running a hundred-and-twenty-cover service without a 'contagiously ill' garnish chef for Christmas Eve lunch, cooking a Christmas dinner for three and a half people was hardly likely to get my Alan Whickers in a twist. He means it, though. He didn't go in for that third helping out of politeness.

'I'm afraid my treacle sponge is going to seem naff after that.'

Emily cuffs him on the arm with the back of her hand. 'Shut up, you. Mum doesn't care. And anyway, I've tasted it already and it's really nice.' They give each other a little look and a smile. They were definitely having sex last night. The murmur of Emily telling him to stop groaning the loudest giveaway, penetrating through the wall to Matthew's room. It will feel strange when they've gone back to Manchester, sleeping in her bed again, remembering Morgan's sex noises.

They might be trying for a baby. The new house, the wedding coming up, it would make sense. Emily does like her ducks in a row. And he is perfect for her: solid, sensible, kind – with his fond way of taking the mickey out of how stubborn she is.

'I heard from Matthew the other day.'

'Did you?'

Can she sense my need to know more? My shame, not wanting to admit that my only knowledge about the empty chair at the table is a text message: *Won't be able to make it for Christmas in the end, Mum, sorry. Things too busy. But I guess you will be too, anyway! I'll speak to you on the day.* A promise which, so far, he has not kept.

'He sounded well. This hotel job sounds like it's working out. He should have asked for some time off, though. I told him he's a selfish prick for not being here.'

'What's the name of the hotel again?'

'Something Spanish. La Tipuana, I think. Even if he'd just come for a day. It's not like it's that hard to get here from Barcelona.'

'I'm sure he tried.'

'Oh, yes. I'm sure he tried really hard, Mum.'

She goes quiet. She is not saying any more about him.

'Have you made any plans with Rebecca yet?'

'Just that we'll go for a drink tomorrow, probably head into Peckham. She said that Paul and Julie might pop over here at some point to say hello, before you go to work.'

'Oh. Great.'

What was it they said in the café a couple of months ago? *Do just let us know if we can be useful.* The thing people say when they have no intention of doing anything useful.

'I'm going to check on Dad. Do you want to get the dessert out now, Morgan?'

She goes through to the living room and Morgan is straight up on his feet, getting the dessert.

'I'll give you a hand, Morgan. Just with the bowls and spoons, don't worry. I won't interfere.'

He collects a pile of plates and dishes and walks ahead of me towards the kitchen. Through the door to the living room, Emily is taking off Patrick's cracker hat. She puts her hand on his for a moment then rearranges the blanket over his lap.

Morgan is at the fridge, taking out the treacle sponge.

'How's the restaurant?'

'Busy. As always.'

'Posh people can still afford to eat, then. That's a relief.'

'Isn't it just?'

He puts the sponge into the microwave. 'Is it open today?'

'No, no. Christmas Day is off limits. Frank, my head chef, would probably open if he could but he'd have a revolt on his hands.'

Morgan turns around from the microwave, quizzical. 'I thought you were the head chef.'

'Sous. I'm the right-hand woman. Why, is that what Emily has told you?'

'No, just the way she talks about your job, I've always assumed that you run the place.'

'I do, really. It's me organises the day-to-day, sorts out the problems. All the power, none of the glory.'

'You should open your own restaurant.'

Fortunately, he is pouring custard into a pan on the hob and cannot see whatever is betrayed by my face.

'One day, maybe.' The image of the place on the green flashes through my mind – the possibility of it once again alive after Peter's news that the buyers have backed out before completion. 'Come on, let's get that dessert out, Chef.'

Emily is sitting at the table again.

'He's fast asleep.'

Something is coming. It's there in her eyes. Something more about Matthew, perhaps: how he should be here now; how his anxiety shouldn't excuse everything he does, or doesn't do.

'I've been thinking,' she says. 'I want Dad to enjoy his life more, live it to the full.'

'Oh, right. What do you have in mind? A safari?'

She doesn't think that is funny. Morgan eats his pudding, saying nothing.

'There must be some things he would enjoy. All he does is sit in that chair, or in bed, waiting for some woman to come and feed and clean him. That can't be all he has to look forward to, surely? So, yes – travel, why not? Even if it was just going to the seaside for the day.'

'He's not able to go to the seaside, Em.'

Our spoons tonk on our bowls.

'You can't take the time off work, you mean.'

Morgan gives her a look. 'Emily.'

'No, you're right. I can't take the time off work. We need the money.'

'You have money!' She looks around her at the dining room.

'The house, you mean?'

'Yes, the house. Your savings. Dad's teachers' pension.'

Any urge of compassion that should now be stirring in me is defeated by a wish to show her how misguided her denial of the situation is making her. 'Our savings won't keep us for long, even though they are, with his pension, just over the assets threshold, which means we have to self-fund.' *My* savings too, that other detail that nobody else thinks is relevant. 'This is only going to get more expensive, you know. His care. Adapting the house.'

'Then sell the house. Move somewhere smaller. More suitable for him.'

Morgan has his arm on her forearm. 'It's probably not that simple, Em.' Nobody has complimented his nice pudding.

'It is that simple.'

'No, it isn't.' They are watching me, waiting for more. 'This is his house, legally. The deeds are under his name, our savings are under his name, everything is under his name and he never granted me power of attorney to make those decisions for him while he had the capacity to.' They will be able to hear the eagerness in my voice at speaking these words.

'You told me that he did.'

'That was welfare. He granted me that. But not property and finance.'

Her expression has lost all of its anger. Now she just looks hurt and confused. 'Why not?'

The real answer coils behind my tongue: because it was my stupid mistake ever to tell him about my restaurant dream.

'Because that was your dad's way.' Which is, of course, just as true.

Emily is silent. Maybe she is thinking about the time that he wouldn't let her take drama A level. Or, further back, the summer he didn't allow her to spend her pocket-money savings on a lava lamp. Whatever she is thinking, she has turned ashen and a need is rising in me to go to her, to comfort her – but Morgan is doing it, putting his arms around her – and instead more words are spilling from my mouth: 'Most of our bills come out of his personal account and if the bank find out he's lost mental capacity they could freeze it – and then I'd probably have to get a court order just to keep the payments coming out.'

She is crying. Morgan is holding her. These words were not meant as an attack, just to let her understand. There is more too that she could be told – that she should know: that me applying to be made his legal deputy, now, will be expensive and complicated; that he made me promise him, before any of this, never to do that to him, never to let him become a burden. And that what remains of our savings should be mine as well, for my own future.

'He does have mental capacity,' she says quietly. 'He does. I had a conversation with him this morning. He was telling me about when we bought the television.'

'He has his good days, yes. Sometimes he starts talking, out of nowhere, then the next minute he's gone again.'

There is no satisfaction in opening her eyes to this, as Peter put it, however much it needed to happen. She stays in Morgan's arms, on the other side of the table from me.

'The pudding was lovely, thank you, Morgan.'

'You're welcome. It's been a really—'

Patrick is in the doorway.

'Dad.'

He is wearing his presents. The scarf, the Velcro shoes. In the crook of his arm he is carrying the creepy synthetic, breathing puppy that Morgan got him.

'Woof!'

Morgan pulls out a chair for him and helps him to sit down. Patrick puts the dog down on the table in front of him.

'Would you like me to get you a whisky, Patrick?'

He looks up at me with open joyfulness. 'Oh.'

Emily is stroking the dog's head. 'Have you given him a name, Dad?'

He smiles, then lowers his head until his face is close to the table. He is showing us something. Morgan, then Emily, begin to laugh – realising, just before me, that he has covered his head with the new waterless shampoo. He wanted to amuse us, and he has. Emily is looking at me. It is not a challenge, though she is communicating the fact that he has proved me wrong. *He does have mental capacity*, she is saying. And no wish to correct her sparks up in me, placing his whisky in front of him like a reward, only happy relief that he has come and given her what she needed.

Everything in this room feels unfamiliar. The dark blocks of the furniture. The sinewy mattress. On the other side of the wall there is the sound of low voices. If they are having sex again, they are doing it quietly. More likely that they are cuddling – after how upset Emily was saying goodnight to her dad. His comic flashback this afternoon long since over-shadowed by the shrieking episode over the commode, and then not remembering who Morgan is.

My phone is lighting up on top of the bedside cabinet. A reply from Peter. The mattress whinges at the shifting of my weight towards it.

How is she now?

My fingers automatically begin typing a reply, then stop. It does not feel right. Here in Matthew's bed, with Emily on the other side of the wall. Why, though? Why should it feel so criminal just to send a text to Peter? To tell Emily about him, even? The timing would not be right. But the timing is never right. If she came home more often, so that every moment of her being here didn't have to feel so intense and we could just go for a walk together and talk about normal things, then maybe it would be possible to tell her. A man called Peter is my friend. Simple as that. Except, of course, it is not as simple as that. Because he is all the time becoming more than a friend; more, too, than Tristan ever became. Peter is steeped now into something else, something bigger, a part of me that Emily has never seen, the part that has wants, dreams, and the fear of having a real conversation with her is actually a fear that she will at once see through me and detect it.

The phone is lighting up again.

It is a photograph of Peter's Christmas lunch: a plastic ready-meal tray of three potatoes, three sprouts, three carrot batons and on top of the turkey slices a stuffing ball that looks drier than a pine cone. *Any time you fancy dinner at mine . . .*

My fingers are spontaneously typing back a message: *Mmm, tempting. Prison food.*

His reply coming through straight away: *Serves me bad for kneecapping those buyers before they were able to complete.*

One final message for him – *And for getting too carried away with your penis vegetables x* – before putting the phone back on the cabinet and finding the lamp switch. It takes my eyes a few seconds to adjust to the light. There is so little in this room. A few Blu Tack scabs on the walls, the windowsill bare, as if Matthew didn't want to leave any trace of himself. Alarm races through me – that it is not possible to remember exactly what he looks like. His face has gone. And there are no photographs of him in here, no school pictures, Polaroids, friends. Nothing in the bare, musty wardrobe. The cabinet. Each stiff tug of the cabinet drawers reveals nothing either. No photo albums, just a hoard of computer games and joysticks. In the bottom drawer, a collection of plastic spinning tops with weapon and monster designs on them – his Beyblades – and abruptly his face comes back: not an adult, but a child at the kitchen table, battling the Beyblades against each other; my chest convulsing at the suddenness of the memory, finding him.

Turned upside down, the Beyblades nestle against my side in the bed with their tips pointing up like shadowy teats. All is silent next door. Emily asleep now, with Morgan in her bed and her parents in separate rooms either side of her, one cuddling a fake, breathing dog, and me cuddling a plastic udder of weaponry, with my other hand over my mouth so that they will not hear the juddery heaving noise that is trying to escape my throat – woken from the cave inside me and calling to him still through the dark, screaming his name into the empty street, willing to give up my life only for him to be safe.

'Have you called her?'

'She'll be in the car, of course I've not called her.' Patrick is putting his shoes on. It has not even crossed his mind that he should be the one to wait for her and be late for work.

'Emily!' He shouts up to her again, 'Emily! Time to go. You need to get your shoes and coat on.'

'She was supposed to be here ten minutes ago. She knows I have to leave now too. Service starts in less than an hour.'

He can hear the blame in my voice. His mother, his responsibility. He carries on getting his things together – 'What the hell is she doing up there?' – all his annoyance focused on Emily.

'Look at me, Daddy!'

Matthew is at the top of the staircase. His shirt is undone and he has his hands down his pants, which have expanded with something he's put in them.

'Go and tell your sister it's time to go to Rebecca's.'

Matthew is investigating around his willy.

'Look, Daddy.'

He pulls out Jim. Round the other side he finds Rosie.

'Fine. I'll call Dad and ask him when she left.'

He pushes past me, going into the snug. Matthew is stepping slowly down the stairs, stretching out the elastic of his pants. He stops, standing directly above Patrick's head. 'Mummy, where's Duck?'

'Dad. Mum's on her way, isn't she? It's ten past four. She's supposed to be looking after Matthew this evening.' He is thrumming his fingers on the underneath of the stairs. 'Well where is she, then?' Above him, Matthew has found Duck. He is holding him aloft, his mouth wide with elation. His dad beneath his feet, grimacing. They've got no in-between, this line of men. 'She has to leave too, Dad.' The eldest member on the other end of the phone, no doubt scratching his head in befuddlement. 'Her restaurant placement, Dad.' He cannot say it – work – even to the muddled old man. 'Her cooking thing, yes.'

Emily is charging down the stairs. She's kicked her brother's toys away. Matthew immediately losing it, completely distraught.

'All right, Dad, I've got to go.' Matthew is slumped screaming against the banister. 'Emily, shoes on. Now.'

'I'm going to be late too, Patrick.'

He throws up his hands, exasperated.

'What can I do? The first parents are in at half four. I only came home to get changed and pick Emily up for her sleepover. I could have just stayed at school.'

They are getting their coats on. They both call a quick bye-bye to Matthew, and they are gone.

Matthew nearly falls over running down the stairs after them.

'Daddy! Daddy!'

He beats his fat fists against the door, not letting me hold him, his body rigid. He pushes me off. 'Not Mummy.' He collapses to the floor, writhing there, wailing. His wet pink chest is picking up all the dirt from the mat. He won't accept my comforting. He carries on flailing about and hits me in the face.

'Fine. You can stay there on the floor, then.'

In the kitchen, the clamour of his fists still beating on the door comes through from the hallway. It is my own hurt that's stopping me from going to him. There is a pause, then he starts again, beating on the door even louder. It is quarter past. Even if Mary arrives right now, and the bus comes straight away, there's no way now of being on time for the beginning of service – and Chef will be keeping a record, to pass on to college. Matthew has gone quiet. Guilt, intensifying, goads me eventually from the kitchen, back out into the hallway.

The front door is open, slightly ajar. A shard of clear blue sky is shining in the crack above it. Duck is there on the mat.

'Matthew!'

The door, swinging open, thumps against the hallway wall.

He isn't on the doorstep, the front path, the pavement. He is nowhere. Goose pimples ride up my arms. The houses across the street are drifting and his name will not come out of my mouth now, until shame – at not being able to shout it out here, for fear of what other people will think – fires me into action, running into the street, looking both ways and calling his name. There is no sign of him. My eyes close. He could be in the house still, hiding. After two deep breaths, my mind is working: taking me back to the door, shutting and locking it, sprinting to the pavement again. Patrick. He wanted his daddy. Would Matthew know where the car was parked? There is a space by the pavement where it had been. Where would he have gone from here? Down the pavement in the same direction Patrick has driven? Into the road? Cars are speeding down the street. A van. They keep coming, one after another, all of them driving too fast. The unbearable truth of what is about to appear further down the road is choking me: knowing that his body will be there, lying on the tarmac – his eyes closed and people running towards him and his naked chest broken and disfigured, not moving.

'Matthew!'

For as far as my eyes can see down the road, he is not there. My breath comes back in a coughing rush. He has to be in the house. He has to be. This is just making sure. My legs are not my own, speeding me untiring down the street – checking every gap between the parked cars, every front garden. At the end of the street he is not left or right. A new terror laying hold of me that he has been taken: a passing car, a man, a hand over his mouth. My vision is shrinking, becoming a tunnel, each piece of me working separately, my throat hoarse from shouting his name even though my ears are not able to hear it. He is in the house. He must be.

Further off, cars and buses are rushing both ways through the village. Lives continuing, uninterrupted. The unreal thought, going towards the village traffic, that mine is over. The last words he heard me say: *You can stay there on the floor, then.* A grey car is coming towards me. Mary. Seconds from now she is going to know. She will realise that he is gone and she will know that everything she and Gordon ever thought about me was right. But it's not her. Another car. Somebody else. They are slowing down, the driver already winding down the window. A woman's face, looking at me.

'Have you seen a little boy?'

She understands instantly, uniting us for a second in shared dread.

'How old is he?'

'Three.'

'Oh, God, no, I haven't. What does he—' She is speaking but every muscle in me is already moving for home, turning away from the woman, needing to be back there, to find him playing with his soft toys on the stairs.

The key is in the lock. He will be able to hear it.

'Matthew!'

There is no noise inside. Duck still on the mat.

'Matthew, please, where are you?'

The house is deathly quiet. The hallway, the living room, the kitchen – desperation soaring, certain now that he has gone. Rosie and Jim are where they were near the bottom of the stairs after Emily kicked them.

He is not in his room, not in any of the rooms upstairs.

None of these things up here – the toothbrushes on the bathroom sink, the washing basket full of people's clothes – make sense any more. They have no connection to anything real, because the house is not real. There is a ringing in my ears. It is like walking through a set: all of these things are props, or exhibits, a museum of another life. The ringing in my ears is increasing, confusing me, bringing me back to that other time when the world came loose and nothing was real any more, the policeman coming into the flat – *There's some bad news to tell you, I'm afraid* – putting the kettle on for him, watching him look out of the window at the world below the tower, everything floating, detached. It is the doorbell. That sound. The doorbell is ringing. Hope rages through me, making me almost tumble down the stairs to the front door, staring from the bottom steps as it opens.

'I got stuck in traffic.' She is taking off her coat. 'You can leave now.'

'Oh, Mary. He's gone. I can't find him, Mary.'

'Who's gone? What do you mean?'

My legs are caving. Her fingers bite into the tops of my arms, holding me up.

'What are you saying? Who's gone?'

'Matthew. He got out of the front door just after Patrick left for parents' evening. I can't find him.'

She is withdrawing her hands from me, stepping back.

'Have you called the police?'

'No. Not yet, no.'

'Have you called Patrick?'

'No.'

She is saying something under her breath, taking her coat back from the coat stand. 'Stay right here. Call the police, then call Patrick at school, then stay here in case he comes back. I'm going out to search for him.'

She is leaving. She's going out of the door and down the path and all of my hatred for her is at bay, watching her get into her car, overcome with relief that somebody else is in control. The noise of her car starting breaks the still, cold air. The car pulling out, driving away.

It is too hot in the snug. My veins are soupy with tiredness and it's hard to force myself to sit up straight. The phone is heavy and strange, the rubbery cord sticky against my neck and it doesn't make sense any more, this sticky, dangling thing, a cuttlefish against my ear. A woman asking me questions: *What is he wearing? Does he have shoes on?* The air around me is so thick. It feels like being underwater, every little movement an effort. An officer is being dispatched to the scene, she is saying, and then she is gone. A small noise from the kitchen, something in me surfacing, alert – but it is just the tap, a dribble of water from the tap. And now another woman – why are they all women? – is telling me that Patrick has started his parent consultations, is the call urgent? Yes, it is. She is waiting to hear what kind of urgent but that is not for her. She will give him the message without delay, she says, she will go herself.

By now, he could be anywhere. How long has it been? Does he have shoes on? Probably not. Socks? Maybe somebody has found him, wandering in the winter cold with his shirt open in the street, and has taken him in and is trying to piece together a three-year-old's understanding of where he lives, where home is. *You can stay there on the floor, then*. The phone is ringing. The sound of it is filling the snug.

'What's going on? I'm in the middle of a parent meeting.'

'Patrick, I'm sorry.'

'What's happened?'

'Matthew's gone.'

'What?'

'He undid the top lock somehow and got out and now I can't find him.'

There is nothing. Not even the sound of his breathing.

'Is Mum there?'

He has confused me. Is his mum here? The first thing he wants to know.

'She came. She's gone to look for him.'

'Good. How long has he been missing?'

He waits for me to figure it out by working backwards to my sulk in the kitchen when Mary still wasn't here and Matthew was jumping up at the door.

'Forty minutes.'

'Jesus Christ. You've called the police, obviously?'

'Yes.'

'Okay. I'm leaving right now. Stay where you are. Wait outside the front door in case he comes back and keep listening for the phone. You and your fucking chef fantasy.'

He has hung up. He doesn't need to hear me crying down

the phone. He needs to know that his mother has arrived and has taken charge.

The streetlights are coming on. Fewer cars coming past. A man is turning on to the street, walking down the pavement. He stops, too far down yet to see me. He's looking at something in his hands. A piece of paper. Now he is going through the gate to one of the houses down there. The cold has turned my legs and bottom numb. My coat is just there, in sight through the doorway behind me, but it feels shameful to get it and put it on. Does Emily know yet? Who will tell her? Paul and Julie? The awful thought coming into my head that Emily might think it is her fault, for kicking his toys down the stairs – but it isn't, she needs to be here before she can think that, for me to tell her that it is definitely not her fault, it is only mine.

My eyes have stopped flicking left and right along the street, fixed now only on the front path. Imagining him walking down it. Looking about for his daddy but not seeing him. Walking away down the street, the world so small to him, here and nursery and Granny and Grandpa's house and the car everywhere in between. In a few minutes he will have been missing for two hours. The police have not found him. Unless maybe they haven't brought him back here and instead they've taken him straight to the police station, or the hospital, and not told me. The possibility of it brightens. Why would they call? The priority is not me. That can come later. Headlights are turning on to the street. The police car again. It comes past and the policeman looks at me through the window, shaking his head. Patrick and Mary will still be searching elsewhere. They will have discussed their search strategy, their outrage at me. Maybe more officers have been sent to search for him now. Remembering the policeman's kindness when he got here gives my thoughts a brief place to rest. After the horror of opening the door, seeing his face there for the second or two before he spoke, waiting for him to say it. *There's some bad news to tell you, I'm afraid.* The pure relief when he didn't and instead started taking notes, asking for photographs, offering hope: 'Don't worry. We will find him.'

It is pitch black now and freezing. My bum and legs and feet solidifying into the cold stone of the step, my flesh and bones slowly disappearing, no longer in the real world of people coming home from work, going into their houses, making their dinners, the blue radiation of televisions through curtains. He has been lost for three and a half hours. Nobody comes outside at the sound of my lungs heaving, the dry scream of his name into the street. A three-year-old does not comprehend that he is loved. He knows that he is not part of me any more but that he is not on his own because he knows as well that my life is for keeping him safe and letting him grow in this space beside me, within my reach. The bare minimum – keeping him safe – and now he is not and even if he is found and he is alive, that understanding, its basic unconscious bond, will have been lost. Please let him not be harmed. Only that. Please let him be alive and untouched and everything else, my life, can go.

Time has stopped. There is no before or after, only the sensation of not existing any more – falling, weightless, through space. Images racing through my mind: a road sectioned off by police tape; blue tarpaulin; the steel bathtub on the riverbank. Shouting for her, not believing, needing to see. Everybody ushering me away.

But she is here, now. She is sitting with me on the step, waiting and watching, holding me.

Patrick. His car is turning on to the street, coming towards me through the dark. The police car is behind it. They are getting nearer, and Mary is in the passenger seat next to Patrick. Their faces are glazed, giving nothing away, but Mary is turning to watch me get up from the step and run down the path towards them – and Matthew is there, he is there in the back, in his child seat. The door won't open. The lock is on and Patrick isn't opening it, Matthew looking at me, saying something to me through the glass.

'Oh, my love, I'm sorry. I'm so sorry.'

Patrick is stepping out of the car and coming round to open Matthew's door. He is undoing his seatbelt, lifting him out. He holds him tightly, kisses the top of his head, carrying him towards the house, the policeman at my side now, taking my arm, supporting me down the path and talking to me: 'It was his grandmother who found him. She said he'd got half-way to your husband's school!' Which is meaningless because Matthew doesn't know where the school is but it doesn't matter, he is alive. He is looking at me over Patrick's shoulder. It is almost five hours since he went missing. They go into the house, Mary following just behind. Love balloons in my chest for her, overwhelming me, making me want to put my arms around her. Patrick puts Matthew down in the hallway. As Patrick stands up straight again he and Mary share an odd, cold look in the doorway, while Matthew picks up Duck from the mat and runs away up the stairs.

The words on the screen are beginning to fog. They make no sense, the language too coded, not about real people. *Prosecutors must apply the public interest factors set out in the Code for Crown Prosecutors and the factors set out in this policy in making their decisions.* How kind of them, the public, to take an interest in his death when nobody has taken an interest in his life during the five years since that first stroke on the ship, even during this terrible, plummeting year since the second one. *A prosecution is less likely to be required if: (1) The victim had reached a voluntary, clear, settled and informed decision . . .* As if there is anything clear about any of this. When was the last time Patrick reached a voluntary, clear, settled and informed decision to do anything? And if he no longer has the capacity to decide for himself, what about the him that was once there, the person who *had* made a clear decision – *I do not want to become a burden* – does he not count any more?

(2) The suspect was wholly motivated by compassion. Compassion. This document assumes that it is a simple thing, that it is absolute. What it does not explain here is that there is a difference between the kind of compassion that assists the end of their suffering, and the other kind that means not listening

to them ask you over and over for mercy, to help them do it an easier, gentler way, because you think that you can save them instead. But there is no punishment for that kind of compassion; not by the law, at least.

It is pointless reading this now, as seems to have become my habit, late at night after a slammed service. The letters, too – getting them out to match against these words on the screen, the six tests, when there is every chance, tired and shaky as this, of spilling something or falling asleep on top of them. But still the white blaze of the screen lures me in. *In the last decade there have been 152 cases referred to the CPS by the police that have been recorded as assisted suicide. Of these 152 cases, 104 were not proceeded with by the CPS and 29 cases were withdrawn by the police* ... It is time to sleep. The bookings sheet slammed again for both New Year's Day services tomorrow. A new care worker to try to prepare him for. It is impossible to stop, though. Page after page of faceless cases and legal itty-bitty, declaring labels for everything – *amateur assistance; manslaughter; murder* – as though each of these cases can be so simply defined as only one thing. What is the term for *not* assisting them, so that they have no choice but to take it in their own hands? *On the question of whether a person stood to gain (paragraph 43(6) see above).* It doesn't make sense. None of it makes sense. *The critical element is the motive behind the suspect's act. If it is shown that compassion was the only driving force behind his or her actions, the fact that the suspect may have gained some benefit will not usually be treated as a factor tending in favour of prosecution.* So they were all wholly motivated by compassion, these 133 Florence Nightingales? How many years – it doesn't say here – does it take of watching the person you knew die before your eyes while your own life runs away from you and your bank balance is sucked dry, for compassion to be considered the only motive? How can the benefit to your own life ever *not* confuse the whole thing?

1995

'Listen up. This evening's private function. We have thirty guests. They've got the whole of the McKenzie Suite. Most of them are hotel residents, Japanese, and their company wants to show them the best of British, which, when you've finished fiddling in your pockets checking if your dick is still there, Lewis, is what we do here. So, to run through what you are going to be putting up – all before service proper kicks in, remember: they will be eating a medley of British game birds. Platters all down one long table. Pheasant, grouse, partridge, woodcock, quail. A medieval bloody banquet. You are all going to go home tonight stinking like hell.'

He is inspecting up and down the line, his big head turning on its rubbery, white squid neck. If his own dick is still there, it's a fair bet he's the only one that knows it.

'Commis chefs.' My skin prickles. They are all about to get an eyeful, laugh at me again in the oversized whites. 'Each of you, our two new recruits included, are going to be involved, crate to plate. I want you to learn from this. So, you have each been assigned a different bird, and you will prep them from start to finish exactly as you were shown yesterday. I want everybody on fucking point for this. This function is a big deal for the hotel.' He is looking directly at me. 'I want service tonight to be as smooth as an otter's cunt.'

'Yes, Chef.'

The chant echoes about the stainless steel. And away we go.

The crates are stacked up in the cold room, feathers bulging from the slat gaps.

'Here.' Mark passes me down a crate. 'These are yours.'

Woodcocks. A dozen of them but the crate hardly weighs anything. They're all feathers. This isn't a meal; it's an exhibition. The soft, lifeless way the birds lie flumped up against each other makes me stop and gag before the cold-room door – their heads, their eyes pressed together like this – my mind moving to that image in the paper of all those bodies piled in the truck, the soldier standing smoking beside it with the haystack burning against the mountain behind him.

'Come on, then.' Mark is holding the door open. 'Let's get plucked.'

Lewis, my fellow newbie, is at the next section, in front of his crate of birds. He's got the grouse. He starts taking them out and lining them up along the top of the garde two-door until Farris goes over to him. 'No, mate. Just one to start with. You're going to show me the whole prep on it before you do the rest.' He picks up a bird and holds it aloft in front of Lewis. 'Tell me you know what bird it is.'

Lewis looks at the bird.

'Pheasant?'

'Grouse, dickhead. Start plucking.'

My hand fits snugly around the breast of the first wood-cock, laying it gently on its side next to the gnome of warm water. The feathers pull out easily. Working down one flank of the bird a patch of dark pink skin is gradually revealed. Mark checks in, not saying anything. More and more feathers are suspended in the water after each finger rinse. The bird's bared flesh rests against the steel as the other side strips away just as quickly, until all that is left is a punky ridge of feathers along the spine.

Mark is back again.

'That's good work.'

Foolish pride flaring, at this first opportunity to prove myself since my placement was made permanent. The other commis are not this far on with their birds. Farris is helping Lewis with his grouse, showing him how to do around the neck. Feathers are stuck to my hands, my forearms. Some have worked their way under the billowing sleeves of my whites. All around the kitchen, feathers are floating under the lights, yellow and red and different browns, like autumn leaves.

'Go on, then. You can start to gut it now.'

Mark stays to observe me opening the neck, then he moves off again. The jacket sleeves are getting in the way. They need rolling back. The small whites that Chef promised still haven't come in the laundry order, it appears. The first-day embarrassment of coming into the kitchen in this fancy-dress costume flashes hot across my brain: Chef's delight – *'It's*

Jimmy Krankie!' – and the rest of them pissing themselves, whether they'd understood his rubbish joke or not. My index finger slides into the bird's throat. There is not much to clear. Pulling out, my fingers are coated with a blackened, clumpy residue. Nothing identifiable. It wasn't eating before they shot it, then. What was it doing? Sleeping? Sitting on a nest? A half-remembered detail from college comes back – about woodcocks being night-feeders, and something about the flocks arriving from the east in winter by the light of a full moon, although probably that was just a Chef Terry fairy story. Three fingers fit neatly through the incision into the stomach cavity, just as Chef demonstrated yesterday, teasing out the intestines, then the liver, the kidney; back inside again to feel for the delicate membrane he described to us until my fingertips find it, stretched like bubble gum, and pop through it to extract the lungs and the heart on the other side.

A purple slurry of offal shines in a bowl next to the dead bird, ready for Mark to turn into a pâté. The heart lies on my palm, a tiny plump fruit. An impulse to hide it shudders through me. To not let them have it.

'Holy fuck!'

Everyone is going towards Lewis's workspace. From the opened throat of his grouse a moorland has bloomed: heather flowers, fern, bright red berries. Lewis is standing back from it, traumatised, as if he's just found the bird's rotting foetus. Farris stepping in front of him, nodding, mouthing something to the bird as he tugs out the flora. He shifts aside a little to allow me in next to him.

'Now, that,' Farris says, picking out the berries and offering them to me, putting them into the hand the heart is not in, 'is a beautiful, wild animal. All right, you lot – chop, chop. You've got a whole crate each to process before staff food.'

The woodcocks are up next. They nestle against each other, legs tucked, trimmed wing tips trussed to their sides and each of their long, elegant beaks – in perfect symmetry down the row – pierced into their own thighs.

The flesh colours quickly in the butter.

'Done.' Mark holds up the pan for me to tong a pair of birds into my drop-tray. Over by the ovens the pheasants are already out. The grouse going in. Further down the kitchen, an audience of naked quails is waiting, last in line. The whole kitchen stinks, ripe and weird as baby poo. Above us, residents are getting themselves ready for dinner, shaving their legs, doing their hair, having sex. A universe away from here, Patrick should be getting Matthew and Emily ready for bed. Both of them need a bath but he probably won't bother. It almost came out of my mouth this morning to remind him, before the instinct not to – the right to instruct him, in his eyes, given up by me taking this job, by my own failure even to keep them inside the house, safe, never mind clean. For a few seconds, as two more birds tense and fizz in the pan, the perpetual longing to go back to that day is taking hold, pulling me from the distraction of here once again into the house, to stand in the kitchen listening to his fists beat on the door but this time going to him, picking him up from the mat and holding him, locking the door. Mark is lifting the pan. A wave of heat washes over my face. Tongs, drop-tray, butter. Two more birds. The need to know myself capable is urging my hands, my mind on through these long, hard hours until the journey home and the final stillness of the bedroom, kneeling at Matthew's bedside, resting my head on the edge of his pillow and allowing myself to be comforted by the quiet rhythm of his breath, his chest, whispering into his dreams for forgiveness.

'Okay, all done. Into the oven.' Mark takes the drop-tray of steaming woodcocks from me. 'Six minutes, let's go. Chaud behind!' He moves quickly past the other chefs, Lewis lowering a steel basket of game chips into the fryer, a waiter appearing at the potwash porthole, scraping plates, going out of sight, then coming alongside the pass.

'Table twenty away.'

Chef slaps the pass steel. 'Away on twenty! Two beef Wellington. Fucking cunts.' He wanted the platters gone before any mains starting coming in for the restaurant, and the floor staff are clearly keeping their distance now that he's fuming at them for letting the early couple order straight away. Something is itching at my neck. Platters cover every section. All around, garnishes and sauces are being brought up — fondant, red cabbage, madeira and bread sauces — the pheasant platters now dressed with roast chestnuts and pickled brambles ready for the carcasses to sit amongst. Is this what it was for, giving up teaching? Being away from my children? To impress foreign businessmen with immaculately murdered wild birds? The itch, my fingers finding it now, is a feather. A little one, from a tummy, maybe. Hard to tell what bird it is from but it goes into my pocket together with the clingfilmed heart, to be buried in the garden tomorrow when they've all gone out of the house, deep enough that the ginger intruder next door can't get at them.

'Go on the toast.'

The toast. My job. Crate to plate, my arse.

The first layer of bread starts to yellow under the salamander. Maybe it's not in fact so different from my old life, this new one; it's still all about making other people continuous toast.

The roasted woodcocks are dripping on a rack. Mark spanks a couple of pans back onto the stove. The toast ready to flip. He drops a wedge of butter into the pan. It sizzles and foams as he pinches in the thyme, then the first two woodcocks to baste.

Chef comes over, watching me take the toast out and stack it into the silver breakfast racks. Mark is lining up the birds on chopping boards.

'Right.' Chef passes me a cleaver. 'The heads.'

This, then, is why he gave me the woodcocks. Why he didn't tell me until now that this part would be my job. It is a test.

'You want me to split them?'

'That's right. I want you to crack those birds' skulls open so thirty fat, Japanese fucks can teaspoon their brains out.'

'Yes, Chef.'

Mark, lining the first platter with ramekins of the pâté he has made from the organs, is not hiding his interest. The knife steady in my hand, its heel poised over the centre of the first bird's head. What do these men want to happen here? For me to break down and run crying from the kitchen? Parts of me are closing down, silenced, so that there is nothing but the task, the bird on the board. Refusing to be defeated.

There is a small quiet snap; the head parting precisely in half.

Chef turns his lips down in approval. 'Okay. Next one. Go.'

Some of the others have broken off what they are doing to watch this red-blooded tribal initiation ceremony, the heads cracking and dividing one at a time while Mark fans the tea-spoons around a saucer at the centre of the pyres of bodies, ready for businessmen to insert into the black voids of the birds' heads. Lewis, arranging his game chips onto a red cloth, has paused, transfixed, jealous. Watching me carry out my work, my face and my hands perfectly composed, while beneath the oversized whites my insides are pounding but a secret, quiet strength is passing into me from where the pock-eted heart is touching my stomach, next to the feather that will be Matthew's later, one for his collection – for him to hold and twirl and feel against his lips – the bird returned, by him, by us together, to life.

'I've finished the potatoes, Chef.'

'Show me.'

He goes to fetch a double G N pan full of potato peel.

'Put it on the scale.'

He is watching the number settle on the screen but he doesn't know what it means, what it is supposed to be. He looks up, waiting for my verdict.

'It's too high. You're being heavy-handed with the knife. Go and peel the next sack. I want it under 1.8 kilos. Seven per cent peel. Go.'

He lifts up the pan and goes away.

'And Dan . . .'

He turns around. Stands there with his massive pan of potato peel, all the boys' eyes on him, enjoying this. God knows what he must say about the Longwool, about me, when he's at the pub with his expensively groomed cyclist mates.

'Look at your apron.'

He looks at his apron.

'It looks like you've just buried a body.'

Jack and Turtle are smiling at each other. They want to

see him taken down, this tech twonk who thinks he can just walk into a kitchen and be a chef.

'Turtle, come and stand next to him.'

Side by side, they look like a washing powder advert.

'That is what your apron should look like, even after service. Use your rag, keep changing that. My first job was in a hotel where they fined you for not keeping your uniform clean. And the head chef here before Frank used to make anyone in filthy whites take their trousers off and cook in their pants.'

Xav is walking up to Dan. He tosses a crumpled ball of baking paper into the peel pan. 'He is the one who got fired for punching a diner?'

'That's him. Stewart.'

Dan is listening meekly to all this. Xav, still close to him, reaches to touch his beard. He pets it briefly. If Dan was asked to take his trousers off right now, he probably would.

'Go and put a clean apron on, then start peeling that other sack. The timer is going on – now.'

After service, going home, it will come for me. The second self that knows it is wrong to treat him like this. Telling myself that it's just the way it is – that he has to stand up for himself and earn their respect if he really does want to be here. Give him an easy ride and the boys would turn against me. He will likely be gone by the end of the month, anyway.

Here he comes. Clean apron. Lugging the next sack of potatoes towards his workbench, where Isaac has on the quiet left a better peeler waiting for him. The only person apart from Isaac who has so far treated him like an individual, actually talked with him, is Peter. When he came in earlier to deliver these sacks of potatoes he spoke with him easily, genuinely, the same as he does with all the boys – the two of them getting into a conversation about meat-free sausage rolls. Would Peter be surprised, disappointed, to see me behave like this? Even if he shrugged it off, said it was just the way of the world, it is hard to ignore the creeping unease that he might think less of me.

All around, the kitchen is in motion. The radio on low and the sticky kiss and thwack of the walk-in door opening and closing – Jack going in with the veal demi-glace he has just passed and reduced; Jonas coming out with a bath of iced water to crisp his veg – the sudden gorgeous smell of truffle that Turtle is grating for the Wellington's duxelle on the other side of the bench from Anton, who is trussing a sirloin, crossing and looping the string with swift, light fingers, as if he's doing a little girl's plait.

'Backs!'

Freddy scurries past Dan and his potatoes with a full used stockpot for the plonge, its hot cloud following him through the kitchen. Dan pauses after he has passed to wipe the lenses of his trendy, milk-bottle glasses with a cloth from his pocket. Then he's straight back to the peeling. There is something more determined about this one. He has stuck it out longer than the last bearded wonder – who has already gone back to his old life, according to Jonas, stalking him on the internet. Software engineering, or web design or whatever it is they do, these men. Lord only knows why they want to try at being chefs. Maybe their lives are that soft, sitting at their laptops surrounded by ping-pong tables and daylight, that they've decided they want to be abused. He is doing a better job of this sack. Handling the peeler deftly, his action faster. That Cordon Bleu training was good for something, then, even if they didn't tell him he'd end up peeling spuds every morning when they took his twenty grand. That the artisanal small plates he thought he'd be creating would have to stay in his dreams while he started at the bottom, a commis, like everyone else.

Anton has finished trussing the sirloin and is cleaning up and slicing the chain he's taken off it. He drops the little meat morsels into a blistering pan, barely cooking them at all while he goes for a plate. A little bit of salt then he tips them onto the plate and starts walking from section to section handing them out to a rhythm of slapped backs and hums of pleasure. It might not be on purpose, he might simply have forgotten he existed, but he has not gone to Dan. As Anton comes up to me with the final piece, Dan turns to glance over and for a couple of seconds his face, pale and resigned through the kitchen smog, is Matthew's.

Dan brings up his pan of peel. He's done it nearly three minutes quicker than the first one. His hands and wrists, lifting the pan onto the scale, are covered in thin red cuts.

'1.76. That's more like it.'

A wish to praise him is stopped cold by Turtle and Jack rubbernecking over. Defying me to do it. It would be different if it was Frank. If Frank praised him they would be pissed off, and they'd be bastards to Dan afterwards, but they would accept it. Frank hasn't had to spend years winning their respect, proving that he is not soft-hearted, a mother. However ironic my own children might find that idea.

'Right. I have another job for you.'

He wipes his hands on his rag. 'Yes, Chef.'

'The two tubs of crabs that came in this morning – Jack will help you bring them in.'

Jack, overhearing, does not need instructing.

They carry the tubs from the walk-in and put them down on the fish-section stainless.

'You can go back to your prep, thank you, Jack.'

The crabs are dragging themselves in slow-motion around the inside of the tubs. For a few horrible seconds their scraping becomes the sound of Duncan's burglar boy, the blood in his organs thickening with cold, trying to haul himself to the freezer door. Dan observes first the numbed crabs then the tools in my hands: tongs, rolling pin, the pass docket spike. He comprehends.

'Watch me do the first one. You are going to do the rest. You're not a vegan, are you?' A few titters behind us.

'No,' he says and puts his hands behind his back, taking a deep breath.

'First, take the crab out with the tongs. It's moving slowly because it's been chilled, but still, tongs. Put it upside down on the board and use the tongs to pin it securely, then – you see this triangular flap: that's the apron. You tease the spike in, like this, and lift it up.' He flinches with the crab as it makes a spasm of movement, all of its legs unfurling and extending, like a Transformer. 'Now, quickly, push the spike into the nerve centre here – tap with the rolling pin – then to make sure, put the spike into its brain here, rolling pin, tap. Okay, lift the crab up for me.'

He holds the crab up. The legs droop limply. Juices are running down from its brain over Dan's trembling arm.

'Dead crab. Right, your turn.'

He has angled himself so that none of the others can see his face. They are all ogling him, remembering the time that they had to do this. He takes off his glasses, wipes them with his pocket cloth, bracing himself. The thought of Matthew comes again, disorienting me. He gives a little start at my hand on his arm, surprised at me leaning in, whispering to him: 'Are you okay?'

'Yes, Chef,' he says, picking up the tongs. 'Ready.'

1996

There is a comical look of concentration on him. His lips all squashy. Little grunts of frustration because he's not getting it right.

'Here, Matthew – like this.'

He studies me rubbing the flour and butter together, then copies me.

'There you go, that's it.' A small smile from him now. 'You should come and work with Mummy.'

He takes his claggy hand out of the bowl and scratches his head a minute, then puts it back in and carries on. 'Can I make people biscuits in your restaurant, Mummy?'

'Course you can. Our customers would love people biscuits.'

'How much money will they cost?'

'Oh, they'll be very expensive.'

He's nodding. He likes the sound of that. 'Emly's not going to work there too. She doesn't know how to make people biscuits.' His cooking stool wobbles a little under his feet as he stretches to help lift and pour the semolina into the bowl.

'Well, she can work front of house, maybe. Or in the hotel.' Which, rash as it probably is to map out their personalities already, does sound about right: Emily the bouncy one out there with the public; Matthew awkward and out of the way in the kitchen.

'Yes. Emly can stay here.'

His back is rubbing up and down against my stomach as we work the mixture into a dough. There's a clump of it in his hair. The heat and energy of him travels through my clothes, my skin, uniting us; his body something separate yet also inseparable, as if he has just climbed out of me.

His hands are on top of mine on the roller handles, flattening out the dough together. As we roll he looks up at the window and starts shaking his head, slowly and seriously. 'Daddy's broken the lawn rover.'

The back bit has come off the mower and a fountain of shaved grass is going up into the air. Patrick cuts the engine, cursing. A green cloud sinks over him. He looks at us through the window, shaking his fist and baring his teeth in a pretend snarl. Matthew is cackling. Green has settled on Patrick's hair, on his clothes. Specks of it start to float in front of the glass. From outside the dream of this moment an obligation to remember it, to keep it safe, is tapping at my skull.

There are only two people-cutters in the pastry box. One with legs, for men; one without legs, just a skirt, for women. Matthew won't let me cut the shapes. He pushes them into the dough, very carefully, swapping the cutter after each one.

Man, woman; man, woman; man, woman, until he has filled up the pastry sheet with faceless couples.

'Now cook them, Mummy.'

The people biscuits fit onto a single tray and go into the oven. 'What do you want to do now until they're ready to paint?'

'Help Daddy.'

Out of the window, Patrick is kneeling on the grass, his face up close to the lawn mower. He's got his screwdrivers out.

'No, let's leave Daddy.'

Matthew pouts, ready to complain, but my resolve to keep this time with him for myself is too strong. 'I know – would you like me to read you something?'

'Yes.'

'I'll go and get a book, then. Which one would you like?'

'*Matilda.*'

'All right. Wait a moment.'

On the carpet he climbs onto my lap to listen to me read. *'It's a funny thing about mothers and fathers . . .'*

He pores over the worn pages, knowing when it is time to turn them without being told because he has been read this story, like Emily was, so many times before. He's listening closely, though, focusing on each of the pictures as if they are new to him, and in the peaceful togetherness of our joined concentration everything feels so perfectly clear, here, now, our limbs twined in easy akimbo, that the thought of there being something broken between us seems far away. And even as the words of the story continue out of my mouth, something else is forming behind them: a need to be witnessed, doing this, being good at it. By who, though? By Patrick, if he walked in on us from the garden? By Mary? Evidence that we have this bond and Matthew is happy and normal and undamaged by me losing him into the dark when he was still so little. Matthew is tracing a line with his finger, quietly mouthing the words. It is not, however, by anybody else – the realisation comes to me with sudden simplicity – this need to be seen, to be acquitted; it is by myself.

'*Chatterbox*,' he is whispering, his mouth shaping the letters, then again: '*Chatterbox*' – perplexed or intrigued by the unusual word, which is in my mouth too now, our lips parting and touching at the same time, reading it together.

The sound of the front door opening. Footsteps in the hallway, running. Emily appears at the door, breathless.

'Hello, Mummy.' Rebecca is behind her.

'Everything all right, girls?'

'We've come back for my Polly dolls. Then we're going to Rebecca's.'

'Okay, just be very careful along the road, please.'

'We will.'

Rebecca gives a little wave. They turn and run up the stairs.

'Can we paint the people biscuits now, Mummy?'

'I don't think they'll be ready yet.' But he's getting up off my lap. On his way to the kitchen.

The biscuits haven't coloured and are soft to the touch.

'I want to paint them.'

The reply of *No, wait*, is on my lips – but for what? They are his biscuits. What does it matter if they're a bit of a mess? 'All right. Let's just put them by the window for a minute to cool down a bit.'

With some help he gets the food paint ready himself – mixing the different colours into the egg cups with the icing, then lining up the paintbrushes on the counter.

'Who are you going to do?'

'Me and Daddy. You can do Mummy and Emly.'

The biscuits are still too warm. The gooey liquid bleeds across the bodies as soon as it goes on them. But Matthew isn't put off: he is painting his own hair quite well, the same black mop of fringe – although he keeps going even when the hair is done, his lips squeezing together, until he's blacked out his whole head.

'Now Daddy.'

He repeats the process for Patrick.

'I need this one now.' He puts a brush into the cup of white paint, and splodges on what must be eyes. Then face-wide mouths. No noses.

'They're lovely, Matthew.' He oversees me finishing off his sister. She has a red dot for a mouth. A cascade of yellow hair. 'Who now?'

'Granny and Grandpa.'

'Good idea. You do Grandpa. I'll handle Granny.'

Mary takes shape nicely: all-black dress, white dots under

her ears, black lips. She goes onto the rack to wait for Grandpa, who is getting a wig, a big black one in memory of his former hair.

We paint Ruth, David, Anna and Ashley, and put them all on the rack. There are three naked bodies left.

'Who's left to do, Matthew?'

He considers it. 'No one.' If he was thinking about Eddie, he's decided against him. 'Can we sell them in your restaurant?'

'Yes. Chef will be over the moon.'

'Who's Chef?'

'My boss.'

'Can we make him?'

'Yes, if you like.'

He doesn't ask what he looks like. Or if it is a him. He gives him the same black hair and then, without being told what a chef wears, he does the body all in white. It runs off Chef's arms and legs until the skin shows underneath. Chef, accurately enough, isn't smiling either.

'Let's leave the last two for Emily to do when she gets back from Rebecca's.'

Matthew carries the rack slowly over to the windowsill. Outside, Patrick is unwinding the hosepipe. He spots Matthew through the window and comes over, puts his nose to the glass and looks through at the assorted lunatics of his family.

'They're really good,' he calls through. 'Is that one on the end me?'

Matthew is tickled pink. 'Yes!'

'And is that one you?' He's pointing at Chef.

'No. That's the man Mummy does working for.'

'Right. And these ones look like Uncle David's family.'

'Yes and that's Granny and Grandpa. And Emly.'

'Oh, right. Well, I can't wait to try them.' He licks his lips and goes back to the hosepipe. If he noticed the woman next to his daughter, he obviously didn't feel the need to say anything about her.

'Can I watch telly now, Mummy?'

'If you want to.'

He stands completely still for me to kneel in front of him and untie his apron strings.

'Good,' he says, and so lightly and casually that it is as if he does not realise he's doing it, he kisses me on the forehead, before he walks off towards the living room.

She is kind, this doctor. Unlike the last one, she is acknowledging that Patrick is actually in the room with us, making a point of directing her words to him as well as to me, even though it's plain enough that he's not fully here – his eyes on the sky above the window blind. Just the walk from the surgery car park has tired him out.

'So, the antihistamines are not proving effective for him, is that the case?'

'Not really, no. They did a bit at first, but now he's awake most of the night.'

'There's some day-night reversal, is there?'

'He's usually drowsy or asleep a lot of the daytime now, yes.'

'It's common for a person living with dementia to experience sleep disturbance, especially as the illness progresses. It can cause problems with their body clock, the sleep-wake cycle.'

Patrick, fittingly, seems to be falling asleep in the chair, his breath coming heavily, in time with the fake dog on his lap. They look, together, completely at peace. Both of them exist only now, in this room, history and the future just an empty space around them. But a remembered love is stirring in me, looking at him there. The judgement of today, that this deception is the right thing to be doing, confronted by a faithfulness to another age: the two of us truly together. For a few happy years, long ago, no one could touch us. Before his illness – and even before that, time, his selfishness, his lie – took it away.

'And what about his sleep hygiene?' the doctor is asking. 'Regular bedtimes, no tea or coffee in the evening, plenty of exercise and outside-time during the day?'

'All of that, yes.'

She is nodding thoughtfully. She does not know that until today he hasn't actually been outside for more than a few minutes since Emily took him for a Boxing Day walk in the Fields three weeks ago.

'Well, I'm wary of prescribing him a sleeping medication – Benzodiazepines, say – at this point, because they could increase the risk of him falling, or getting more confused, so what I'm going to do is recommend just a small supply, for now, for you to use as and when he most needs it over the next few weeks.' She is starting to type at her computer. 'And if the sleep problems persist, or get worse, come to see me again and we can think about a more prolonged course. Does that sound reasonable?'

And as the doctor smiles now at Patrick, the magnitude of what has just happened – the possible future that she does not know her action has opened up – makes me for a moment unable to reply. She is looking at me patiently.

'It does. Thank you.'

There are no empty containers in the kitchen cupboards.

Inside the fridge – a half-full jar of raspberry jam, which, opened, is blooming with mould. It will do. It is big enough. The action of spooning out the spoiled jam, turning on the tap and washing out the jar is so normal, so habitual, that none of this is registering yet.

He is fast asleep in his chair. The television garbling away. It is 10.20. Not, in truth, the most perfect sleep hygiene. An alien part of my brain is doing this. One disconnected from the part that, going up the stairs, is starting to feel nauseous, and has made the decision that Matthew's room is where they are going to be kept.

The pills pop out of the pack onto the carpet. These first ten, tinkling into the jar. As easy as that. Only when the jar is sealed and stashed behind the Beyblades in the bottom drawer of Matthew's bedside cabinet does my body shut itself down, remaining before the cabinet on hands and knees, unable to get back up.

1997

The kitchen waits in the dark. Even the KPs are not in yet. In fifteen minutes the whole place will be bright and banging, voices, hungover breath, coffee, everyone tearing into their prep lists while the hotel guests sleep on above us, dreaming about their dippy egg and soldiers. It is time to get changed – but, just for a few more seconds, it feels good here in the cool peace of the kitchen, the hum and gurgle of fridges, the blue glaze of the hot starters metal under the fly light. An unseen smile pulling at my lips. My section now, boys.

There is nobody on the floor either. The wood shines with wet patches where Maria has been over it with the mop. The chairs upside down on the tables; wine-bucket stands grouped in a corner in front of the decanter cabinet. She's given the bust of the bald bugger who built this hotel his weekly once-over and left him sweating in the middle of the bread trough, like a canoeist, for the floor staff to lift back onto the cabinet.

The door of the women's is propped open with a bucket. Inside, Maria is scrubbing at one of the sinks.

'Morning, Maria. Can I come in to change into my whites?'

She shakes her head. 'Not yet, sorry.'

'Can I use the disabled instead?'

'Is not ready. Use the chambermaid room.'

No use telling her it will take fifteen minutes to get up there and back and sous will do his nut at me being late. There is still nobody in the kitchen, though. Or the dry-store corridor – past the detergent kegs and towers of till rolls – the rest of the breakfast shift about to shamble in like always at two minutes to six. The light is off in the locker room. Inside, it stinks. Feet. Antiperspirant. It feels illicit, unbuttoning, taking off my shirt in here. Their space. There's no sign above the door, but they have claimed it. The diners' toilet for me and the waitresses. The mouths of most of the lockers hang open, some of the doors bent or missing, a pair of dirty trainers in one, energy drink bottles, talcum powder. Lewis |||| Abbo ++++ has been scratched into the metal. The talcum powder looks fairly new. A little puff of white smoke exhales with each tap, coating the red skin of my armpits. It will sweat into a paste by the end of breakfast, but it's better than nothing. The door is opening. Lewis. He sees me, in my bra, a tiny aggravated movement of his mouth. He doesn't apologise for walking in on me. He doesn't say anything – he is going straight to his locker, walking right past me hurriedly disappearing into my white jacket in a reflex of shame. The talcum cloud dances in his draught. He's thinking that he is the one who is owed an apology, for this trespass into his territory, into his fantasies – the bodies he dreams and wanks

over that don't look like this one he's just been made to witness: the thin lines of powder that have compacted in the
rucks of skin around my armpits; my chest, this place once
known by my still-asleep children. His back is turned. He is
close enough that his breath is audible inside the metal box
but he has decided to act as if there is nobody here; only the
apparition of a younger woman.

He leaves without a word. Through the corridor there is
the noise of them baying and whistling in the kitchen. Only a
few years ago, before Matthew, maybe, he would probably
have wanted to run his eyes over me. When did they decide?
When did they relegate me from a novelty to compete over
or threaten to somebody instead to erase? Anguish picking up
now – not at Lewis, childish little prick that he is – but at
myself, for automatically letting that just happen, for taking
part in it, a pact of invisibility.

The noise of them is louder at the entrance to the kitchen.
There is some commotion going on near the cold room. All
of the breakfast shift crowding around the pass, fidgeting and
laughing. Maybe they're torturing something – a whelk, a
crab – while Chef is in the office.

My section is clean. Abbo has left it spotless from last
night, ready for me. A strip of ticket roll is pinned under a
mug with today's lunch hot starters and a list of prep and
there is time now, before the breakfast rush, to get going on
the starters mise. My own section to organise and direct, even
if they have averted their eyes from me; perhaps, in fact, why
they have averted their eyes from me. Starting from fresh like

this it is possible to block out what has just happened and get into the rhythm of work, gathering, ordering, the radio going on over by where the others are still messing about at their game. Rachel is coming into the kitchen, carrying two iced pints of Coke on a bar tray through into the plonge. Both KPs stop what they are doing and thank her – Mauricio putting his palms together in prayer to her. She turns around and sees me.

'Oh, hi. I didn't know you were in. Do you want a drink?'

'I'd love a cup of tea, thanks.'

'No worries. I'll just fetch the butters and I'm right on it.' She sees the boisterous pack of chefs ahead of her. 'Oh, great, here we go.'

They are betting, or trading, Lewis collecting notes from a couple of the others. He catches sight of Rachel drawing near and for a second his smile falters, then everyone else notices her and they all burst out laughing. She's poking her head into the melee to see what it's all about. When she straightaway pulls back Lewis thrusts his face at her, windscreen-wiping his tongue over his bottom lip, before she escapes for the cold room.

There is another flurry of excitement when she comes out again with the tray full of butters and jams. A wolf whistle. Lewis is saying something to her, waving his fistful of notes in the air as she walks away. She rolls her eyes when she goes past me. Without looking back, she calls out, 'You can keep your dirty cash for yourself, mate.'

Curiosity, more than my prep list, tempts me over. They

don't see me approaching. Through a gap between the fat gammons of their shoulders a pile of DVDs is visible on the pass, glistening in the lights. The picture on the top one is hard to make sense of – a man's back? – and my first thought is that it's a bodybuilding video, but as they become aware of my presence and step away there is no stopping the small cry of shock leaving my mouth on realising that there is a woman underneath the man. There are other piles of DVDs lined up along the pass, most with fivers or tenners on top, and pro-truding from behind some of the notes are the legs and arms and inanimate faces of more women.

My face is hot with humiliation, turning to a fury that it is me, much to their obvious amusement, who is the one who feels ashamed.

'Too late, Chef.' Lewis is shrugging his shoulders at me. 'The good stuff's all gone.'

'How many are we talking?'

'Hundred and ten.'

'Fine. Bring it on.'

'All second seating, though. I saw the reservations sheet. It's all together – slammed at nine.'

'Twats,' Turtle says. It's not clear who he thinks the twats are, but a line of heads is bobbing in agreement down the table. It could be the diners – though more likely it's the receptionists. Still, they get called worse. Even, as is evident from some of the Sharpied graffiti on this clothless table, when they are being admired. Everyone carries on eating their fish fingers without chat, an atmosphere of wired energy building at this end of the dining room. Chefs, floor staff, readying themselves for service. When they get up from the table in a few minutes' time they will be hyper, blood sugar roiling after the Saturday staff meal. All the way down the table plates are still piled high with fish fingers, chips, beans, a ketchup bottle farting continuously, being passed around with the two big jugs of blackcurrant juice – a children's birthday party.

'Seen this?'

Jack is pulling up his sleeve. There's a recent, wet wound up the inside of his forearm.

'Fuck. What was it?' Turtle taking hold of Jack's hand, pulling the arm closer.

'Flat-top. Didn't know it was on.'

'Silly cunt.'

'Yeah, I know.'

Jonas moves a ketchup bottle and lays his own arm down on the table. 'I'll show you a real scar.'

For a few minutes there is a freak show of burns, lacerations, deformities, Turtle's partial fingertip amputation saved, as usual, until last. They are scanning across, not subtly, for the reactions of the waitresses. Xav calling over to Sandy to ask if she wants to touch his. None of them, of course, ask to see my scars. At the other end of the table, the bearded wonder, Dan, is sitting with the waiting staff, who are talking amongst themselves. He has made it to a month. His technical aptitude becoming more apparent each week, not only to me and Frank but to the boys, too, constantly taking the piss, threatened as they obviously are by his difference to them – the things he understands that they don't, his connection to the world outside the kitchen. He is talking to Richard now, clearly more at home with the floor and their conversations about politics and films, his cultural equals, even if Jimbo on the other side of him is presently arranging his fish fingers into a Jenga tower.

Frank arrives on the scene. He stands by the table, gives me a nod. 'This lot ready?'

'They are.' All of them looking at me now. 'Come on, boys. Jump to it.'

Frank picks up a chip from Jack's plate, eats it and walks off. As one, they get up to leave. The floor staff, a moment later, start to follow on. Outside the window, it is beginning to snow.

'You must have some war wounds too.' Sandy is still eating. She and Karolina beside her are the only ones left with me at the table.

'Twenty-five years' worth.'

Both waitresses make faces of astonishment – at me being that old? At anyone being that old? There is a moment of shyness. They don't know if they can ask me to show them.

'Do you want to see?'

They lean closer to look at the welts and lesions on both arms that have been there so long they've become unnoticeable to me. The two girls are looking at them intently, however. There are new injuries in with the old ones. The gash Patrick gave me during the bathroom fight a few months ago a hard ridge now, permanent.

'Do you want to see my favourite?'

Under the double-breasted flap of my jacket, one button down, the red weal of my first major, hospital-visit fuck-up. Karolina visibly recoils, Sandy asking, 'What happened?'

'Sous vide. It was when we first started using them and nobody had a clue how to operate the bloody things.'

Karolina is getting up from the table. Maybe it wasn't fair, showing them this, frightening them into the vulnerable truth of their own bodies. Snow is whirling at the window as Sandy stands up with me. She walks in front, carrying her plate to the plonge. There is ketchup on the floor in front of the passthrough and she arches her body over it to scrape her plate, half her meal uneaten, into the bin. When she's finished she turns around to go and join the other floor staff preparing the tables, then stops. She is waiting for me to finish scraping my plate.

'Look.' She lifts up her shirt – to reveal a long, straight scar up the side of her stomach. 'Beats any of theirs, doesn't it?' she says, smiling, tucking her shirt back in, going back to work.

1998

A small movement in the mirror gives her away. How long has she been standing there in the doorway, concealed by the din of the hairdryer, the steady lull of it against my head?

'Hello, Emily. What are you up to?'

She comes into the bedroom. In the hush of the switched-off hairdryer her feet pat on the carpet. She nestles into me, pressing her cheek against my warm shoulder. 'Mummy,' she says, then nothing else. Her question forgotten – or maybe it wasn't a question, something more basic: a statement, a claim.

'Is everything okay?'

'Yes.' Her cheek is still on my shoulder. She does this. She is more physically affectionate than the rest of us. Her skin, her face, the soft smell of her more familiar to me than any other person's. She lifts up her head. She is inspecting me. 'Mummy.' It is still Mummy, most of the time. When did Matthew, two and a half years younger than her, stop calling me that, reduce me to Mum? 'Why don't you have any hair on your face?'

'What do you mean, sweetie?'

'On your cheeks. And here.' She puts her finger to my top lip.

'Like your dad, you mean? Women don't have hair on their faces.'

'I do.'

'No you don't. Don't be silly.'

'I do. Look.' She is pointing at the downy hair that has been noticeable for a little while on her cheeks. Hair that Patrick first pointed out after she had gone to bed one night, disturbed at its appearance.

'That's nothing to worry about. All boys and girls your age have hair like that. It's normal.'

'Nobody else in my class does. They say I've got a beard. They call me Noel Edmonds.'

'Who says that?'

But she doesn't want to say any more. She is burrowing into me, letting me pull the dressing gown around her, wrapping her up, tightened by a livid desire to go into her classroom and cut the little bastards down to size. She has got distracted by my jewellery box on the dressing table. She wriggles out of the tent of my dressing gown to touch it, run her finger over its lid. She sits herself on my lap, her long lollopy legs bonking against my shins.

'Whoever says that to you is mean, Emily.' It is not enough. And it's not the point. 'They're wrong. You're just normal.' What would the men in the kitchen have to say about a girl's facial hair? Or a woman's? Didn't Laurel and

Hard-On make fun of someone at college – Kerry – for just that? *Shouldn't she have a net for that thing?*

'Look up at me, Em.' She twists around. 'In a couple of years everybody in your class is going to have hair growing in new places.'

'I know. It's called puberty.'

Someone has told her already, described it to her, before me.

'You never have to feel ashamed of your body. We've all got one.' The truth of these words feels convincing, observing her take them in, even as another part of me wants to warn her that she will, she will be made to feel ashamed of it, even though she should not have to. She is taking hold of the lapels of the dressing gown, pulling it open. My instinct, idiotically, to stop her, cover myself up. She hesitates, until she understands that she is being allowed and she opens it up. She examines the hair between my squished thighs, then lifts her hand towards my chest. It comes down, lightly, on my collarbone. With one fingertip she moves down, tracing the join of my breast to the sternum, following the fine lines of stretched skin to the top of the other breast.

'Is that uncomfortable, Mummy?'

'No, it's not uncomfortable.'

She comes inside the dressing gown again, wrapping it around her herself this time. The time will come, soon enough, when she won't do this. Already she is private about her body with her dad, and her brother. Who told her that this is how it should be? Her nakedness to be kept to herself, her room? It was not me – although she never heard me tell her any different, either, while Patrick, without having to say anything, closed the door on that easy naked time in her life. He is the one who has stepped away from her, disowning her body.

'Would you like to finish drying my hair for me?'

'Yes.'

She takes up the hairdryer and points it at my head. She is unsteady with it, hot bursts of air gusting at my neck and into the dressing gown.

'Here, Em, watch.'

Her rigid little fist relaxes inside my hand, letting me guide her, more slowly, until she is able to continue on her own, concentrating so hard that she doesn't notice the figure of her brother in the mirror, watching, his face looking like he wants to come into the room and be with us, but instead turning around, leaving.

Commuters are streaming past on both sides, irritated at having to go around me. A man tutting before he carries on up the steps, taking them two at a time. There is no reason to turn back – it would be madness to do that – would make me late, for one thing, behind for prep, not ready for service, chasing all day. There is simply not enough time, even after setting off early to avoid the care worker in the first place, but Peter's voicemail has bled me of the energy to move forward and what is instead sucking me backwards, home, is a compulsion to check on her. To know that she is not being unkind to him – alongside an angry, selfish need to make sure that we are getting what we have paid for. A big rucksack bangs against my shoulder. The man not apologising, not noticing. How long is it possible to stay here for, indecisive, between worlds? What about sitting down on the steps? Not making any decision at all. Just sitting here with my head resting against the wall to listen to his message again while the angry train-catchers hurry towards their heart attacks and the care worker gets on with her job undisturbed and Anton and Freddy bring things into order at work. A crazy thought, bunking off from all my responsibilities. It would not be allowed. Someone would come and put a stop to it.

But nobody is. Trousers and tights keep coming up and down the steps. Snow on their shoes. How long before somebody comes looking for me? Before they record me as missing? Low down here at a small child's level everything moves in a blur and my eyes, as if they have entered his three-year-old's vision, are gaping at the onslaught of legs coming past, the rush of cars on the road above my head; the terror of being lost.

Peter's voice brings me, my phone cold against my ear, back to the disappointment of his message: *Anita, can you give me a call? I'm afraid these new lot have put in an offer and it's been accepted. The agent called me first thing this morning to let me know. We delayed too long. I did keep telling you.*

On the third time of listening to his message, the recrimination in his voice is the only thing that my ear can pick out. *I did keep telling you.* A new whispering of anxiety planting me here on the steps a while longer with the forbidden thought that, now the restaurant is gone, Peter will be too.

She is upstairs already, seeing to him. As the front door shuts there is a bustle of movement up in the bedroom. Another unhinged thought: that here it is, all these years after his secretive dealings with other women – the moment of finally catching him in the act. A care worker is coming out – a new one – noticing me from the top of the stairs, scowling.

'You are the wife? They told me you will be at work.'

'I forgot some things that I need.'

She's too sharp for that. She is folding her arms. 'I have much work to do. The man is dirty. Everything needs changing.' She's not hiding what she thinks, then. The wife has left him here, alone and dirty, for another woman to deal with. There is a dull moan from the bedroom but she doesn't budge. Where is she from? Romania? Bulgaria? There is something about her eyes, her cheeks, that is like the waitress from Sofia who shook the restaurant up for a few months last year – a sudden panic coming over me that it is the same woman.

'You will get your things and go back to work, yes.'

It doesn't sound like a question. She has no patience for whatever is happening here. Why should she? This return home makes no sense to me now either. She thinks that the wife should be doing this. Attending to him. Keeping him clean. It is my duty. A yowl from the bedroom. We both start towards him, the woman turning quickly on the landing. Black, foreign words are tattooed on one of her ankles.

He is upright in the bed. His face and neck shining with moisture. She has already begun cleaning him. He looks dappily content. He's not aware of me by the door, as she gets straight back to work, adjusting the towel underneath him, starting to mop his chest with a flannel. Now he sees me. His face puzzled. Disappointed.

'I had to come back to get some things.'

He looks crestfallen. Maybe he was enjoying himself. A

young woman has arrived and started flannelling him but now, just as unexpectedly, here is the wife to put out any fantasy that might briefly have lit up in the dying matter of his brain. He is gazing at the top of the woman's head. In twenty minutes she will be gone. Unless she adds on the couple of minutes lost to my interruption. Why should she, though? Why make herself late for her next client, this woman who is paid the same as a KP to do the dirty work of a country that doesn't give a monkey's about her? She gives a quick, bitter look behind her. Why is the wife still here, she is thinking – this woman who came home unannounced to check up on me and does not look after her husband but will be inspecting her jewellery box when I have left? Inspecting as well to make sure that the jar in Matthew's bottom drawer has not been discovered. Although that thought is just for me.

'I should go. I'll be late.'

'You have these things you forgot?' she says, pulling down the covers to uncover his stomach.

'They're in the kitchen.'

'Ah. They are in the kitchen.'

She is gloating now. She is the one in the right. She peels away the covers and tells Patrick that she is about to clean his feet. 'They are unclean,' she is saying. She starts to swab the soles – something none of the others have ever done – and he breaks into a big silly grin at the sensation. He likes her. He's gone dippy for her, like a baby. Pity lunges in me. That this woman knows nothing of who he was, only what he has diminished to. This room and its stink of piss and chemicals. *I don't want this life.*

'I'll leave you to it. Thank you.'

In the kitchen, pretending to retrieve my things for a few humbling seconds, the pity that came on so strongly just now recedes, leaving behind the fixed presences of guilt, anticipation and – darkly appearing amongst their shadows – resentment. Upstairs, at the sound of my feet coming down the hallway, the woman gives a short fierce laugh, as though she can see and hear everything, knows every inch of my selfishness, knows very clearly who it really is that does not want this life.

1999

A perfumy smell. Maybe something they spray the tablecloths with. Or a hint of floor detergent. It could be one of the other diners, or the floor staff, but not our waitress – she's much too cool for a nasty perfume. She is at the bread station, scanning over her section, another waitress now coming towards her, a wink and a little smile between them. What you can't smell is the food; the kitchen buried away, out of sight. If it wasn't for the clockwise trail of floor staff through where the in and out doors must be, you wouldn't even know where it is. Patrick is taking the bubbles out of the bucket. He flannels the bottle down with a smooth, surprisingly sexy motion, the same way he does his chin after a shave. He tops us up and puts the bottle back. It sinks back into the ice as he raises his glass for us to clink again.

'Well done us.'

The bucket is still tottering in its stand. There is an old folded piece of paper under one of the legs: . . . *and aubergine stack* poking out, a dish they've still got on tonight's menu.

271

'I was thinking, you know, we should do something fancier for next year's.'

'What have you got in mind?'

'Don't know.' His face is about to make a joke. 'Dirty weekend?'

'Lucky kids. A holiday with Granny and Grandpa.'

He tilts his champagne flute at me. 'Oi. Be nice.'

It feels good, getting on like this. The mains still to come, dessert, maybe even a drink afterwards so that we get home later than he told Mary and catch her unawares, rattling on the sofa. Instantly, worry is pricking at me: has she remembered to put the landing light on for Matthew, and to leave his bedroom door open? Of course she has remembered; whether she's done it or not is the question. Our waitress is floating through the tables, seeing everything. She clocks that Patrick has topped our glasses up himself, sees the table next door aren't ready to order yet, that the old couple beyond them are still scratching at their puddings, and now she's coming towards her friend again, the two of them exchanging a couple of words at the edge of their territories. As they part, our waitress – blink and you'd miss it – gives the other a pinch on the bottom.

'Anyway, it's looking more likely I'm going to be made Head of Department, so I might be able to take you away somewhere properly fancy next time, make up for not being able to do it for our tenth a few years back. Paris, maybe. How about that?'

'The head been dropping hints again, has he?'

'Oh, he's always dropping bloody hints. I think it might come to something this time, though.'

Our waitress is disappearing behind the kitchen wall partition. Who – the question comes to me out of the blue – would pinch me on the bottom? The other chefs? Probably not. One or two of the floor staff, at a push – Rachel, maybe, but the floor and the kitchen don't mix, except sometimes to get drunk after service. It's hard to imagine making any real friends in that place. My choices have always taken me away from easy friendships: moving to a street, a school, posher than me; cheffing; Patrick. And all the friends from before – Deb, Chrissie – who hadn't already stepped away from me ignoring their pleas to stop reeling down the street and into strangers' parties, off my head after Mum died, have their own lives now. By twenty-one, twenty-two, however old this girl is, the few people in my life who weren't Patrick were all sat in a pub watching me get married to him. He is looking out eagerly across the restaurant towards the kitchen. He has taken me away from all that mess. He's let me turn into someone better – even if, sitting here now celebrating another year of proving ourselves normal, it is hard to know for sure that there isn't another person, hidden inside me, waiting for something more.

'Here they come, look.'

The waitress is walking towards us with our steaks.

'Medium fillet?'

Patrick raises a finger. 'Thank you very much.'

'And the medium-rare sirloin.'

She places my food on the table, holding my eye for a second, long enough that something is communicated between us. What does she see? Does she see herself, and where her own life might be headed, or is the future too distant, too unthinkable, to concern herself with it yet?

He tucks straight in. He's hungry; he won't have eaten since the school canteen. 'Not bad, eh?'

'It's good, yes.'

It's not good. The steaks have hardly been rested for any time at all. They sit on our plates in thin, pink puddles. Patrick's has had half a minute too long on the grill, not that he's noticed. It is their busiest stretch, the chefs in their cavern hard at it now, itching inside their costumes, the ticket machine gunning. Still, steak is one thing you'd expect them to get right, in a steak restaurant. The grill chef with his tongs and his greasy timer, turning, mapping the bleeding deck of meat laid out over the bars. So much about this place has been got wrong. Or made average, the same as everywhere else. The grey shirts of the floor staff. The pewter side-dish bowls and the stencilled cows on the reception walls.

'Do you know what I'd do, if this was my restaurant?'

He mops his meat juice with a chip. 'Go on.'

'I'd get rid of the crap music, for a start. No music at all. Tables closer together, but at different angles, none of these straight lines. This place is set up like a classroom. And I'd brighten it. Wall lamps. Why does it need to be so gloomy in here?'

He is nodding, chewing. 'Sounds good. What else?'

'No front-of-house uniform. The floor can wear what they want, but they'd get a bit of extra money every month to spend on their work clothes.' The ideas are running through my mind, crystal clear, exciting. 'And flowers. Fresh flowers, in simple vases. None of this orchid nonsense. And that wall there.' He turns around to inspect the wall behind him with its jauntily arranged black-and-whites of charismatic, ugly male chefs. 'That's getting knocked out, so we can see into the kitchen.'

'You never know. One day, maybe.' He looks out contemplatively, as if the thought of this is his original idea, one that hasn't occurred to me during all the thirteen-hour shifts, sending plates into the dark.

'Yes. It's what I want, one day.'

We eat our bland, wet steaks, thinking our thoughts about this.

'And what would it be called, this restaurant of yours?'

'I don't know. Brilliant Cow.'

He is putting his knife and fork together on his plate, frowning. The cogs turning. 'People might think it means you.'

'Bloody right they will.'

The same howl for the last ten minutes. It is clawing at the floorboards, but still no muscle in me will move. The longer the noise continues, the heavier my body is becoming, filling with the revived self-doubt of all those nights of letting the children, letting Matthew, cry himself out, the feeling returning now so intact that it is as if those nights never ended, the same desperate faith that this is the right thing to do rooting me to the spot, helpless, fighting the unnatural urge to howl back now through the ceiling in imitation.

He stops at the opening of the bedroom door – my face appearing – then he starts up again.

'It's okay, Patrick. Shush now. It's okay.'

He is reaching for something under the covers. The mound of his hand moving as it searches about, until eventually the top of the fake dog's head emerges at his side. He lifts it up – to throw at me. It doesn't reach the end of the bed. 'No!' He is shouting. 'No! No!' The same word, coming at me over and over, following me through the room, down the stairs – turning into the same long howl as before – and out of the front door.

It is freezing outside. A raw wind is blowing down the

street and my fingers have immediately gone red and stiff around the phone. At the end of the gravel paths between each house, the skeletons of the recent snow lie in the grass.

Please can you come?

A strange force is steering me, away, outside of myself – a memory coming back: fleeing the house, running, my vomit sliding down the side of a van, a tiny brown shrimp in it, and the lapping of water onto a shoreline, sand pushing softly up against the back of my head.

His text comes straight back: *Of course. Where?*

The right thing to do is to turn around and go home to drug and settle Patrick. The need to see Peter, though, to be free of the responsibility, will not let me go.

Can you come to me? The bowling green in the Fields?

My pulse has quickened, waiting for his reply.

I'll be with you in twenty minutes.

The florist's window is a drama of Valentine's bouquets. The busiest service of the year ahead tonight: the whole restaurant rearranged into lines of young couples silently comparing themselves to the couples next to them. Inside the café, a high-pitched scream of frothing milk makes my flesh contract. It is crowded in here. Pre-pickup mothers. Laptop workers. A little group of people standing waiting for their coffees. The girl behind the counter is signalling to me. 'What would you like?'

'Long black, please.'

She calls the order to the girl at the machine without turning around.

'What's your name?'

The question halts me. *Chef. Mum.* An impulse to tell her something made-up – Tracey, Tallulah, Twiggy, she doesn't know any different – does not reach my tongue.

'Anita.'

She writes the *A* in large red print on the side of an empty cup, a scarlet letter, before the squiggle of the rest. She passes it back to the other girl. The cup stands there on the worktop, embarrassingly conspicuous, and it feels acutely like everybody must be looking at it while the girl takes forever to pump the shot and tamp and slot the portafilter into the machine, before she picks up the cup and fills it with hot water, then carefully pours the shot over it. He probably does not even know that he has been left alone in the house, crying out to nobody.

'Anita!'

For a moment, as she slips the cardboard cardigan over the writing, it is somebody else's name. She is looking at me, smiling, holding out the coffee.

'Is this you?'

The Fields are littered with brown piles of snow, the relics of snowmen. My hand around the coffee cup is the only part of my body that is not cold. Everybody else has wrapped up warm, in scarves and gloves. With each step the house is becoming more distant – on to the river path now, the water very dark, the trees on both sides bristling in the wind, adrenalin carrying me ever faster away. The care worker will come soon. Will she know better than me how to deal with him? Will she understand exactly what is wrong and be able to calm him down? Beyond the trees there are children running about in the playground. A shaft of sunlight, through the trees on the other side of the river, shines on the dusty surface of the water, illuminating the floating leaves and rubbish. The wind is travelling in the direction of the current, miniature waves forming, pulling at the river's skin, urging it north towards the Thames, passing the towers where Mum started her walk from the flat that night, then moving through the creek where she had stopped days earlier to collect the round, heavy stones that she stitched into the pockets of her overcoat. My legs are moving still quicker, my mind letting the memory come: the image of her in my bed – *I just want something that will help me* – and remembering the policeman's face at the door, the blue tarpaulin shelter still up on the riverbank; the wide, steel bathtub underneath it that they put her into; remembering now as well shouting for her but not knowing if she was still in it and none of them letting me get close enough to look.

A clear, cold energy stops me in my tracks – a young woman behind almost walking into me, muttering her indignation. Patrick is in bed, still howling. He does not deserve to suffer like this. If he could see himself – what he is shrinking into – he would be appalled. There is no doubt, any more, that he would be. *I do not want this life.* The electric conviction flowing, as my legs start up without me towards where Peter will soon be, that it is the truth: whatever he does deserve, he does not deserve this; neither of us do.

'Can you just put your shoes on, Matthew?'

He doesn't stop whatever he's faffing about with on the hallway floor. A pack of cards that he keeps ordering and reordering.

'Matthew.' It's right there under the surface – my temper, out of control, and he knows it, he's waiting for it. 'You are going to be late for school. Put the cards down and get your shoes on.'

He stands up, lets the cards fall from his hands then just looks at them scattered there on the floor. 'I need to get something,' he says quickly and darts for the stairs.

'Oh, for crying out loud, Matthew.'

Emily is ready by the door. 'He doesn't want to go to school.'

'What do you mean?'

She is looking up the staircase. Under her school shirt, there is a small bulge where she's rolled up the waistband of her skirt. 'I don't really know.'

'Then why did you say it?'

'There's some mean boys in his class.'

'Is he being bullied?'

'I don't know. I don't go to school with him, do I?'

'But he's said something?'

'Not really. Little things sometimes. And just the way he is at the moment.' She keeps looking up the stairs towards his room. All of us are going to be late now. Still my first month in the new restaurant and this will be the second time already. How *is* he at the moment? Has he been behaving differently? He's seemed exactly the same to me. But Emily probably does know more – she sees more of him, understands his unpredictable moods better than me. The truth of it making the anger mount again, making me want for an instant to shout at her to roll her bloody skirt down. Matthew is coming back down the stairs.

'Are you ready to go now?'

'Yes.'

He starts putting on his shoes.

'Matthew, is everything okay at school at the moment?'

He is intent on his laces, doing them up with great deliberation, following Patrick's instructions in his head, maybe remembering as well his dad's words that a boy his age should be able to tie his own shoelaces, for God's sake.

'Is anybody being mean to you?'

Emily lets out a sigh. Annoyed that she's late for school, clearly, but there's judgement too: *That's* you dealing with it? *That's* your parenting? When Matthew at last gets up with his laces tied he won't look at me and he seems on the verge of tears. He stays very still by the door.

'Because if they are, you're going to have to stand up for yourself.'

My stomach knots, hearing myself speak these cold words to him.

Emily is shaking her head. 'Mum, can we go now?'

'You understand that, don't you, Matthew?'

He nods once and follows Emily out of the door. They walk side by side a short way ahead of me up the pavement. This clear view of the pair of them, here in front of me talking to each other, Matthew looking up at the side of his sister's face, is starting gradually to calm me: with the determination that even if it means working myself to the bone, it is still me, without Patrick's help, who is here for them. The quiet knowledge settling that this is what they need me for: to be always here following, at a remove, watching over them and keeping them safe, resisting the temptation to look back in search of any other of my own desires which lie behind in our shared wake – for fear of turning round again to discover that either of them, my children, has disappeared.

His fingers close slowly around the pen. He starts to copy out the *M*, my hand guiding his, although his grip is quite firm and steady today. It is my hand that is shaking.

'That's good, Patrick, well done.'

Together we have managed the *M* and the *A*. It does not matter if he can't finish it this morning. It is working well, this method, a few words each day – and he wants to do it, that much is clear. There's a stiff tenacity about him as he moves the pen, as if this is a coordination exercise that the occupational therapist has set for him.

'Shall we try *T*? Yes? That's it – an easy one, that. Let's do another next to it.'

Grotesque as the truth of what he is actually being made to do might be, this has become an enjoyable routine for him: me helping him for ten minutes or so with the magnetic vege- table garden that Emily sent, before turning the board around to use as a desk for the envelope.

If he did know what he was doing, he would be in agree- ment. He would. His old self would agree. *I do not want to become a burden.* And yet my hand will not stop shaking, as much now as it has all this past week doing Emily's envelope.

The concentration on his face, the tip of his tongue appearing between his lips, is making me doubt myself, watching the strength of his will to accomplish this task, to please me. But although he is still able to use his will, and still understand pleasure, he will only get worse from here – and he has already told me what he wants: that he needs me to help him. Faith speeds through my blood, into my arm, my hand – this is the right thing – trying desperately to ignore the whispering exhortation that the possibility of a future, of something better than this, is so close.

We have finished his first name. We can do the surname tomorrow, start the address the day after that. Whether it is the right hotel is another matter. La Tipuana. It will be hard to resist – later tonight, before continuing with my nightly study of death and the law – searching for Matthew again in the website photos. The busy restaurant shot with the glimpse inside the kitchen at the back of it; the *Where's Wally* street scene outside the front of the hotel. Maybe he is there, maybe he is not. Maybe he was there and has since left, moved on somewhere else, restive, fleeing endlessly from this house, still carrying with him all the rage towards his dad that he left with a year and a half ago.

But the letter will exist, either way. After it is sent it will land in this place, addressed to Matthew – evidence, the same as Emily's, whether he is there to read it or not.

The hall is bouncing. Excited anticipation. The gabble of parents. Next to us on our row there are two pairs of them jabbering at each other over the heads of their other children, sandwiched between, calm and smiling and dressed up smart. Matthew is slumped in the chair beside me, still in his school uniform. There is a brown streak down the front of one of his trouser legs, from yesterday. He doesn't want to be here; he wants to be alone in his room, playing his computer games, killing people. He keeps swinging his legs, kicking the chair of the dad in front. They're out in force this evening, the dads. The ones who didn't have to stay late at work for a departmental report-writing meeting.

'Please can you stop that, Matthew?' He stops, tilts his head back to glare upwards. The smooth pink fillet of his throat is lit up by the roof lighting.

'Why do we have to be here?' he moans, spinning his Beyblade in his palm and kicking his legs again. The dad shifts in his seat, disgruntled.

'Stop it, Matthew.'

Straight away he is crying. One of the mothers next to us watching, commenting to her husband.

'I want Dad.'

'Well, he hasn't come, has he?' He is still crying. Other people turning now to look. 'Let's just calm down. I'm sorry.'

He tenses up at my hand stroking his thigh, everybody no doubt able to see my guilt and embarrassment, if not the silent shame, like a continuous underground current, that it is not his fault he is like this. And if Patrick was here, he would be glaring at me too, like these other parents: my responsibility, my fault, still, for Matthew's behaviour.

'Look – it's about to start.'

Children are walking onto the stage from both sides. Loud applause. Emily is there. She seems relaxed. Serious. She looks so young, for once, taking her place in the second row, all the older ones lining up behind her. In the audience a few hands are waving – and there are smiles from some of the smaller children. Emily keeps looking straight ahead. She doesn't seek me out. She's focused on her teacher, who is stepping out in front of the choir with a gesture for them that the audience can't see, something funny and reassuring because they're all grinning now, even the older ones, the teacher's arms lifted, poised, total stillness.

My skin tingles at the lovely, bright peal of sound. Even Matthew bucks up, craning to see through the heads.

'Where's Em?'

'She's there at the front, look, in the middle.'

She has put her hair back since she left the house this

morning. It is shining a brilliant yellow under the lights. From this distance, her hot face given over to the song and the union of voices, she has become someone new.

The teacher-conductor is working hard, her ponytail swishing across her shoulders as she looks left, right, nodding and pointing at her choir. The faint steam of their breath rising into the stage lights.

Matthew has lost interest again, staring at his Beyblade. There is applause as the piece comes to an end. The next one beginning before it has died down. The melody is gradually recognisable as the tune that has been coming through the ceiling these past few weeks, the one Emily has a solo in. When did Patrick last come to one of these things? All through primary school her concerts and performances were too early in the day because he was teaching, and by now it has been too long assumed to be my responsibility, not his. He doesn't think about the cost to me of dropping a dinner shift. His meeting will probably have finished by now. He'll be out with his colleagues, one of his colleagues.

The choir quietens. The teacher raises both of her arms – from the back of the choir a long, buttery note of deeper voices swells up – and with a flick of one hand she directs the whole hall's attention to Emily.

Her voice carries above the bass, clean and beautiful, a part of her released. There are murmurs of appreciation around us. Matthew watching and listening avidly now, pulled from his funk by the call of his sister. Patrick does not know, right now, that she is doing this. He is not thinking about her. His attention is elsewhere, on someone else. Matthew's face turns around. He sees me crying and he frowns, confused. 'Mum?' He lets me take his hand between the seats, unaware that in the contentment of this moment my own mum is here with me too, with us, the three of us joined together watching and listening to Emily. She must be near the end of her solo, her voice gaining confidence, but anxiety is starting to thump in me, making it hard to breathe normally, willing her not to get it wrong. When the rest of the choir comes in, gathering her voice into the chorus, relief and thundering pride sweep me up inside the folds of the song, people in front of us standing to applaud – so many bottoms! – and when they sit down again Emily is smiling. She looks out, at her teacher, who must have given her a wink because Emily flushes with delight and in this moment it is clear to me that she is a separate person, this girl who was once a portion of me; her life now, unstoppably, her own.

His key in the door. An extra couple of seconds of waggling that means he's been drinking. He must hear the television on in the living room but he is going straight through to the kitchen. The rustle of the freezer drawer being wrenched open; a few seconds later, the tinkle of ice in his tumbler, then he is coming back through the hallway and is on his way upstairs. There is a quiet knocking up there and then his voice, Emily's voice too, through the floorboards, before he makes his way back down the stairs.

He comes into the living room.

'She says it went well.'

As if that covers it – all he needed to know.

'It did. She was amazing.'

He is behind the sofa. His hands, one of them cold from the whisky tumbler he has just put down on a bookshelf, inching cannily around the base of my neck. He has already moved on from thinking about Emily – his intentions written into the circling of his thumbs on my shoulders.

'You're back late.'

'We went to the pub afterwards. Didn't get finished until nearly eight.'

'Busy meeting, then.'

'It was.'

He has stopped fondling my neck. 'Shall we go upstairs?'

'I need to sleep. I'm knackered. We did eighty for lunch and I need to be in earlier than normal for prep tomorrow, after missing tonight.'

'I'm sure they coped.'

He's still there behind me, calculating whether it's worth the effort of coaxing me some more.

'She would have really liked you being there tonight.'

He gives a phlegmy snort. 'The meeting was important. I couldn't just drop it.'

'They couldn't have coped without you, then, your colleagues?'

'No, they couldn't.'

'Any in particular who would've missed you?'

He is silent.

'I'm going to bed,' he says eventually, leaving the room and closing the door behind him.

With the television off, there is only the distant swoosh of cars through the village. It is so many years now since teaching at that place, Lord knows how many turnovers of staff – but still it is hard not to try to catalogue them, the women. To guess. Whoever she is, though, if she does exist, it is not just her that has come between us. We are not joined together like we once were. Time has separated us, given us other demands, each one binding us tighter together while pulling us further apart.

It is starting to rain. The natter of it against the glass is soothing, making me sleepy. It doesn't feel that long ago, standing in that orange grove with the wasps droning around us, the only two people in the world. How long ago was that? More than thirteen years, it must be. The whole of Emily. The picture of her up there on the stage comes back to me, the sound of her singing flowing again through my brain, transporting me from here, from the chair, lifting me up momentarily to float inside her voice like in a cloud. Where did she come from, that girl? Not from us, it doesn't feel like. She has made herself. And she will remember this day. This staging post in her life, and who was there to watch it.

He has turned all the lights out. My legs are so tired they have become sides of beef, lumbering up the stairs, into the bedroom, the bed taking shape in the gloom. He's not in it.

On the landing, carefully, my ear presses against the black block of the bathroom door. There is a sound inside. The shaving light, through the crack of the door, is on. His breathing unmistakable now, thick, escalating, and another noise too: the quiet, fleshy flapping of his hand, speeding up – until a final sharp sigh and the plunk of the toilet water breaking, like a coin in a wishing well.

'Anita.'

He is on the pavement by the restaurant entrance.

'Peter?'

He takes a step away from the entrance, drawing me towards him, until we are close enough to touch.

'I – well, I just came to see you.'

The small space between us feels immediately charged, dangerous.

'I'm about to go on shift.'

'I know.'

Inside the glass front of the restaurant, Richard has seen us. He notices me glance at him and looks away.

'I need to go in.'

'Yes.' He puts his hand on my waist and a sudden memory of Tristan diffuses through my hips, my thighs.

'This isn't the right time, Peter.'

He gives a short, hard laugh. 'No time ever is, is it?'

'I don't know what you want.'

'No, Anita.' He takes his hand away. 'You've got it the wrong way round: I don't know what *you* want. I've really got no bloody idea.'

Richard is still there behind the glass, watching us.

'Peter, I have to—'

'I know, I know. It's not the right bleeding time.'

Richard has come closer to the glass to look, like me, at Peter walking away – disappearing into the pavement crowd, the sensation of his touch still kindling inside my skin.

Inside, the normality of the restaurant is helping to compose me – floor staff flitting about, Sandy changing the water in the vase of flowers on the bar – letting me shut away what has just happened and the knowledge that something irreversible has altered between us. Richard is busy for the moment at reception and my steps quicken towards the kitchen, past the bar where Barman Danny is banging out the kitchen coffees – the Sports Direct tankards queued up along his drip tray – a triple shot for the boys' first break of the day: coffee, smoke, piss. *Do they know what they're doing to their bodies?* Patrick asked me once. *They're young men*, my reply, *they don't think about their bodies.*

It is humid in the plonge. Isaac is sweating. He has scrubbed all of the deck oven trays already and is on with hosing down the stock bone roasting tin.

'Hello, Isaac.'

'Good morning.'

'Have you taken a break yet?'

'Soon.' He points to a dirty cup of tea on the passthrough, the teabag still in it. He stops the hose. His gaze resting on me.

'Are you okay, Lady Boss?'

'I am, thank you.' He must sense the jitteriness of my hand by the pile of oven trays but he is too kind to move his eyes to it. 'Go and take your break now, Isaac.'

'Yes,' he says, but goes back to finishing the tin.

The boys pause at me coming into the kitchen. They are all looking at me and a nervous tension kicks in my stomach at the sense that they have seen me outside with Peter.

'How are we looking? Everybody cleaned out their fridges?'

'Yes, Chef.'

'Good, because I'm coming to check them.'

Jack is watching me approach the garnish section, his coffee waiting for him on the pass until his fridge is given the all-clear.

Inside the cold chamber of the fridge my breath is speeding up. Here with nobody looking at me the encounter with Peter is set loose and replaying in my mind. The unexpected intensity of his words: *I don't know what you want.* Understanding that the truth of them has for so long been avoided, buried, that even to myself it is impossible to be sure whether the problem is me not knowing either, or me not being able to admit what my own wants are. The voices of the kitchen, all of them waiting for me to let them go on break, are distorting. Snatches of conversation filtering down: 'Hey, Fucknuts, your garlic's burning.' If Richard had not been watching us, what would have happened then? If Peter had stayed longer; if either of us had said something more? Jack has left a thin puddle of soapy water at the bottom of the fridge. A baby carrot is floating in the bubbles like a tiny, fat thigh. The sight of it, even though the rest of the fridge is clean enough, the shelves washed, everything labelled, is beginning to rankle me, filling me with irritation.

'Jack!'

The plastic grid of the runner gurgles with the slop of his soap water as he walks over then stays far enough back to let me reverse out of the fridge. Control, on standing up, returning to me.

'The bottom of your fridge is flooded.'

He stands there staring at me.

'Yes? No? Bollocks? Mop it up – now.'

'Yes, Chef.'

He goes to the plonge for the C-folds but my annoyance is still lurking, welling up, agitating me with the need to take it out on somebody.

But not Dan. It isn't a surprise, by now, to find the fish fridge immaculate. It barely even smells of fish. Freddy is right: he's different, this one. He wants it – and he's good, Freddy delegating ever more of his technical prep to him, while the other commis, Jack and Turtle, who've been here a year, are still picking herbs.

It is Turtle's fridge which is a hole. It doesn't look like he's cleaned it out since last night's service. Anton should have checked this, or done it himself. The shambles in here proof of just how hammered this section was last night. All those fuck-ups. The chateaubriand that came back, overcooked, its cooking temperature entered wrongly into the Micros. The ox cheek pithivier that collapsed when Karolina put it down in front of the diner. Frank's face, watching it come back to the pass – picking up the plate and carrying it through to the plonge to drop the whole thing into the bin.

'Turtle!'

He has already gone to the fire exit. The kitchen is deserted, even though there are sweating onions catching in a pan at garnish and Anton is obviously behind with meat prep – and my anger at their slackness is turning into a desire to scream at them, the nervous tension again in my stomach, moving me towards Jack's bucket and sponge where he's just left it in his section, then returning to Turtle's fridge to kneel down before it and pull out the tubs and trays, a strange energy pumping through my arms, working at the pink stain on the back wall of the fridge where a bag of mince has been resting against it. It fades with the first wipes of the sponge but it is deep set and won't come away fully. The scouring side of the sponge doesn't make a difference, my breath resounding inside the fridge now, working harder at the stain, needing it gone. The kitchen radio chimes with pips. Eleven o'clock. An hour to service. The care worker coming into the house. Keying in, going up the stairs. Waking him up and rolling him over, propping him with pillows, removing his bedclothes. Noticing that the gummy skin on his back is getting worse. The sore, rosy blotches up his spine. She will begin at his neck, dabbing, sponging his armpits, the small of his back, his buttocks and, if he will let her, the damp mess of his genitals. Please let her be kind. Gentle. There is enough of him left to feel the indignity of it all and it is not fair, my own quiet whimper echoing in my ears with the pointless scraping of the scourer, all of my anger dispelled and instead a sharp needle of guilt, damnation, accusing me with every swipe – that it is me, the end in my sights, that is not fair.

'Chef?'

Turtle's feet are behind me.

'Chef, you all right?'

What will he think at the sight of my face, the state it must be in?

'Turtle, this fridge is a shithole. Sort it out. Now.'

'Sorry, Chef.'

He stays where he is, awkwardly waiting behind me, not understanding why his boss still isn't getting out of his fridge.

It's only been three days since his promotion but Yann thinks he's a big man now, lording it at the pass, strutting about telling the CDPs even though he was one of us last week that our prep needs to be quicker, more precise; barging into garnish to take over Sam's capocollo prep then abandoning it for Sam to finish and wrap. From the bar the grumble of the coffee grinder is beckoning but Yann won't let us break yet. The floor staff, beyond the open border of the kitchen, are all hard at it buffing the glass walls of the restaurant, their shapely, unkitchenlike bottoms haloed by the bright sunshine streaming in above the other glittering skyscrapers of moneyland. My ravioli are almost ready. The pan water at temperature. My thumbs kneading out the last pockets of air, their twin brains working together to massage each skin of dough tightly around its filling – the steady pleasure of feeling the ravs come to completion, of creating something perfect, circulating through me.

Yann is by the pasta machine, having a go at Lucas. How effortlessly he has got into character, as if being sous is second nature to him. As if his own food, just by changing his job title, is not in fact shit. He couldn't create a dish like this – the ravs plumping up nicely now in the simmering water – not even in his head, but Il Maestro doesn't care about that, or that Yann's food is slapdash and salty and the Genovese sauce he made the same day Il Maestro called him into the office for a beer to tell him he was being promoted tasted like spoon wash. Or that he's been here at Lo Stambecco six months less than me. None of that matters, because he's fast and he'll work any hours with the coke zipping through his veins and nobody else to think about in his life except himself. The sauce is done. The ravs steaming in the sieve. Yann agitated at the pass, an hour to service, louring over at me.

'That starter ready for you to show me yet?'

'It is.'

'Bring it up, then. Come on.' He claps his hands twice quickly together.

Today's motivational quote is up on the pass, the Da Vinci one that Il Maestro goes potty for – blatantly why Yann's put it up, knowing he's coming in today – *Simplicity is the ultimate satisfaction*. Not that the quote seems to have motivated Yann's own cooking, if the lobster terrine with Cabras bottarga and clarified octopus milk on the lunch specials is anything to go by. He is studying my ravs, sniffing at the three warm parcels sat touching on the plate. He takes the little jug and pours on the sauce. Past his head the floor are putting out tablecloths and linen-wrapping the grissini. The

City's spires and rooftops, through the pristine window walls, glow in the gaps between the skyscrapers. Yann is cutting into one of the ravs with his fork. It comes gently apart. The pink threads of beef inside the sticky, dark peposo hold their shape as he pushes the fork in and brings it to his mouth. His face giving nothing away, chewing the soft purse of four-hour miniature stew, twiddling his fork.

'Not bad.' He keeps chewing. 'Needs more power, though, more precision, more seasoning. It's too homely.'

He walks off into the kitchen, leaving the plate on the pass. Too homely. 'One hour until service!' he shouts. 'Go! Go! Go!'

Sam, meeting my eye, is shaking his head. 'Fucking prick,' he whispers. After all that time spent on the ravioli dish, my mise is behind. There will be no coffee break now. It will be straight through from here until end of service. The mood in the kitchen is downbeat, nobody talking, no music – although on the other side of the pass some festivity has broken out on the floor. Happy greetings. Laughter. Il Maestro is here. He is striding from the lift, hugging and kissing the floor staff. As he moves through the restaurant he plucks a grissini bundle from a table, slides one out and takes a bite. He looks back over his shoulder and gives a cheeky wink at Federica, slapping his own hand, then leaves the bundle on another table.

Yann meets him at the pass. They shake hands under the hot lamps and Il Maestro leans into the kitchen. 'Buongiorno!'

'Buongiorno!' everybody shouts back, not a single Italian among us.

Il Maestro is looking at my dish, still on the pass. He does not sense me watching him, craving his acknowledgement, wanting him to realise that it was me who he should have promoted. He picks up Yann's fork and cuts a rav into four. He prods one of the pieces, swirls it in the sauce, eats it. His face lifts to the ceiling, his monstrous Adam's apple mounting inside his slack, tanned throat.

'Beautiful.' He looks at Yann. 'This is on today?'

'Yes. I wanted to come up with something standout for the specials.'

'Very good.' He shakes Yann's hand again. 'Very good, Yann.'

Xav is like a gremlin at work, here in his private corner of the kitchen: scuttling about and talking to himself, frowning, tapping his foot as he pours a three-litre of milk into a pan. Here at pastry the kitchen feels subtly different. The air less full, quieter. A place to hide. My eyes run over the docket on top of the steel without taking in the words and figures; my mind on Peter. The boys will not have noticed me arriving early each day this week, waiting outside the restaurant a short distance down the pavement from the entrance, trying not to work myself up over why he has not come again except for his delivery yesterday – which he kept short, steering clear of me to speak only to Frank – and why he hasn't met me at the park either since that charged moment on the pavement. The horrible, increasing possibility – *Can't meet tomorrow. Maybe next week* – that he doesn't want anything more to do with me.

It is time to get to work, to stop these thoughts. Everywhere there is activity, laughter, bodies moving about, water running. In the heart of the kitchen Freddy is opening an oven; seconds later a breath of heat is on my skin. The lulling vapours of Xav's milk coming to a boil are misting inside my brain, putting me into a trance powerful enough that it is possible, momentarily, to imagine that Matthew and Emily are about to appear before me in their brightly coloured aprons and clamber onto their cooking stools. The buzz of the hand mixer jolts me out of it – Xav whisking the blobby lavas of yolk in a big steel bowl, moving the beater hooks around and around until the egg starts to turn pale and ribbony. He is more obviously aware by now of me standing near him. There's the hint of a haughty flourish to his actions, in the way he breaks up the chocolate into a bain-marie, splashes orange blossom water into the milk.

'If you were putting an alcohol in, Xav – whisky, say, and maybe a strong measure – would you add that at this point?'

Xav shrugs his shoulders. 'Normally you boil off. It depends how sober you want the mousse.'

Anton has stepped out of the kitchen and left Turtle to man the meat section. Turtle, though, is showing Jack something on his phone, taking advantage of Anton's absence and my distraction. Dan walks past them, looks in at the phone, smiles and shakes his head.

Xav's nose twitches minutely while he stirs the yolks and the milk together. When he has finished he motions for me to move back as he lifts the bowl of melted chocolate to pour into the yolk-and-milk mixture.

'Would you use the same proportions if it was milk chocolate?'

'Milk chocolate?' He closes his eyes. 'I do not use milk chocolate.'

'But if you wanted a sweeter mousse, less bitter, you could use the same quantities?'

He is beating the separated egg white in another bowl. 'You could, yes.'

The egg white is starting to stiffen. A memory of Emily, screwing her eyes closed while Matthew, on his stool, turns the bowl upside down above her head, the white holding fast and both of them squealing in delight. What would they think of this plan that is becoming by the week more real? Will they ever understand, if they find out the truth, that it was what he himself had once asked for? Although Matthew, the dark thought comes, might already have imagined an end like this for him too. Xav begins folding the egg white into the chocolate mixture, his spoon twisting rhythmically at the end of his thin arm. This will be the moment to add the pills. Crushed to a fine white sand with a pestle and mortar, folded inside the sweet, alcoholic mousse, clingfilmed, to set in the fridge.

There is movement in there. Mattress springs. His feet dropping onto the floor – making me pull back from the door and turn towards the bathroom, an explanation already forming in my head: *Just going for a wee before I set off for work, Matthew. Your dad will be back in an hour, but there's pasta on the hob if you get hungry before he's home.* Please eat it. Please come out of your room. Just to show me your face, to let me see that you are okay. The bed springs tense again. Maybe he is laid out doing his homework, because there is no sound from the computer – the continuous grunts and yelps of dying Nazi soldiers that fill his room, his brain, from the moment he gets home from school until after my return from the restaurant late at night, too tired and cowardly to go in and tell him to go to sleep. It's just his age, Patrick says. *They're all like that. It's normal.* Is it, though? The question that never goes away. Is he normal?

My ear has gone dead against the wood. He'll come out eventually. To get the pasta, or expertly raid the fridge for something else. It is just us in the house; this door between us. Emily won't be back from Rebecca's for a while yet. Nothing abnormal about her. Unless revising with your friend counts as abnormal, as it would have to me at her age. Then again, at her age, normal was not having a mum any more and getting wrecked in strangers' houses and vomiting in their beds before passing out and being woken by a man's hand crawling up my leg. Emily, no question, is the most normal of all of us. Got lucky, maybe: dodged the bullet of whatever was wrong with Mum – and Matthew has been hit with it instead, right between the eyes, falling into a trench with one of his dead soldiers. A current of need slices through me. Wanting to touch him, to have him on my lap. Another mother would know how to talk to him. Would know, at least, what is wrong with him. Although, knowing what is wrong with him and when it began – and whose fault it was for losing him then – has never really been the difficulty. Doing something about it, breaking down this unspoken wall around him, has always been the difficulty. There is the sound of him getting back onto the bed. The familiar vision surfacing – as clear and real as the day itself, the goose pimples still riding up my arms – of his little pink body walking, lost and afraid, into the dark.

He could come to the restaurant with me this afternoon. Is that such a stupid idea? And immediately it's obvious that yes, it is. He would be terrified of the chefs. Like the time he came with Patrick and Emily and he refused to even go through the entrance to the kitchen, struck dumb by the threat of men. The question he'd asked me afterwards, before he went to bed: *How can you work in a place like that?* And for a moment, then, out of his own anxiety, he had looked at me openly and he was the only person who has ever properly understood what it's like, being the odd one out. My legs have gone weak. My body is not letting me up, forcing me instead to stay here on my knees, and pray, for him to be okay, for forgiveness. My lips touch the door. My mouth pressing against it.

'Matthew. I've made you some food, my love. I'm going to work now.'

His reply, when it comes – 'All right, Mum' – so simple and ordinary that there is nothing else to say.

He is huffing in annoyance. He will not permit me to do this for much longer.

'Just keep still.'

The clippers dig into the nail, hinge straining, but they won't bite shut. It's like a snail's shell.

'This is silly. Wait here a minute.'

Old habit, from when the children were little, keeping my knife wrap above the wardrobe. The weight of it in my hands is reassuringly familiar; capability, order, entering my fingers and travelling up my bloodstream.

He raises his mad eyebrows when he sees it. Draws a finger across his neck.

'If you don't keep still, yes.'

He watches me – unfolding the wrap on the bath mat, sliding the poultry shears from their pouch.

'Do not move a muscle.'

The big toe nail carves off in one easy, arcing slice. 'Now we're talking.'

It takes less than a minute to complete all of his toes, then his fingers, until the wreckage of his nails lies all over the bathroom floor. He uses the opportunity of me bending down again for the wrap to play-act sneaking away: turning his body a little and shuffling his feet. Increasingly, it is not easy, seeing him as docile, as guileless as this, to hold on to the fact of how cruel he became; to remember what he did.

'Stay put, you. I'm not done with you yet.'

He doesn't resist, he looks like he's even enjoying himself, as my forty-pound Japanese fish-bone tweezers set to work on his eyebrows. 'God knows what we'll find in here. And look at your ears, too.' A crust of dark brown wax is growing inside them both. It was the ears that the doctor seemed to notice first – her little joke, before she signed off the new pre-scription with the longer course of Benzodiazepines this time, about sleep hygiene being only one of a number of hygienes to keep on top of.

Eyebrows done, a quick scrape with the precision tongs in the first ear makes the wax start to flake up enough to be picked off. The care worker, even if she was contracted for ears and eyebrows, would not have been able to do this.

'Well done, Patrick, we're finished. Now it's sweetie time.'

He doesn't try to move. He seems calm, ready to accept today's first round of medication without fuss. If he detects the anxious note underneath my forced cheer, he gives no sign of it, opening his mouth to put out his tongue for the first pill, the Warfarin. A sip of water. Then the blood pres-sure one. 'Good, Patrick, well done.' The beta blocker. 'There we are. All done.' There is no rational need to conceal the blister pack, with its lone unopened plastic mound – it's not as if he will notice – but instinct nonetheless makes me slip the pack quickly into my pocket while he isn't looking. 'Back in a minute.'

Blood surges through my arms and into my hands, pulling open Matthew's bottom drawer. The stashed kit – the letters now in their envelopes, the jar – is all there, safely in position.

The pill bursts through the foil and spills onto the carpet, then goes into the jar with the others. The rising tide of pills getting closer, each day, to my Sharpie line.

2004

They are clambering over the seats for the stereo, eleven
backsides scrummaging like piglets for a teat. Frank takes his
hand off the steering wheel to block them off, telling them to
get back to their seats. Marcelo ignoring them, smoking out
of the passenger window. He's got the CDs in his door
pocket. He takes one out and twists round to hold it up in
front of them all. 'My choice it is, pussies.'

Dance music fills the minibus. We might as well be in the
kitchen. They're all moving back to their places, protesting
or getting their headphones out, or just staring at the early-
morning traffic. The commis boys on one side, CDPs on the
other – except, of course, for the new girl, who has somehow
ended up here at the back next to head chef Stewart. He is
amusing himself with something. Little sniffs of laughter. He
elbows my forearm and points at Max and Johnno in front of
us, who look like they are still sulking at not getting their CD
choice. 'Little babies,' he says, the most he's spoken since we
left the restaurant – pretty much the most he's spoken to me
this first three weeks in his kitchen. Stewart is old school, he's

made that clear enough. Only speaks to his sous, Frank, who speaks to me and the other CDPs, who speak to these meatballs in front — but the line is broken today because of the trip, and the need to say something in reply to him is making the music beat louder in my eardrums.

'What music do you listen to, Chef?'

He keeps looking out of the window. 'I don't listen to music,' he says.

The conversation, apparently, is at an end.

My thoughts wander back to this morning, the mess of leaving: Patrick giving out about the early start, even though he's known about this for a week. *Devon? Are you bloody joking? Do you know how much I've got on at the moment? I really needed to get in early today.* The usual argument — how important this new job at the Longwool is to me after the disappointment of Lo Stambecco and how little it seems to matter to him — averted, temporarily, by my sharp exit. The satisfaction of leaving while he was mid-lecture. Still, it will be late tonight when the minibus returns, so he won't have to worry about me finding out what time he gets home himself. Something in it for him too, then.

A couple of the boys have their heads against the windows, falling asleep. Is it possible to track when it turned this way: arguments, distrust, the need we once had for each other quietly fading away? Probably not. There was no single moment; just a slow retreat from the way we used to be. Outside, traffic swarms around us, the same sides of faces reappearing, disappearing as we stop-start towards the motorway, my own face coming to rest against the glass, a dull, throbbing sadness coming on, thinking about the loss of that short, happy time we gave each other.

No one except me has eaten any breakfast. They come out of the service-station toilets and all head straight for the burger outlet. A team of professional palates, on their way to visit a rare-breed farm, feeding themselves on packets of desinewed, antibiotic-infused meat. Even Chef Stewart has gone over with them. Although maybe that's just to get away from me.

Countryside rushes past the windows. Trees, fields, roads dark with hedgerows. Who lives out here? What is there for them to do? The air of the minibus stinks of burger farts. Chef is reading a book with an embossed tear of blood on the front. He reads books. Strange to think of him having any kind of life outside the kitchen. Although, to be fair, you could say the same about any of us. Maybe he would be surprised to know about me being a teacher, before, or that there are still books which that time opened my eyes to by the side of my bed. He has gone back to his unspeaking mode, pent-up, the opposite of Il Maestro. It dawns on me that he can't drive, which must be why he's back here with me: it would make him lose face to be up front in the passenger seat as Frank's sidekick, and he's obviously itching to get to the farm and take charge again.

*

Tristan is at the gate to greet us. He shakes Chef's hand. Then the rest of us, one by one. He leads us into the farmyard, telling us about his cows. He looks different here to when he's been in the restaurant. At ease. Native. Not that he is, obviously. He's too posh. A lifestyle farmer with cow shit on his Hunters. He wants us, all the same, to see that he's proper – the pliers and the syringe tucked into the pocket of his quilted body-warmer – but even city chefs who've never sucked in this much blue air before know that real farmers don't give their cows names. At the bottom of the yard there is an outbuilding with its shutters open. A pair of quadbikes inside it and a massive tractor parked in the entrance. A fair bet nobody here has ever seen one of those before. We stand gawping in front of it – a metal elephant. Tristan is grinning. 'Would any of you like to sit in it?'

He lets us climb one at a time like children to sit inside its cockpit and put our hands on the steering wheel. A few giggles below as they watch me step up into it last. It is clean inside. The dashboard is a bank of dials and switches and levers and behind it there is a plastic well that he's filled with the tiny, white skulls of field animals. He's seen me notice them and he's laughing. 'Bit disturbing, I know,' he calls up. 'It gets lonely out on the fields.'

'A few more of these little skulls for your collection today.' We look at each other over the heads of the boys, who haven't clocked what we're talking about. 'You'd have room in this compartment for most of them.' It's not much of a joke but Tristan's laughing, still looking at me. From up here the farmhouse is showing above the yard wall. It's ugly. New. He's probably built it himself. Two intermingled colours of brick, an orange one and a yellowy one, the visual effect of which is like a rash. There will be a wife inside it. Posh, ruddy children who he'll be teaching how to run the business with him one day, once they've finished school, university, Inter-railing.

He waits for me to come back down before he continues his tour.

'Right. Would you like to meet the girls?'

They're all stood there dumbfounded.

'You silly sods.' Some of them turn, surprised to hear me taking the piss. 'He means the cows.'

Everyone follows him through the sliding doors of the rare-breed barn. A security-code box is bolted onto the concrete wall outside. Tristan starts explaining that heifers are what he supplies the restaurant with. He doesn't finish them quickly, he says, he raises them in a stress-free environment. No one has anything funny to say about that. They're too respectful of him. Most of us have come from nothing, not like him, and his poshness is silencing. Everyone gathers around the first of his luxury cows lolling its glossy head over the top of a stall, and listens in. While he's talking, the cow starts licking on the metal bars of the stall gate.

'Fuck me,' Max says. 'It's got a tongue like you, Johnno.'

He's right – it is like Johnno's – a pink surfboard.

'Do you know why cows have tongues like that?'

Nobody knows why they have tongues like that.

'They use them to pull out the grass. They don't need to bite on it like sheep. Sheep have got tongues like me.'

He puts his tongue out. It is small and pale. Through the group of heads, it is me who he's showing it to. A farmer is sticking his tongue out at me. He draws it back in.

'Right.' He rubs his big hands together. 'Shall we go out onto the fields?'

The earth stretches out before us, soft and green. Max makes a dash for it. Johnno straight after him. They chase each other over the field, everyone else turning to Tristan, wondering if this is allowed, but Tristan is smiling – and at once we are all at it, even Chef Stewart, running across the damp grass, some unseen force taking us outside ourselves and carrying us all away together over the open land towards the calm faces of the hills on the horizon. Johnno has caught up with Max. He leaps at him and they both vanish into a hollow. Their happy shouts ring out across the grass: 'Fuck off, you penis!'

When the rest of us get to the hollow, out of breath, dizzy, the two boys are lying side by side, gazing up at the galaxy. We line up around the rim, looking down at them.

'You pair of wallies,' Frank says, and jumps in. Whooping and hollering, they all jump in after him, until the hollow is full of chefs, giddily writhing about like children in a ball pit. Only me, Chef and Tristan remain standing above them. They so little expect any of us to go in too that there is an explosion of surprised laughter when my bum lands in their midst, somewhere soft, and straight away their squirming mass takes me in, individual faces and limbs unidentifiable in the silly chaos of bodies, everybody laughing uncontrollably, somebody yelping – 'Oi, my nads!' – a wriggling litter of new-born pups, Chef and Tristan standing at the lip of the crater, wondering what the hell is going on.

Lunch is waiting for us in the farmhouse. Tristan doesn't take his wellies off to go in, but Chef does, so we follow his lead. It is a state inside: yellowed sheets of newspaper over the floor and dried mud everywhere. There is a stack of plastic crates at the entrance to the kitchen with two blue syringes on top. In the kitchen, a long wooden table is spread with food. There's a block of cheese. Bread loaves, butter, jam and a line of plates heaped with thin, blood-wet slices of beef.

'Tuck in, lads.'

He shoots me a look but doesn't, thankfully, correct himself. The steak strips are cold, tensed-up, delicious. We sit quietly around the table, eating, while Tristan cuts up the bread. Above the sink the branch of a big, sprawling shrub outside is trapped in the window frame, the inside part of it gone dry and black. Tristan looks up like he's just remembered something. He goes out of the room. Comes straight back in with two earthenware flagons, which he thumps down on the table.

'Cider?'

A cheer goes up. Tristan looking in a cupboard for glasses. When there's obviously not enough he starts bringing out mugs and an assortment of worn, plastic children's beakers. Each chef without fuss automatically takes whatever size of vessel matches their rank in the kitchen, mine a small John Deere mug, as Tristan talks us through the variety of breeds we're chewing through. He's different inside the house. He's not got his confidence of outdoors. It's obvious he's put this midnight-feast buffet together himself – and that if there is a woman running this house then she must have gone off her head. My eyes search for clues of her whereabouts. Taped to the back of the kitchen door, in amongst all the disarray of dockets and inventories, is a clutch of photographs. Children in them. Two girls and a boy, the same three faces getting older as the photos spread outwards across the door – on a beach, on the tractor, the field, the building site of this house half-constructed – until the youngest girl, at about thirteen or fourteen, disappears. Her siblings, in the few remaining photographs, growing up without her. Tristan is in one of the earlier photos, doing a goofy pose. The image of him sticking his tongue out comes back. In none of the photographs is there any sign of a mother. And it's her absence – in the photos, in the crude buffet that's been put out, the lack of glasses, the shit heap everywhere – that makes the house feel queer. Her and the disappeared daughter. It is because of them he's not right with himself inside his home. Not that any of these bloody-chinned dimwits have noticed.

The care book has been left open on the hallway table. In the stillness of the house, the presence of the last woman lingers. A shift in the air. There are two new logs. Jittery anticipation drawing me towards them.

> *Client upstairs on entry. Confused when woken and did not want washing at first but finally came to bathroom and was able to put him on stool. Washed top to toe. Dried off with towelling. Gave medication. Helped him downstairs to sitting room and prepared cheese and tomato sandwich. Client still confused so made him cup of tea and sat with him until departure.*

The four o'clock log is in a different handwriting.

> *Client in the maze for long time. Tell me to go, he say this many times. Empty commode. Heat soup. Medicines. Leave television on for his comfort.*

Client in the maze. She makes it sound like a corporate away day. She's got it right, though: isn't that the best way of describing it, his brain – the dead-ends and retrodden ground

319

and sudden faces and disorienting half-sounds from unseen places? The handwriting of both logs looks new. Flicking back through all these pages of logs reveals a roll-call of women, five or six hands now, miniaturising his days into dozens of little elegies. The Bulgarian woman, Petya, long gone. Her last entry five weeks ago. She is the only one who has used his name. *Patrick ate all of his cheese and tomato sandwich*. A good thing, it is becoming clear, thumbing through this winter of visits, that he still likes cheese and tomato sandwiches.

Even after the effort of service, this morning's injection of hopefulness is still at work inside my system. Peter's message felt like him again – as if the infrequent, clipped language of the last few weeks, instructing me only that we would not be meeting, was from somebody else: a sulk, a jilted lover, who has now gone away. Lover. How preposterous that word sounds, like a character from a TV soap. But isn't a lover simply somebody who loves another person in a way that is more active, more actual, than other kinds of love – love that is more than just habit? So, yes, maybe it is true that we are lovers. We do love each other. It is not so difficult, any more, to admit that to myself. Yet it is not possible, still, to admit that there is in fact more to it than that – that there is something else, too, that is always there, curling at the ends of our fingers. Although, now that we have agreed to meet, later the same day of his delivery next week, there can be no ignoring it any more. For all that the pretence of things going back to how they were has soothed me today, he has already ensured that they cannot stay that way. *I don't know what* you *want.* The cat, after all this time, is out of the bag.

A thin light is coming through the door crack to his bedroom. The bedside lamp, because the television is off. He must have done that himself. He looks peaceful. But for the rattle of his breath, he could be dead.

'Hello, Patrick.' The quiet words at his ear sparking a confusing flash of remembrance: whispering into his ear in the dark, the smell of the classroom storeroom, his breath hot against my neck. How much easier it is, now that my decision has been made, to remember the good things there once were. Easier, as well, than thinking about the things that lie, seductively, in front of me.

He is opening his eyes. They clamp to me. He lets out a desperate moan, hoarse and frightened. 'Can we go now?'

'It's okay, Patrick, it's me. It's just me.'

'Can we go now?' He is flapping inside the duvet. A woken strength in him. 'Can we go now?'

'Go where, Patrick?'

'Can we go now?'

He tries to slither away and it is difficult to pin him down. 'Can we go now?'

'Patrick, stop, it's okay; it's just me.' But he doesn't know me; he can only see another intruder. A spurt of energy is still coursing through his body and it takes all my strength to restrain him, holding his shoulders to the pillow, his eye darting madly.

'Stop now. It's okay. You can stop now.'

The eye is abruptly still. Focused on me. A shadow of understanding passing between us. The other pillow beside his head. It would be so simple, so much easier this way. His eye still staring into me, communicating, pleading.

Word has got around that Johnno has thrown up next to the track. Everyone crowds to the window, misting it up with drunk breath, looking for him, until Frank spots him, a shrivelled whelk up against the advertising hoardings. Some of the boys start pounding on the glass, shouting his name. He's too far down to see the sick, unless he's lying on it. Another race is about to start. People's attention moving to it, or back to the tables.

Meat shines darkly in the cave of my pie. 'You are not betting?' Marion asks, sitting down next to me.

'Already spent up. Lost every race. What about you?'

'I have done a few. I still do not know how it works. I just like the dog names.'

Most of the Longwool staff are milling about now. A few drinks closer to fighting or fondling each other later. Everything has got more mixed up than when we came into our area and all sat at tables with our own — kitchen, floor, management, suppliers, KPs — like a dressed-up staff dinner.

Only the KPs are still at their table. Most of them not drinking, a game of cards going on.

'I'm going outside,' Marion says, standing up. 'I will see you out there.'

At the other end of the grandstand restaurant a table erupts – a pint of beer in the air, drunk men and dolled-up women hugging, jumping about, tits, heels, the whole lot of them gone bananas. It's another world here. Hen dos and old boys in flat caps. Businessmen. Couples. A separate room of sad, slumped men at the machines. The smell of fat fryers. Dank, patterned carpet. In the car park, a line of vans with back doors open, ready with water bowls and bedding for the dogs inside. The safest bet tonight is that there'll be a pissed-up chef or two crawling into one of them later, thinking it's our minibus. My legs are unsteady getting up and the tabletop tilts in my grip. Another throat of wine. On all the abandoned plates around the table the gravy is skinning over.

It is nice by the window. Calm. The glass a screen on to something not real. A painting. Dozens of miniature dramas are unfolding: two children playing with a slinky on the aisle steps of the grandstand; a row of men in long, white coats looking at a monitor; our lot gathered laughing around Johnno, hoisting him up to his feet by the track barrier; old men studying their booklets, lifting their faces to the drugged dogs going round and round after a mechanical hare that they're never going to sink their teeth into.

'Have you had a flutter?'

Tristan's lips are stained purple. As he smiles at me an

awareness is pricking up, looking at the simple outdoors man-
liness of him, that something new has just entered the
evening.

'One or two. Lost every time, though.'

'One of your lads is down three hundred quid, your lamb
supplier just told me.'

'Who?'

'The one who's just been sick by the track.'

'Johnno. That's his whole week's earnings.'

He purses his lips. 'Boys will be boys, eh?'

He obviously didn't know how to dress for tonight. What
would the woman not in the photographs think of his
choices? The jeans and the black, tasselled loafers and short-
sleeved salmon shirt, tucked in, like a dad on a stag do.

'He's the tight-lipped type, your head chef. Can't be the
easiest to work under.'

'Stewart's a good chef.'

'Yes, I know. I mean, I know his reputation.'

Our eyes are on each other. The yellow fug of the flood-
lights outside. Black night closing around the stadium. He
licks at the wine on his lips. There it is again, that little
tongue. 'Got to say, I'm glad there won't be any dancing this
time.' He laughs. 'I'm not a dancer.'

'No, you're not. We all remember the last Christmas party.'

He's looking at me, until it's too much, my eyes too pissed
to hold his anyway. A few tables away the new Kiwi waiter
with the goatee beard has got himself in with the hen do.
Things already heading the way they always head. The

madhouse that last Christmas party became: Marcelo and Frank brawling in the toilets, Karen weeping into my lap in the back of the taxi, her snotty face on my thighs – *It's all right now, sweetie, it's all going to be all right now* – stroking and stroking her hair and thinking about Emily, already planning her university applications, all the nights like this she has ahead of her. And thinking about what it will be like without her at home. Not understanding how the years went by so quickly.

'Do you want to go outside?'

'Okay.'

The KPs are still on with their card game. Nobody sees me follow him out into the noise and cold. My ankle folds on the steps and he is taking my arm, leading me down. Farm strength in his arm. Stronger than Patrick.

'You all right?'

'Yes.'

There is a rabble of people around the bookies but Tristan pushes through, knows what he is doing. He goes up to a man in a leather jacket writing on a board and puts his mouth to my ear. 'What do you reckon?' he says. 'Pirate's Daughter? Emerald Isle?' He must think there was some answer from me because he's talking to the man, reaching into his pocket. We move to another part of the trackside. Marion is a bit further along. She's seen me and she is curious. There is the bang and whine of the hare setting off then a small cheer from the crowd as the dogs are released.

Lord knows which was ours, but it has lost. 'Ah, well,'

Tristan says. He rubs the tops of my arms. 'You're cold. Let's go back inside and get a drink.' He takes my hand. Feeling me not respond, he lets it go.

It is a different bar, not the restaurant, somewhere quieter. He has bought two pints of lager. He takes a long drink. The glass in my hand is so heavy. It's like holding a pot plant. He has an attractive smile. 'You don't have to drink it, you know,' he says, his own pint almost half downed already. The bottoms of his jeans lifting – sports socks – as he slides off his barstool. 'Come with me.' He is taking us into another room full of gambling machines. A man in a baseball cap has his back to us, pressing buttons. Tristan is raising my chin with his finger. The track outside the window a blur of colour. He is kissing my eye. He is kissing my eye! 'What are you—' His mouth moving down my face and our lips and tongues are together and this is wrong, everybody down by the track must be looking up at the window, this scene lit up in the flashing lights of the machines. His hand is at the base of my spine, my legs weakening with sudden wondrous abandon as he presses me to him – until he senses me moving away, stepping to stand back from him.

Outside, a man is kneeling in the sand by the finish line, clasping the head of a dog in both his hands, their noses touching.

'I'm sorry.'

He shakes his head. 'No,' he says. 'Please, don't be sorry.'

The boys have gathered around, in his spell, oblivious to the communication that is passing unspoken, through them, between me and Peter. He keeps glancing at me as he talks. What to say to him when we have our walk later today is still beyond me, out of my grasp, but he is letting me know, even as he's regaling the kitchen with some daft story about a vegetable picker getting trapped inside a mountain of cabbages, that he expects something from this conversation we will soon have.

'I swear down,' he is saying, 'the guy was almost a goner. All these cabbages are tanking down on top of him and no one's any the wiser until right at the last moment when his face is about to go under.'

'You're shitting us.' Turtle looks round at Jack, then at Dan, unsure if he's the only one not in on a joke. Peter is at once deadly serious.

'You think it's funny, do you, a man almost drowning in cabbages?'

A pause – then they're all laughing, spanking worktops, each other. All of them behind on their mise.

'There was a man once who did die on a supplier's farm.'

That's got their attention. They are staring at me, wanting more; Peter, too, stepping towards me.

'What happened?'

'The supplier killed him.'

Dan, in a dramatic flourish of incredulity, takes his glasses off. Without them, his eyes are round and small and wrinkly, two startled arseholes. Peter puts his hand, for a second, on top of mine on the pass. 'Looks like you better tell them that one.' Distracted, the boys do not seem to have registered our touching – but my whole arm is pulsing now with fresh blood.

'Our old lamb supplier, Duncan. A burglar got into the outbuilding where he kept his power tools and the rest. The driver in a van hidden in the woods behind the farm. They'd been casing it for weeks, knew where everything was – but he tripped the alarm and the next thing he knows the farmer's there with a gun.' Every one of them has their attention fixed on me. Even Xav has wandered over from pastry to listen. 'The farmer told this boy to put his hands behind his head and walk further into the building. He did everything he was told. Even got into the walk-in freezer and shut the door behind himself.'

'No!' Jack, in childish wonder, turns his head to see Dan's reaction. Dan saying, 'Oh, yeah – I think I remember seeing this on the news.' Peter is looking at me with intrigue. At the story, maybe, but probably more at my desire to tell it, wanting to hold the boys' attention, his attention.

'The police took twenty-five minutes to arrive. No ambulance because the farmer hadn't said where he'd detained him. By the time they got into the walk-in the boy had burrowed himself under a shelf of meat, drenched in his own half-frozen wee and sweat, his organs shutting down, blood as thick as Jack's gravy.' Jack doesn't seem to register the joke, he's too enthralled by the story. 'Saddest thing was, he probably would have lived except the police locked him in the police car, put the heating on full whack and he went into ventricular fibrillation.'

'What does that mean?'

'His heart exploded.'

Jack's mouth is wide open. Turtle asking, 'What happened to the farmer?'

'He got two years, suspended. Involuntary manslaughter.'

Dan, as the rest of them continue to gawk at me, looks quickly at Peter then back to me.

'Right, you lot, back to work. Mise, mise, mise.'

They return to their sections, chattering.

'Cheery story, that one,' Peter says.

'I'm not good at cheery stories.'

'You don't say.' He leans forward, speaking more quietly: 'That's why you'll be staying well clear of the diners, when we do find our place.' An impulse to touch him, to put my hand on his neck, his jaw, is so strong that it feels, almost, like it is actually happening.

One of the receptionists is running towards the pass. We step back from each other.

'There's a phone call for you. I can't quite understand her but it sounds important. She says she's been calling your mobile. Something about an ambulance.'

He is coming back from the toilet. His hair a bit wet where he's run his hand over it. Shirt re-tucked.

'Another?' he asks, arriving at the table.

At home, Patrick will be going to bed about now. If he is at home.

'One more.'

As he heads for the bar a twitch of excitement, guilt, moves in my legs. It's still a surprise that this is happening, still new enough that it feels like somebody else's life. He is giving the barman his order. A few words between them, the barman smiling, some small joke. Tristan standing with both his big hands on the bar top. Can the barman see what this is? Probably. It's not difficult to spot. It doesn't feel humiliating, though, the obviousness of it, two lonely forty-somethings girding themselves for the taxi ride to a cheap hotel room. It feels – Tristan walking back from the bar with our drinks – like absolution; these hours together the only release, temporarily, from the shame of waiting for them.

'I got us some peanuts,' he says, sitting beside me in the booth. 'Didn't know which you prefer, so I got dry-roasted.'

'Sexy.'

He is nodding in amusement as he takes a drink of his pint. His leg is pressing against mine. He tears open the foil of the peanut bag in a smooth, easy motion, which is, in fact, unexpectedly quite sexy.

'What do you think to us going for a meal next time I'm up?'

He says it as if it's just a casual thought. He knows, however, what he is asking me.

'I don't think so. I like how it is now.'

'Fair enough,' he says, putting his hand on my thigh. 'So do I.'

He is turning his body towards me and without hesitation we are kissing. He doesn't care, neither of us do, that the whole bar can see us, might right now be marvelling at the unusual sight of two people our age reaching for the backs of each other's heads, clutching ourselves together. It is a long time before we stop, pulling apart, both of us breathing heavily. The barman has certainly noticed now. He is looking this way, his face frozen, scandalised, as if he's just discovered his parents going at it over the breakfast table.

'Let's go,' Tristan is saying. He takes a handful of peanuts and a final, long drink of his pint, then puts out his arm to pull me from the booth.

In the taxi we don't bother about the driver – even bolder than in the bar, his hand under my shirt, moving up my stomach. However wrong this is, it is made easier by the thought that Patrick has probably been doing it too, for longer. His own secret life, after school, seems to be growing. Every week there are more signs that it is becoming more serious, or that there is a new one: the patterned shirts that have started appearing in his half of the wardrobe; the way he looks at me on those nights he gets home late, disappointed, critical. What is there, the quick wild thought baits me, to stop either of us from doing it: moving on? Now that the children have their own lives, the words almost form in my head; would form, if it was true, if Matthew was showing any signs of a life. And would this always be enough anyway, for me, for Tristan? What will it be like when this fervour for each other, inevitably, cools? The driver is listening to a phone-in show on the radio. One angry caller after another taking the opportunity to say their hateful words into the dark: *At the end of the day it's their own choice to be out there, and if they already know there's other ones who've been killed, then just get off the street.*

'Can you stay this time?' Tristan is stroking my cheek. His fingers smell of dry-roasted peanuts.

'Of course I can't.'

He resumes kissing me, unshaken. Now that he doesn't have to talk and he can let his body take over he is a different man, more at ease with himself. The taxi is pulling up outside our hotel. Tristan leans forward between the front seats and pays the driver, then opens the door for me to get out before him. We walk towards the entrance, into the hotel, our movements and the silence of the lobby all the more intense now that we are not touching. As soon as the lift doors close behind us we come together again, his hand on the small of my back, pushing us closer, a beeping noise – and the doors are opening again before the lift has moved off. A man and a woman. Not much younger than us. They come in, Tristan asking which floor they are going to, pressing the button for them, posh and gentlemanly as ever, regardless of the dangling evidence that he had already begun unbuckling his belt just before they arrived. They know what they've walked in on but the moment for it being a shared comical event has passed. They're embarrassed. They are married. Our floor is the one before theirs and we are all waiting awkwardly together in the small, breathy space until the doors open for us and Tristan says goodnight to the couple, stepping out, taking my hand, leading me down the corridor.

It's a different room this time, but it is identical to the last one – the same curtains, same arrangement of the tea tray, same coiled-metal bedside reading lights, same bedding – except that everything is laid out the other way round, against the opposite wall to the last room, a mirror image. Tristan is lifting me, putting me down on the bed. He is unbuttoning my jeans, sliding them down now, a sensation coming over me of being able to see myself on the other side of the room, a month ago, stretching out unafraid on the bed for him to pull off my underwear, my socks, the figure on the other side of the room arching with me at his first touch – and the hotel filling with past and future visions of myself, letting go simultaneously, all of us gloriously irresponsible.

'Let's find somewhere we can talk,' the consultant says, as though we are at a party. He must surely have his own office, somewhere in the hospital, but we are not going there; he is taking me somewhere closer to hand, somewhere more routine.

'This way, please.'

Hospital staff shuffle past in both directions. All of them segregated by uniform, shift, skin colour, like in a restaurant. The same hierarchy – with the worst jobs inevitably given to the African workers who, like Isaac and Musa, might have night jobs elsewhere while everybody else is resting.

'Here we are.'

The room is almost bare. A computer on an MDF desk. A pair of plastic chairs that he is pulling away from one wall, examination bed against the other. Flat, white light fills the windowless space. There is nothing personal here.

'So, the scan has given us a clear picture of the damage to his brain caused by the blockage. We can also see multi-infarct deterioration to several areas of the brain, mini strokes that appear quite recent, when we put it up against the scan from his second major cerebrovascular event of' – he looks at the computer – 'just over a year ago.' He pauses for me to take this in. 'I'm afraid you're likely to see a marked down-turn from his previous level of function, possibly in several aspects . . .' This man delivers this news day after day, patient after patient, before he exits this place and picks up his kaffir lime leaves from Waitrose on the way home. Impressive, really. '. . . recognition, getting lost, nominal dysphasia – that is, knowing what things are called. And the damage to the frontal lobe might mean personality changes too: sudden dis-inhibition, emotional incontinence, aggression.'

'He's made a head start with some of those already.'

The consultant is nodding, seriously, even though he's not thinking about what his list might actually look like, smell like, inside a house. His work is academic. He doesn't have to touch the bodies. There are other people for that: foreign nurses; women.

'Do you have any help at home? Family, other carers, a friend?'

My brain immediately working to block out the instinctive thought of Peter.

'We have a care package. He has two visits a day while I'm at work.'

'It's likely you will need more help. And you may need to consider taking a period of time off work, I'm afraid, at least for the foreseeable future. What work do you do?'

'I'm a chef.'

'Okay, so, you can hopefully arrange some time off, if it's – what is it, a school? Private catering?'

'No – I'm a chef.'

And now my mind is made up: he is definitely a dick.

'Right, I see.' A sly glance at his watch.

'They've told me before that the average survival length for somebody with dementia is seven years from diagnosis, maybe less for vascular like his. Is that right?'

He is shaking his head. 'There is no' – he cocks his forefingers – 'average. Every case is individual. I don't think there is any benefit to be found in looking for a guide.'

'It's been five years since his first stroke, but because he was early-onset, does that make a difference?'

'As I say, every case is individual. However, the fact that he is still relatively young is favourable. Although, he is now technically beyond the age of early-onset.' A small, pleased-with-himself smile is coming to his lips. 'He has graduated.'

The smile disappears as soon as he sees me stand and push the chair back.

'At the next consultation, I would like to see Dr Mosse instead.'

'Oh, right – well, you are of course entitled to speak to any member of my team that you wish to. I would point out, however, that I am the clinical lead on this unit.'

He is standing up, obviously ruffled.

'I know that, thank you. But as you say, Doctor, every case is individual.'

A window is open near the front, cold air pouring in; the girl underneath asleep, curled up against the glass. The bus is moving through a street of illuminated, empty office towers. Not far from here, up in the sky, the chefs will have finished the clean-down at Lo Stambecco. Another day of perfect, macho food, the dishes flawlessly repeating themselves up in Il Maestro's temple in the clouds.

The top deck is fairly quiet. A few sleepers. Men on their own. A young couple at the front with their heads nestled together. The screen at the top of the staircase, every six or seven images, captures me – the smudge of a woman in glaring whites. It was foolish not to change, the magnet the whites are for some men, but service was too much tonight, it's done me in. The bus has been stopped a while. The strip of bars along here chucking out now. Tired and drunk young people are appearing one after another at the top of the stairs. They find places to sit, most of them up near the front. They slump down, laugh, kiss, eat their stinking food.

Lo Stambecco. How many of those chefs, disappearing now

into the late places of the City, will drink or snort or cry themselves to sleep tonight? Yann's sneering words on my last day: *Good luck. I'm sure you'll end up somewhere that suits you better.* Where will Yann end up? In a magazine? A clinic? There is no anger any more, however, remembering Yann, or Il Maestro. Let them keep on making their executive food high in the sky. The Longwool's food is less pretentious and Stewart is a fairer head chef; it does suit me better. And one day, in my own restaurant, there will be nobody at all to worship. The happy thought of that lulling me with the vibration of the engine, the motion of the bus picking up speed across the river. Desire is growing in me — to believe that it is not a dream, that it can happen. To create a place of my own, where each cook has a voice, a space to try new things, a name.

My temple bumps the window. A quick check outside — south of the river but not near home yet — and the exhausting thought of getting another bus back the other way steels me not to nod off again. Tomorrow, after service, will be a Tristan night. The anticipation of it, his hands, his mouth— Matthew. He is on the bus, at the top of the stairs. My brain struggling to understand whether he is real or conjured from guilt, dreaming him into existence. He is looking for a seat. All of me alert now. It is really him. Has he seen me? An instinct to call out to him jams in my gullet. He is sitting down on this side, ten or so rows in front. Where has he been? Weeks like this one, all lates, he thinks there's no point telling me what he's doing, so he tells Patrick. He has probably been playing computer games at one of his nameless friends' houses. He shouldn't be coming home at this time. Not my place to tell him – and it's too late to say anything now, after letting him sit down without going to say hello. If he turned around would he believe me pretending that he'd sat down without me noticing? He wouldn't want me intruding anyway. The CCTV screen is just to the side of him, but he's staring straight ahead. A need to go towards him is tearing at me, inciting me to leave my seat and walk the short distance down the aisle to just say hello and sit down there and talk to him. Hold him. Ask him how he is; whether the pills that the doctor prescribed him are helping. The white blob of me has appeared again on the screen. What would he do, if he saw me on it? Maybe he'd think it was funny. Or maybe he would pretend not to notice me either. Would he even – the image changing again – recognise who it is?

'Hello there.'

A man is sitting down next to me. Even with my face turning away to the window, his boozy breath is in my nostrils.

'Thank you for my dinner.' His leg pushing up against mine. He is in a suit. It's either a crap joke or he was in the restaurant tonight.

'You're welcome.'

My pulse is already quickening. Every part of me alert to the danger, remembering the Christmas that the man from the office party followed me home from the restaurant, stepping off the bus after me at my stop.

'What's it like, then, working with all those men?' *All those men.* Maybe he is a spy, sent by Mary and Gordon.

A fizzy drink bottle is rolling back and forth under the seat. His hand is spread on his thigh, the tips of some of his fingers touching my leg. Why is it so hard to get up and just move away? To let him have to himself this space that he has laid claim to. Why should it be me, not him, who feels ashamed here?

'Excuse me, please.'

He is looking up, smirking and scowling with fake offence. He doesn't move aside, he makes me squeeze past, as if it is me who is in the way, out into the aisle. Matthew is still facing forwards, not seeing me. The man muttering behind me: 'Stuck-up cow.' Nobody turning around. So what? Why should it matter? At least he is staying put. That should be reason enough to be thankful – so too the fact that this doesn't happen as often as it used to, in all these years of coming home on the bus after service, while Patrick keeps the car for himself.

'Hello, stranger.'

'Mum?'

'I didn't see you there. Where did you get on?'

'Few stops ago.'

'Have you had a nice night?'

'Yeah.' He smells faintly of weed. 'Have you?'

'Not really. Service was dog shit tonight.'

He is smiling, not used to hearing me speak in kitchen language. He doesn't budge at me sitting down beside him, my head coming down to rest on his bony shoulder.

'Wake me up when we're home, will you, my love?'

'All right, Mum.'

The reek of pee hits as soon as the door is open. It enters my airways, my pores, finding its way into me.

'I've got the milk! I'm just going to put it in the fridge then I'll come up and see you.'

The sink is full of yesterday's washing-up. Bowls, beakers, soup pans. The dishcloth, over the arch of the tap, has dried out into a stiff toupee. There is a build-up of work to get done this morning: his sheets, his meds, new batches of soft-slop food for the freezer, a decent wash. Monday. This would have been a park day, before. A Peter day. My movements quicken – milk into the fridge, beaker of water – not permitting myself to think about that or what Peter might be doing now or the conversation that Patrick's stroke interrupted; able only to think about now, making sure that he is comfortable.

The bed covers are on the floor. He is lying on the mattress, looking at me. His underwear is hugely swollen over the incontinence pad and the smell in here is unbearable. Dead herb water. Can he smell it, each time he wakes up, or is that another function that has gone now?

'I've got the milk. I see you've been battling with the duvet.'

He lets out a barrage of coughs. With a heave it is possible to lift him into a sitting position. My hand on his back, patting, stroking – 'There, there' – the coughs slowing down.

For some time, his breathing regular again, we stay in the same position. It is soothing, touching him like this. With my eyes closed, breath held, he is almost him again. An old memory of intimacy is transmitted for an instant between us – broken by a new cry of pain.

'Oh, I'm sorry, Patrick, I'm sorry.' He allows me to bend him slightly forwards to inspect the gaping mouth of the sore at the base of his spine. 'We need to dress this. It's getting worse. And I'm afraid we need to change the pad too.' His arms and shoulders are going rigid. 'I know, I'm sorry, but it's getting a bit smelly. Let's just change it quickly, shall we?' He will not let me move him. His fingers are gripping the sheet and the mattress protector underneath. 'Please, Patrick. Let's just get it done.' His legs are kicking and without putting my weight down on top of them he would injure me. There is no other way. It needs changing. Simple as that. Those words – *Let's just change it quickly, shall we?* – once more in my mouth, in my head, echoing up from the past. His hands clamping to my knuckles, refusing, the tug-of-war over his pants and the force of my will sapping, afraid to look at his face and see his humiliation – *No, no, no* – which is mine, too, knowing that he shouldn't be wearing a nappy any more, he should have been trained out of them long ago, if he was normal, if he had someone more competent than me who could encourage him and who could protect him from the boys in his class who know he still wears them at night and tease him, follow him to the toilet and make fun of him outside the cubicle door – his shame at it raging with every kick, every scream, all directed at me.

Patrick's pants pull free, sliding down his thighs. One quick motion and the pad is unglued from him. His body has gone floppy; he has given in. Underneath the pad, his penis and scrotum are squashed together like a trampled field mushroom. He needs wiping down but it is too much now, he has been subjected to enough, and while he is staying still it's a simple job to slide the new pad underneath him then pull his pants back up.

'There we are. All done.'

His eyes flick to me. They track me kissing his forehead. He is there in them, close to the surface.

'Okay. I'm going to go down now and make us some broccoli and potato soup.'

The fridge needs a clear-out. There are things in here – an opened yoghurt, a bunch of parsley in a Mason jar – from before he was admitted to hospital. Inside the vegetable drawer the head of broccoli has gone off. The florets have yellowed and the film around it is slack, a little pool of liquid collecting at the bottom of the stalk. *Serves you bad*, Peter would say, suffocating it in plastic. It was brainless of me not to think about buying another at the shop just now. Tinned tomato soup for lunch it is, then. The broccoli head is trailing a line of drips on the way to the dustbin. The stalk in my hand soft and fleshy. At the release of the bin lid the smell of used pads wafts up as the head plunges into the darkness, coming to rest near the bottom, and in the half-light in the depths of the dustbin the plastic bag is starting to twitch – sucking in, out, the head gasping for breath – Mum's face, before the lid closes, pleading, looking up at me.

2008

Something is not right. My fingers around the door handle have stopped functioning. They won't move. My other hand shaking inside my handbag. The street on both sides is dead still, filling with the sound of my breathing getting louder, a pressure of air growing inside my lungs. Please let none of them be home yet. The house keys jittering at the lock. Whatever this is, it will pass over. An overwhelming need is sinking through me, to just lie down, on the bed, the floor, to just let it pass over.

There is nobody in the house. It is not stopping, this strangeness in me. A crushing sense of suddenly not knowing myself, of being completely lost, is constricting my lungs. There is no controlling it, my breath choking, a rope of air being hauled in and out of my throat. My handbag has fallen onto the mat. Things spilling out of it. The door still open.

My feet move down the pavement. Every window filled with eyes. *What's she doing now, the silly woman? She's legging it, look – she's trying to get away!* Past the bus stop, and into the village, there is no stopping me. Escaping. The thought of Tristan comes, disorienting me even more, his lips pressing against mine in the hotel room. He is not a real person. The thought of him feels like an invention. Is he all that is left, this monthly man? Is that my life? Something is wrong – something internal collapsing, like my plug's been let out. My breath hot and raking and my legs starting to go faster, running. The slap of my shoes on the pavement. Running! When was the last time? A lifetime ago, another person, not me. This is someone else's body – a man walking the other way staring in confusion – bearing me onward through people, commuters, hospital workers, a homeless woman, a mob of children outside a chicken shop, into the Fields and to the river, all of these places familiar, everywhere knows me. Some force is pulling me backwards, the past reeling me in. The last time running like this has caught up with me, the memory of it at once in my legs: the search for Matthew. People are stopping on both sides of the road to watch the spectacle – a nearly middle-aged woman sprinting, gasping for breath – each of them then looking behind, to see if someone is after me.

On, away, out of the Fields and along the river, under the rush of traffic. What will Patrick, the children, think? She finally lost her marbles. The river has gone out of sight, underground, beneath the roads and the concrete. Bile is racing up through me. Outside a builders' warehouse, behind a van, it all comes up. Vomit sliding down the side of the van. It drips off the undercarriage, onto the ground. There is sick on my legs, some of it seeping into the top of my socks. By the base of the wheel a tiny brown shrimp sits on a little damp bed of samphire; my only meal today was somebody else's. Something has come loose in my brain – and it's not finished, it is carrying me away again, out of the forecourt, on and on across the grey landscape, across the New Cross Road, traffic slowing to figure me out, to understand what is wrong. The need to get away, to flee, feels overpowering. The violent lust to escape is beating at the walls of my chest. Tears gutter across my cheeks, cooling in the rush of air – but they don't connect to anything, they are coming from elsewhere, as if there is another person inside me, under the skin, wanting out, but another person inside her too, and another, surrounded by themselves, a small voice echoing from deep inside them all – *He's right: my head's gone* – her yellow eyes looking out of the dark: *Promise me you'll turn into someone else.*

My knees feel hot and torn and my stomach is cramping, slowing down now, leaving the road behind. It is quieter here, near the creek. Everywhere there are tall glass apartment buildings under construction. An art studio. Some of the old routes are still here, though. By the side of an empty, glass-fronted gym, the narrow cobbled alleyway down to the river beach is unchanged. The great, tireless river in front of me.

The beach is deserted. Nobody sees me walking towards the water, needing to be near her, dropping to my knees on the pebbles. The strength is gone from me. Further back, a short crawl away, there is a patch of sand. The distant sound of a boat's engine; the lapping of water onto the shoreline. It is peaceful here. The lovely, soft give of sand against the back of my head. The urge to escape has passed. They need the whole of me. Emily and Matthew. Patrick. The chugging of another boat increases, then fades away. High above, a plane is slowly unzipping the sky, cleaving it open to expose a secret dark forever of gas and dust and silence.

The foil splits open and the pill falls from the blister pack, straight into the jar. The Sharpie line getting nearer, a month away.

He has been happy this afternoon. Stroking his dog, arranging his magnetic vegetables. He is comforted by my being here. He knows, but does not really know, that my leave from work is ending soon. The lid closes tightly in my palm. Can this be the right thing, still? He is too far gone for it to be possible to understand what he wants now. There is only the evidence of the person before to speak for him. But do they both, really, want the same thing? What he wants now is his dog, his vegetable magnets; maybe the truth is that this is enough for him. Except that he is getting rapidly worse. Even this, these small enjoyments, will be gone from him soon.

The jar makes its quiet tinkling sound as it slots back into place, propping up the letters at the back of the drawer. The line so close now that it is possible almost to imagine the days, the shifts, the mornings with Peter, until it is reached.

Tristan is still asleep. Neither of us thought to close the curtains last night and in the early-morning light his face looks different, new sober details of it revealed: a small bulge in the flesh of his left eyebrow; stiff, white hairs in his sideburns. Watching him sleep, the possibility of a life with him is laid out clearly before me. His quiet strength and tenderness, wanting me, forever grateful for filling the empty space of his family. Making a home of the farmhouse. The calm spell of the countryside. And it is just as clear, in this moment, that this life cannot happen. Patrick would move on, in all likelihood; he might already know who with, if his continued late nights staying behind after school are anything to go by. The idea of leaving him – sharply real for an instant – is coolly untroubling. Even Emily would probably get used to it eventually. But how well would Matthew cope with the distress of it, the new damage it would cause him?

'Tristan.'

He is not moving. His faint snoring continues unbroken beside me. He is not the type of man to show his intentions, but he wants more than this – the monthly tumble each time he comes up to meet with his stockists. Perk as it is. He had obviously planned his words last night carefully, opening up about his family for the very first time, offering me a new kind of closeness. An invitation into his life. All the same, it was so unaffected, the way he told it. No plea for sympathy, no bitterness, just a series of events that were not one person's fault: his wife's increasing unhappiness on the farm and his unwillingness to give up what he had built and leave with her; the youngest daughter getting in with an older group in the town; the arguments with the daughter as she drew away from home and into this group's circle, their drinking, drugs, before the accident. Even when he described his wife packing up and leaving with the daughter for a new life far away, there was still no hint of judgement in his voice. If not for the removed photographs of the wife on the back of the kitchen door, it might even be possible to believe that he feels no anger, or regret, at all. He is stirring, his shoulder shifting a little. He looks content. Maybe it was a relief, telling somebody. In the years since they left, and then the older children left too, for university, he has probably never spoken to anybody at that length about his life, and he was making it plain, when he changed the subject, that he had said as much as he wanted to. All of my unasked questions – how often does he get to see the daughter? Have the older children sided with one or other of them? – suspended for another time. Not that he got anything in return from me, has ever got anything from me except for three years of hotel sex. What would it be like, to talk to him about my own relationships with my children? To tell him that my son once went missing when he was only three years old because of me shouting at him then leaving him on his own to cry and slip out of the door to get lost on the streets in the dark looking for his dad. And that when he did finally get found and brought back, by his grandmother who despises me and his dad who will never forgive me for it, there was a part of him that never returned, that has still never come back to me.

Matthew and Patrick will be waking up in their own hotel room about now. Going down for breakfast, getting the bikes ready for the last leg of their route. Maybe, when they come home tonight, Matthew will have a new spark about him. Patrick might have been able to talk to him properly, to encourage him to do something with his life – if not university, as Patrick will of course still have been pushing him towards, then something else, a direction, anything that isn't lying in his room in front of his game console. A car horn sounds on the road outside. Tristan is sighing, close to awake. A pang of old faithfulness propels me from the bed: not to Patrick, himself, but to the bond that we once had. This, here, Tristan, is not my future; it cannot happen again. Duty, at last, has got the better of me. My only thought now is to be at home.

Tristan is opening his eyes.

'Good morning.'

He looks around at the room in daylight, as if he can't fathom where he is. 'Morning.'

He is a decent, kind man. He will be hurt, alone on his farm in the months to come, but he will understand.

'Come on, farmer. Let's go and have breakfast.'

A light rain is falling. Peter is unbothered by it, walking along the avenue deep in thought. He doesn't know, understandably enough, quite what to say, except that all the things he did want to say, before, are now off the table.

'So.' He looks up, above the trees, seeming to notice for the first time that it is raining. 'Deer or ducks?'

'Ducks.'

On the way to the pond the rain starts to come down more heavily. The avenue brightens with umbrellas, people dashing for tree cover or up the hill to the Observatory.

'Come on,' he says, 'let's take shelter.'

We run underneath a horse chestnut tree. Rain is lashing the path, throwing up a dense mist. My clothes cling to my skin. A powerful feeling of being trapped here is taking hold. The care worker is in the house now. Will she know to check his pressure sores, his pad? Will she respect his need to leave those things alone, if it is too much for him? These thoughts are a distraction, of course, an excuse. Accusation pens me beneath the tree. Who is *not* with him? That is the real question. What kind of person would be here instead? The sky is all of a sudden clearing. The rain passing over – gone. The lingering mist and the dripping of the tree the only signs that it ever happened.

'Right we are. To the ducks.' People are emerging from the trees, shaking off umbrellas. 'I've not asked you about Emily's visit.'

A small child streaks across our path. He dives onto the wet grass. The mother chasing behind, calling to him in frustration.

'It was difficult for her.'

'Course it was.'

'He was so happy to see her, though. He knew she was there. The whole time, he knew.'

'She coming down again?'

'As often as she can, she says. Morgan, too.'

'That's good, that's good. What with you going back to work as well.'

'Yes. She's not finding the thought of that so easy, believe it or not.'

'I suppose that's to be expected.'

We carry on towards the pond. Peter has gone quiet. He keeps looking across at me, often enough that maybe he wants me to notice, for us to pull up here on the path so that he can say to me whatever it is that he is thinking – my legs, walking on, fighting against a hankering to stop walking and make him. For him to stop being endlessly attentive and return us to where we had been cut off, about to really talk to each other at last.

'If I can ask,' he says finally as we keep moving onwards, 'how are you getting by for money?'

'He's going to have three care visits a day now. And the

house has to be adapted. I need to be going back to work this weekend, put it that way.'

'You wouldn't, I mean, think about selling up the house, like? Move somewhere, you know, easier.' It is rare to hear him so hesitant. For all that he is holding back, he knows that this is new ground.

'It's not mine to sell. He never gave me financial power of attorney, while he was capable.'

'And it's too late now?'

'Technically, no. But it wouldn't be simple.' A party of foreign teenagers in matching red jackets is coming past, leaving the pond. 'He didn't trust me with our money.'

Peter smiles, good-natured as always, at me pretending to make a joke of it. 'He knew you'd blow it all on a restaurant, did he?'

'Something like that.'

'Well.' He pauses. 'You can understand it, in a way.'

'You can, can you?'

'He was needing to control something, maybe, while he was losing control of everything else.'

The sun comes out from the clouds as we stop at the edge of the pond. The water, all the way across, is perfectly flat. Peter is standing very still, looking out. 'I got a bit that way, myself, if I'm honest, with the divorce and that. Not the same thing, obviously, but like, when you feel everything's slipping away from you it can make you dig the heels in, you know. Back then it was about the girls for me, mainly. There's things I did then, things I said, that I wish I hadn't.'

All these years and he's never really spoken about this part of his life. Always until now he has been without a past. Clean. It is jarring to be reminded of the fact that he has one too, that he's had his own share of shittybollocks and that sometimes he probably wasn't good either, like Tristan, refusing to leave his farm, like everybody else. Peter moved away from where his children live, free to start a new life for himself, without baggage. Even if his ex-wife was not still alive and living in a Right to Buy in Hartlepool – if he was a widower – the world would have expected all the same for him to move on. As a man, he would not have been judged for it.

'If he hadn't tried to control everything so much, Peter, it would be easier to care for him now.'

'Aye, well, that's how it goes when you hold on that hard. You can't see you might be pissing on your own chips.'

An old woman on the far shore has exploded a loaf of bread into the water. Birds are sailing towards her. A coot rushes out from the bushes beside us, followed by her brood of chicks, all of them doing their funny little run over the mud before splashing into the pond. For a moment the woman is cast in sunlight and she lifts her gaze to it, smiling. A memory is twisting through me, Mum's face, making my breath falter.

'Or that you might end up pissing over everything.'

The heartless words, out of my mouth, paralyse me. My legs are going – and a long, thin noise is at once coming out of me, a continuous sound, Peter trying to lift me off the ground, the old lady staring across the pond, shocked.

'Here now, pet. It's okay, here now.'

My clothes are streaked in mud. All of me limp. A weight in his arms. The noise still escaping from me, unstoppable. It was wrong to ask him to meet me. He is holding my hand, leading me away from the water, up to the bench. The sky is a blinding white. Our hands still in each other's. What is it, this unnameable thing between us? How is it possible to need so badly to be at home doing the right thing, the only conceivable thing, but at the same time to keep wanting, wanting, wanting? Peter is sitting me on the bench and my whole arm is thickening, as though a pressure cuff is squeezing the flesh, the confusion of blood hurtling, onward, into the future – but back too, back into a past that is always racing towards me, looking up at me from the bed, *You don't need to say anything, my love*, squeezing my hand, *you just need to promise me you'll turn into someone else.*

'Check on. Eight covers. Three sweetbread, two asparagus, two scallops, one duck. To follow: four sole, two pork, two gnocchi.'

We are getting slammed, the fourth order in the last five minutes, this one the birthday table. Chef Stewart finishes calling it and leans out of the pass to shout at Jo to tell the floor to hold off any more fucking orders. Everything that is not the dish in front of me pares away from my brain. My hands and arms working automatically now, keeping going. Reaching for a C-fold, patting the next two soles dry, dusting them with flour, adding oil to the pan. There are no voices in here. Only the sound of pans, knives, the cheeping of clogs on the runners. At the next section, Andreas is going down. He's in a flap, ducking up and down for his service fridge, not finding something, swearing to himself, 'Shit, shit, shit.' He has been hit hard by the last order. Seven hot starters, his tag rail stuffed with checks. He crashes a pan onto the flat-top and something slides out of it, falls to the floor. A scallop. He leaves the pan on the stove, scrambling back for his mise as all around us the Ramencos start spitting out another order.

'Check on!'

Andreas has forgotten the pan. His eyes are locked on the tongs in his hand and he doesn't seem to have noticed me coming in alongside him, his hands shaking, not doing what they should be doing. His section is a tip: damp salt and chopped herbs everywhere, his boards slimy, his spoon wash brown, a ticket fallen into his velouté.

'Bloody hell, Andreas, this tag rail looks like a ballerina's washing line.'

He doesn't smile at the old kitchen joke. He hasn't even heard me. Christian on the other side of the section has been infected by Andreas's panic, stirring and stirring hollandaise over a bain-marie with dead-eyed purposelessness. The floor is littered with small bones, as if a fox has been at the bins. Andreas steps back to let me reach across and wipe his board. 'The pan, Chef.' He understands and takes it off the flat-top, the butter inside dark and burnt. 'Wipe it down and go again.'

He is doing it. Cleaning his pan and setting it down with new butter. Starting his scallops and blanching the asparagus spears; cracking two duck eggs into ramekins and tipping them steadily into the water. 'That's it, Andreas.' My voice a whisper. His cauliflower purée is good – soft and creamy. It pipes smoothly onto the plate, holds the sweetbread beignets nicely. 'You're doing well. You're on top of this.' A thought from the outside world finds its way in – Matthew – an abrupt longing to be with him, to talk to him like this, encourage him.

'Away on fourteen! Two sole.'

Chef Stewart knows what is happening here. He is allowing it. There are tickets dangling off my Ramenco now and Nathan is clearly sweating it, left at the section on his own, but Chef has judged that this is the least bad option for us getting out of the shit. Andreas's bollocking can wait for him or Frank to deliver in the morning. Andreas is getting control of himself, breathing, flipping the scallops, giving instructions to Christian. He's not ready to be left alone, though, not yet. One more minute. Another order is coming in. Andreas adds butter and a squeeze of lemon and takes the pan off the heat then straight away puts a spoonful of romesco onto each of the scallop plates and draws a swift smear with the back of the spoon. He lifts his scallops from the pan, perfectly caramelised. A wave of tiredness is sweeping through me, the kitchen slipping in and out of my vision. Last night's hot wakefulness catching up with me: the second night this week of erratic, shredded sleep, listening through Patrick's relentless snoring to the strangled cries of Matthew's computer game across the landing, to reach the morning with all of my joints still stiff and aching.

'You good, Andreas?'

'I'm good.'

A few of the boys glance over at me returning to my section to line up the new checks onto the rail. Chef has turned around too. He meets my eyes. Gives a slight nod of his head. My limbs, four aching stumps which have another two hours of this to get through and need to rise again for another double tomorrow, are, right now, floating on the air.

Soap bubbles surf across the metal. Everywhere there is the shush of sponges on the worktops. 'Chaud behind!' Chefs and KPs are hurrying between the kitchen and the plonge. Every bit of me hurts and wants to be home, in bed, but the exhilaration of service is keeping me going, urging me on. A clarity of purpose is directing my movements – knowing that the future, no matter what anybody else needs from me, is beckoning. To channel my energy into this life: cooking, moving up the line; a restaurant, one day, of my own.

Andreas is walking over. He stands next to me, just as we were before, and gives a gentle nudge with his elbow, his hand dipping for a second into my pocket – my skin suddenly pulsating all across my hip at the already forgotten knowledge of being touched – and now he is going, out of the kitchen, his clean-down completed. There is motion all around, everybody wanting to finish and leave and get fucked-up.

In my pocket, gleaming expensively like a ring box, is a petit four, stolen from pastry.

It's a dog's breakfast out here. Always his domain, the garden — and there are still a few remnants of his labours, here and there. The thin, gnarled stump of that bushy thing which used to flower outside the kitchen window. A row of little blackened coffee stirrers along the back border, his neatly labelled plant names swallowed by rot and the plants long gone except for the cluster of daffs by the fence, escapees from next door. This lawn that he used to mow once a fortnight without fail is not really even a lawn any more, bare as it is, with just a couple of thriving patches of jungle grass, like his own head. Still, he would probably enjoy sitting out here. What does he care, any more, that it's a wreck? It is a sunny afternoon and it would do him good to get outside. The garden chairs, at least, are in all-right condition from being stowed away in the shed, and they open out smoothly enough. A bit musty, although with the sun on them, side by side here in the fresh air, they might make for a welcome change of scene for him.

'Patrick!' It is dark inside the house, coming in from the sun. 'Let's go and sit in the garden. It's a lovely day.'

He is not in his armchair. He has moved off somewhere,

all by himself. The strangeness of it takes me by surprise, making my heartbeat immediately quicken.

He's not in the kitchen either, or the dining room, the downstairs toilet. Impossible, surely, that he's managed to get upstairs. 'Patrick!' My breath is getting thicker. This doesn't make sense. He could hardly walk to the toilet earlier.

The bed is empty, and a recollection comes to me. 'Oh, Patrick, you're not playing bloody hide-and-seek, are you?' But he isn't. The gap behind the bed has only a mass of fallen rubbish down it.

The bathroom, Matthew and Emily's rooms, everywhere is deserted. The landing is starting to spin. The falling sensation of losing control, of orders piling in, time swirling around me and this still, small moment of choice in the eye of it – of resolve or surrender – an automatic reflex taking over, shouting his name louder, checking the rooms again and hurrying down the stairs, thinking clearly now: was he wearing his Velcro shoes? Where is his cane?

The front door is open, slightly ajar. A shard of clear blue sky is shining in the crack above it. The fake dog is there on the mat.

'Patrick!'

The door, swinging open, thumps against the hallway wall.

He isn't on the doorstep or the front path. The pavement both ways looks empty. How can he have got so far this quickly? A car comes past and a stupid thought seizes me, that he has been taken. Bundled into a van and driven away. Stupid. Stupid, stupid. At the pavement, indecision brings me to a standstill, not knowing which way to turn, trying to piece together the broken logic of his mind, to guess which realm of history he has slipped into – his commute to school or taking Emily to choir practice or going to his parents – the savage irony of this last thought making me move, spontaneously, in the direction of their old house. Is it possible that this is where he is heading? That the map of these streets still exists in his brain and he is going to walk all the way, expecting to find them still there scheming in the living room; the three of them reunited to devise their pact over a cup of tea? If he wasn't wearing his shoes his feet will be cut or he will have fallen. Instinct makes me check between each parked car – every time hoping, for a split-second, to find him there, but there is no sign of him. He is nowhere. What was he doing, saying, in his armchair this morning? Only the usual: *Can we go now? Can we go now?* A car is slowing down. The driver has seen me, desperate on the pavement, and they're wondering if they need to stop. A woman is lowering her window.

'Is everything okay?'

No words will come. For God's sake, speak. Yes? No? Bollocks?

'Are you all right?'

'Have you seen a man looking lost?'

'No, I don't think I have.'

'Infirm. Probably with a cane.'

She is shaking her head. 'Do you want me to help you look for him?'

'No. Thank you. No.'

She stays parked on the road, watching me in her mirrors walking away, breaking now into a run. Please let him be okay. There is the quiet idling of the car's engine. Shrill bird-song in the pavement trees. Down the gravel paths, children are playing in the back gardens. It is my fault, forgetting to lock the door. Even though his mobility is worse still since the last stroke it shouldn't have made me drop my guard. The consultant's warning: to expect the unexpected. Please let him not be harmed. The image of him wandering, vulnerable and lost, is too much. My vision is contorting, a mirage of him here on the pavement bleeding into it, but the car engine is still there behind me. What is stopping me from asking her to help me? To knock on every door and enlist all the neighbours? To call Peter? My face is sweating. Shame thumping at my chest with each stride. What was on *my* mind while he was wandering from the house? What was distracting me when my only duty should have been to make sure that he had everything he needed and he was safe? At the end of the street, checking left, right, he is still not anywhere. A determination kicking me on, making me turn around and set off back the other way down our street – passing the postbox again and remembering Matthew sobbing in his bedroom, finally telling me – that he has to be okay.

How long has he been gone? It must be only a few minutes. Too soon to call the police. They would not come, not yet. It would waste time. The faces of policemen – Matthew's, Mum's; *there's some bad news to tell you* – are merging. The woman is there, still in her car, watching me come past her in the other direction, past the house again, tempted to go back in and check if he has returned by himself, or if he was there all along, hiding from me. He has to be close. He can't be more than a hundred metres from here. If somebody stopped him, would he be able to tell them where he lives? He might. Yesterday and last week and last year are lost in the fog of his brain but his address, decades old, might still be there in the roots.

He is there, outside Paul and Julie's house.

'Oh, Patrick.'

He doesn't seem to be aware of me running towards him, his gaze fixed on the door. He is in his socks. His face, his hands, all of him is cold.

'You're here, my love. I've found you.'

'I knocked,' he is saying. He wriggles out of my arms and hits the door twice with his cane.

'Paul and Julie? They're probably away for Easter.'

He is frowning. 'But. The barbecue?'

The woman is driving away. As the noise of the car increases, something buckles inside me, needing him home, comfortable and safe with his dog on his lap.

'The barbecue was another time, my love.' He lets me take his arm. 'Come on, let's get you home.'

My skin is crawling. The tiny prickle of it is only just perceptible, although knowing that it has started is enough to make me fully awake, as if a nest of spiderlings have hatched deep within me and are now beginning to swarm into my chest, my arms, my legs. My neck, where a few loose strands of hair are touching it, is already burning. It helps – taking off my nightshirt and spreadeagling across the empty bed – but it is coming now and the inevitability of the rest of the night is, for a short time at least, calming. There is nothing to do except wait and be thankful that Patrick isn't in the bed and that tomorrow, however many sleepless hours lie ahead, is a day off.

Heat is flowing like magma under the surface of my skin. The thought of Patrick's reaction, the first time, coming back to me: *Jesus Christ, woman, this is insane. It's like your waters have broken.* Revealing, maybe without him even realising it, how traumatised he still must be by that particular milestone. He probably still dreams about that stain on David and Ruth's sofa. There is no point changing the sheets yet. Better

369

to wait until it has passed and the whole bed is damp, lying here until then reliving tonight's service: the refire on all of twenty-three's mains, coaching the CDPs back from their panic, appeasing Jo and the floor, all while this second fatigue was slowing my movements like some creature growing inside me, feeding on my reserves.

As fast as it came on, it is starting just as quickly to pass. The sheets, the new mattress protector, the pillowcases, peel from the bed. The prospect of Patrick seeing them in the morning, wet and crumpled on the carpet, spurs me into action, gathering them up to carry downstairs and hide where he will never find them, in the washing machine. From the landing, the reverberation of him snoring soundly in Emily's bedroom makes me pause outside the door, indulging the passing fancy of suffocating him with these sodden sheets. From Matthew's room next door there is no noise any more. He is asleep. His console, at some point between three and four o'clock, at last switched off. A yearning to look in on him sleeping, at peace, is beckoning me towards his room – until my sanity returns to guide me away down the stairs. If he was woken up now, by his mother naked and glistening with sweat, he would probably never sleep again.

Even with the washing machine on and the shower running, neither of them will stir. Used as they are to my late, post-service showers. This second one of the night every bit as blissful as the first.

The bed, with the clean new sheets on it, is cool and comfortable, but sleep will not come now. My mind is jumping.

To Matthew never leaving his room. Mary coming over tomorrow. Patrick's snoring has taken over the air of the whole upstairs. *Jesus Christ, woman.* How long did it take him – the second time, the third? – to decamp to Emily's room? More restful for both of us, he decided. Not his issue to deal with, or talk about; something to be put up with in silence and kept apart, from him, from Matthew, from work. The idea of confiding in Chef Stewart! My ankles hurt, Chef, and sometimes in the middle of service my vagina itches like hell and my heart pounds so hard it feels like it's going to explode. He might be kind and let me drop a shift or two, even though he wouldn't understand and he would definitely remember it the next time he hears me knocking on his door wanting to talk about a promotion.

It is already late. Past a respectable time to get up. She's having a lie-in, is what they will both think, unaware that this is my first proper rest since last night, that sleep didn't arrive until the light was starting to come up outside the window. Ten past ten. Just five more minutes. There is the sound of voices downstairs. Mary. She has probably driven here, against Patrick's wishes – never mind he still hasn't the courage to tell her that it isn't safe for her to drive any more. The thought of her in the old, grey car plays in my head like an unbroken dream, in which she's still driving up and down these streets, searching for Matthew. Their voices have got quieter. They've gone into the kitchen. Patrick making her a cup of tea, telling her to sit down. Her perfume has already invaded the house. It feels out of joint, now that she is old and weak, to remember how he used to hang on her every word. The power she used to hold. Although, in fact, didn't that shift in their relationship – the parent and the child – really begin years ago, even before she got old? Did it not actually start to tip the other way long before, from that day she rescued Matthew, seventeen years ago next week? How protective Patrick became of her after that, wanting more than ever to keep her apart from me. And the strangeness that has grown between them, did that start then too? Looking back, all these years in between slowly pulling a veil over their private tension, it probably did. The coded glances. The disapproval of Matthew's idleness, as she calls it, and Patrick's snappiness with her whenever she has a go about Matthew wasting his life. Their voices downstairs are louder again. Mary's words clear now: '. . . and I keep trying to get Gordon to do his speech muscle exercises like the doctors want him to but he just won't listen.' Her voice getting louder still. They might be coming up the stairs. In one swift movement the bedcovers are off. Dressing gown on. A quick look in the mirror, smoothing my hair down, and it is time to show my face.

Mary is at the foot of the stairs. Patrick close beside her, listening to her reassurance that his father is fit and well, recovering from the stroke, that he does not need to worry. She notices me on the landing above her. In her eyes that old critical look, so scorched into my memory that Patrick may as well still be holding Matthew tightly in his arms next to her.

'Morning, Mary.'

She casts a look at her watch.

'Good morning. A busy shift last night, presumably?'

'Yes, it was.'

She must be able to see the sleeplessness on my face, and it strikes me for the first time that she must be able to relate to it. She will remember what it was like, this woman who has lived more than twice the life of my mum. She will have changed her own bedsheets in the middle of the night and never spoken about it. As she peers up at me peering down at her, at the painstakingly preserved set of her hair, her aged, blotched skin, sympathy lurches in me – witnessing her there still attending to her son, her husband, doing her duty to the last – understanding, finally, that she never really had any power at all.

'Mum.' Patrick's hand is at her elbow. 'Come and sit down.'

She meets his eye – and there it is, moving between them: their shared secret knowledge; their pact. He is ushering her slowly away into the living room. She moves jerkily, as though some part of her is in pain. Her body, disappearing through the doorway, is so frail now. Her mind, though, still boiling.

'Mum.'

Matthew is approaching quietly from his room.

'Is Granny here?'

'Yep.'

He gives me a smile, a wink. My son who has also been up half the night. 'Best go and say hello, then,' he says, turning back for his room so that we can both get dressed and go downstairs to face the rest of the morning together.

He looks tranquil, here in the garden chair. His dog on his lap and the late-April sunshine on his face. His forehead is already turning pink; he should have suncream on – but he'll be fine for a few minutes longer, no need to disturb him yet. Next door have got the radio on. Somewhere further down there is the twittering of children and a man and woman talking. Families we don't know. My hand folds around one of the smooth pebbles in the tub by my chair, caressing it a moment, trying to distract my thoughts from where they are wanting to go – Peter – before tossing it onto the dead lawn.

'Do you like what I've done with the garden?'

He starts to rock. He seems, maybe, to comprehend the sarcasm.

'I've been keeping it in check for you, mowing, weeding, watering the flowers. Looks nice, doesn't it?'

He stares out at the warzone of the garden. 'Yes.'

His hand is becoming more curled up. He can't stroke the dog with the flat of his palm any more: it's his fingertips and thumb that are moving across the fur. The dog looks happy, mind you. Breathing with Patrick's strokes, enjoying the easy bliss of sun and new batteries.

It is reassuring to think that Petya has been sitting out here with him too during this sunny spell. Whether it was just a quirk of the care computer, or because she requested to come back, it helps to know that she is with him each day at the same time, that somebody else is doing this with me. That to him it might feel like we are working in tune together. It's probably me imagining things, but her entries in the care book increasingly give the impression of messages written to me: *We sat in the garden today. Weather good again, I will try to get him in shorts if good again tomorrow!* The little faces she draws on my own notes to her – *I can't believe you got him to eat that tin of carrot soup!* ☺ – confirmation that she reads them, that she doesn't mind, as if we are sending postcards to each other.

His lips are quivering. He is making some internal noise, a quiet keening, his head tilting to the side – the first splinter of panic making me get up from my chair and go to him. 'Patrick? Are you okay?'

It is a smile. He is listening to next door's radio. He's following the sound of the music, his lips squeezing with attention on whatever it is, something classical. Fleetingly, it seems possible that he recognises the tune. An old concentration is on his face, a hunger for the pleasure of the music, for this moment. Those lips. Everything else might be going to seed but the lips are still his. He switches his attention sharply to me. He's noticed me absently lobbing pebbles onto the lawn and is frowning. 'Woof!' Whatever frequency of compos mentis he'd just tapped into has gone again. 'Woof!' He lifts up the dog, pointing its head towards the lawn.

'Oh, I see. Doggy wants to chase the stone?'

'Woof!' He is passing the dog to me. He chuckles at my pretend yap back to him, laughing even more as the dog jumps down from the chair to sniff at the earth.

The dog's fur is warm, its belly breathing in my hand as we cross the wasteland searching for the pebble. What would the neighbours think, if they happened to look over the fence now? The dog has found the pebble, nosing up to it. 'Look, Patrick, she's found it!' This dog, unlike all of Emily and Matthew's childhood soft toys, is going to be a girl. Patrick claps his hands together – watching me journey back on hands and knees, the dog gambolling across the ground towards him, barking, and Patrick barking back, as if they are communicating with each other. There is no doubt in my mind any more that he thinks the dog is real. Maybe it is me that he thinks is not real – who knows? – but we are here together, nonetheless. Me, the dog, him, all still here.

The beautiful, earthy smell of the stall pulls me towards it. A tower of beetroot crates is stacked up by the till next to a row of cauliflower heads, all along the counter, firm as old lady perms. The vendor is out back, inside a little storage shed. 'Be with you shortly,' he calls out. At the next stall a man is pouring a cascade of ice into a display trough. The sounds and smells of the market are bringing me back to my very first days at the restaurant, walking round here between shifts, giddied by it, while the rest of them went to the pub. The veg man comes out with a clap of his large, soily hands. 'I'm not rightly open yet but seeing as you're here.' He gives a big smile and two deep wrinkles open at the corners of his eyes. 'What can I help you with?'

'Vegetables.'

'Ah, well. You've come to the right place, then. Any in particular that you're after?'

'White and red onions, cavolo nero, snow peas, heritage tomatoes. A twenty-five-K sack of Kerr's Pinks and another of fingerlings. Garlic, ruby chard and Jerusalem artichokes.'

'Well. Now, there's a start to my day.'

'I'm from the Longwool. Our veg supplier's let us down, again.'

'You one of the chefs there, are you?'

'Senior sous, believe it or not.'

He makes a hum of approval. 'I'd best make a good impression, then. I haven't got all that lot exactly as you said it, but what I don't I'll have something in the neighbourhood. Will you write down what amount you need of each while I go and fetch the potatoes.' He unspools and tears off a slip of till paper, then hands it to me with a pencil.

While he is in his shed, the market is everywhere full of life around me: shouts rising to the rafters; the whir of a charcuterie slicer; the smell of bacon from the market café. He glimpses through the doorway at me, then goes deeper inside the shed. What will Frank think of my initiative, coming here for these vegetables that will undoubtedly not be cheap – only a couple of weeks after my promotion, while the memory of Chef Stewart's diner-punching disgrace is still raw and Frank is himself under pressure to prove himself up to the job of replacing him?

He returns heaving the first sack of potatoes, using the strength of his shoulders to heave it, the tendons and radial muscles of his forearms tightening. He sets the sack down onto the ground before me and the gorgeous smell of the potatoes gusts up.

'It'll take my KPs all morning to clean these. It looks like a bag of coal.'

He laughs. 'They're scruffy, all right, but your diners will be happy, believe me. Your potatoes usually come in wrapping paper, do they?'

'And ribbons. When they do come.'

The unexpectedness of this exchange, its light-heartedness, is rousing a forgotten version of me: bold, naughty.

'Tell you what, then – if you'll give me a minute to price this lot up before I box and bag everything, I'll walk you over with the cart, deliver it myself, how's about that?'

'That's okay, thank you. You don't need to. I'll send a couple of the boys across.'

'No, I've offered now and I'm happy to.' He picks a potato in each hand from the sack and clonks them together. A scab of soil falls to the ground. 'Highlight of my week, this.'

He goes back into the shed, taking out a large wooden crate and a couple of smaller sacks, then starts gathering the rest of the order together, unaware or unbothered by me watching him. When he has finished, he wheels out of the shed a rickety wooden cart with two long handles.

'That's dirtier than your potatoes.'

'Hey, don't knock the chariot,' he says, loading the sacks and boxes into it. 'You'd be surprised the effect its rustic charm has on some of my buyers.'

He takes a sturdy hold of the handles and starts to push. We move together through the market, the usual weight of my fatigue lifted, this morning, by a new vitality.

'Look – see how jealous he is,' he says, giving a short wave to the fish vendor, who is watching us over the top of a polystyrene box of prawns.

We are exiting the market onto the street, which is busy already with people on their way to work, some of them turning their attention to the curiosity of this cart trundling through the commuters.

'Are you sure you don't mind doing this? It's at least a five-minute walk, even without an antique wheelbarrow.'

'Not at all.' The wooden wheels are clacking along the pavement. 'I'm not one to pass up on a good thing when it walks right up to me.'

It is only as Isaac starts singing that the silence of the kitchen becomes so noticeable. At every section they are inside their own worlds of prep, each of them suspended in a trance of cooking, all breathing the same air of smoke and garlic but their minds in a time and space apart, a dream. Isaac is singing something soft and continuous, the song emanating from deep within him, in his bones. From here by the deck oven his head is framed by the plonge entrance: his face tilted downward, eyes half-closed as he sponges a dish. It is an easy thing to imagine him standing over one of his children, when they were little, tending to them. He glances round at me coming into the plonge but he keeps singing, smiling a thank-you to Sandy when she puts his tea on the passthrough. In a few minutes Peter will be here. The thought makes me step forwards towards the plonge, restive, needing to move. Isaac has stopped singing to take a first hot sip of his tea.

'That was lovely, Isaac.'

'Thank you, Lady Boss. It is a song from when my boys were babies. Michael Bublé.'

'Oh.'

'Yes. They liked this song a lot.'

On the other side of the passthrough, in the service gangway, Sandy and Karolina are shrouded in a mist of boiling vinegar-water, chatting as they polish a bucketful of cutlery. Something above the gangway wall distracts them momentarily. Karolina stands on her tiptoes to peek over the top – but it is Jimbo, his face appearing above them now, laughing; Peter is not here yet. The remembered sensation of his hand on my waist outside the restaurant is spreading across my hips, provoking me to move again, picking up a nest of cleaned terrine moulds from Isaac's for-kitchen shelf. Isaac is putting down his tea, wanting to take the moulds from me.

'No, that's all right, Isaac. You go on break whenever you're ready.'

Back in the kitchen the boys are moving around, talking, the trance broken. Anton is showing something on his board to Dan. Jack and Turtle coming over to the section too. Dan is asking Anton something, Anton nodding, starting to unpeel the clingfilm from whatever it is on his board that is definitely not an element on today's menu.

'What is that, Anton?'

'Just an experiment, Chef.'

He pulls free the last of the clingfilm – revealing a perfect, strange cylinder. He takes a knife and cuts through it near one end.

'Look – magic!'

Running through it in swirls, like a Swiss roll, are different tones and textures of poultry tightly packed together.

'Please don't tell me you've used meat glue in there, Anton.'

'I bought it online. It's an experiment. I bought the goose and the chicken myself too. Mad, isn't it?'

'Something is. Meat glue, Michael Bublé. Why did no one tell me this morning that I'd woken up fifteen years ago?' And if it was, the thought flashes across my mind, then it would be Tristan, not Peter, who was about to walk into the restaurant. It never felt like this, though, waiting for Tristan to arrive.

Dan is bent over, inspecting the bird roulade. 'Could you use this on anything? Fish, too?'

'Nobody here is putting out any dish with meat glue in it, Dan. That's all you need to know. Right, everybody, show's over. Where are we with lunch prep?'

Jack and Turtle go back to their sections. Dan lingering a little longer for a final study of Anton's chickoose. He wants to understand how it works, what he can learn from it. He will try this at home.

'It's an enzyme, Dan. It bonds the proteins. Come on — let's get back to prep.'

Dan returns to the fish section, where his own prep is already finished, neat, on point. He has made a place for himself here. Watching him now, with Freddy, coordinating the fish dishes for lunch service, a little flush of satisfaction warms me, knowing that it is because of me that he feels safe here, that he has been able to develop like this. Although, to be fair, he's got some unexpected balls, too. Telling the rest of them to stop having a go at Karolina last week after her wrong-table-away mistake. They're still taking the piss out of him for it, but they respect him, more with every week that goes by. It is not difficult to see his direction from here, how swiftly he is going to progress: CDP in a year or two, sous in three or four, maybe even head chef somewhere before he's thirty-five, if he plays his cards right. All of it years quicker than me; a different track, worn smooth by men's feet.

'Chaud behind!' Xav is coming through with a GN pan full of fuming pink liquid.

Dan has started to prepare his spoons for service. Even at this, his fingers are quick and precise. It would have made me resent him, once – to predict how effortlessly he will go up the line – but it doesn't now. My name is not on the menu, or monogrammed to my whites, but this is my team. It is me who teaches them, who makes them respect each other, respect the waitresses, me who watches over them.

'Potato Man!'

My shoulders cramp in anticipation of seeing him. Jack and Turtle are moving straight away to say hello and help him with the bags and crates. Peter is in the service gangway. He greets them and looks across, between the pass shelves, to call good morning to me. He comes inside the kitchen, going towards the meat section. In his hands is a small, golden pineapple. He places it down on Anton's board, next to the glued bird.

'Straight from the tree for you, son.'

Anton is grinning. 'How much do—'

'Don't be daft, man. It's for you. Enjoy.'

'Go on break, Anton. All of you – you can go on break.'

Anton is immediately crafting his pineapple with a paring knife, slicing away the skin and, as the others gather around him, removing the eyes and the core and chopping it into wedges to share out. They all leave for the fire exit. Peter is standing in front of me. From the floor there is the creaking sound of the awnings being wound out on the terrace.

'Shall we go to the office for a minute, Peter?'

He follows me out of the back of the kitchen. Our feet are falling into step, echoing down the empty corridor. Behind us there comes an outbreak of laughter from the fire-exit court-yard. My limbs are in control of me, taking me onward. Whatever is about to happen, whatever the other parts of me want now to happen, it does not feel wrong. It feels, arriving at the office door, uncontainable.

It is hot and stuffy inside the office. There is an atmos-phere of Frank's antiperspirant. At the first gust of the fan, the walls start to flutter with pinned-up dockets and rotas.

'I feel like you're about to fire me, Anita.'

'No chance. Your vegetables are too good.'

A silly thing to say but it relaxes something, makes it feel less out of the ordinary how closely we are standing together in this hot little room. Peter quietly clears his throat. His fin-gers are touching mine.

'You doing okay?'

'Yes.'

'I've been worried, not seeing you this last couple of weeks, with how you were in the park that last time.'

'Thank you. I'm fine, though.'

Our chests have come together. The fan and the fluttering paper loud now. Peter's cheek is against my temple, his mouth almost touching my ear, all these months, years of need pouring through my nerves and bones and skin. My fingertips press at his back, pulling him towards me. The office is roaring around us as my lips touch his neck. There will be a reckoning for this – but my body is unafraid, in control.

A loud knocking on the door makes us both jump.

'Chef!'

For a few seconds neither of us moves.

'Chef – are you in there? Chef? We can't find the bookings sheet.'

2013

'Well, here she is, look, the lady chef.'

'Hello, Peter. Are you closing up?'

'This very minute. You wanting an order for tomorrow, are you?'

'No. I'm just walking through on my way to the station. Finished for the day.'

His head disappears beneath the counter. From down there he calls up: 'I'll walk with you. I'm about done with my close-down.'

He goes into the storage shed. The shouts and clatters of the market packing up resound about the place. All the lovely, expensive produce being locked up or loaded into vans to leave the city for the night.

'All done.' His hands are shining wet. His thin hair damp too where he has just wiped a hand across it. The fish man gives a goodbye salute to Peter as we come past. 'Only lunches for you this week, is it?'

'Yes. I pay for it next week, though. Five doubles in a row.'

'Hell's teeth. I don't know what makes you do it.'

'The money.'

He understands, smiling, that it's a joke. 'Well,' he says, 'if we all did what we do just for the money, the world would be a pretty dull place.'

The street outside the market is busy already. After-work drinkers are standing outside the bars. A group of young men in suits has spilled onto the pavement and we have to step around them, onto the road.

'Five doubles.' He whistles in admiration. 'How long have you been doing this for, Anita, if you don't mind me asking?'

He waits for me to calculate the years, taking them away from the children's ages. 'Twenty years, more or less.'

He breathes out in an exaggerated way, like blowing on a child's food. 'That's a long time in that game.' A young man on a scooter cuts suddenly across our path – Peter gently taking hold of my elbow, safeguarding me. 'Sorry if I'm nebbing here, but do you have children?'

'Two. They're grown up now.' Although one of them, it feels shameful to tell him, has never moved out. Never, fully, grown up.

'I have a couple of those myself.'

The station is up ahead. We have slowed, approaching it.

'Do you see them much?'

'Not enough. Their lives are up there. Boyfriends. Their mother. They come down from time to time, like, and we have a giggle.'

Currents of people are coming past us outside the station. It feels wrong, parting at this moment in the conversation, the first time we have spoken about anything so personal.

'I'll be seeing you, then,' he says.

'You will. Have a nice day off tomorrow.'

'Will do. Enjoy your doubles.'

He turns back for his bus stop and at once has vanished. For a short while my eyes search the mass of heads – a strange, empty feeling growing, needing to catch sight of him, but he has been lost to the crowd of commuters.

My hands and fingers feel different somehow, even doing something as ordinary as this, washing up this morning's mugs and plates, as if there is fresh blood inside them. Every movement, in some small, sensitive way, is bringing me back to those moments together in the office last week. Petya's voice is coming through from the living room. How long since my last check of my phone? Fifteen minutes? Less? But as soon as the washing-up is finished, my hands move involuntarily to pick it up. There is no new message. The last one is still mine: *Thank you, Peter. I agree we should talk. I know I'm always keeping you waiting but I just need some more time. Still not sure what I feel.* It's like something written by a teenager. Angsty and confused. Except that my feelings are in fact only too identifiable: need, desire – and bound to them, sly and inseparable as meat glue, the guilt of wanting to allow them in, aware all the time that upstairs inside the drawer the Sharpie line has been reached, the jar ready, waiting, to answer Patrick's plea.

Petya's voice from the living room is briefly louder: 'He is lazy, your dog. Lazy dog!' A whicker of delight from Patrick. He really did seem to understand earlier when she told him that she will be doing all of his care visits from now on. And when she made her joke – 'Maybe I should move in' – the impromptu picture of it, the three of us living together in this house, Patrick cared for and content, me and Petya sharing the load, free to live our other lives outside the house, held me for a little while. The idea of it now, however, standing here at the sink, feels barmy.

Petya is in the kitchen doorway. She sees me putting the phone into the back pocket of my jeans.

'All okay in there?'

She presses her hands together, moving them to the side of her tilting head.

'Good work.'

She stays where she is, observing me.

'Would you like some lunch, Petya?'

Silly to feel embarrassed about asking her something so basic. It has never come easily to me, friendship.

'Yes. I have my lunch.'

She goes out into the hallway to her rucksack. Only with Peter has it ever come easily. If friendship is ever what it really was, rather than a cover for something else, and that in truth every interaction between us over the last seven years has always had this under its skin. It will never be possible any more to know. Petya is returning with the rucksack. At the table she unzips it and takes out a white plastic box.

'We can eat together,' she says.

She sits down at the table with her box in front of her, waiting, watching me take things out of the fridge – saucisson, cheeses, the kipper pâté that Freddy over-prepped yesterday – to put down in the middle of the table with a loaf of bread, butter, cherry tomatoes, a sharp knife, two plates and two forks.

'Let's eat, shall we?'

Petya looks impassively at the spread. 'Yes.' She unclips the lid of her box and holds it out to me. 'Try.'

There is a bright salad inside: roasted red peppers, cucumber, spring onion, tomato and a grated, briny white cheese, the first forkful of it sharp and satisfying in my mouth.

'That's very nice.'

Petya is nodding, although she has already started on the bread and the saucisson. 'This is good,' she says. 'Posh food.'

'It's from the restaurant.'

She turns around, chewing, and points down the hallway.

'What was he like, Patrick?' She turns back to me. 'What man was he?'

How plainly she states her judgement: that a different person, detached from the past, is sitting asleep in the living room.

'To be honest, Petya, he was a bit of an arsehole.'

She is nodding again, tucking now into the pâté.

'Maybe not at first, he wasn't, but later.'

'My boyfriend, he was an arsehole too.' She pauses to finish her mouthful. 'Very nice in the beginning. Then . . .' She mimics hands closing around her throat.

'What did you do?'

She shrugs her shoulders. 'Buy a plane ticket.' She puts her fork down and mimes waving goodbye. It is endearing, how much she uses her hands to express herself. This, probably, is how she communicates with Patrick. 'In the beginning,' she says, 'they make a space for you. It is a gift they give. Patrick, he gave you something like this in the beginning?'

Our forks are working side by side at the salad now that Petya has finished the pâté and the saucisson.

'Yes. I felt safe with him.' She is looking at me, making a noise of understanding. 'He made me feel normal.'

And it is the truth. He never did, really, turn me into someone else, someone better. He didn't need to. Just being with him was enough for me to do it by myself.

'What about you and your boyfriend, Petya?'

'Ha!' She wipes a hand across her mouth. 'My boyfriend is always an arsehole. But his gift is he has a very sexy body.'

She puts her head back and launches into a belly-laugh so long and rapturous that it is impossible not to join in.

The red roofs of the town are coming into view. A horde of seagulls has occupied the ship. A couple of them have landed in the pool and are bobbing up and down, cackling, cocksure as pitch invaders. Patrick is gripping the handrail, his sight on land. He looks queasy as hell. Another hot, tiring excursion to come — temporarily releasing us from this ship-island of each other. To think it was my idea, this cruise, to avoid a party by going away instead for our joint big birthdays, alone together. The wind is hard here by the rail. The new earrings flap against my neck. We are both weighed down with clichés. Not that he wore his cufflinks at the botulism buffet last night, although he obviously ate plentifully enough from it, looking at the state of him, his face white and peculiar — as if he's about to tell me something grave, or throw up into the sea.

'I've been thinking about Christmas,' he declares.

If, through the sea spray, he spots me rolling my eyes, he's not rising to it until he's finished his speech.

'I think we should all go away together somewhere. Emily

395

would love that, and Matthew might even come too for some of it if we can find the right kind of place. An announcement blurts from the Tannoy. It is barely audible over the hiss of the sea. *Gathering point . . . guides . . . lunch*. At least he's chosen to have an argument that can move onshore.

'How long are you thinking we go away for?'

'A week. We could stay on for New Year.'

It is bait. A whole bloody week? We haven't spent a week together, the four of us, since they were children. Does he really think that Matthew is going to agree to this?

'You know I can't take that long off at Christmas.'

He is opening and closing his left eye against the spray.

'Oh, yes, of course. The restaurant. You have to get your priorities in order.'

'You know it's our busiest time.'

His hand clenches to the rail. His face, when he reels round, is bleached and gleaming with seawater. 'How long *are* you prepared to take off, then?'

'The same as always. A few days. Frank has already said I can have Christmas Day and Boxing Day, maybe the twenty-seventh.'

'Isn't he kind?'

'He's my boss. It's only his second Christmas as head chef, and it's already looking like a mental one.' A party of shore-trippers has started to gather on the deck below us at the entrance to the Aquatheatre. The ship's engine growling as we angle into the harbour. 'I can't pick and choose when I work. I am an employee, remember.'

'Oh, now I understand. That's what this is about. The neighbourhood restaurant fantasy.' Water gulps and slaps against the hull. 'And if you were your own boss, you'd give yourself Christmas off, would you? Ha! Your place would be that profitable, would it?' He looks even more unsteady. Self-righteous anger has washed him out. He looks withered and ancient, clutching the rail like a Zimmer frame. Wretched pity snakes through me. He should come away from the edge, go back to the cabin and lie down while the ship is docked.

'You are a selfish cow, aren't you?'

He closes his left eye and keeps it shut, looking at me foully out of the other. He is listing against the rail. The sudden thrilling image of him, plummeting, the fluttering of his shirt tail above the white fizz of water. He is mumbling something, incomprehensible in the roar of the engine: 'Only. Only. Finish, you. Finish.' He collapses to the deck. People further down the rail spin around to look. He is not moving.

'Patrick? Can you hear me?' His ear is hot against my mouth. 'Can you hear me?' His chest rising and falling. 'Leg,' he gasps. His open eye is glazed over. His arm laid out on the deck, the hand upturned and pale at the end of it, a dead crab. A man crouches down beside him. Another man touching his neck with the tips of his fingers. 'Is this your husband?' The two men start lifting him by the armpits. 'This man needs a doctor!' Down below, the party of faces shine in the sunlight. One of the men shouting to them, 'Is there a doctor down there?' The faces all stare back. 'We need to get him to the infirmary, now!' The men are lugging

Patrick away. His shirt has come untucked. A bit of his stomach is showing. They move off down the deck and Patrick's new boat shoes drag behind him, leaving two slug trails in the film of moisture.

As the front door closes, a wall of heat surrounds me and it is as though service is still going on and there was no journey, no gap, between work and here – my own fault for leaving boiler instructions for Petya in case he says he's cold.

Unusually for her, she has left a block of cheese unwrapped on the kitchen counter. A crumbed plate and a bottle of Tabasco standing next to it, exhumed from somewhere in the past. The pile of post is in a mess, like someone has gone through it, and under the toaster the bits-and-bollocks drawer is slightly open. Something is wrong. In the quick terror that takes hold of me it is hard to recall with certainty whether the front door had been locked.

Up the stairs, the bedroom door has been left open – and in the dream of heat and panic Patrick is here, sitting on the bedside chair – but he is young again, a ghoul from a former time, the teacher smiling at me in the staffroom.

'Hello, Mum.'

My arms are numb and won't lift.

'I let myself in. I've still got a key.'

Patrick is in the bed, asleep.

'You didn't tell me you were coming.'

'I'm not here for long. I presumed you'd be at work.'

He has brought grapes. Big red ones. If Patrick tried to eat those he could choke. Why is he here? Almost two years without a single visit, all this time not knowing if he's on his knees somewhere, and yet here he is, alive and well, sneaking back into the house. It is how healthy he looks, irrationally, that is provoking. How obvious it somehow makes it that he has chosen, until now, not to come. He has left it to Emily. The daughter's job.

'You should have told me you were coming, Matthew. He's not well enough for surprises.'

'Sorry.'

'When did you get here?'

'Half an hour ago, maybe.'

He is looking down at the carpet. Don't push him away. Not after all this time. He is waiting for it, the excuse not to come and see Patrick again. Do not push him away.

'Has he been awake?'

'He was when I got here.'

'And did he—'

'He knew who I was. We spoke.'

This must be untrue. Is it possible? An impulse to tell him that he's wrong forms in my mouth.

'That will have made him happy.'

Matthew sits staring at Patrick in the bed. 'Whatever he is, Mum, he's not happy.'

And as he says it an acceptance moves in me: that this is wrong too. He *is* happy, sometimes. The person Matthew knew – and, when he left, could not bear to be near – might be gone, but this new person, in his way, can be happy. Stroking his dog; sitting in the sun; eating cheese and tomato sandwiches.

Matthew is looking at me. 'You've moved out.'

'What do you mean?' An instinctive vision of Peter appears so vividly before me that it feels like Matthew must be able to see him too. 'No, I haven't.'

'You've moved into Emily's room.'

He has been in the bedrooms. He must see the alarm on my face, remembering only now what is hidden in his bottom drawer.

'When did you do that?'

'Months ago. He needed more space.'

'Oh, right, makes sense.'

He has not found them – the pills, the letters; the one addressed to him – thank God. They will need to be moved, as soon as he goes to the toilet, into my own chest of drawers.

'Will you stay the night?'

'No, it's okay. A friend said I can stay at his.'

'I'd like you to stay.'

He hesitates. 'All right. Thanks, Mum.'

'Can I feed you as well? Are you hungry?'

'Yes. Starving.'

He is standing up, coming towards me. Hugging me, quickly, stiffly, like the boy who used to live here, about to go to school for the day. He leaves the room to go downstairs – as if it's an everyday thing, hugging his mother who cannot at this moment move after him down the stairs because her legs have turned to wax from wanting so intensely to be with him, to hold him for longer.

He is taking note of the grab rail at the bottom of the stairs. The non-slip runner along the hallway. What is he thinking? His dad doesn't need these things? She's stolen that runner from work? A smile forming on my lips. Here we are again. How quickly things return to normal. Less than ten minutes back home and already the same old question: what is he thinking?

He sits down at the kitchen table.

'What would you like to eat?'

'Not fussed. Anything.'

'All right, then. I've got some British asparagus I took from work.' And again the guilty thought of Peter interrupts me: my whispered instruction during his delivery this morning, to meet me next week. 'I could put some in an omelette for you.'

'Yeah, sounds nice.' He is taking his shirt off. His arms, in just his T-shirt, are surprisingly muscly. 'It's so bloody hot in the house, Mum.'

'Tell me about it.'

The first little melts of butter run bubbling into the grooves and scratches of the old pan. When the asparagus spears go into it and begin to sizzle, the green, happy smell of them comes alive. Matthew leans back in his chair. He is sitting, maybe he doesn't realise it, in the same place that he always used to sit in, closely watching me act out this scene from his childhood: cracking the eggs into a bowl, thumbing the last of the albumen out from the shells, beating, removing the asparagus and pouring the egg gloopily into the pan to work with a fork until the edges start to set and the spears, four sunburned alien legs, can be pushed softly into the omelette.

'There you are, my boy. Done.'

As soon as the plate is before him he goes at it hungrily.

'You make a good omelette, Mum.'

'Thank you. I do.'

'Aren't you having one?'

'I'm not hungry. Too tired. Always too tired.'

He thinks about this for a moment. 'Em says that Dad's got a carer.'

'A care worker, yes, he does. I can't manage on my own any longer, Matthew. It's too much.'

'He won't like her touching him.'

'Unfortunately, that's her job.'

'It's weird, thinking of a stranger with him like that.'

He has almost finished his omelette already. It should not be this difficult to resist pointing out that he is taking an interest in his father's care visits six months too late; to tell him that, then, yes, they were strangers, a troop of them, but the one he has now seems genuinely to care for him. To let Matthew have his selfishness.

'I know it's difficult, Matthew.'

He has gone very silent. Is he thinking about his father with concern, with love, even? He has chosen to come here, so something about the way he feels must have changed. In his silence, though, there is no way of knowing whether the hostility towards his dad is still there, or if it has passed, consumed, like everything else, by Patrick's dementia.

'What did you speak to him about?'

'Nothing, really. Hello. He just kept saying that. Hello. Hello.'

He doesn't cry, he doesn't allow anything to break from him, but he lets me hold him properly now, letting me press his head to my stomach, the heat and energy of him travelling through my clothes, my skin, uniting us.

'He wouldn't have wanted to live like this, Mum.'

'No, he wouldn't. He's not that person, though, Matthew, not any more.'

Backs. Backs of heads. We follow on at the rear, the four of us moving in step behind David and his family, some half-familiar cousin in front of them, each party shuffling forward towards her pit. Emily and Matthew have hold of Patrick, either side of him, by the arms. He is burst. His shoulders going, the breath shuddering through his nose. The first mourners have come to a stop by the graveside. Long coats. New, black gloves. The bright winter morning clean against their faces. David is streaming too, but his children don't cling onto him; it's Ruth who they've gone to. Patrick and David have picked up where they left off last night, side by side for the first time in years to receive the body that lay before them in ecstasy: her sons together wailing through the Rosary. Which of them chose the photograph on the stand? A person, a scene, that must once have existed: Mary a young woman laughing with her children – gentle, happy. Was there a time, the photograph seemed to be asking, before Gordon closed her inside the house and removed the doors to the world, when she didn't feel afraid of failing at the life she had been handed; when she had dreams for herself?

We gather around the hole.

The priest starts reading a verse of scripture. Next to the hole the mound of earth has hardened. Crystals of frost glow with cold, ready to shatter on top of the coffin that other men have carried. Neither of her sons willing to do it. On the other side of the grave Ruth has bowed her head. To my surprise, she is crying. My own indignation after the liturgy, when Mary was wheeled outside on her dessert trolley and the only longing in me was to kick it into the car park, is softening – into an acknowledgement, now that she is dead, that so much of my resentment for her was really because she, his mum, was alive. Because she got to live. Something that Patrick always took for granted. And now a new thought is unfolding, towards this woman who badmouthed me to Patrick and my children and probably to most of these stiff, red ears gathered round ready to commit her to the ground, that maybe some of her resentment for me and my choices came from the simple fact that she was never allowed any.

David is shaking. His blasted cheeks are blowing in and out, watching his mother hover above her grave, no doubt thinking about the flask of whisky inside his coat pocket. Slowly she gets eased in beside Gordon, saving her place for her from the grave next door, ready to retake possession of her. Together again at last, rejoined for more of the same buttoned-up misery they used to share before it got broken off by Gordon's massive stroke in Forest Hill Sainsbury's.

For a few quiet seconds my eyes remain on the coffin.

Briefly, it is not Mary inside; it is Mum. She is smiling, and a powerful wave of peacefulness passes through me at the thought of her, happy now, at rest.

A cloud of breath has collected above all the heads. Life, floating to the sky. Patrick is turning to me. Not with need – he's got the children for that today – but with curiosity. *What is* she *thinking?* The answer, if he really wants to know, now that his mother has entered the ground and the Lord's Prayer is bounding through the chill air and she is no longer here to judge me – this wicked daughter-in-law who gave up a stable career and who once let her child go missing – is, quietly and unexpectedly, forgiveness.

There are groups of people on every stretch of grass, enjoying the Spring Bank Holiday sunshine. Some of them have brought rugs and picnics with them. A party of young men with their shirts off are taking it in turns to walk across a tightrope they have strung between two tree trunks.

'Champion day, isn't it?'

'It's beautiful.'

He keeps adjusting his baseball cap, taking it off and putting it back on again. Either he is nervous or he's just not used to wearing one. The avenue is getting more crowded as we get closer to the Observatory, so we peel away in unspoken agreement down a quieter path. An awareness is growing in me: that all of this has changed. Peter can feel it too. Outwardly he is just himself, cheery, gentle, but there is something altered between us, a tension. There is no way back to the pretence of this being innocent any more: every word, every movement has a new meaning, loaded with the memory of that morning in the office and the palpable desire in both of us now to return to it.

'So, Matthew's stopping a while, then?'

'It looks like it. He's on leave from his hotel for another couple of weeks.'

'That's great, Anita. Must be nice, having him home?'

'It is. He's as quiet as ever, and he takes himself away to his room or he just goes out without letting me know – so, all told, it's like he never left.'

'And he's been spending some time with his dad, has he?'

'He has.'

The image of Matthew sitting each day in the chair by the bed, wordlessly watching over Patrick, stays with me for a few seconds. The impossibility of knowing what he is feeling. Whether it is care – love – or if his anger is still there, the condemnation behind his eyes as fierce now as it was the day he left.

'And now Emily's coming at the weekend.'

'Full house, then.'

We fall into silence, continuing down the path. Both of us are waiting for the other to say something. What is there to say, though? That morning, everything felt clear, out of our control – and that same hunger to abandon control is coiling inside me now – but here, walking in the sunshine with our hands and bodies apart, there is only uncertainty. An ice-cream van is parked in the clearing ahead of us. Children beetling about with cones and slushies.

'Would you like an ice cream, Peter?'

He is smiling, surprised.

'A ninety-nine, please. Flake, sprinkles, raspberry sauce.'

'Anything else? Glacé cherry on top?'

'No, that's all, thank you.' He stops at the edge of the flower garden. 'I'll be just here waiting.'

There's no queue at the van. The man inside is sitting on a stool, scrolling on his phone. He stands up and puts the phone down on a chest freezer.

'Please can I have two ninety-nines with flakes, one with sprinkles and raspberry sauce.'

The man nods, glancing down at the space beside me, probably expecting to see a grandchild. He turns to the machine to pull on its handle and ice cream discharges from the spout. As the cone fills, twisting with the delicate movements of the man's hand, an old film is being projected onto the backs of my eyes, of Tristan demonstrating how to milk a cow. The man finishes the first ice cream and puts it in a small stand, pausing to take my payment before he starts on the second one. On the plastic side of the slushie tank the faint, lurid blue reflection of Peter is visible, and a surge of devotion courses through me. For just a moment, it feels so simple, to love somebody.

'There you are. Two ninety-nines.'

'Thank you.'

It would not be fair, though, on anybody. It would not be right.

'Enjoy,' the man says.

From the little rail of the flower garden, Peter is watching me approach. He takes his ice cream, thanking me, and examines it for a short time.

'Doesn't matter how long,' he says, his voice oddly self-conscious, as if he has been rehearsing this. 'What I just said about being here waiting for you. That's what I want to tell you. I'm not going anywhere.'

2016

'The house?'

'Yes.'

'The bloody house? Have you lost your mind, woman?' The same thought, to be fair, that struck me too when the financial adviser explained the process.

'It's standard practice. It doesn't mean that we'd have to sell it. It would be put down as collateral.'

He glowers at me like he would a pupil he is about to punish, after he's told them how stupid they are. 'It is not standard practice with my house.' He turns his attention to the kitchen wall, exasperated, lifting his hand up to rest against it. 'How long are you going to carry on with this silly fantasy? Even if you did have any backers, or a proper plan, a site, any capital or any business experience what-so-bloody-ever, it would still be a pipe dream. You know the figures. Most new restaurants are dead within a year.' He breaks off. Pouts. 'Do you know how long, how hard I have worked to get us to where we are?'

'I don't know. About as long as me, at a guess.'

'You selfish cow.'

He sits down on a chair, fatigued with anger. Maybe he's thinking about the last time he called me that — what happened to him when he did. Or maybe he's remembering the months the selfish cow took off work after the stroke, taking him back and forth from the hospital and the doctor's, cooking all his meals, helping him with his physio, his speech exercises, his shoelaces.

'You're fifty-two. You don't need something new to fail at.'

He is stroking a hand up and down the table top. Poor man: the bank is going to take his kitchen table away from him. Another precious object that's going to up and leave him. Just like the children. His mother. His hair. *Something new to fail at.* Does he have a list of these failures written down somewhere? He might do, actually. And not hard to guess what he will have put at the top of it. Motherhood; career. That three-legged race to nowhere.

'I do have a plan.'

A little laugh.

'I've been thinking about this for so many years, Patrick. It's not a dream. It has always been my plan.'

'On your own? Without any backers?'

'I will find backers.'

'Who? The economy is in . . .' There is a lapse as he looks at the table, trying to find the word, tapping his finger in annoyance at not being able to. 'Meltdown. For years, in meltdown. Who can risk their money on a little independent restaurant? However lovely I'm sure it would be.'

The change in tone is disorienting, but he will not make me cry.

'Anyway,' his voice has changed again, 'whose name do you think is on the house deed?'

Matthew is in the doorway, looking into the room. Patrick, noticing him, goes quiet. None of us speak – Matthew staying where he is, looking coldly at Patrick. Something is passing between them, some private understanding. Whatever it is – this conflict that has grown between them over the past year – it looks from Matthew's face like this might be the moment that he finally breaks his bitter silence – until, just as suddenly as he appeared, he is gone.

They've done a nice job of the sign. A bluebird, flying above the green. Hand-painted, by the look of it. All of the outside tables are full, the café bustling, its merry clamour drifting across the road now that the traffic has stopped for the lights. It really is a good location – right on the corner, in the middle of the two main footfall streets around the green. Peter's voice comes back to me as the lights change: *That's why you'll be staying well clear of the diners, when we do find our place.* The thought of him, momentarily, brightens in my mind – picturing him by the ice-cream van holding his ninety-nine, looking at me intently, ready with his promise.

A man in a big car is hesitating, waiting for me to cross, irritated by my dawdling. He utters something to himself at me finally stepping in front of him, not returning my smile, and speeds grumpily away as soon as the road is clear.

Closer up, it's easy to see that the clientele have money. Old couples in expensive beige clothes. Sunbathers who have stepped across from the green for lunch. Posh teenagers. Families enjoying the end of the half-term holiday – a holiday that we used to enjoy too, once upon a time. A holiday, imagine that. A proper one. Quiet, white villages. Paper tablecloths. The sea. A man is standing next to me, looking at the menu in the window. He goes in and is followed by a woman who, inside, sees another woman with two young children and greets her with a hug while the children stand close to their mother's legs. A waitress is coming out with plates for one of the outside tables. It's a quiche and cold-counter type of operation, and the food looks decent enough. They are still hiring, according to the notice underneath the menu. *Bubbly, experienced staff wanted*. The waitress is going back in. Before the door closes behind her an urge to see the place is pushing me inside. Immediately it is loud. They've exposed the brickwork and the space is bouncing with voices. There are tables of customers only drinking coffee. Big mistake. And the walls have been covered with bric-a-brac – plates and dangling cups – alongside an exhibition of crap art for sale. Still, they've got other things right. The floor is beautiful. They've done just what Peter wanted to do: lightly lacquered the wood and buffed it to a soft shine. The tables attractively but efficiently distributed across the L-space; reclaimed stone troughs with tall plants beginning to lean in to the daylight. The floor aprons are a good choice, too: charcoal tabards over jeans. One of the waiters is coming towards me, displaying his teeth with a big smile, unquestionably bubbly.

'Hi there. Are you wanting a table?'

'No, I just wanted to come in and take a look.' The service door to the kitchen swings open – a chef with both hands in the air, another laughing – then swings shut again. 'Another time, though, thank you.'

*

He is waiting for me outside the restaurant, a few metres from the entrance. The first words out of my mouth, from habit, are almost to ask him why he hasn't gone in ahead of me – until a more powerful intuition checks it. This is who he is.

'You're late, Mum.'

'I know – sorry.'

He lets me lead the way inside. Richard is coming across the floor to greet us. He says a friendly hello to Matthew, shaking his hand, then kisses me professionally on the cheek. A first.

'You found the place okay, then?' Richard says, grinning at me and touching me on the arm as he turns to take us through. This tone is new: warm, cheeky, the tone that young men use to flirt with their grandmas. Although not the young men and grandmas in our family. Matthew is alert, studying everything: the restaurant, my exchange with Richard, the floor staff – who have noticed us and are waving hello, Sandy blowing a kiss.

'Here we are.'

Richard has given us a table on the terrace. Matthew, from the tiny relaxation of his posture, seems pleased, possibly for the extra layer of distance from the restaurant, the kitchen.

'I'll leave you to get settled. Sandy will be over in a minute.'

Matthew is looking out over the foliage fencing at the City. Does he know how much he looks like Patrick? His hair, his forehead, the lips. Of course he doesn't. He wouldn't want to hear it, either.

'Are you hungry?'

He shrugs. 'I'm always hungry.' He turns his face to me. 'Food any good here?'

'Better when I'm on the other side of that wall.'

He gazes through with me at the partition between the floor and the kitchen, my eyes at once moving over it past the service gangway and into the heat and racket and perfect machine of service, craving – for a moment – to be inside it.

'Here she is, look.'

He's pointing at the entrance, where Emily is chatting to Richard. Richard takes her travel bag from her, showing her through, Emily saying hello to waiters she has never met before, instantly at ease on the restaurant floor as she walks towards me and Matthew, who have never really been at ease anywhere. Matthew is already standing up. She steps into the sun of the terrace and goes straight to him.

'Hello, brother.'

'Sister.'

They hug each other, for a long time. When were they last together? Two years? Can it really be as long as that? When they finish and Matthew sits back down, she turns to me.

'Hi, Mum.' She kisses me, briefly holds me tight.

'How was the train?'

'It was fine. Long. Morgan says hello, by the way.' She looks about her at the terrace. 'This is a treat.'

We sit down with Matthew at the table. Sandy, through the open sliding doors to the floor, is advancing with a tray of champagne flutes.

'Well, well,' she says as she comes out onto the terrace.

'Don't you scrub up nicely?' She places the flutes down, one by one on the table. 'From Richard.'

'Thank you. Sandy, these are my children: Emily and Matthew.'

Emily says hello and smiles; Matthew looks at her and nods.

'I hope you're better behaved than her other children.' Sandy gestures towards the kitchen, then walks away towards it, her waiter's knack of leaving on a neat line.

'She's cute.' Emily takes a sip of her champagne, smoothing her hand over the tablecloth. 'Are you showing off, Mum, bringing us here?'

'Not really. I only pay cost here. Pizza Express would have been more expensive.'

Matthew is looking down the tables of the terrace, filling up now with businesspeople. 'I would have preferred Pizza Express,' he says.

Emily is shaking her head at him. 'Tit.'

Both of them laughing, surveying each other.

'How's Morgan?' Matthew asks.

'He's sorry to miss you. Rare opportunity that it is.'

'You can tell him that I'll be at the wedding.'

Emily gives him a black look. 'You bloody well better be.'

'I will. I've already booked the time off work.'

'Have you?' She leans forward, resting her forearms on the table. 'Thank you.'

'It's your wedding, Em. Of course I'm going to be there. I'm not going to miss something like that.'

She is smiling at him, moving her hand to rest under her chin, too pleased it seems to point out all the other events he has missed over the last couple of years. Sandy is returning, carrying three plates of amuse bouche that we have not ordered.

'The kitchen say hi.'

Matthew and Emily tuck in straight away to the smoked eel potato cakes.

'Oh my God.' Emily lifts her face to the sun. 'Poor Morgan.'

They both keep taking from the plates in quick succession, eating without pause, like hungry children.

'So, brother,' Emily says, biting on a prawn, 'how much longer are you staying for?'

'Until the end of next week.' Information he has not told me.

'Catching up with anyone while you're here?'

'No, I don't think so. I want to spend some time with Dad.'

We are both looking at him, the same thought clearly going through our minds: while he is alive. With the last of the amuse bouche finished, Matthew picks up his menu and starts to read it. If Emily is upset, she is not showing it. She looks amused, in fact, her eyes on me.

'So, Mum, what's this with you and the care worker?'

'Petya? We're going for a drink one night, that's all.'

They are smirking at each other. Me – a friend? While we're at it, me all surprises, perhaps they'd like to hear about Peter too.

'I think that's great,' Emily says. 'It's a bit left-field, you know, Dad's care worker, but it's nice. Does he know? Does he understand?'

'I don't think so.'

Is that true, though? He might well not know what it means, my friendship with Petya, just as he doesn't know any more what our marriage means, or what it used to be, unable as he is to piece them together, all the floating parts of his life — but his mind is alert to this shift in his surroundings. He understands, as the sound of us in the house talking moves through his brain, that he is alive.

'Mum, I know this is selfish, but I really want him to be well enough for the wedding.'

'I can't promise you that, Emily. I want him to be too. That's not selfish.'

Sandy is near, coming for our order. She hovers at the terrace edge, judging the scene at our table, then goes back in.

'Thank you, Mum.' She taps on the menu. 'Tell us: what's good here?'

'It's all good.'

She smiles, beginning to read it. Both of them are poring over it carefully, their eyes scanning across the lines. A thought speeding: of them opening their letters, starting to read them.

Emily is standing up. 'I just need to nip to the toilet. Should have gone on the train. If she comes can you order me the celeriac croquette and the monkfish?'

Matthew carries on reading the menu after she has gone. If there was ever a moment to speak to him, without the walls of home around us, it is now. He is putting his menu down on the table, his decision made.

'I know that this wasn't an easy thing for you to do, Matthew, coming back to be with him.'

He circles a finger on the tablecloth, thinking about this.

'It wasn't that hard. I can't feel angry at him any more. He doesn't even know who he used to be.'

Holding Matthew's hand on top of the table, injustice flares – that Patrick might yet escape the guilt which for so long he let me suffer for him. This barrier that has always been there between me and Matthew, shadowing every moment together with the constant presumption of my responsibility for his troubles – the lie that Patrick put between us – telling myself ceaselessly that a child doesn't remember all the times their parent did well; they remember, and carry into their life, the times the parent failed them.

'And what about me?' The need for his acceptance is too strong to keep in.

'What do you mean?'

'Do you forgive me too?'

He is scowling at me across the table; my lovely, awkward boy.

'Forgive you for what, Mum?'

Do other families do this? Normal families probably sit around the table to talk, or go for long, muddy walks and bare their souls. Not this creeping across the landing to spy outside each other's rooms. There is the sound of something heavy being put down. A drawer closing. If he is still angry or upset from earlier, it's hard to tell through the door.

'Matthew?'

He stops what he is doing. We both wait for the other to speak.

'What is it, Mum?'

'Have you got a minute?'

He's considering it.

'What for?'

'To talk.'

It is not, he's thinking, a particularly appealing offer.

'I just want to make sure that you're okay, after this morning.'

'Yes, I'm fine. I don't really want to talk about it.'

'I would. If that's okay.'

The mattress is creaking. His feet moving across the floor. The door opens and he steps aside to let me in. All over the carpet there are piles of his things.

'You're leaving, then.'

'I am. You're getting shot of me at last.'

He goes to sit on the bed. There is nowhere else for me to sit other than next to him. He doesn't seem to mind. After a moment, he angles his body towards me, our knees almost touching.

'And are you sure this is the right thing? That you're not rushing into it?'

He laughs. 'I'm twenty-seven, Mum.'

'No, I mean, after your fight with Dad.'

'Which one?'

He is looking out of the window. The whole pane is covered with the faded tattoos of his childhood stickers, the afternoon light shining through them.

'I've been thinking about this for a while, Mum, you know that.'

'I know.'

He is still staring out of the window.

'When are you going?'

'Today.'

A dizzying sensation is rushing through me – like waking up to find myself at the edge of a sheer drop. He is leaving right now? How can he suddenly not be here, after all this time, without me even preparing for it?

'Where will you go?'

'A friend's.'

A friend's. This is all he wants to tell me. Twenty-seven years. If he ever said more than the bare minimum, maybe he wouldn't feel so badgered by all the questions that pile up behind his silences. Which friend? For how long? What are you going to say to your dad?

'And after that?'

'I want to go travelling. I've been thinking about Spain. Or Morocco.'

The vision of him on his own in a foreign place, unreachable, gone, is too much – a desperation rising, escaped thoughts knuckling at my temples: that this is my fault for not spending more time with him over the last couple of years, over all of his years, doing more to help him through his anxiety. For not doing more to mend his relationship with Patrick. Another vision now taking shape: of the foreign place that this house will be without Matthew, alone here with Patrick.

'Please don't leave before he comes back home, Matthew.'

'Don't worry, I'm not that childish.'

'I know it's been difficult recently, but it's not because he doesn't want you here. He does. It hasn't been easy for him these last few years since the stroke. He's not fully in control of his moods.'

'Don't defend him, Mum.'

'I'm not. I'm just saying that we have to accept he's maybe not exactly the same person he was before.'

He is glaring at me, incredulous. 'I remember exactly what kind of person he was before.'

He moves his eyes off me, back to the window.

'He was a better parent than I sometimes was, Matthew.'

He is frowning. Fleetingly, it seems like he's about to say something, but he holds it in. His hand, close to my leg, is clenching at the bedcovers.

'I'm going to tell you something,' he says. Words so unusual for him that we are both left speechless. He continues to stare at the window, for long enough that it begins to feel possible he has decided against saying any more. 'About Dad.'

His face has gone tight. He is deliberately not looking at me.

'When Granny died – that night, after the wake, you remember how he was. Him and Uncle David had been drinking and Dad was just, I don't know, he was in pieces. I'd never seen him cry before. When we got home after the wake and you and Em had gone to bed, me and him sat up in the living room. Do you remember?'

'Yes.'

In pieces is right. The memory of Patrick then is still clear. As well, how he had shut me out, even at the funeral, and wouldn't let me hold his hand in the taxi back home.

'When it was just the two of us he got all weird and started saying all this stuff about Granny. How she'd never meant to hurt anybody, it was just the way she was, how it was a maternal instinct at heart. And saying over and over that there was really nothing he could do, he'd been in an impossible position.'

'I don't understand, Matthew.'

'No, I didn't either. He went on talking gibberish for ages

until I made him stop and tell me what he was going on about.' His face has coloured. 'That day I went missing, when I was little.' The rhythm of my hand on his back is interrupted, my muscles tensing, not expecting that. 'She didn't find me when she said she did.' My brain is scrabbling to remember, still not understanding what he is saying. 'She found me earlier, much earlier, but she didn't take me home.'

The clunk of a car door on the street outside makes us both start. For a few seconds there is only the sound of Matthew breathing unevenly while we wait for the front door to open. Time has stopped. The past racing to catch us up. But the door is not opening; it is not Patrick.

'You understand what that means, don't you?'

'Yes. I think so.'

'She took me to her house. I kept asking him why but he got all weird again, saying she just wanted to get me safe and warm, how that was the most important thing, even though it's bullshit.'

He is sobbing now, his head and shoulders moving gently up and down against my chest.

'Can you remember where you were when she found you?'

'I think I have a memory of our street, of being next to the postbox, but it's all so confusing when I try to remember. I'm sorry, Mum. I'm really sorry.'

'Shush, no. You were so little. It's not your fault.'

'I have this other memory too, of being at her and Grandpa's house, upset because I didn't have a toy or something with me. And Dad's there as well. I'm sure he was there too.

I can see him sitting drinking tea with Grandpa and Granny, talking to them, I'm sure I can, but I just can't remember anything else.'

Every fibre of me is alight with understanding. About Mary's speed of thought on finding him, only as far as the postbox: deciding instantly that she would remove him to her own home – as a reproach for letting him out of the house; for never being the kind of woman she wanted me to be, Patrick wanted me to be. The understanding too that Patrick took part in it – a five-hour persecution – and he could never bring himself, even after his parents were dead, to admit what they all, together, had done.

'I can't be around him any more, Mum. I've tried, but I just can't. I need to be away from him.'

'Why didn't you tell me, after he told you this?'

He pulls free from my arms and sits up straight, facing me.

'Because he asked me not to. He said it wasn't fair to upset you with it, it was something in the past and it wasn't really such a big thing. I didn't come to any harm, he said. But I should have told you, I know. I'm sorry. It's just – it's hard to explain. It wasn't long after his stroke, and then I thought that if I stayed at home I could be here more for you, but actually all I've done is sit in my room or fight with Dad. And the stroke shouldn't be any excuse for how he is. He's mean and selfish. To do that to you. He treats you like shit, he always has, and I know that I should stay and—'

'You don't need to stay here for me, Matthew, or for him.'

And as he starts to sob again into my chest, something, it

seems, is let go from him. He is crying in my arms like a child. For so many years all this worry and remorse over him has grown from a lie – and yet the simple understanding that he might now be free from this house and its past, able to get on with himself, is releasing something in me, too. A knowledge at the same time strengthening that Patrick should not be allowed so easily to steal away from what he has done.

Matthew is reading a message on his phone while we wait for the coffees. Smiling to himself as he types back. On his leg, poking out beneath his shorts, is what looks like the bottom of a tattoo.

'Who are you messaging?'

He doesn't look up from his phone – probably objecting, understandably, to the needless intrusion – but then he says, still typing, 'Just Emily. Morgan's made her go to a wedding fair.'

'Yikes.'

'I know.'

It is only since she went back to Manchester yesterday that it has really struck me how unexpectedly natural it has felt, this past week of the two of them in the house together, talking, teasing – friends. The girl is stepping forward with our coffees. Matthew puts his phone in his pocket and takes the tray, smiling at her. *M* is written on each of the cups, although she didn't ask for his name when he ordered, despite how busy it is in the café, the Saturday crowd of couples and dog walkers all milling around the counter.

Her eyes move off Matthew to me getting her attention: 'Please can we get one of the cherry pastries too?'

Matthew is looking at me, curious.

'For Petya.'

'Ah, right. Here, I'll get these, Mum.'

He hands me the tray and pays, picking up the pastry from the counter before following me out of the café.

He takes the tray back and passes me my coffee. The village is lively this morning. We walk along the pavement, through other people's conversations, past the bright display of flowers outside the florist, the sun on our backs.

'I didn't know you had a tattoo.'

'This?' He stops. He lifts his knee and hitches up the leg of his shorts to show me. The small design is of a woman sitting on the ground, her head turned, looking away. There is writing, Spanish, curled around the top of her.

'What does it say?'

A tall young man and his wheezing pug come past us, the man and the dog glancing simultaneously at Matthew still standing on one leg.

'I love my mum.'

People keep coming past. Matthew puts his leg down. He looks serious.

'I've got one of Dad on my arse.'

Now he starts laughing.

'Git.'

We walk on together, Matthew still smiling. 'It's Spanish. It means: the world is a handkerchief.'

'Okay.'

'I know. I was drunk, obviously. To be fair, I might as well have got an I love my mum.'

We are leaving the bustle of the village now, Matthew getting his phone out again as we turn towards home.

'Are you going straight back to Spain this afternoon?'

'Yes. Working again on Monday.'

'Do you think you'll stay there?'

'The hotel? I think so. For the rest of the year, at least. But I'll be back for the wedding – and obviously,' he pauses, 'if I need to be here before then.'

We carry on without speaking for a while. My phone vibrates in my pocket – bringing on a rush of expectancy that it might be Peter – although, from the look of Matthew's face, amusedly absorbed in his text conversation, it is possible that it might be Emily.

'I'm sorry I haven't been around more, Mum.' He looks over at me. 'I know it was selfish.'

'No, it wasn't. You did what you needed to do. I don't blame you.'

'I do know what a good job you've done, managing everything.'

These awkward words hang between us, and for a few seconds it is possible to ignore all of the things that he does not know.

'Thank you.'

'He's going to die, isn't he?'

Through a hedge, a child is counting loudly in a garden.

'There's no way of knowing that, my love.'

'I hardly recognise him now. I know he's there, but I can't get to him. It's like there's a wall.'

'He's had two strokes since you saw him last.'

His face looks tense. He might feel accused, but he is nodding slowly.

'You're right, though. He is getting worse. But that's not to say he won't stabilise, even stay like he is for a long time. We just don't know.'

We are almost home. Turning onto our street, the postbox is just up ahead of us. Does he feel anything when he passes it? Does he think at all about his childhood, all those moments that are so stitched into me – does he remember them all too? Some of them he will, probably, some of them he won't, and even the ones that he does he will remember differently. The truth of it clear before me, as if it hadn't been all along, that his memories might not be as complicated, by time and guilt, as my own – and that the way he seems now, content, in his own fragile, peculiar way, could be all that matters, all that he is. His past has become somewhere new. Looking at him today, walking brightly down this time-scarred road, it is equally clear that so too has my own. He does not know, forgettable as they will have been to him, everything that his simple words last week – *Forgive you for what, Mum?* – have released in me. It is not possible, holding on to all of the anguish of before, to truly turn into someone else. The past needs to keep changing; a person needs to keep changing. And if she was here now, watching the man that her grandson has become, walking me home, she would be able to see that, in fact, we both have.

'What about you, Mum?'

He has caught me off guard, disoriented. 'What do you mean?'

'Do you think about the future?'

'Sometimes.'

We continue walking, both of us obviously sensing the difficulty of taking this conversation further – and yet it is me who is, saying to him, 'I'd like to open my own restaurant one day.'

'That would be cool.'

'It would. It's something I've wanted for a very long time.'

'Could you afford it?'

'It would be difficult. I've got a friend, though' – the words coming out as if not my own – 'who might go in with me.'

'Oh, right. Who's that?'

'Peter.'

'Really – Petya?'

'No, not Petya. A different friend. He's called Peter.'

We have slowed down, reaching the house. My heart is beating strongly in my chest.

'Okay,' he says. 'Is he someone you know well?'

Anger lights in me for doing this – threatening everything right as he is about to leave again, his bags already packed – but the compulsion to tell him something, to not lie to him, makes me keep speaking.

'He is, yes. He's one of our suppliers at the restaurant. I've known him for some time, and he's been a support to me.' We remain at the front garden gate. 'We've become quite close.'

He says nothing, his hand on one of the pickets, then he

opens the gate and goes on up the path, leaving me here a moment alone, composing myself.

He has opened the door and is inside the hallway. Petya has arrived. He is giving her the pastry. She steps into view, telling him thank you and lifting the pastry package to her lips, kissing it. They are looking at each other, Petya smiling slightly in amusement before Matthew moves past her into the house. This funny way they have together. He likes her, he can see how good she is with his dad, but he can't quite figure her out. He's still a bit intimidated by her, which she knows, and their mutual recognition of it has become a kind of constant tease, maybe even, by now, a flirtation. Something to ask Petya about, perhaps, when we go for our drink later. At the bottom of the stairs he turns to watch me coming into the house.

'I'm going up to get my bag,' he says.

'Okay, Matthew.'

Patrick is in the living room, awake, in his armchair.

'They are watching the television,' Petya says. The faithful dog is on the armrest, a sentinel, facing the screen. 'I will heat his soup now, for when you are gone to work.'

'Yes, thanks, Petya.'

Patrick registers me coming into the room. He looks pleased. Petya has wiped his face, seen to his hair.

'I'll be going to work in a minute, Patrick.' His attention is on me. 'Matthew is about to leave as well. He is going back to Spain.'

'Yes,' he says, matter-of-factly, whether he understands or

435

not. His hand is lifting from the armrest, hovering shakily, like a remote-control helicopter.

'Do you need something?'

He doesn't speak, but his fingers are closing tightly around mine and bringing our hands down together onto the armrest. Matthew is walking across the ceiling, in his room. A woman shouting on the television. In some small way, we are reaching each other. Time is dissolving and it is possible to understand, holding his hand and knowing he feels it too, that while the past might run through everything, every action, every choice, it is not fixed – and in the gentleness of this moment it pulls back and, briefly, is gone. There is only the stillness of now.

Petya is coming back into the room with his soup. Behind her, Matthew is in the hallway, his rucksack leant against the wall.

'I'm just going upstairs a minute, Matthew. I'll let you have a moment to say goodbye to him.'

He moves aside to let me past him.

Going up the stairs, Matthew's voice is softly in the background, talking to him, talking to his dog. Petya's question, eating lunch a few weeks ago, coming back: *What man was he?* Is he really a different person, though? Is he so much more changed than any of us are, eventually? Even if it is possible to condemn somebody who no longer remembers what they once did, or what they once wanted, it doesn't feel like what matters any more. He does not remember, but it is still him. Just as Matthew can't, fully, remember that day that he was lost – but it is nonetheless part of him, who he is, even if the parts aren't all there to fit together, in order. Matthew is still talking, some of his words rising upstairs, 'thirty-four degrees in Barcelona', as my hands take the jar and the letters out of the drawer. They are unaware of me moving calmly now out of the bedroom, the long-held solution here in my hands, going back down the stairs – glimpsing him knelt beside Patrick – and into the kitchen. The promise of a future is coursing through me and it is not a surprise, in the end, how easy it is to let go. Not a surprise either, watching the pills, the letters, plunge into the darkness, to realise that they had already gone, that there is another life already waiting for me.

In the living room, Petya is holding the bowl of soup. She's over by the window, a considerate distance away from them. Matthew is standing behind the armchair now. His hands are on Patrick's shoulders. He bends down, their faces getting closer, and kisses his dad on the cheek. He says something quietly in his ear, then stands back up, to walk towards me.

'All right then, Mum. I'll be going now.'

'Let me know when you've got there, please.'

'I will.'

He pulls me into a hug.

'I want you to be happy too, Mum,' he is saying, holding me firmly, my body inside his, suddenly at peace. 'It's okay for you to be happy, too.'

Emily is kneeling before him on the carpet. Fussing. He lets her put his feet into the weird slippers the hospital has given him. He stays quiet and calm, although he wouldn't let me put them on him earlier. Until she arrived, he wouldn't allow anything to be done for him.

'What else do you need, Dad?'

'Nothing. Thank you.'

'I just want to make sure you're comfortable.'

'I am.'

'Good.' She gets to her feet, leans down to kiss him on the head and puts her hand over his on the armchair. He snatches it away with a tiny yelp.

'Dad, sorry, I—'

'No, no, not your fault. All of me just bloody hurts.'

Emily looks at me for an explanation. She is confused. Wounded.

'They told us to expect heightened reactions. Skin. Joints. His shoulders. He said yesterday that he feels like he's wearing somebody else's skin.'

'I'm going to be a cranky old git for a while, basically.'

She seems heartened by this flash of humour. 'More than normal, Dad?' she says, stepping away from him to come and stand next to me.

For a moment he stares, glazed, at the carpet – then, slowly, he is smiling. 'Yes. Yes.' He looks up at us. 'You're both just watching me.' He is amused. 'You should be running around.'

'He's perkier since you arrived, Em, that's for sure.'

She smiles, but it is quickly gone from her face. She wants reassurance. Answers. He was four years on the road to recovery. This wasn't supposed to have happened again.

'How long are you staying with us, my love?'

'Just tonight. I need to get back to Manchester tomorrow. I've got a big meeting on Monday morning.'

Funny how unquestioned it is, the importance of everybody else's work.

'Well,' Patrick says. He looks tired with the new effort of conversation. 'Thank you for coming. We know how busy.' He is speaking more slowly now, almost slurring. 'I should have these turns more.'

She is not laughing. 'Do you want a cup of tea, Dad?'

He is looking at the television.

'Dad. Tea?'

He turns to her, muddled. 'Oh. Yes.'

In the kitchen she waits for the cover of kettle noise. She wants to ask me things but is starting to cry instead, nestling into me, pressing her cheek against my shoulder. What answers are there, anyway? They are the same as after the first stroke, only louder. She is wearing a perfume yet still the soft smell of her, her skin, her face burrowing into me, is just Emily. It silences me, not having thought properly until now about the absence of this body that was once as known to me as my own. This time tomorrow she will be gone. The simple truth of it holds me to her, unfairly begrudging of her independence; wanting as well to protect her, and Matthew, from everything that is to come.

He has fallen asleep. Emily puts his tea down on the stool and comes to sit with me on the sofa.

'So, what did the neurologist say?'

'I told you most of it on the phone. It was bigger than the last one. He needs to rest. He's weak and stiff – they've given him a cane, which of course he doesn't want to use – and he might have some cognition difficulties, sleep and swallowing issues, unpredictable emotions.'

She sits with her knees together, taking this in, working out solutions. The dry language of prognosis will be making it easier for her, connecting her; she can google all these things from Manchester. She did not have to see him in the hospital, the fleshy mess of that.

' "Unpredictable emotions" means what?'

'That they could be triggered more easily. When I told him you were coming, he went straight to change his trousers because he didn't want you to see him looking like an old man in dirty pyjamas, he said, but when he couldn't put the new ones on and I told him it didn't matter, he shouted at me to shut up and slammed the door on me. He tried to, anyway.'

Emily takes in the one-sided account of this event: she does not see me blocking the door from shutting, or the anger that had leapt in me at him.

'And how long will this last?'

Asleep in his chair, Patrick gives a long sigh. We both watch him as he shifts about for several seconds then goes back to rest, his face completely serene, guiltless.

'They can't say. The risk of another one, as you know, increases each time.'

'So, what, this just keeps happening until – what?'

She will know the answer to this already too. She'll have looked it up. She wants me to say it, though, to give her confirmation.

'Let's just concentrate on now. Help him get back on his feet.'

The television burbles away, always on, saying nothing.

'And what about your outgoings, with you both not working?'

Here it is, the assurance she wants from me. Her eyes imploring me to concede that there won't be as long a period off work this time.

'We will be fine for a while.'

'Morgan and I can help, you know. Don't feel ashamed to ask.'

They've already discussed it, then. Decided how much they can afford, how much it will be worth to turn me into his carer. Has Matthew been involved in these arrangements? Doubtful. Yesterday's phone conversation is likely to be as involved as he will get. However unwell his dad might be, he obviously still doesn't want to come back from wherever he is to see him. The fact of his absence hits me once more, a physical pain wrenching through me – wanting to know that he is okay; and wanting Patrick to hurt too, for all these years of letting me blame myself for Matthew's anxious aloneness.

'I might make a start on dinner, Mum. Can he eat?'

'Yes, but he probably won't want to. You could mash some potatoes. There are carrots too. Ham, if you're feeling ambitious.'

She gets to her feet and goes to pick up his undrunk tea.

'Thank you, Em. I might step out for a minute, while you're cooking.'

'Oh – out?'

'Just while he's asleep. I've not left the house since we came back from the hospital. I'll only go to the shop and back, get some more milk.'

'Okay. If you need to. That's fine.'

As soon as the door closes, the fresh afternoon air on my skin, something lifts. Some element of me separates from it all. Emily didn't catch me slipping my phone into my bag. Not here, though. On our street. Ears and eyes. Familiar faces. Do any of the neighbours even know that he has had another stroke? They must. The ones with children at the school will certainly have heard by now. All the juicy details. The Year 11 girl who noticed he was slurring the constitution of the Weimar Republic and knew to check whether he could lift his arms up. The PE teacher who carried him like a bride out to the front of the school.

The Fields are busy. Joggers and families. A group of teenagers clowning about on the playpark swings. The phone is poised in my hand. Why does it feel so wrong to call him? It shouldn't. There's no one else to talk to. Near the playpark there is an empty bench. A quiet place to sit, just briefly, and be alone.

A loud squawk from the swings makes me flinch. It takes a long time to regain my composure; the thumping of blood slowly getting quieter.

'Hello, Anita – hold on a moment, I'm just coming in the flat.' For a few seconds, there is the clacketing of keys. 'There we are. I've not heard from you in a while. You been off?'

'Patrick had another stroke.'

'Oh, hell. How is he?'

'He's at home now. It happened on Tuesday while he was teaching. He's tired and frail but he's okay.'

'I'm so sorry. How are you holding up?'

He can hear me steadying myself, suppressing the threat of breaking down.

'Shall I come and meet you?'

'No. Thank you, Peter. Emily is here. She's staying the night. I need to go back in a minute and help her with dinner.'

'I don't know what to say, pet.'

'You don't have to say anything.' One of the teenage boys

lets out a wild roar. A couple of the girls falling about in hysterics. 'They said he could have more of them. That there's a high risk of dementia, vascular dementia, further down the line.'

'Oh, hell. I'm so sorry, Anita. Does he know?'

'He doesn't. I haven't told the children yet, either. But Emily probably knows it.'

'And Matthew? Is he coming home?'

'I doubt it.'

'You know that I'm here. Anything you need.'

'I know you are. Thank you.'

Emily is calling. The phone flashes in my hand like an alarm. 'I have to go, Peter. It's Emily. I'll be in touch soon.'

A temptation to let her go to voicemail drugs my hand as the phone continues to ring. It is selfishness, however, and not fair on her.

'Where are you, Mum?'

'I'm on my way back. Is everything okay?'

'He woke up agitated because he didn't know where you were. I told him you'd gone for milk and now he keeps doing this weird laugh and saying, "She's gone, she's gone." What should I do?'

'Tell him I'll be home in a couple of minutes. Put something different on the television for him.'

'Okay, Mum, I will.'

He is my duty, clearly, mine alone. Fifteen minutes out of the house to buy milk is too long away because this is the life that has been appointed to me: his life, whatever course it takes from here. My job to take responsibility for him, my husband, this man who has not and now maybe never will have to take responsibility for all that he has done.

The house stands before me in the early-evening sunshine, waiting.

The milk. Crap.

Emily takes the dinner plates back to the kitchen. Patrick's has barely been touched, despite Emily wanting to leave it sitting on the carpet for the last hour, just in case. He is fidgeting a bit in his armchair.

'Are you okay, Patrick?'

No response. He's still acting funnily – trying to punish me, possibly, for going out of the house. Emily is coming back in. 'Do you need anything, Dad?'

'I want to go to bed.'

'Good idea. I think I might too in a bit, after I've called Morgan.'

He is trying to get up. Emily going to help him.

'Do you need the cane for the stairs or can—'

'No.'

He lets her take his weak arm, all the same, and he moves unsteadily out of the room, tired out again. They take the stairs slowly, Patrick's toes catching on the lip of each step as they move up together ahead of me.

Emily stops outside our bedroom door. She doesn't help him in, sensing perhaps how he might react to that. She kisses him on the side of the head, then gives him a hug.

'Goodnight, Dad. I'll see you in the morning. Night, Mum.'

Patrick toddles into the room, leaving the door open. He goes to stand by the bed, then lowers himself with both hands until he is sitting on it.

'Do you want me to do anything?'

Again, he ignores me. His right hand is shaking on the duvet. He closes his eyes; reopens them – and looks up at me. 'Please.' He raises the shaking hand to stop me coming towards him. 'I don't want to be an invalid.'

'You're not an invalid. You just need to rest.'

'I don't mean now.' He wants me to hold his hand. 'You will need to help me.'

'I don't know what you mean, Patrick.'

From Emily's room, there is the faint sound of her voice.

'I do not want to become a burden,' he says, his speech starting to drag. 'A drooling fool in a home.' He is squeezing my hand. 'You must promise me.'

His eyes stay on mine for the first time since the stroke. Something unsayable is passing between us.

'I promise.'

As we look at each other, a new strange fire is starting to burn inside me. After a long time, he lets go of the hand and lies down slowly on the bed.

The house is completely still, Emily asleep now, her muted conversation with Morgan long finished. The laptop screen glows in the darkness of the dining room, lighting the hospital leaflets strewn across the table. There is a noise upstairs and my fingers freeze on the keyboard. It's probably just Emily going to the toilet. Wait. Just be calm and wait. With the laptop closed, the room goes black. *I do not want to become a burden. A drooling fool in a home.* Isn't this – the words my fingers are about to type, even if he could not bring himself to say them – exactly what he was asking me? The noise comes again. It is outside, not in the house. Just a neighbour, closing windows.

How to begin? How to spy into the future and predict how capable, whenever the time comes, he would be to write this. My hands move to the laptop before my resolve, the fire inside still burning fiercely, can fail me. His final voice in my fingertips.

Dearest Matthew,

This is not an easy letter to write to you. Or to your sister.
If there was a better way to do it then I would.

He is patting the duvet. He wants me to sit next to him. His dog is on his lap and he looks jolly – rolling over onto his side – my hand shooting out to grip his nightshirt to stop him from falling off the bed. He is reaching down for something. The space between the bed and the wall is gathering ever more rubbish. However messy and stinking it might be getting, though, it's too late to clean it up. He is hoarding things there, in this small remaining territory that is his.

He comes back up holding a butchered hospital letter. A shape has been cut out of it, with some parts coloured in with felt tips. He can't have done this by himself. Petya, surely, has helped him. He holds it up in front of me. It is a person. A mad doll.

He is pointing it at me.

'Is this me?'

'No.' He is handing it over – and is pleased at me taking it. He's off again, rolling to the edge, and he returns with another one, for himself.

We sit together, holding our dolls. Mine has yellow hair. Two dots for eyes, no nose, and a line across the whole face for a mouth. There are legs, arms, cut into the paper. The writing on the letter tattooed across her body: . . . *this gentle-man in clinic today and discussed* . . . He has started playing with his doll. He's giving it a voice, too quiet and gobbledy-gooky to make out, walking the doll up his tummy. His has a squiggle of short, black hair. The little pantomime plays out in the corner of my eye and a long-forgotten instinct – as if happening upon one of the children immersed inside some private magical world, playing with a teddy or a stone or a classroom of carrots – warns me against watching too bla-tantly, in case he stops; afraid to break the spell for fear that something might be lost that will never come back.

The doll goes still in his hand. He looks up at me – then at the door. He moans, agitated, maybe seeing something that is not there. Dandruff jumps from his thin remaining hair as my hand strokes the back of his head, gradually calming him, a slow spreading satisfaction calming me too, at being able to soothe him, of knowing myself capable.

'Would you like me to read you something, before I go to work?'

He doesn't understand.

'A book. I could read a book to you.'

A flicker of happy surprise. 'Oh, yes.'

'All right. Wait a moment. I'll go and find one.'

There is enough time – at least twenty minutes until it will be time to leave, before Petya gets here. It should have occurred to me before, to read to him. There are shelves and shelves of books here on the dining-room walls, all of these beyond him now. The rows of his history books, his thrillers.

My Victorians. Poetry. These books that usually bored my pupils to tears but opened up a world to me. Would he want me to read Sylvia Plath to him? Unlikely. The old him always hated her; the new one probably has that in common.

Everything that is left of the children is in Emily's room, my room, in the big cupboard now blocked by nappy packs. It's all inside cardboard boxes, the choice cuts, the stuff that couldn't be chucked. Packed and Sellotaped and, not very helpfully, all unlabelled. But the book boxes are obvious enough.

The first one opens onto a jumble of all ages. Baby books, early readers, bedtime stories – the memory of each one as instant as looking at a photograph. Would it be unkind to read him one of these? To confirm that he is a child once again? It does not feel unkind, though. It feels – the worn-out book pulling free from its tight wedge – like something that will make him happy.

He is sitting up in the bed on my return, with his dog and both of the dolls beside him, eager for his story. He waits for me to get into position in the bed – sitting next to him with the book on my lap and the two dolls between us, propped up against a pillow.

'I found this one in Emily's room.'

He nods, attentive.

'*It's a funny thing about mothers and fathers. Even when their own child is the most disgusting little blister you could ever imagine, they still think that he or she is wonderful.*'

Tears are forming in my eyes. He is enjoying himself. This absurd scenario that we are now beginning to act out, the two of us sitting here with his dog and the dollies of the children nestled between us, all listening intently to the familiar story, the old silly voices coming back to me unconsciously and the compounded loss and love of each of them growing, echoing through the pages.

In the concentrated peace of prep, an alien sound is mingling with the extractor fan. Walking about the sections, watching the boys at work, it's difficult to figure out what the noise is. Something from the street outside. A murmur in the extractor engine. Under the pass lights, ready on the metal, the hindquarter is waiting for me. Each of the floor staff, who keep coming by on the other side of the pass, slows for a few seconds to look at it. The new one is walking down the gangway steps. She sees the quarter cow and stops. She is taking out her phone – Richard appearing now, telling her to put it away and get on with setting up the floor.

It is Jack, the noise. He's humming. He is absorbed enough in his prep, peeling the leaves from an artichoke, that he doesn't notice me moving closer to him. On the other side of the section, Jonas is humming along with him, both of them so focused on their boards that they don't seem to know they are doing it. The tune is hard to pick out, disguised – Michael Bublé? Is it possible that somehow, without anybody realising it, Michael Bublé has become a constant presence in the kitchen? Jack, spotting me, looks up as if he has been caught out.

'Carry on, Jack. As you were.'

He slices across the top of the artichoke's heart, a bit embarrassed, then scoops out the hairy choke with a table-spoon. He puts it on top of his tidy pile of leaves. The rest of his board and metal spotless.

'Neat prep. Well done, Jack.'

He keeps his eyes down, starting to brush the heart with lemon juice, the side of his neck turning pink from my atten-tion. A couple of steps behind him, Dan is bent over measuring cod cheeks with a ruler. Turtle watching him from meat, shaking his head. This odd collection of people, as dif-ferent from each other – loud, anxious, mean, funny – as siblings. Nobody else understands what happens in here. The invisible mouths beyond the gangway wall are more inter-ested in the upbringing of the chicken on their plate than in the person working a seventy-hour week for four hundred quid who has cooked it. But it is not for them. They are not the reason these chefs are here, hidden away together in this closed-off world, a family.

At the pass, placing my hands on the cow, the chill of the walk-in still in its flesh, a calmness is seeping through me: at the brief thought of Peter, then remembering Matthew's mes-sage last night – *Do you give your lot food this good?* – the photo of him in his work uniform eating a white bean and chorizo stew with the other hotel office staff. A new sureness has stayed with me since he left, that the change in him is real. As though the boy who disappeared from home all those years ago has finally returned, grown up, surprisingly playful. It is wrong, however, this interpretation of him. Probably he is the same as he has ever been; it has just taken until now for me to see him properly, without looking at him through myself.

'Chef?'

Anton is grinning at me. My hands still braced on the steer.

'You look like you haven't had your coffee yet.'

'Good point, Anton. No, I haven't.'

'I'll make you one.'

He goes off, out of the kitchen. A few words and a joke with Jimbo and Karolina in the service gangway, sharing out slices of pineapple, before he leaves for the bar. Here on the pass steel he has prepared the break-down for me: C-fold laid out under the metre board; boning knife, filleting knife, fresh pile of C-folds, bone tray, commis chef – Turtle appearing now at my side with the saw, like the assistant to some gruesome magic trick.

The rough buzz of the saw's teeth through the vertebrae brings the kitchen to a halt. Floor staff start wandering over too, drawn to the spectacle. A woman with a meat saw. The rhythm of the saw needs all of my strength and focus – a straight line deepening in the lumber, rump and sirloin cleaving slowly apart, until the gap is wide enough to be finished off with the knife. Anton is back with my coffee. He puts it down on the metal, watching me knife-scrape clean the sawdust from the bone.

'Thanks, Anton. Wait here and I'll take the fillet off for you.'

A few soft strokes of the knife detach it from the sirloin. The fat and sinew pulls away with a single rip to reveal the smooth, purple fillet. Anton is rolling out a sheet of film on the metal, while Turtle takes away the rag of sinew to render down for the staff-food roasties. As soon as the fillet is placed down on the film Anton starts wrapping and rolling, then twizzling the ends, tightening the tube as he walks away to begin processing it into today's tartare and carpaccio and chateaubriand special for the businessmen idiots. My blade follows the ribcage along the sirloin, the wave of bones, nipping and stroking with the knife in one hand, pulling apart with the other, my own body swifter and stronger than it has ever been, the knowledge of years of work collected at my fingertips. There is an audience on both sides of the pass. Their small movements of faces and arms visible but faraway, outside of this space which my body has claimed for itself. All of them are standing back, studying me work. Men who will only ever understand the world through the pair of eyes they were born with and will never know what it is like to be more than one person, always shadowed by the image of themselves. In this moment – the sheet of bones pulling free – they are all watching with my eyes, learning with my hands the beautiful architecture of this animal, its musculature and composition, the curve of its pink bones.

Turtle is ready with the tray.

'You can take it, Turtle.'

He picks up the sheet of bones, lifting it into the tray. He knows now how to trim away the connective flesh for mincing and how to make a stock from the bones, how to process the chain that will be cut away next for braise and render and morning break titbits. They are all still there on both sides of the pass. On my instruction they will shortly disperse and go back to work but, for a moment longer, they are part of the deep sensation of peace that is filtering through me, knowing that this space is mine – and that, in time, it will one day emerge somewhere else and will keep expanding, with work, with people, to feed and teach and grow with and love.

'Back to it, everybody.'

There is a flurry of movement, talking, waiters streaming away along the service gangway, the clang of a pan behind me. Within seconds they have all gone, leaving me alone, the knife still in my hand, with only the primal cut remaining, ready on the board in front of me.

I am thankful, as ever, to Peter Straus, for his guidance and friendship. And, for the years of editorial encouragement and insight invested in this book, to Michal Shavit, and to Ana Fletcher — to whose sharp eyes and gentle elbow I owe a great deal. I would also like to thank the rest of the teams at Rogers, Coleridge and White and at Vintage, with particular thanks to Cecile Pin, Joe Pickering, Isobel Turton, Alison Tulett and Alex Milner.

For their insights into the experience and infrastructure of social and medical care, I am grateful to Fiona Pereira, Laura Checkley, Caroline Methuen, Richard Whittell, Suzy Harvey and to Lewes Depot's dementia-friendly screenings.

For all things cooking, thank you (with a few recommendations for readers) to:

Calum Franklin (if you *really* like pies, go to the Holborn Dining Room in London, where Calum is exec head chef — and try out his book, *The Pie Room*); Liz Haughton (if you are in Bristol and fancy a local, organic, tasty lunch, go to her place, the Folk House Cafe); Ravneet Gill (check out her hospitality community movement Countertalk for discussion around the promotion of healthy work environments in the industry – countertalk.co.uk – and if you like baking, have a look at Rav's books: *The Pastry Chef's Guide* and *Sugar, I Love You*); Sherri Dymond (for a friendly neighbourhood cafe serving beautiful food, visit Italo in Vauxhall); Maria Elia (*Smashing Plates* and *The Modern Vegetarian*, if you like Greek food, and vegetables); Tony Moyse (if you are in London Bridge and in the mood for a fat, straight-from-the-market steak, go to the Market Porter pub; Chantelle Nicholson (formerly chef-owner of Tredwells, author of *Planted* and – if you are ever looking for a high-end, environment-conscious, hyper-seasonal eating experience, treat yourself to a meal at her new Mayfair restaurant, Apricity).

I am grateful too – for sharing with me their knowledge as well as their contacts – to Amy Wood, Kristjan Bigland, Joe Nixon and Elliot Sheppard.

Finally, to the hundreds of chefs, cleaners, waiters, kitchen porters, hotel staff, bar staff and union organisers I have worked alongside over the years in the UK, Ireland and France, thank you. I miss working with you.

Acknowledgement also to Robert Hazard, songwriter of 'Girls Just Want to Have Fun'; to Jeff Barry and Andy Kim, songwriters of 'Sugar, Sugar'; and to Roald Dahl and the children's novel, *Matilda*.